BILL K. UNDERWOOD

UNBROKEN

Other books by Bill K. Underwood

The Minotaur Medallion
Resurrection Day – A New World Novel

A NOTE ABOUT THE LANGUAGE:

When Columbus sailed west from Spain and found what he thought was India, he called the islands the West Indies – which name they still bear – and called the residents of those islands "Indians." In 1519, the setting for this book, the Spaniards still believed they were on the outlying islands of India.

The people they called Indians called themselves the Taino. They referred to their enemies on other islands as the Caribe so the Spaniards named the sea surrounding the islands the Caribbean.

What none of these people were called was "native Americans." An Italian explorer named Americus Vespucius was aboard a vessel in 1502 that mapped enough of the coastline beyond the West Indies to suggest it might be a continent. In 1507 a German mapmaker produced a very early global map and he named the hint of the new continent "America," though the name didn't catch on for another sixty years.

Some other vocabulary oddities you may find herein: In 1518 horses had a single rein, not "reins." Some men wore a *pantalon*, not pantaloons. Clocks didn't have minute hands. (When I found that out I went back and tried to remove any references to minutes – I hope I caught them all.) Similarly, distance wasn't measured in inches, feet or miles and money was neither dollars nor pesos. The only firearm was a muzzle-loading trigger-operated gun with a bell-shaped barrel called an arquebus (ark-wah-boose) and the gunmen were called, appropriately, arquebusiers.

Mayan words and names don't roll off the tongue. The "x" is pronounced 'sh' or 'ch', so xocolatl is 'chocolatl' and Ox-Ha-té is 'Osh-haw-tay.'

Aside from those glaring differences I have not written this in the language of the day. First, because I don't speak Spanish; Second, even if I did, it wouldn't be the Spanish that was spoken back then. I've tried to put in enough 16th century phraseology to give a flavor of the time without making the story unreadable. At the same time, I've tried to avoid as much 21st century slang as possible.

Prologue

February, 1519

Felipe wasn't worried about dying. Sick as he was at the moment he thought he might welcome it. He felt like he was living through a nightmare.

The seasickness he'd experienced briefly when they departed Havana two days ago was back and worse than ever. The wind screamed through the rigging. The waves pouring over the rail struck like a solid mass. The masts and yards groaned in agony. The world spun; his ears rang; his head felt like it was being squeezed by a pair of enormous, cruel hands. He believed if he threw up again he would start seeing pieces of his insides.

And now, far more worrying, Isabella was showing signs of distress. Until now, the mare had been taking the journey in stride; as if living in a cramped stall on the open deck of a three-masted Spanish ship was perfectly normal.

Not Majesty of course. The stallion continued to neigh and rear and shake his head, trying to pull loose from the ropes that secured him. White showed all around his eyes as if the storm were attacking him personally. Streaks of sweat slathered his slick black coat. It had taken all Felipe's skill to calm him, to prevent him from hurting himself or kicking down his stall. Again. Each time the ship rose to a new wave he jerked against his ropes.

But Isabella withstood everything. She'd endured with bland calm the sails rattling like thunder above her head and the noise like a gunshot when one of them blew out; Sailors rushing past to take in the flailing rags of sailcloth and the cursing *sargentos* swinging starters at laggards; The constant thrumming of the wind through taut ropes; And the constantly rolling deck. As long as she had hay and water in front of her Isabella was content. Even the lazy Estefan could keep up with that. But now she was getting sick and Estefan was nowhere to be found. No doubt he'd found a dry place below decks to hole up until the storm was over. Perhaps she was seasick. Did horses get seasick? Felipe didn't know. If only his stomach would hold still. If only the pain and dizziness in his own head would ease he could think about it more clearly.

There were six horses on *Concepcion,* the flagship. Another ten horses were divided among the rest of the fleet… if "fleet" wasn't too grand a description for the ragged flock of boats that had left Havana two days earlier. Most were small open brigantines, little more than fishing boats; too small to carry a single horse safely, let alone several. But the *Trinidad* and the *Santiago*, each of seventy tons, carried four horses apiece. And the wallowing, grandly named *Santa Maria de los Remedios,* fifty tons, managed not to sink despite a pair of horses in temporary stalls on her open deck.

Ideally there should have been a groom for each horse. Felipe was supposedly tasked with caring only for Majesty. But the rapid departure from Havana had left them with only himself, Pedro and Estefan to care for the six horses. But Pedro's expertise had been needed on the *Remedios* to help with a sick horse and, thanks to the weather, he was stuck there. Estefan rarely came around. When he did show up he wobbled and smelled of sherry. The day before, in one of his rare appearances, Estefan had cross-tied Isabella so she could barely move. She couldn't get her nose away from the dusty hay Estefan had jammed into the canvas manger in front of her. Felipe couldn't stand to see a horse so mistreated. He corrected her ties to allow her to move her head. He pulled the hay out of the canvas manger, rinsed the dust from it and put the right amount back. How was it possible that he, not yet a teenager, knew to do these things but old Estefan hadn't learned them?

And now Isabella was sick. Or something. Pedro had taught him horses needed to keep using their leg muscles for their digestion to work properly. An improperly boxed horse could be lost within hours. Felipe again checked the sling under her belly to make sure it wasn't lifting her legs off the deck. It wasn't.

Through the fog of his own misery Felipe finally, reluctantly, allowed the thought he'd been trying to avoid to creep in: Isabella, big as an oxcart, was going into labor in the middle of a raging storm.

CHAPTER ONE

Six months earlier

Felipe knew someone was coming. Majesty, in the corral on the south side of the barn tossed his head and neighed loudly. He smelled or heard the visitors long before Felipe detected them. His loud call indicated there was at least one mare coming. If it had been a strange stallion Majesty's neigh would have been much more challenging. Felipe went to the corral and poked an ear of corn through the bars and the large stallion, having established his authority, accepted it gracefully. Felipe then went to the house and put on his tunic. His father had taught him that Spaniards found naked children uncivilized.

When the stranger finally rode into the stable yard Felipe wondered for just a moment whether he might be the king of Spain. He had never seen such finery associated with a single individual. The tall, severe-looking man had a long thin nose pointing down to a long thin beard. He wore a red velvet coat with two rows of gold buttons down each breast, more gold buttons on each sleeve and gold braid around all the edges. A thick white ruffled collar seemed to limit movement of his head. The black leather boots rising over his knees were polished until they gleamed. His skin-tight white leggings had not a single spot of mud on them. Over his head a banner fluttered limply in the slight breeze. Felipe could make out the king's crest on one end of it. The legend across it in Spanish began *"Don Hernando Cortes de Monroy y Piz..."* There was more, but the banner was folded back on itself. Felipe had been to the nearby village, a cluster of a half dozen homes, many times. Once he had even been to Santiago, nearly a full day's ride away. It was exciting compared to the village. But even if the stranger was from Santiago it hadn't seemed grand enough to warrant all this ostentation.

By contrast the tall man's horse was a small, sad sorrel mare that looked as though she couldn't wait to be relieved of her burden. She nickered when she saw Felipe, perhaps recognizing a kindred spirit. She was not in foal, which was unusual here in Cuba at a time when horses were scarce and expensive. Felipe wondered if perhaps she was barren. He ran to scoop a bucket of water for her from the rain barrel set under the eaves of the barn.

Only after he returned with the water did he notice the monk on a donkey following the magnificent man. The mare stopped. The monk jumped from his donkey and ran to kneel below the left stirrup of the tall man, who stepped on the monk's back as he alighted. The tall man sniffed and slowly turned his head, surveying the primitive surroundings with disdain: the simple palm log-and-thatch house; the rough-hewn barn; and the raw branches tied together to form the corral. Felipe had never been ashamed of his home before, but he was now.

"At last!" Felipe heard the tall man say to the priest, in Latin. "This will be a worthy animal for me."

Majesty neighed again and Felipe told him in Spanish to quiet down. He'd almost addressed the horse in Latin, so shocked was he to hear Latin in common use in his own barnyard.

"Where is your master?" The man addressed him in Spanish.

Felipe didn't have a master. He knew the man had to be referring to his father but the odd question, together with the linguistic puzzle, had tongue-tied him. He struggled to form a sentence but nothing came out.

"I seek Señor Ferrer. Where is he?" When Felipe still didn't answer the tall man raised his whip, evidently having no qualms about striking a child, even if he was a stranger.

"I will abide no impertinence from you, Indian. I just heard you speaking Spanish to that horse. Answer me!"

Felipe found his tongue. "Pardon, Señor, my, my apologies. I have no... my, that is to say my master Señor Ferrer is...

"What's going on here?" he heard his father bellow. Miguel Ferrer stepped out the door of the barn just in time to see the raised quirt. He was bare-chested above his *pantalon* and sopping wet, wiping his hands with his wadded-up tunic. When he'd heard the strangers enter the yard he'd stripped off the tunic and dumped a bucket of water over his head. But the raised voice of the stranger made him decide the niceties would have to wait. While not as tall as the stranger his body rippled with the muscles he'd acquired over years of raising, taming and shoeing horses.

"Ah! Señor Ferrer I assume. Finally. This Indian is insolent. If you do not discipline him he will come to no good end."

"That 'Indian' is my son. Now I asked you a question: What's going on here?" he repeated quietly.

The tall man looked away. "Perhaps you'd be so good as to cover your nakedness. I'm here to discuss business."

Ferrer looked at him intently for a moment then pulled his tunic over his head. He couldn't afford to offend such a wealthy potential customer. "Happy to oblige, Señor. Now what can I do for you?"

"Allow me to present myself: I am *Don Hernando Cortes de Monroy y Pizzaro*, Alcalde of Santiago and Captain General of Governor Velasquez' new expedition to explore Yucatán and the islands beyond. I desperately need horses. I will pay top price for all you have."

Ferrer knew Cortes was the mayor of Santiago but this last tidbit was news. "Another expedition to Yucatán? And you will be leading it? Allow me to congratulate you."

"Thank you. How many horses do you have?"

"I have a couple I could sell I suppose. A filly and a colt, both sired by this noisy fellow." He couldn't conceal his pride as he pointed at Majesty. "The best stallion in all Cuba. Come back here. I'll show them to you." Ferrer turned and walked away. He picked up a bucket and tossed several ears of corn into it. He stood where the fence joined the far side of the barn and noisily shook the bucket, at the same time whistling shrilly. In short order there was a thudding sound as hooves pounded the pasture. Then two small heads poked over the fence to grab the corn. "Meet Aquila and his half-sister, Priscilla."

"They're babies!" Cortes snorted. "What am I supposed to do with those?"

"They're eight months old. In six months time they will be in training to the saddle and carrying a small rider. In a year they will be fine mounts. I can show you their dams if you like."

"I don't have six months. I'm preparing to leave soon. I need horses that can be ridden now. Let me see the mares, their dams."

Ferrer was perplexed for a moment. Then he grasped what Cortes wanted. "Oh! I see. No, I don't own the mares. I simply meant I can show them to you. They are within half a day's ride from here. These youngsters were given to me as payment…"

"If they are within half a day's ride from here I have likely already seen them. I probably already own them. How much for this one then?" He pointed at Majesty.

"Sorry. He's not for sale."

"Everything is for sale. I have the king's own funds behind me." That wasn't true. But Cortes had told the lie so often that he had almost come to believe it himself. "Name your price."

"Majesty is not for sale at any price." A hard edge crept into Ferrer's voice, stopping just shy of disrespect.

"A thousand maravedis."

Ferrer scoffed. The maravedi was a copper coin minted in Spain specifically for use in the New World. It had no intrinsic value. But as there was a shortage of them and it was the only legal tender, they had almost become worth their weight in gold.

There was an even more crucial shortage of horses in Cuba. Spanish explorers led by Governor Velasquez had arrived in Cuba from Hispaniola eighteen years earlier with just eight horses. At Columbus' suggestion and by the king's command every ship coming from Spain to the New World, regardless of its cargo, also brought more horses, and had been doing so for over twenty years. Few enough of those had made their way to Cuba. Only a few survived each trip across the Atlantic. The "Horse Latitudes" got their unfortunate name because of ships getting caught in the doldrums and having to pitch overboard the bodies of horses that died from lack of water. By now Hispaniola had over a thousand horses. But there were still only somewhere between a hundred and perhaps two hundred horses on all of Cuba.

Thus even under normal circumstances an average horse in Cuba was worth seven hundred maravedis. If Cortes was buying up as many horses as he could get, he would have driven the price up substantially.

And regardless of what the market price was, Majesty was in a class by himself.

"Señor," Ferrer said respectfully. "I'm sure I don't need to tell you that most of the Andalusians given to Columbus by the king or sold to captains since then by horse breeders never left Spain. Few of those captains were horsemen and the sailors usually traded the Andalusians secretly for jennets, barbs, or even plow horses; anything to put a few coins in their pockets for drink. And of the Andalusians that did make the crossing, few survived the Horse latitudes. Majesty, as I'm sure you can see, is a true Andalusian. His value as a stud is beyond measure."

Cortes sneered. "'Majesty'. If Charles knew you'd named a horse after him he'd have you flogged. I'll pay fifteen hundred Maravedis."

"He isn't named for Charles. He's a four-year-old. He was named for Ferdinand. And he's not for sale."

Cortes was startled. Not only that this simpleton would turn down fifteen hundred maravedis. But even more so that a dirt-poor horse rancher knew who the current king was; knew who the previous king was; and even knew when Ferdinand had died. Perhaps the man was smarter than he appeared.

"Two thousand. That is more than fair."

"No."

Cortes drew himself up to his full height and glared down his nose at the horseman. Ferrer calmly held his gaze. Then he relented a bit.

"Sir, I mean you no disrespect. But Majesty is my main source of income. He covered nearly thirty mares this past spring at ten maravedis per live birth. Next spring I will be charging fifteen maravedis, and I have already booked thirty-five mares. I expect him to end up covering over forty. And as I said, he is still young. You would have to pay me his earnings for the next ten years to persuade me to part with him. I'm sorry."

Cortes decided to change tacks. "Why don't you and your horse come with us then? *El Gran Cairo* is said to have pagan temples full of gold. After a month in Yucatán, two thousand maravedis will seem like the money you throw to a beggar."

Yucatán and its surrounding islands lay west of Cuba. Even further west lay India. These islands, Ferrer knew, were just beginning to be explored. But none of the expeditions had so far included horses. And none had been found there. While Ferrer had heard the stories told by the few sailors who had returned alive from Yucatán he was skeptical. "Don't tell me you believe the stories about a city of gold?"

Cortes appeared to ponder the idea. "I agree the tales of gold cities are probably exaggerations. If Yucatán is like Cuba, '*El Gran Cairo*' will probably turn out to be a village of grass huts." The returning explorers told stories of Yucatán natives living in huge cities with stone buildings, paved streets, running water and even, if they could be believed, a pyramid. The pyramid had caused the name *El Gran Cairo* to be coined. "What is as good as gold, however, is that we could easily come back with a thousand or more slaves."

The local Taino Indians were not slaves, technically. Twenty-five years earlier Queen Isabella had forbidden enslaving the Indians. Columbus, trying to skirt the edict, had instead declared them subjects of Spain and required them to pay a 'tribute' to their new sovereigns: a small copper hawk's bell was given to each male above fourteen, a novelty they'd never seen before and could be counted on to cherish. But it was to be brought back full of gold every three months. Any who showed up empty-handed had their hands cut off and were left to die. A priest, appalled at the practice, had written to the Queen to stop the slaughter, and recommended instead a system called *encomienda* – protectorate – whereby the Indians were forcibly converted to Christianity, clothed, and fed by a protector assigned by the crown. In exchange they were expected to gratefully give the protector their full-time labor in agricultural pursuits for a pitifully small allowance. It was little better than slavery. It had simply been given another name.

But *encomienda* only applied to the Indians who were natives of Hispaniola and Cuba. Indians brought in from other places were legal slaves, just like Africans. The chief legal distinction between *encomienda* and slave was that slaves could be sold. A healthy adult Indian slave was worth about two-thirds of the value of an African male, who in turn was worth nearly as much as a horse.

Ferrer was unmoved by the offer of wealth. "No, I'm sorry. I'm not interested. My needs are few. And I don't need wealth. I wish you well." He tried to keep his disgust from showing on his face but he hated the idea of slavery. He was convinced it was an unchristian concept and no amount of rationalization would change his view.

Cortes looked thoughtful for a moment. Finally he shrugged. "Very well," he said. "Perhaps we'll speak again before I leave." He turned back to

9

his sorry mare, the monk knelt and Cortes stepped on his back and mounted. Cortes left the yard without another word, the monk on his donkey following behind.

Ferrer was sure that Cortes' parting remarks were not casual observations. And he wasn't wrong.

CHAPTER TWO

"Why did that man behave so?" Felipe asked his father. They had just finished their modest supper of beans and cassava fritters. He wasn't confident enough to use the word "arrogance" but his father knew what he meant.

"Unfortunately, *mijo*, there are more people in the world like him than are like us. He has great ambitions for himself. He is arrogant, prideful. He believes he elevates himself by pushing other people down. Can you tell me what is wrong with that kind of thinking?"

Felipe groaned. He should have known that asking a question would result in a lesson. His father had been his schoolmaster for years and there was no reason to think he was about to abandon that position.

Felipe closed his eyes and mentally scanned through all the pages he'd read and written. His memory was nearly perfect, especially when accessing things he'd written himself. His father had noticed this trait early on. So Felipe had spent a few hours each day since he was little more than four years old reading one of the Bibles and copying the words. First it had been simply copying the letters of the Latin Bible in charcoal onto dried pawpaw leaves. But Miguel had noticed the exactness of the copies, even those he'd done days later from memory. Then Felipe had done the same with the Greek of the Epistles and the Evangels, and finally the Hebrew of Job and the Psalms and the Proverbs. By the time he was seven he was fluent in all three languages in addition to Spanish and his mother's Taino. He had even applied the Latin alphabet to Taino – a language that did not have a written form – and had taught his mother how to read and write her own language before she died.

Miguel Ferrer was not the adventurer that many of his neighbors were. And his name was not really Ferrer. Often as not his neighbors claimed some obscure noble title that fooled no one. Many of them had been given a large swath of land but they wouldn't lift a finger to work it. Labor was beneath them; that was what Indians were for.

Miguel on the other hand really was from a noble family. His father was the second duke of *Arjona*. The duke had sent Miguel, who was to become the third duke one day, to university in Salamanca when he was sixteen. The son quickly discovered an affinity for languages and in no time had read through all the classics in Greek, Hebrew and Latin. His language skill had brought him to the attention of Cardinal Cisneros, whose team was working on a polyglot Bible. Its Old Testament was in three columns: First, the original Hebrew, second an interlinear with Latin words beneath each Hebrew word, and the third column containing the Latin Vulgate. The New Testament was being laid out the same way with Greek, interlinear, and Vulgate in three columns.

Miguel, as most students do, asked questions. Why didn't the Latin Vulgate say the same thing as the original? Did the Church have the right to change the words of the Bible? And most importantly, Why was all this work being put into a Bible that could only be read by scholars? Why not translate it into Spanish so the people could read it? The answer he got – 'Because the pope said so' – was not good enough. So Miguel began creating a Spanish translation himself. When he showed a couple pages of his work to Cardinal Cisneros he didn't get the praise he was hoping for. As he read, the cardinal's face grew almost purple. Then he ripped the pages to pieces.

"How dare you! Who do you think you are? Have you never heard of the Inquisition?" With that his voice dropped as he realized what he was saying. He looked around as if expecting an inquisitor to jump out of the woodwork. "Stop this work immediately. Never speak of this again. If word of this got out you could be burned at the stake!"

Miguel never spoke of it again but he didn't stop the work. He immediately rewrote the two pages the cardinal had torn up and continued his work on a Spanish translation every night after the others in his dormitory had gone to sleep. In due time of course, one of his classmates got in trouble and used Miguel's nighttime project to deflect attention from himself. This time when he came to Cisneros' attention, there was no escape. It was 1508 and the Inquisitors were actively looking for the slightest hint of disobedience. But men were needed in the New World. Cisneros gave Miguel a hundred gold *reales* – each worth over three hundred maravedis – and demanded that he ride for Pontevedra that very night. "There are ships leaving from there for the New World nearly every month. Change your name. Keep out of sight until you sail. I'll think of something to tell your father," Cisneros said. "I'm not going to have you burned at the stake. Your father would stop his endowment to this University. And that would be the end of my polyglot."

Exploration, adventure and gold prospecting in the New World did not hold nearly as much interest for Miguel as his studies. As he packed his saddlebags he took only a single change of clothes. But he packed three Bibles: Latin, Hebrew and Greek, all of which he owned. And he used Cisneros' cash to purchase from a fellow student a new Latin-Spanish dictionary the student had likely "borrowed" from the University Library. He also went from room to room spreading around more of Cisneros' gold coins to acquire as much paper as his classmates were willing to part with. He left town with nearly five hundred sheets of the valuable commodity and boarded a caravel in Pontevedra as Miguel Ferrer – a name he borrowed from the author page of his new Spanish dictionary.

***

"Felipe, tell me: what do the scriptures say of arrogance?" his father nudged him. It was not a question he would have raised even to a learned priest. It was a ridiculously difficult question for one as young as Felipe. The concept came from a rather complex Hebrew idiom that would need explanation. But he also knew Felipe's was no ordinary mind. He could see the concentration on his son's face as he scrolled through all the memorized verses. Then his face cleared and he began to recite:

"'Raise not thy horn on high, nor speak arrogantly with a stiff neck.' Book Three of the Psalms, the third psalm of Asaph. But Don Cortes doesn't have horns, does he? Do you think he had a stiff neck?"

"His stiff neck is an attitude, not a medical condition. Imagine if Majesty had horns. Now..."

Felipe burst out laughing. "He would be a bull!"

"True. Nevertheless try to imagine him with horns. When the horns are up high, what is Majesty thinking?"

Felipe raised his head proudly and bellowed. "'I'm the greatest stallion in Cuba!'" He did look a bit like Majesty. Well, actually, he looked more like the arrogant Don.

"So what do you think the psalm means when it talks about a person raising his horn?"

Light dawned. Felipe's face lit up as he understood the lesson. "So that is what 'arrogant' means?"

"Yes. But we must never call someone arrogant. They would be insulted. What is the opposite of arrogant?"

Again the somewhat disconcerting, unfocused stare as Felipe accessed the invisible pages of his memory. "'God resists the proud, but gives grace to the humble.' The Epistle of Santiago. What's grace?"

"That is a lesson for another time. For now, can we agree it is better to have a gift from God than for him to resist us?" Felipe nodded vigorously. "Okay then. So, for us to call someone arrogant, would that make us humble or arrogant?"

"I see," said Felipe. "It would be arrogant to call someone arrogant. Is it okay for me to think someone's arrogant as long as I don't call them arrogant?"

"Not really. It is not our place to judge."

"But if I'm only thinking it, not saying it, is that judging?"

13

"Still, better not to even think it. Not until you are older. Better, for now, to assume you simply don't understand someone. Come on, time for bed."

CHAPTER THREE

Two days later Cortes returned. He was still riding the sad, sorrel mare and followed by the monk on the donkey. This time, however, they were accompanied by four soldiers on foot, each wearing steel armor and helmets and carrying pikes.

"Señor Ferrer," Cortes bellowed. "Don't try to hide. I know you're here! Present yourself immediately!"

Ferrer, who'd been working in his cornfield when he heard the group approaching, was nearly to the house when the words reached his ears. What on earth? He wasn't trying to hide. He strolled into the yard brushing mud from his legs. "What is the meaning of this?" he asked.

One of the soldiers unrolled a piece of parchment and began to read from it. "'In failing to respond to charges made against you in the king's court in Santiago-'"

"What charges? How could I respond? This is the first I've heard of it!"

"Don't interrupt. Where was I...'you have been found guilty of assaulting the person of the alcalde of Santiago...'"

"You!" Ferrer whirled and pointed a finger at Cortes. "You snake! I never assaulted you! I never laid a finger on you." He turned to the monk. "You, sir: I call you as a witness. Before God, upon your soul, did I attack this man in any way?"

Cortes didn't wait for the monk to answer. "Your opportunity to question witnesses was at the trial yesterday. You did not. It is too late to do so now. You have already been found guilty. By the court's decree you have been fined two thousand maravedis. Do you have it?"

"What? Of course I don't have it! No one has that kind of money!"

"I thought not. I paid the fine for you. I will take your livestock as collateral. These men will remand you to the prison in Santiago until you have repaid the debt with interest."

"You criminal! You son of a viper! How am I supposed to repay a debt I don't owe from inside the prison?" Still rattled, the realization finally dawned. "This is nothing more than a ploy to get Majesty from me! You're worried how you will look at the head of your 'expedition' sitting on that sorry excuse of a pony!"

"As I said, the matter is closed. You will come along; peacefully or otherwise. But you will come."

"Papa? What's happening?" Felipe had been fishing at the far end of the farm when the delegation had arrived. He had run as fast as he could when he heard the commotion. But he knew in his heart that something bad was happening and that there was little he could do to extricate his father from whatever was going on.

Miguel turned and grabbed the boy, scooping him up in one massive arm. "This- this gentleman has a piece of paper that says I am guilty of striking him and he's taking Majesty."

"He can't do that! You didn't strike him!" Felipe turned to face Cortes. "You can't do that! Majesty is ours! He's not for sale!" He struggled to get down from Ferrer's grasp but his father held onto him, worried what the boy might do.

"Yes, Majesty is still yours," Cortes explained to the boy. "I'm merely keeping him for a while until your father pays the debt that he owes." He turned to Ferrer. "Not just Majesty. The order specifies *all* your livestock. I'll be taking Majesty with me today. I'll have some of my *encomienda* run your farm and take care of your other animals while you are in debtor's prison. Only until the farm pays the debt of course."

Felipe's eyes filled with tears and he fought them back. "You can't throw my father in prison! He's a good man! He's a better man than you! God will punish you for your arrogance!"

Cortes loosed his most scornful look upon Ferrer. "Is this what you teach your child? To insult others? That you are a better man than me? Or perhaps it is his Indian nature speaking?"

Ferrer said nothing. His mind churned, trying to find a way out of this predicament. But he could see none. He didn't believe for a moment Cortes' promise of running the farm. He'd simply take the livestock and abandon the fields. The corral, barn and house would crumble and gradually be devoured by the jungle. It would never contribute one maravedi to his debt.

But he had another overriding concern. What was to become of Felipe now? If Cortes forgot about him he'd be alone on the farm, with no livestock and no way to feed himself other than fishing and picking whatever grew wild. The boy himself would grow wild.

On the other hand if Cortes remembered Felipe he might easily decide to throw Felipe into the same prison as his father. The prison was notorious for squalor and disease. Felipe wouldn't last more than a few months. As he quickly churned through these few options another slim possibility, nearly as painful, presented itself.

Cortes had walked to the corral and reached through the bars to pat Majesty's nose. With a yelp he quickly drew back his bleeding hand and stuck a finger in his mouth. "He bit me! Why haven't you trained him better than that? How am I supposed to get him saddled?"

"Felipe, go calm Majesty and put Don Cortes' saddle on him."

16

"Papa…"

"Go!"

"Yes, sir."

As Felipe worked with the tall stallion Ferrer furtively watched Cortes. As it began to dawn on Cortes that Felipe was quite proficient at handling the high-spirited animal Ferrer made his suggestion.

"I think you'll be needing a good groom for the horse."

"I have grooms."

"They may not want to lose any of their fingers. You need a groom that can get this horse to do your bidding."

Cortes watched Felipe as he looped the bridle over his wrist and cupped a handful of grain, holding it down low. When Majesty dropped his head for the grain Felipe easily slipped the bit into Majesty's teeth, tied the straps on the bridle, and dropped the rein to the ground. The horse stood as if the rein were attached to a stump. Felipe then came over to the mare and uncinched the saddle. Carrying it over one arm he went and retrieved a box to stand on and placed it beside the stallion. He stepped up on the box and threw the saddle over Majesty's back then cinched it under his belly. Majesty stood still the entire time.

"Very well," Cortes said. "Perhaps he'll be useful. I'll take him along."

Ferrer breathed again. He hadn't realized how much he was counting on this decision. But he wasn't done. "What is your pay rate for grooms?" Ferrer asked.

Cortes shot him a look. "Be thankful he's not going to be rotting in prison with you!" he hissed.

"Don't tell me you convicted him *in absentia* as well as me? No? Then he's free to work for you. All we need to determine is his rate. 'The workman is worthy of his wage' after all. What are you offering?"

Cortes blew out a sigh. "Fine," he said. "Room and board and a maravedi a week." Ferrer didn't dare to look relieved. A maravedi a week was about a third of the wage a grown man would receive. Still, by offering any wages, he was acknowledging that Felipe was free, not a slave; a crucial distinction.

"Two maravedis."

Cortes shook his head and stepped up to the tall stallion. The monk knelt and the Don climbed into the saddle. Majesty immediately reared and twisted to his right. To Ferrer's surprise Cortes kept his seat. He yanked on the rein with his left hand, while pulling the short whip from his boot with his right.

"No!" Felipe screamed. He ran straight at horse and rider, throwing up one hand to block Cortes' blow while reaching for Majesty's rein with the

17

other. The horse stopped bucking and lowered his head to nuzzle Felipe's hair. Cortes, in turn, dropped his arm, returning the whip to his boot.

"Very well. Two maravedis a week," Cortes said to Ferrer. "We'll apply it to your debt," he added smoothly.

At two maravedis a week, Ferrer knew he would be in prison until Felipe was grown with a family of his own. But it was the best he could do for his son.

CHAPTER FOUR

November, 1518

The town of Santiago was barely four years old. It smelled of fresh-cut pine and rang with shouts, clamor, the banging of hammers and the thunk of axes. A start had been made building it five years ago on the other side of the harbor. But the town had been plagued by fire ants and some of its citizens, trying to burn them out, had burned the town instead. Some believed it had not been an accident.

The new town had an enormous plaza. There was a fountain in the middle but so far no water pulsed from it. It would require an aqueduct from a nearby hill to provide the necessary water pressure and the aqueduct hadn't been built yet. The square was surrounded by buildings on three sides, the largest of which was Government House where Cortes lived. The fourth side was open to the harbor where another important construction project still remained unfinished: a wharf.

All shipments from Spain to Cuba landed first in Santiago. Cargo had to be offloaded into boats and rowed ashore. Loading the ships with gold, corn, cotton, hides, pineapples and other Cuban goods bound for Spain also required rowing out to the deep water where the ships were anchored. The wharf was sorely needed.

Children are resilient. Felipe was adjusting to his new life. He and half a dozen other grooms slept in the hayloft above the stable behind Government House. While the others slept on the wooden floor Felipe went into the jungle and cut arm-loads of a long, pliable grass, twisted it into rope and wove himself a hammock. While the older stable hands looked skeptically at the native contraption, some of the younger ones asked for his help making hammocks for themselves.

A cook brought out a large caldron of food twice a day. Felipe had learned to push his way through the crush of other stable hands to get a bowl for himself. It wasn't really about the food; he could and did feed himself quite well from the jungle. It was about establishing himself as an equal to the other older, larger hands.

About an hour after the sun rose each day Cortes and dozens of others would arrive at the plaza to practice maneuvers. Felipe and the other grooms saddled the small herd of horses and led them to the plaza where the recruits waited. Majesty had finally, grudgingly agreed to allow Cortes to ride him. Cortes gave each of the men who expressed an interest in riding a try-out. Most were rejected within an hour.

When he'd settled on ten good riders and another ten adequate riders Cortes began putting them through their paces. The men practiced riding in formation, progressing from walk to trot to canter to gallop; on command raising and lowering their lances, and thrusting the lances at targets on the ground, at waist level and head level; dropping their lances and pulling swords. Some of the targets were man-sized posts with melons on top. Everyone laughed when a lancer finally managed to split a melon. Felipe didn't find it funny. It was too easy to picture a lance doing that to a man's head.

Then gun exercise would begin. The guns were not large and certainly not accurate. But they were loud. And Majesty hated them. The first time the guns fired Majesty reared and kicked and took off at a dead run, Cortes sawing uselessly on the rein. They returned after a few minutes, Majesty spent and covered with sweat, Cortes disgusted. "Get him properly trained," he told Felipe. "If he does that again I'll shoot him."

"If you shoot him my father owes you nothing."

"Well then maybe I'll shoot you. Get him trained." And he stalked off. Felipe began a program of purposely startling Majesty: dropping buckets, flapping blankets, pounding loudly on the wall of the stable. He scolded Majesty when he started from the noise and rewarded him with a handful of oats when he ignored the surprise. Within a week Majesty was able to stand next to the guns without flinching as they fired; well, not too much.

Cortes insisted that the cavalry maneuvers continue at one end of the plaza as the guns were exercised at the other, firing at a raft floating in the harbor. This was done not only so that the horses would learn to ignore the noise and commotion, but also so that the gunners learned the order and timing of the cavalry maneuvers.

A battle was a dance. In European warfare infantry took the field first. When enemy cavalry appeared, the infantry knew to form up in tight squares, with lances pointing upward and outward on all sides of the box. If the men in the square kept their nerve and stayed in the formation it was virtually impossible for the cavalry to break them. But once the soldiers were crowded into the tight squares, the horses would peel away and the guns would pound the large, square targets.

Of course Cortes thought it unlikely that the Indians would know of such maneuvers even if they had cavalry. But it was the way he'd been taught to execute a battle, and he saw no reason it wouldn't work even more effectively on an enemy who didn't know the dance. So the cavalry rode in unison and peeled off in unison; the guns fired; the cavalry moved in while the guns were reloaded; then the cavalry moved out of the way in time for the guns to fire again.

Another exercise involved men in line of battle loading and firing arquebuses and crossbows. Every man had either a pike or a halberd – staves taller than a man tipped with an iron point or axe head – in addition to most having crossbows and the few who had arquebuses. Rarely were they given leave to fire at will. Instead they fired only when a Sargento commanded them. They were in two ranks. After firing, rank one held their halberds or pikes pointing at the enemy while rank two reloaded. Then on command they traded tasks. Further complicating this part of the dance was the fact that reloading a crossbow took less time than a man counting slowly to ten. But you could count to sixty or longer while some of the less skilled arquebusiers reloaded their crude machines. So they practiced every day.

After the daily maneuvers, once Majesty was cooled out, washed, watered and fed there was little for Felipe to do until evening when the owners came around to inspect their horses. He'd been shocked the first time a strange man had cuffed him because he didn't like how his mare looked. Felipe wasn't even responsible for the mare; he was simply the closest. He'd discovered the man liked hitting people he considered beneath him. But he was careful to choose victims who were the least likely to hit back. After that Felipe made sure all the horses looked their best at evening stables. He also made sure to stay out of reach of all the horse owners. Another life lesson learned.

Most afternoons he tried to visit his father. At first the jailers drove him away, telling him his father wasn't allowed visitors; when he came back anyway they told him a jail was no place for a child. But he persisted. He learned their names and the names of their wives and children and politely asked about them. He went into the jungle everyday and picked papayas and guavas and pineapples and caught fish and gave these to the jailers. Within a week they were looking forward to seeing him. By the end of the second week Bernardo, the large, unctuous day-shift jailer agreed to let him see his father. "But you can't take that in with you," he said. He pointed to the knife in the sheath tied around Felipe's waist.

"If I leave it at the stable someone will steal it," Felipe replied.

"I'll hold it for you." Felipe pulled the knife from the sheath. "Leave the sheath, too," Bernardo instructed. Felipe untied the belt and handed over belt, sheath and knife, using his medicine bag to hold his tunic closed. Bernardo gave a cursory inspection to the contents of the bag and allowed the boy to keep it.

The cell was built of rough cut pine boards laid horizontally, as thick as a man's hand and three hands wide. The lower half of the walls had been smoothed not by the builders but by the bodies of the various occupants. A single window near the top of the outside wall had been formed simply by cutting a notch in one of the boards large enough to allow light and rain to get in, but too small for a man to get his head out. In the dim light provided by the window Felipe was shocked at what he saw. Ferrer senior had been fed almost nothing – a single bowl of cassava gruel in the morning and another at sunset. His only source of water was whatever came through the leaky roof and window during the almost-daily late afternoon downpour. He'd dug a basin in the floor under the most prolific leak to serve as a reservoir for those days when the rain failed to materialize. He had only one bowl and it needed to be empty every morning to get his allotment of cassava.

"Papa," Felipe whispered to him. "You can't eat the cassava the way they give it to you. It is poisoning you. Mama said you must squeeze it, hard… get all the juice out of it. Then you can eat it."

"I know, mijo. I'll try to do better." The bowl of cassava was so watered down that squeezing it would have accomplished nothing. As Ferrer had gotten hungrier and weaker he'd simply slurped down the contents of the bowl as soon as it arrived, praying that whoever prepared it had squeezed it properly before watering it down for porridge. Spaniards had been unfamiliar with cassava before coming to the West Indies. The Taino, on the other hand, had been eating cassava for centuries. While the root contained unhealthy amounts of cyanide, the Taino had discovered long ago that the poison could be removed simply by grating the root and squeezing the pulp dry. Still, even properly prepared, a man couldn't live long on a diet consisting of nothing but cassava.

Felipe pulled a papaya from his medicine bag and handed it to his father. Ferrer bit into it hungrily, spitting out the seeds. "Eat the seeds too, Papa. Mama said they're good for you." Out of respect for the memory of Felipe's mother Ferrer picked up the seeds he'd spit out and began chewing on them.

When Ferrer had arrived in the islands he had at first been shocked by the nudity of the natives. In Catholic Spain everyone covered every inch of their skin save their faces and hands. The shock had soon worn off and the native nakedness had become perfectly unremarkable. It gave new meaning to the Genesis account of Adam and Eve being naked until they discovered guilt. On his third night in the new land he'd woken to screams. When he went to investigate he'd found a drunken Spaniard trying to rape a young Taino woman. In a seething rage, he'd dealt the man a single tremendous blow that had rendered him senseless, and the beautiful young woman had spoken to him through her tears. He'd had no idea what she said, but immediately vowed to learn the unfamiliar language. The next day the woman and her family found him. They brought baskets of food, cotton fabric with intricately painted designs, and jewelry. The young woman pointed to herself and said, "Macu," and Ferrer realized his language lessons had begun. Over the course of the next few weeks he'd picked up a few words of Taino, and Macu rapidly became fluent in Spanish. He taught her about the Jesus of the Bible. She presented herself to the priest and was sprinkled with holy water after which they were married.

"What else do you have in there?" Ferrer muttered, nodding toward Felipe's shiny black medicine bag decorated with bright red paintings of frogs and storks. No one else had such a bag. Macu had made it for Felipe. She'd caught three large bats, the meat of which had gone into their stew pot one day. She cured the wings in a concoction of fruit, herbs and urine, tanning them into the strongest, lightest-weight leather Ferrer had ever seen. When it was empty it shriveled up to the size of his fist. But it stretched; He'd seen Felipe stow as many as a half-dozen papayas in it.

When he'd been forced into servitude to Cortes, Felipe had quickly run to the house and filled the bag with some food, his sling, fishing line and half a dozen fishhooks, a pocket-sized portrait of his mother Ferrer had commissioned from a traveling painter about a year before she died, several small clay pots of his mother's special herbs, and his father's Toledo steel knife.

Felipe's stable mates, the jailers and in fact most of the people of the town of Santiago had grown accustomed to Felipe carrying the black bag. Sometimes he wore it strategically strapped around his middle like a breechcloth. He opened the mouth of the bag enough now so that his father could see the contents.

"Bernardo would only let me bring the one papaya. He wouldn't let me bring the knife in," Felipe said.

"That's okay. He's afraid I'll use it to escape," said Ferrer. "I was hoping you might have some paper."

"Do you want me to bring some?"

"If you can. Bernardo probably wouldn't allow it. Perhaps you could leave me that line though, and one of your fishhooks." He explained what he had in mind. Felipe was delighted.

Felipe dug through the collection of small clay pots at the bottom of the bag. He pulled out the largest and gave it to his father. "Some of Mama's medicine. Put some of this in your food everyday, Papa. It will help with the cassava poison."

"Time to go!" yelled Bernardo from down the corridor. Felipe gave his father a fierce hug and left.

***

Felipe stopped in front of Bernardo, looking up expectantly. Bernardo's corpulent belly rose and fell slowly as he pretended to sleep. Felipe gently poked him.

"What?"

"My knife, Señor."

"What are you talking about?" Bernardo rumbled.

"You were holding my knife while I visited my father. I'm leaving now; I need my knife back."

"I don't have your knife," Bernardo said.

Felipe pointed to the handle jutting out from the top of the large man's breeches. "My knife, right there."

"That's my knife. Are you trying to steal my knife? Do you want to end up in a cell? Get out of here!" He cuffed the youngster on the ear. "Go!"

Felipe fought back tears. The man was going to steal his father's knife and there was nothing, nothing legal, he could do to stop him. Felipe dropped his head and trudged away.

CHAPTER FIVE

Toledo steel was the finest in the world. When the Muslims were fighting their way across southern Europe in the previous centuries, prevailing in country after country, it seemed nothing could stop them. It wasn't until just fifty years earlier, when their scimitars rang against the steel swords made in Toledo, Spain, that they met there match.

While it was not unusual for Cortes to have an expensive Toledo steel sword it was most irregular for the seemingly low-born Felipe to have a Toledo blade. Bernardo had coveted it from the moment he'd seen it.

Felipe continued to take his jungle fare of pineapples, guavas and fish to the jail as if nothing had happened. Bernardo wore the knife and sheath on his belt proudly, daring Felipe to make another accusation. He didn't accuse. But he always asked.

Felipe now carried a long mahogany stick. He'd picked up a suitable stone and used other stones to shape it into a usable stone knife – which he never brought to the jail. He'd used the stone knife to carve a pretty good likeness of a small sea turtle onto the top of the walking stick and he was working on carving his name down one side. The stone knife was a poor substitute for the Toledo knife. Everyday Felipe politely asked for his knife and everyday Bernardo proclaimed that the Toledo blade was his. Felipe always reacted as he knew a child should when he was being bested by an adult. But he was working on a plan to get the knife back.

The large man lived with two women and several children in a palm hut a short distance from town. The hut was accessed by a narrow trail that seemed to have no other purpose than Bernardo's trips to and from the jail. Felipe had seen no one else use it. At one point, as the trail crested a low ridge it jinked sharply sideways to skirt a large agave plant. Felipe knew Bernardo would be travelling the trail shortly after the bells on the ships at anchor rang, marking the evening meal or simply acknowledging sunset, he didn't know which. He was in his carefully chosen hiding place when the bells rang. He'd removed the cotton tunic his mother had made for him. She wanted him to look less like a native when he was in town. He'd painted his chest, face and arms with yellow and red plant pigments in the patterns his mother's people had taught him: three red stripes down the right side of his face, from forehead to chin; his left cheek blackened with soot; a large yellow circle below his eye; alternating red and yellow horizontal stripes across his bare chest.

As Bernardo came over the ridge Felipe rose from the brush behind him, spun the sling quickly three times over his head and let fly a small pebble. It struck the large man on his left thigh, exactly where Felipe had aimed. Bernardo yelped and jumped to his right, extending his right hand as he did so. As the tip of one agave sword bit into his hand he quickly withdrew it, which only served to unbalance him further, and with a shout he fell completely into the agave.

Felipe ran silently forward. He paused at a distance and observed the large man. By the time he decided it was safe to approach, Bernardo was snoring. Felipe had smeared the tips of all the agave swords with a paste made from *konamey* leaves, being careful not to cut himself on the blue, sharply pointed agave fronds as he did so. Bernardo had managed to cut himself in two dozen places, the swift poison infiltrating each wound. Felipe had often used the paste to stun small animals and fish when hunting, but he'd never used it on so large a prey.

Carefully avoiding all the agave points he untied the belt from the big man's waist and pulled. It took several pulls to get it loose. Bernardo was beginning to stir as the knife, sheath and belt finally came free. Felipe saw one eye begin to open.

Bernardo saw only a blurry image of a small, fierce, naked, painted Taino warrior before the eye drooped closed again.

***

The next day, Felipe appeared at the jail as usual, carrying a string bag of pineapples and guavas for the jailer. He'd learned Bernardo preferred pineapple to papaya. He stopped, seeming shocked, when he saw Bernardo. The rotund man was as swollen as a gourd and covered in angry red welts.

"What happened to you?"

"Nothing. I fell into a poisonous plant."

Felipe propped his stick against the wall and rummaged in his medicine bag. "Here," he said, handing his enemy a small clay pot. "Rub some of this on your wounds. It will help them heal."

Bernardo reached for it eagerly. He even thanked him. Thanked him! Felipe was ecstatic. But the ruse needed to be completed. He looked to Bernardo's waist.

"Where is my knife?" he demanded. Bernardo hung his head. "Where is it? Have you lost my knife?"

"Someone stole it," Bernardo mumbled.

"How could anyone steal from you!" Felipe said incredulously.

"The plant made me sick. Someone, I don't know, one of your people, a savage warrior, huge! With evil markings painted on him. He looked like Satan himself! He took it." Bernardo shook his head, sadly. "It was a beautiful knife. I'll never own another one like it."

26

No you won't, thought Felipe. "I'm sorry for your loss. I'm even sorrier for mine. Now: may I see my father please?"

Bernardo tried to rise, but fell back into his chair with a groan. "Show me your bag," he said. Felipe opened his bat-wing bag. He lifted out the huge papaya he was bringing to his father and tipped the bag so Bernardo could look down on the small clay pots and feathers that covered the bottom of the bag. Without a word he handed Felipe the key to his father's cell. "Make sure you lock up again when you're done. If you forget, no visits for a week."

Felipe thanked him and ran down the hall to his father's cell. He thrust the huge key into the lock, which screeched loudly as it released. Ferrer was standing against the far wall facing the door.

"Papa!" Felipe rushed to hug his frail father. Father and son both wiped away tears.

"I was afraid Bernardo wasn't going to let you back in again unless you brought something else as valuable as the knife," Ferrer said.

"No, he likes me. I'm helping him heal his wounds," he said. Ferrer looked at him curiously.

"Wounds?"

"He was attacked by a savage Taino warrior," Felipe repeated, loudly enough for Bernardo to hear the story from where he sat. "He got several wounds fighting him off."

"Yes he's very brave," his father chimed in.

"Sadly, he lost the knife he was holding for me. The knife you gave me."

Ferrer's face clouded. He knew Bernardo would steal from his son if Felipe kept coming here. He raged inwardly that Cortes had created this scenario that left his son so vulnerable, that kept him from protecting his son.

Oddly though, rather than being downcast at the loss of the family knife, his son was grinning from ear to ear. "Okay, Mijo," he said softly. "What really happened?"

"It was just as he said," Felipe whispered with a grin. "He was set upon by a fierce Taino warrior." He proceeded to tell his father about the trap he'd sprung to retrieve the knife.

"You can't wear it anymore," Ferrer whispered. "If you embarrass Bernardo he will hurt you. Possibly kill you. Do you have a safe place to hide it?"

"Yes I do," Felipe answered. "Very safe. And I have a plan to pay your debt."

***

Felipe returned to Bernardo, commiserated on his wounds and encouraged him to keep using the salve for a few more days.

27

"I can't thank you enough," Bernardo said. "I feel better already."

"In a few days you'll be as good as new." Felipe retrieved his stick from the wall, waved goodbye and walked away.

He was relieved the fat man had ignored the carved walking stick as he'd done on previous visits. Had he looked closely, Bernardo might have noticed that the "Felipe" carving on the side was completed, and very precisely crafted. But no matter how close he looked Bernardo would never have seen that the primitive-looking walking stick was now in two pieces. The banding Felipe had woven out of green bark and wrapped around the stick below his name hid a seam that would allow the stick to slide open, granting quick access to the handle of a fine, and very valuable, Toledo steel knife.

CHAPTER SIX

Felipe had gold fever. At first he couldn't believe it. But sure enough, there were small flecks of gold in the sand at the bottom of the bowl, lifted from the stream he'd been swimming in all his life. When he thought about all the times he'd passed right by the gold he could have collected he mentally kicked himself. He'd never in his entire life given any thought to money; never cared about it at all. But now that his father was in prison for not having any Felipe wanted it in the worst way. Not the wealth of castles. Not the lavish silk clothing of Cortes. Nothing so extravagant. He simply wanted, desperately needed, two thousand maravedis' worth of gold to free his father.

He'd overheard the other stable hands talking about it most evenings. He'd never understood the attraction before. When he was gathering his meager belongings into his bat-wing bag it hadn't occurred to him to grab the gold necklace his mother had worn – he'd thought only of what things he might need to survive. But listening to the grooms discuss their hours spent prospecting, where they searched and the various techniques they used he had begun to believe that gold would solve his father's problem. If gold could be scooped up from the bottoms of streams he needed to start scooping, and quickly; two thousand maravedis' worth.

Estefan, the old groom who was responsible for Sedeño's pregnant mare Isabella, was no wealthier than any of the others. He had nevertheless set himself up as something of an expert on finding gold. Felipe had listened carefully as Estefan lectured.

"Gold is heavier than anything else. So when the rain washes it out of the mountains and begins to carry it downstream it falls to the bottom quickly, as soon as the water slows down. So look for places that slow the water. In a curve of the stream the water moves more slowly on the outside of the curve than on the inside. Also look where the stream suddenly widens into a pond; the gold will likely be at the upper end of the pond. Look below waterfalls; look at sand bars. And don't forget to look for dry cuts and paths where streams used to flow or that only flow when it rains."

He had gone on to explain how to use that same gold-is-heavier-than-everything principle to make the gold flakes collect in the bottom of a shallow pan while slowly swirling the water to carry away the mud and sand. He had also mentioned something about black sand but he got vague on that point. Felipe suspected that Estefan was simply repeating what he'd heard from someone else and didn't really know what black sand meant. Felipe didn't either. But he knew where to find it. He'd swum, waded, fished and hunted along every inch of every stream within a day's hike of his home. And, thinking about it, he'd seen black sand in many of the places Estefan had described.

He didn't have a pan but in a refuse heap behind Bernardo's house he'd found a shallow wooden bowl that looked like it might be the right shape. Thus armed, every day after the morning maneuvers he'd headed out to where he knew he could find black sand in the curve of a creek. He would use the bowl as a shovel to loosen the sand, building a large pile of it, then scoop up a small amount, stoop and scoop in some water, and swirl and rinse and swirl and stare into the bottom of the bowl until his back muscles screamed like they were on fire, straining to spot the tiny gold flecks against the dark sand in the bottom of the bowl. When he spotted some, no matter how few, he carefully picked them out with his fingernails and dropped them into one of the small clay medicine pots he'd emptied just for the purpose. Every few days, after ensuring that the servant Cortes had appointed over their farm was nowhere around, he crept up from behind the barn and deposited his precious finds into a larger pot he'd hidden under Majesty's old watering trough. He had also rescued his mother's gold chain from the house, shocked it hadn't been pilfered, and added it to the pot. In his mind he would weigh the amount in the pot against a gold *Real* he'd once held in his hand. Including the chain, he believed he might have gold worth three hundred maravedis. Only one thousand seven hundred to go! He knew that it would take years to collect the gold needed to pay his father's debt but, as they had discussed, he had a plan to get it paid off much sooner. Thinking of his father made him look up to gauge the position of the sun. Then he took off running for a pineapple patch to collect Bernardo's bribe so he might let him see his father.

***

Bernardo had greedily accepted the pineapple but had refused him permission to see his father. Felipe left, dejected. But as soon as he was out of sight of Bernardo he raced around the building to a spot directly under the small window of his father's cell. Peering closely, he spotted the thin cotton fishing line with the hook attached. He pulled from the bat-wing bag a small, rolled up piece of leather. Inside was another page he'd torn from the Latin bible – at his father's direction – and five more sheets of the paper he'd salvaged from their farmhouse, rolled around a new quill. His father now had nearly thirty sheets of the precious commodity. On earlier visits he'd delivered an inkhorn in the same fashion. Ferrer senior had found a gap under one of the boards where he was able to scrape away some of the dirt floor to create a cache for his precious writing project. Felipe jabbed the fishhook through the end of the leather roll and tugged on the line. A moment later the leather-wrapped package rose up to the window and disappeared inside.

CHAPTER SEVEN

The news flashed through the town like lightning: Governor Velasquez was unhappy. He believed Captain-General Cortes was behaving less like a captain and more like a general, and he was going to replace him. He had asked his advisors about picking a replacement to head up the Yucatán expedition.

The news, of course, reached Cortes as well, and it galvanized him. He was determined not to be replaced. Having been given such a golden opportunity he was not going to allow it to slip through his fingers. He stormed into the stables. Felipe was there, fortunately, with a couple other grooms. Bernardo had been in a mood and had refused to let Felipe visit with his father so he'd returned to the stable early.

"Get the horses on board," Cortes demanded. He pointed at Majesty, Isabella, a sorrel mare and a bay mare. "These go on the flagship. Divide the others among the rest of the fleet." When the stable hands slowly stood and looked at one another Cortes yelled. "Now! I want them loaded immediately! We leave tonight." His magenta cape billowed as he turned on his heel and stalked out of the stable.

As soon as Cortes left the hands began buzzing about this turn of events. Felipe, on the other hand, wanted to comply with the orders to move immediately but wasn't sure where to begin. Fortunately, an older groom named Pedro knew what to do and wasn't interested in gossip. He'd come out from Spain with horses that had off-loaded in Hispaniola. He'd also helped transport one of the first small herds shipped from Hispaniola to Cuba ten years earlier.

"Let's go," he said. He tied a lead to the halter of the sorrel. He pointed at Felipe. "Hold back with Majesty until we deal with the others. We don't need him trying to prove what a great stallion he is! Bring one of the mares." He opened the stall of the sorrel and led her out. Since Estefan was missing Felipe caught Isabella's halter and led her after Pedro.

When they arrived at the water's edge Pedro waved over the owner of a rowboat. He explained what he wanted, promising him Cortes would pay his bill. Then he and Felipe climbed into the rowboat, still holding the lead ropes of the two horses.

"Slowly, slowly," Pedro told the boatman. The boatman leaned on his oars and began to row toward the *Concepcion*. Naturally, the horses balked a bit when the water got too deep to walk. But Pedro and Felipe insisted, tugging on the lead ropes and whistling encouragement, and the horses began to swim. The strange-looking flotilla – rowboat, two men, a boy and two bobbing horses' heads – made its way to the side of the ship. The sailors had seen them coming and had already rigged a line over the end of a yardarm. The line ended in a sling padded with old sailcloth. Pedro deftly fished the sling under the sorrel mare, fastened the brass fitting tight at her withers then signaled the sailors. The line came taut and the horse rose dripping from the sea, head lowered, looking not at all like the proud mare she had appeared in the stable.

The sling dropped back down and Felipe tried to fish it under Isabella as he'd seen Pedro do. But she was too broad and his arms were too short. He had to defer to Pedro. Pedro signaled the sailors to give him more slack. He formed a loop in the line and threw it into the water in front of her nose. He let it sink beneath her feet then drew it up under her. He clipped the sling and straightened the wrinkles out of the canvas under her belly as best he could Then he jerked a thumb up to the sailors. Isabella emitted a sad-sounding neigh as the pressure increased on her pregnant abdomen but then she, too, was hoisted from the water. Pedro hung onto the rope and got a free ride up. As his feet cleared the railing he jumped to the deck. Felipe waited with the boatman, wondering if there was something he should be doing. Just as he was thinking he should probably climb up to the deck somehow and help, Pedro dropped back into the boat. "Let's go," he said. The boatman rowed them back to shore.

They made another trip, taking two horses out to the *Santiago*. Some of the other stable hands had managed to load three horses onto the *Trinidad* but then they'd left, deciding to snatch their last opportunity to get drunk. Pedro and Felipe led Majesty and the one remaining mare to the shore for the trip to *Concepcion*. Majesty, white-eyed in terror, swam out of necessity. But he fought and tugged against the lead the whole way to the ship. When it came his turn to be wrapped in the sling he wouldn't let Pedro get near him. Finally, Felipe stood and stripped off his tunic. He took the end of the rope in one hand and dove into the water. Surfacing on the other side of Majesty he clipped the sling tight as he'd seen Pedro do. Majesty continued to squirm and kick. Felipe climbed onto his back as if he was going to ride him and muttered in his ear. Majesty calmed, Pedro signaled, and both horse and boy rose into the air.

As they settled on the deck Majesty found his footing and Felipe looked around, trying to make sense of the tangle of ropes, wood, sails and men. He spotted the other horses in temporary boxes at the rear end of the deck, just ahead of where there was a step up to another deck. He led Majesty over there and coaxed him into one of the empty stalls. He looked at how the other horses were secured and did his best to copy the arrangement with Majesty.

"No, that's too tight." Pedro had come up as he was working on the sling under Majesty's belly. "It is not a *hammock*," he said, grinning at the new Taino word he'd learned from Felipe. "It should not support any of his weight. It is only there to keep him from falling to his knees if he loses his footing."

"Thank you, Señor."

"Stick with me, I'll make you a seagoing horseman, or a horse-riding seaman, in no time."

***

While they'd been loading the horses every boat in the harbor had been pressed into service to ferry soldiers, sailors, food, water and other supplies to the ships. One of the sailors said Cortes had traded a gold chain for the entire contents of the town's only butcher shop. The townsfolk didn't know they were going to become vegetarians tomorrow. The gunners had loaded their cannon from the beach using tactics even more complicated than loading the horses. Each gun barrel had had to be removed from its carriage and suspended on a sling between two boats, tilting both precariously.

Felipe caught a ride back to shore on one of the empty boats and raced to the jail. He didn't bother to approach the jailer, who would never allow him to see his father this late at night. He simply ran around to the back of the building. Along the way he had snagged a piece of charcoal from a dead fire. He scoured the ground and finally found a piece of wood small enough to fit through the window. He quickly sliced one side of it smooth with his knife so he could write on it.

In biblical Greek he wrote to his father: "Voyage begins tonight. If you get free look under Majesty's watering trough. I love you. Your son, Felipe." He drove the fishhook deep into the wood and tugged on the line. Tears came to his eyes as the wooden message rose. He wondered if he would ever see his father again.

33

CHAPTER EIGHT

December, 1518

They didn't sail very far.

Cortes had instructed one of the captains to take his caravel to Jamaica to purchase all he could for the expedition and meet the rest of the fleet back at the western tip of Cuba. The rest of the small fleet he instructed to meet him in five days at the village of Trinidad, three hundred miles further west along the southern coast of Cuba. Before heading there himself, Cortes took the flagship to Macaca where there was a royal storehouse.

His red velvet jacket now sported several brass buttons in amongst the gold as some of the Santiago merchants hadn't been willing to extend Cortes credit. Nevertheless, donning the long-suffering jacket and escorted by eight soldiers holding aloft his extravagant banner Cortes cowed the local quartermaster into believing he was on the King's business. He came away with three hundred rounds of iron balls for each gun, two tons of gunpowder, a dozen pigs and forty tons of cassava bread. With a flourish he signed the invoice presented by the quartermaster and told him he could send it to Governor Velasquez but that he'd likely get paid sooner if he sent it directly to the king. The quartermaster vowed to put it on the next ship bound for Spain. While Cortes was taking care of that all the ship's water casks were being taken ashore and filled.

There had been two previous expeditions westward from Cuba. In 1517 Francisco de Cordoba and a hundred Spaniards had set out in three ill-prepared ships. The pilot, Anton de Alaminos, had been one of Columbus' navigators. Cordoba's stated mission was to claim lands for Spain; the unstated mission was to collect slaves and gold.

The mission was a disaster. Their water casks leaked. When they went ashore on Yucatán to refill the casks they were nearly all injured in a battle with the locals. Half died of their injuries, including Cordoba.

A year later Juan de Grijalva set off from Cuba with four ships and a couple hundred men, including the pilot Alaminos. Velasquez's instructions to Grijalva had been to offer glass beads and other trinkets to the Indians in exchange for gold and to capture slaves if possible but, in accordance with standing orders, not to alienate the natives. No one seemed bothered by the contradiction between those two objectives. What Velasquez really wanted, however, was for Grijalva to read between the lines, ignore the orders about not alienating the natives and expand the territory over which Velasquez was governor.

Grijalva failed to read between the lines. More cautious than Cordoba he took possession of a small island when the locals fled into the jungle. On the Yucatán coast he traded for some gold and jewels but, aside from naming a river after himself and mapping a bit of the coastline he accomplished very little. He returned to Cuba less than a month before Cortes' rapid departure with little to show for his efforts.

Cortes was determined that he could be successful where his predecessors had failed. When he rejoined his fleet in the harbor at Trinidad he reassessed their equipment. Their armaments totaled only five five-pounder cannon, eight lighter guns called falconets, thirty-two crossbows, twenty arquebuses and one hundred Indian servants. So far he'd acquired only nine horses.

After horses his most critical need was men. He had left Santiago with nearly three hundred. While many who were down on their luck volunteered in the hopes of finding their fortune in gold, he rejected most of them. A man had to bring something to the table: special skills like blacksmithing; a horse; weapons; or money. If a man couldn't supply either weapons, skills or a horse he had to pay for the privilege of joining the expedition. In exchange he would receive a share of the gold and slaves the trip was expected to garner.

Most were blinded by greed. A few, like Felipe's new mentor Pedro, had enough experience to know that things so easily taken for granted on Cuba could be life-threatening in unexplored territory. Things like water. Pedro had been greatly concerned when they'd left Santiago with nearly empty casks and was relieved the casks were now full.

"Just these few horses," Pedro remarked, "will go through more water every day than the entire crew does." Felipe didn't know how many men were on board – fifty, sixty, perhaps a hundred? He knew Majesty could drink a lot of water but he'd never measured it. Pedro continued. "If the men don't get enough water they will be thirsty, they'll complain. But if the horses don't get enough they'll die. And quickly."

Cortes knew horses as well and he'd evidently been thinking about the same thing. Orders came to the harbor: The horses were to come ashore, followed by all the soldiers. Since Trinidad like Santiago had no dock, the horses again had to swim for it. This time, however, they were not lowered over the side in a sling. A piece of the rail was removed and a ramp was installed that reached down to about two paces above the water. The horses were released from their boxes and driven down the ramp in a bunch. They leapt into the water and swam for shore. Majesty, of course, tried to balk. But the sorrel mare crowding down the ramp behind him pushed him into the water. Felipe was petrified that Majesty would either hurt himself or run off. He didn't hurt himself; but he did run off.

When Felipe got to shore a short while later he learned a new word. Several of the soldiers were calling *mostengo, mostengo*! Apparently it meant 'loose horse!' Majesty and one of the mares was nowhere to be found. Felipe walked around the small town whistling as loudly as he could and shaking some corn in a wooden bucket. It didn't take long for Majesty to come looking for his treat. And the other missing *mostengo* was right behind him.

CHAPTER NINE

Cortes rented a house in the center of Trinidad to use as a recruiting center and hung his banner outside of it. He made inquiries about a caravel anchored in the harbor. Finding it was owned by a local merchant he purchased it, confident he could fill it with men and supplies. He also managed to buy three more horses. One was completely untrained. A second was nearly too old to be much use. The third was a fine black mare, well reined. Felipe couldn't help wondering what pressure Cortes had applied to Señor Maron to convince him to part with her.

There were two blacksmiths in town. Cortes pressed them into service making ten additional crossbows and hundreds of bolts for the crossbows. A ship arrived with dozens of crates of kitchen implements. Cortes purchased them all. He set the blacksmiths to hammering ladles into lance and pike points. Both men joined the expedition.

The guns were ferried ashore and practice continued. The practice was greatly needed. After a gun was fired its crew of six had to wheel it back to its starting point. The rammer drove a wet swab down the barrel to extinguish any remaining sparks and withdrew it. The powder-man poured powder from a keg into a measuring-cup-like device with a long handle. He delivered it down the barrel and withdrew it. Next, another crewman stepped forward and shoved a wad of plant leaves down the barrel. He used a rammer and tamped the leaves down hard, both to compact the powder and to form a seal so the powder would explode rather than simply burn. Crewman number four then dropped into the barrel an iron or stone ball, and it too was rammed home. By this time the powder-man had filled a smaller measuring cup and poured more powder down the touch-hole at the base of the gun, then stepped back out of the way. The chief gunner stepped forward and sighted along the barrel. The gun was wheeled left or right as needed and the wheels chocked. Wooden wedges were either driven under or removed from under the barrel to adjust for height. With a last look around to make sure no one was standing where they would be struck by the recoil the chief gunner reached out with a long stick that had a smoldering fuse attached to one end. He held it to the touch-hole for a moment then quickly jumped out of the way. The gun fired and the gun crew strained to see where the shot went. Cortes began to count, loudly. By the time their hearing began to return the gun crew heard him saying "twelve, thirteen…" as they quickly started the loading and aiming process again. When they were finally ready to fire, Cortes would be intoning, "three hundred ten! Three hundred eleven! Three…" He wanted it under two hundred. So they practiced.

One benefit to all the gunnery practice was the spectacle. People came from miles inland to see the show, and word spread about the new expedition. Some of the men who had so recently been with Grijalva's half-hearted exploration came as well. Many of them, having returned less than a month ago with a little stolen gold in their pockets, had gotten no further than the bars nearest the harbor. Those with more restraint had returned to their homes, most of which were within a few days' ride of Trinidad. Watching the guns work got them thinking about their superiority of firepower over the Indians and about the hints of gold they'd seen on their recent trip. They forgot about the dangers, the arrows, the thirst and the homesickness. In all, nearly a hundred of them joined Cortes.

The other benefit from the gun practice came quite by accident. Often, the roughly-shaped stone balls fractured when fired from the cannon, rock shards flying in a short arc rather than a long straight line. This happened once to the gun at the end of the line closest to the jungle and the resulting shot, instead of sending a ball a quarter of a league down range, spewed a short, deadly cloud of gravel that shredded several nearby trees. Cortes saw it happen and it gave him an idea.

After consulting with several of the experienced gunners they began experimenting with different loads. They gradually worked out the ideal load. Then Cortes gathered together all of his sailors and put them to work sewing small sailcloth bags. Each bag was filled with five pounds of iron scraps, nails or gravel and sewed shut. Practice proved that if they were fired in an upward trajectory as with a ball, the iron and gravel when it fell was little more than an annoyance. But fired level, a cloth bag of gravel and nails fanned out in a short but devastating swath.

***

Felipe quickly bored of watching the gunners practice and spent his time exercising Majesty. Estefan claimed Isabella was too far along in her pregnancy to be ridden by a full-grown man, so the task of exercising her fell to Felipe as well. Felipe knew exactly how far along Isabella was. He had first met her when Señor Sedeño had inquired about having her covered by Majesty but in the end decided not to pay the premium. That had been almost nine months ago… though it seemed a lifetime. He knew Isabella would be happy to carry a full-grown man for at least another month but he knew better than to argue with the older man. Between the two horses Felipe became familiar with all the trails within ten leagues of Trinidad.

His thoughts turned often to his father. Though he'd never been this far from home he knew if he ran off and kept moving east he would eventually come across landmarks that he recognized. He knew how to live off the land. He could be back in Santiago within a month or two. If he took Majesty he could be there even sooner. If Cortes sent men after him Felipe had no doubt he could elude them.

But Cortes wouldn't send men after him. He needed all the men he had. No, he'd simply send word back to Santiago to throw Felipe in jail as soon as he was spotted. He had already proven he was vindictive – he might simply order Felipe's father killed.

He missed his father terribly but running away wasn't the answer. He needed to find a way to cancel the debt and exonerate his father.

CHAPTER TEN

Felipe ran faster through the moonlit trees. It was the third time today he'd made this trip and his legs felt like lead. A low hanging tree branch whipped across his face, leaving a stinging red line, but he slapped it aside and pushed on. He wished now he'd taken Majesty. But Cortes in his anger and frustration had ridden Majesty hard that afternoon. If Felipe broke him down there was no telling how Cortes might retaliate. The deciding factor, though, had been the man's nature: If Cortes found any reason to visit the stables this evening he was unlikely to notice, or care about, Felipe's absence. But he would immediately notice Majesty's absence.

***

The day had started simply enough. Of all the men from Grijalva's expedition who had re-enlisted with Cortes one had been noticeably absent: Alaminos, the pilot. Cortes had waited, confident the expert navigator would show up. As days passed and the pilot remained absent Cortes grew impatient. He sent a delegation offering a sizable bounty to lure Alaminos to the recruiting office and he waited some more. When Alaminos still didn't show Cortes asked around. He soon discovered that the man was living with a native woman on a land grant of twenty *caballerias* somewhere near the trail that ran out of Trinidad toward Havana. He was said to be engaged in building himself a castle.

Cortes decided to seek him out. Felipe had saddled Majesty for him and one of the mares for his ever-present priest, Diaz. The small band that left the stable that morning had consisted only of Cortes, Diaz, and a couple soldiers holding high a smaller version of Cortes' grand banner. Almost as an afterthought he ordered Felipe to join them.

"I don't know exactly where this supposed castle is," he said. "We may have to ask for directions from an Indian. If so I'll need you to translate. I assume you speak Indian?"

Felipe paused a moment. "Taino. Yes, sir."

Felipe had found the excursion to be a pleasant break from his routine. Cortes and Diaz walked their horses so the soldiers had no trouble keeping up. As boys do Felipe ran ahead, left the trail to inspect this plant or that rock or those animal tracks and then jogged to catch up with the small group. When his stomach began to growl he again ran ahead, caught several fish and had them sizzling over a fire in the middle of the track when Cortes and the others caught up with him. Cortes was clearly pleased to be presented with an unexpected hot meal. He wondered, but was too proud to ask, how a small, nearly naked boy had built a fire, caught and roasted fish and cut pawpaw leaves to serve as plates while apparently carrying no tools. His hunger quickly overcame his curiosity.

After the meal, about an hour further along the track they heard faint sounds of hammers and axes and followed the noise to the construction project. The project resembled not so much a castle as a pile of stones and a log cabin. Alaminos greeted them courteously and introduced Cortes and the priest to his wife, Ana.

Felipe greeted her in Taino. "Good day Auntie."

"Good day to you, child," she replied. "I am Anacoana." The woman had quickly thrown a shawl around herself when the riders approached but the priest, Diaz, still looked at the beautiful woman with disapproval.

"Why do you wear that?" he asked, pointing at the heavy, gold cross hanging around her neck. It was larger than his own crucifix. "Do you know what it means? Have you been baptized?"

"She certainly has, Father," answered Alaminos. "And I'll thank you not to speak to my wife in that manner." Alaminos didn't want the father to look too closely at the cross around Ana's neck. It wasn't actually a crucifix of the Holy Roman Church. Rather, it was part of the loot he'd acquired from the natives on his last trip.

Felipe didn't understand what had transpired but Cortes mumbled something to the priest, who walked away and sat down in the shade near his mare and the two soldiers.

Alaminos smiled at Cortes and Felipe, his high spirits restored, and showed them around the new building under construction.

"From here," he said, pointing north, "you look down on that river. I'm calling it the Nuevo Tinto. You have been to Palos, yes? Of course! You must have sailed from there when you came out to the Indies. Well, to me, the bend where the Tinto passes through Palos just before it reaches the harbor looks much like this. Or at least it did look like this before Don Columbus made Palos famous. If you look down there to the west you can just see where it meets the bay. When the hacienda is finished there will be a balcony just here, with the finest view in all of Cuba."

Cortes barely glanced at the finest view in all of Cuba. "It will be a nice place to retire, when you're old. Right now I need you."

"Señor, I am old! I am retired!" He grinned. "Soon I will be forty. But," he added ominously, "I will not see forty if I keep making these foolish trips to the west."

"Foolish?"

"Yes, foolish! The Indians there are not simple, peaceful people like our Indians here. They do not speak any language we understand. They live in

41

cities of stone, not huts. They don't lay around eating fruit from the jungle. They run, they fight one another, and they wear armor!"

"Armor?" This was news to Cortes.

"Yes, armor. It is only cotton armor but it is thick. It is enough to protect them from sticks and stones. It will even deflect a sword stroke unless one strikes very hard. And they hate Spaniards! Hate us! If you give them the chance they will split you open and sacrifice your still-beating heart to their gods while they drink your blood! No, my friend. I've seen enough of those savages to last me a lifetime. If Yucatán is an island it is not like these islands. And if it is truly part of India we should leave it to the Indians!"

"We will be coming at them with much more than sticks and stones," replied Cortes. "We have guns, arquebuses, crossbows, Toledo steel and horses. More than that, however," he added as his voice rose. "We have an obligation from our savior – and a commission from our king – to bring Christ to these benighted children of his. To baptize them into the mother church!"

"You may," Alaminos nodded. "You may be able to get some of them to agree to baptism, perhaps in exchange for some glass beads and mirrors. But you will not really change them. Not like my Ana," he said, pointing to the girl carrying a metal cup of water over to the priest. "She is a true believer. But those Indians over on Yucatán will still be ripping the hearts out of captives as soon as your back is turned. And calling it Christianity."

"Well then that will merely make our job simpler," Cortes responded. "If they convert they will pay tribute. If they remain in their heathen practices then they will not have Christ's protection, and they will become our slaves. And they can do so willingly or they can die and stand before His judgment."

***

Cortes was in a foul mood as they returned to Trinidad. Alaminos had adamantly refused to join the expedition. Felipe knew instinctively that no young-boy antics would be tolerated so he simply padded along silently behind the small group. He heard Cortes speaking and moved closer to see if the man was addressing him. Instead, he realized Cortes was conversing with the priest. And they were speaking Latin.

"Without Alaminos my expedition will fare no better than Grijalva's," Cortes was saying.

"If God wants you to succeed you will succeed. Perhaps God himself will be your pilot," the monk replied sanctimoniously.

"With all due respect to God, I'd rather have Alaminos. He knows the pitfalls. He has records of the coastline, the soundings, where to water the fleet... I must have him!" Cortes pounded the pommel of his saddle in frustration and Majesty sidestepped skittishly. They rode on in silence for a bit.

"If this were Spain…" the priest mused, then trailed off.

"'If this were Spain,' what?" prompted Cortes.

"Well, sir, you know such things better than I. Did you see how the woman was dressed before she saw us?"

"Yes, yes. I saw you staring. So what? I don't care about his wife. Get to the point." Cortes demanded.

Diaz was not to be rushed. "I don't know how it would be done in Cuba. There is no convent here. But in Spain the inquisitors, or someone delegated by them, would simply charge the woman with blasphemy – I mean, wearing the savior between her naked – um…"

"Yes you've made that point. How does blasphemy –"

"Well," the friar continued. "If she were charged with blasphemy, it would be necessary for her husband to commit her to a convent. Purely for contrition from her sins, you understand. And certainly no one would question the man's decision to join your crusade against the heathens while his wife is being purified… Certainly no one would question his committing her to the safety of the Church while he is away. For her chastity, one might say; for her protection even."

"Yes but he's not going to decide to accompany me, is he? And he certainly isn't going to commit his wife to… wait. Are you suggesting…"

"The man clearly is enraptured with his young woman. It's the carrot and the stick," the friar replied.

"Holding the man's wife…yes. That's the stick. I just need a carrot," said Cortes half aloud. Cortes spurred Majesty into a trot and said something to Diaz that Felipe missed. Diaz dismounted and pulled out a piece of paper and a quill and began scribbling. He beckoned the soldiers to him. They were relieved to have an excuse to stop trying to keep up with the horses. Cortes and Majesty continued down the track

Felipe hesitated a moment. Was he supposed to stay with the others or go on with Cortes? A gesture from Cortes settled his mind on that score and he jogged to catch up. He had no idea what a stick and a carrot had to do with anything. But he knew the two men had just hatched a plan that would turn out bad for Ana.

***

When they arrived back in Trinidad they didn't ride to the stable. Cortes rode instead toward the church. Just as they reached it Diaz caught up with them. He led them around the church to the back door of the primitive presbytery attached to the back of it. A fat, bald priest in a dirty cassock met them at the door. His girth, his dull gray eyes and bulbous pimple-covered nose clearly conveyed that he did not practice the self-denial that he so often preached to his congregants.

43

"Welcome Father, Señor! You honor my humble home. To what do I owe the pleasure?"

Cortes glanced around before replying, in Latin, "We have some business to discuss."

"Not on an empty stomach certainly. Come in, come in! You look tired. I'll have the maid set two more places." He glanced at Felipe. "Three perhaps? Consuela!" A short, round woman with a mole, wearing a severe expression and an ornate black Spanish robe and a shawl over her head came to the doorway behind the priest. "Three guests for dinner. Quickly!"

"Just two." Cortes turned to Felipe and reverted to Spanish. "Take Majesty back to the stable. Then get your supper. I won't need you anymore this evening."

"Yes, Señor." Felipe wanted to know what they were discussing with the fat priest. He suspected Cortes was planning to cheat Alaminos and Ana just as he'd done with Felipe's father. Surely there was something he could do…

But he had his orders.

***

As he approached the stable he heard Pedro practicing, badly, on a wooden flute Felipe had made for him. Good. He wasn't busy.

"Pedro! Please. I need your help," Felipe said as he rushed inside. His plan was to leave Majesty in Pedro's care and run back to the priest's house to listen under a window to see what he could learn. Pedro quickly ended that plan.

"Everyone needs Pedro's help tonight," Pedro said.

"Who?"

"Those two soldiers who went with you this morning. They just showed up with two others. They said they were on a special mission from the master himself and needed five horses immediately. Only one of them can ride. I had to help the other three mount! God knows what…"

"Five horses?"

"Yes, five. Five saddles and bridles to clean whenever they get back. Who knows what kind of damage they'll…"

"Where were they going?" Felipe asked. But he already knew the answer.

"You think they tell the stable boy what their mission is?" Pedro responded. "No idea. They order, I jump. Why – were you supposed to go with them? Majesty doesn't look like he's up to…"

"Pedro, could you take care of Majesty for me? I'll help clean everything up when I return, okay? Thanks." He tossed Majesty's rein to Pedro and ran from the barn.

Four soldiers. Five horses. Felipe knew where they were going, what they were planning. They might walk the horses. If they trotted, they'd be sore tomorrow. Some of them might even fall off. Only one of them was an experienced rider. If they galloped, some of them would definitely fall off. No. They would walk or trot. Felipe ran.

***

He was too late. Over his labored breathing and the blood pounding in his ears Felipe almost missed the sound of the riders. At the last possible moment he heard and he dove off the trail and crawled under a bush. Cactus spines dug into his belly but he lay frozen. As the riders came abreast of his position he turned his head just enough to watch out of the corner of his eye as they trotted past single file. Two soldiers, then Ana sitting stiffly, quietly indignant, then two more soldiers, bouncing like sacks of vegetables, hanging on for dear life in the dappled moonlight. They were heading back to Trinidad.

He stood when they were gone. Ana. He was sure they would have taken Alaminos. He considered following them but he knew his legs weren't up to it. Besides, he was pretty sure he knew where they were going. He turned and continued up the trail toward Alaminos' house.

When he arrived he found Alaminos sitting on a log, facing the finest view in all Cuba. A nearly empty sherry bottle lay on the ground beside him.

"Señor?"

Alaminos looked up hopefully at the sound. Then he slumped again when he recognized Felipe. "You. Go away. I already agreed. What more could your master possibly want from me?"

"He did not send me, Señor. I came to warn you. But… I'm sorry. I'm too late."

"Yes, well, thank you for, for whatever you were trying to do, but – look," he said. He turned and stared intently into Felipe's face. "You are a child. There was never anything you could have done. Your master Don Cortes is evil. Or perhaps not evil. He does not think he is evil. He believes he is simply determined, stubborn. And he believes that everyone else must bend to his will. Even God." Abruptly he stood up.

"The soldiers came into my yard," he explained. "Two of them held swords to my throat. When Ana came running the other two grabbed her. If I could have gotten loose I'd have killed them!" The air seemed to go out of Alaminos, and he sank back to the ground. "My Ana," he said. "One of them read a paper declaring me, by orders of the great Cortes, 'Principal Navigator' of the expedition and in line for a tenth of the profit. Assuming there is a profit. Assuming we survive." He shook his head. "When I said I wouldn't take the job even if they offered me half of the profit, the soldier read another paper supposedly written by me, committing Ana to the care of the Church while I'm gone. And they took her away."

"I'm sorry, Señor. He did something similar to my father. I so wanted to warn you."

Alaminos shook his head. "Neither you nor I can stand against him. He is in charge. What he wants he gets. He wanted me to pilot his voyage, and he got me." He heaved a sigh. "And now he has my Ana."

"Do not despair, Señor Alaminos," replied Felipe. "I think I know where she is. I couldn't save my father from Cortes. But I think I know how to save Auntie Anacoana. Perhaps, if I do, you will help me save my father?"

CHAPTER ELEVEN

Felipe was star-struck. Alonso de Avila was the most handsome man he'd ever seen – tall, well-muscled, with bronze skin and golden hair. And he rode a horse like he'd been born on its back. There was not a move a horse could make that Avila had not already anticipated. Horses seemed to want to please him.

Cortes had assigned him to ride El Arriero, one of the new horses. El Arriero was jointly owned by Ortiz the musician and Bartolome the gold miner. Neither could ride or sail or, presumably, fight. Felipe suspected Cortes had added them to the expedition only because of El Arriero.

Cortes was in an upbeat mood after securing the services of Alaminos. Imbued with an air of determination he moved smoothly about the small town arranging last-minute details. One of his lieutenants, a man named Puertocarrero, had no horse and couldn't afford one. Cortes couldn't afford one, either. He had overextended his credit line with the local merchants by over four thousand gold reales. No matter; he lopped off two more gold buttons from his much-abused coat and purchased a reliable gray mare for Lieutenant Puertocarrero.

***

A messenger finally arrived in Trinidad from Governor Velasquez: If Cortes appeared he was to be arrested immediately. Even in this, though, Cortes' air of authority and sense of mission carried the day. He had already won the mayor over.

"Your town is growing rapidly. Trinidad hasn't seen this much business in more than a year, Alcalde, yes?" Cortes had asked him with a wide smile. The two were walking side by side, counter-clockwise around the town square just before sunset. Other men of the town with time on their hands paraded behind them, forming a line that ringed most of the square. Outside their ring was another: the young (and not so young but hopeful) women of the town paraded in the opposite direction.

"Yes, Don Cortes," replied the mayor. "But Don Velasquez seems quite put out."

Cortes continued as if he hadn't heard. "And what is good for Trinidad is good for its mayor, no? I assume you are receiving your fair share of the proceeds from the shop owners? If any are hesitant to pay, point them out to me. They will quickly find it to their advantage to give you what you deserve."

"Thank you, Don Cortes. You are most kind. No, all the businesses have been quite generous to my office. But the summons..."

Cortes waved it away as if it were a mosquito. "Purely a miscommunication. I'm sure when you write back to Velasquez you will update him on the progress we are making in preparing the ships and men for the expedition he authorized." Cortes paused to let the last two words sink in. "You could also point out to him that it doesn't seem prudent to attempt to arrest someone who has several hundred armed, trained soldiers at his disposal. Tell him you fear for the town, if not your very life." Cortes said this last while nodding to a particularly lovely señorita waving her fan as she passed. As if he was not really implying a threat to the mayor's life at all, not really. "Lastly, you could congratulate him in advance on how rich he will be when I, his faithful servant, return successful."

"I'll write to him at once, Don Cortes. And I'll convey your most positive greetings to him, just as you said." The mayor took a moment to consider his next words carefully. "But please, Señor. It would be so much better if you and your men and ships and guns were to be on your way as quickly as possible. Lord knows what would become of Trinidad if Don Velasquez were to send troops to arrest you."

***

Cortes still needed more men but he wasn't going to get them in Trinidad. He had been reduced to accepting a man whose sorrel mare was even harder to control than Majesty and another who owned a heavy chestnut mare with three white stockings whose greatest talent seemed to be eating.

The thought of Velasquez sending armed soldiers spurred Cortes on. He called an impromptu meeting of the entire company on the practice field. Felipe came too, though he hadn't been invited. He needed to know what was on the agenda.

"Lieutenant Puertocarrero will take charge of loading all our supplies aboard the fleet. Obey him as you would me. I wish to be under way by sunset tomorrow. The fleet will go east around Cuba, stopping at every port," he paused. "Except Santiago." The men who knew about the arrest warrant laughed, and the others joined in. "At each port of call, the captains will offer a bounty to every horse owner or experienced soldier to join us. The rest of you, buy drinks for those who have something to contribute, but don't encourage the lazy, drunkards or dreamers. We need fighters."

"Why east?" someone called.

"Most of the fleet will go east. Master Sanchez and I will be taking *Concepcion* to the west, and we will also be looking for recruits. We will

48

meet you in Havana in three week's time. The horses and their minders, and those needing riding practice, will go overland from here to Havana under command of Señor de Avila. They, too, will be recruiting everyone they meet. Any more questions? Good. Let's get busy."

***

Frantic activity reminiscent of their sudden departure from Santiago ensued. Everything Cortes had bought, borrowed or stolen was ferried out to the ships along with most of the men. Even though it meant using up precious supplies, most of the men viewed hiking the two hundred miles to Havana as beneath them.

The expedition was not just Spaniards. Most had brought from one to as many as ten encomienda and many of these also boarded the ships – the higher the individual's opinion of himself, the more encomienda he needed to keep with him to make him comfortable. In general these were designated as servants, but in most cases they'd been brought along to flesh out the soldiers' ranks. In the end the Taino would outnumber the Spaniards on the voyage three to one.

Felipe heard Cortes' voice outside the stable yard. "As I said, I want you to take charge of all the horses." At first Felipe thought he'd gotten a promotion. But he quickly realized Cortes was addressing Avila who was walking beside him. "There must be more horses available between here and Havana. Stop at every farm along the way." He handed Avila a small bag Felipe had seen before. It jingled but not nearly as loudly as it had when Felipe had first seen it. "Show the men the reward they will get for signing on but don't actually give them anything. Promise them they will get the signing bonus when we depart from Havana."

He turned to Felipe. "You will do exactly as Señor de Avila says. I'm sending along you, Pedro, and some of the other stable lads. I'm also sending soldiers whose riding is deplorable. Teach them what you can; just don't let them kill themselves. More importantly, don't let them ruin or lose any of the horses."

"Yes, sir." This was more responsibility than Felipe had ever had before. He felt as if Cortes had made him second in command to Avila. But that thought was immediately dashed.

"Just do whatever Pedro or Señor de Avila tells you and do it quickly." Cortes turned back to Avila. "Anyone who wants to join must know how to be a soldier. If they own a Toledo sword or a good horse, they're in. If not, test them."

He spoke as if Felipe weren't standing right there. "If someone does own a horse you, Felipe or Pedro must inspect it. I don't need more worthless horses; but I do need horses. If it can be ridden, if it has a few more years in it

49

and it moves fairly well that's good enough. You alone will ride El Arriero. Ortiz and Bartolome are not to go anywhere near him. Put them on the slowest, most reliable mounts." He turned back to Felipe. "I expect everyone who goes with you to be able to ride at a gallop without falling off by the time you reach Havana. Is that clear?"

"Yes, sir." Felipe couldn't imagine full-grown men listening to his riding tips. But he would do what he could.

Cortes turned on his boot heel and left the stable without another word. Avila looked Felipe up and down, as if trying to decide why Don Cortes even bothered speaking to this waif. In the end, he too stalked out of the stable without a word.

***

Two nights had passed since he had failed to save Ana. Felipe had spent every waking moment trying to figure out how to rescue her. He now knew the church, the grounds and all its outbuildings as well as he knew the jungle around his own home.

Ana was being held in a room in the cellar of the church. He knew this because it had a small window, barely bigger than Felipe's hand, right at ground level. He'd heard her praying aloud as he silently slipped past the church in the dark. He stuck his face close to the small window and whispered in Taino.

"Auntie!"

She came to the window. He could see only the top of her head and her eyes. But they were shining with tears. "Child! What are you doing here? Where is my Antonio?"

"Cortes is keeping him busy with the ships. Can you get out?"

"No. I am locked in a small room. The woman brings me one meal at daybreak, nothing the rest of the day. She tells me it is to purge me of my wicked ways. She tells me..."

"Wait a moment." Felipe jumped up and disappeared into the darkness. He returned as quickly as he went, carrying two sugar apples. He handed them one at a time through the small window. "Tell me about the woman."

Ana continued her story. "She wants me to spend the day praying for God to forgive me for being Taino, for pretending to be Christian. I'm not pretending!"

"I understand. Is it the large woman with the black lace on her head and the-" he didn't know the word for 'mole' but he pointed to the left side of his chin.

"Yes! You know her? She smells horrible!"

"I know her. Have you seen anyone else?"

50

"The father came the first night. He said he wanted to hear my confession. He put oil on my forehead and told me I needed to change my clothes. He stood watching while I removed my dress. I knew what he was planning. But when he saw my cross he backed away without doing anything. The smelly woman came the next day – yesterday I think? – and made me take my clothes off again. She yanked my cross off and broke the chain. The father came back tonight, supposedly to bring me a clean dress. But I know he is simply determined to see me naked. Why is that? He and every other Spaniard on the island must see hundreds of naked Taino every day. But let one put on a dress and become Christian and suddenly they can't wait to see you naked."

"What happened next?"

"Without my dress or my cross, I think he must have believed I would be defenseless. He found out that I am not. He will not try anything for a few days. But I do not know what he will do when he recovers." Felipe grinned at the thought of Ana protecting her honor from the lecherous father.

"Anyone else? Does anyone else work here or live here?"

She thought for a minute. "There is a woman that cooks and cleans. A man came with wood for the stove yesterday. He must come often. Also a boy delivered things from the market. Other than them I have seen no one. Why?"

No surprises. Felipe had already seen the people she mentioned. "What do you remember –" Felipe dropped flat to the ground and lay still as two men staggered arm-in-arm past the church a few feet from him, singing drunkenly. He was acutely aware of how exposed he was but he was determined to carry out his mission.

"What?" Ana asked.

He rose to a crouch again as the drunks moved on oblivious. "What do you remember about the cellar outside your room? What kind of lock? Which way is the entrance?"

"They brought me down a ladder, um, that way," she pointed toward the back of the church. "It was just inside the back door. On this side." She gestured with her right hand. "I don't think there was a lock. Just a sliding bar."

"I'll come get you out," Felipe said.

"Wait!" she whispered. "You can't. The smelly woman is in the next room!"

Felipe stopped. He realized he could faintly hear the woman in black lace snoring beyond Ana's room. He thought about that for a bit then jumped up.

"I'll be back," he said.

"Where are you going?" Ana cried.

"I need *bibijagua*," and he darted off into the night.

51

CHAPTER TWELVE

Felipe worked through much of the night preparing his rescue of Ana.

He found a wild tomato bush and picked a dozen of the small, bright red fruits, careful not to crush any of them – he didn't want the smell on his fingers just yet. Next he needed aphids. He found them at the base of the tall grass in a wet spot a stone's throw from the church. He knew that where the aphids were the *bibijagua* would be close by. He found a couple dried up gourds and began scraping the aphids and the milky sap they'd produced into them until the gourds were nearly half-full. One of the gourds he stoppered with a wad of grass and put in his bag. He then scouted the ground for the *bibijagua* and when he found some he followed them to their nest. The nest was about midway between the aphid-grass and the church. Right where he was hoping it would be.

He set the open gourd on the ground a few paces from the nest on the church side. Then he attacked the aphid-infested grass – pulling it up by the roots and tossing it into the nearby pond. He spent an hour working at that task. When he stopped to rest he inspected the gourd. Some of the *bibijagua* had found it. Good. He moved it closer to the church, dribbling some of the sap as he went. Then he went back to the drudgery of tearing up the aphid-grass. Another hour, another inspection, more *bibijagua*, move the gourd closer to the church. When most of the aphids were gone he took a tree branch and vigorously scrubbed the ground between the aphids and the *bibijagua*.

Back to the gourd. It now practically crawled with *bibijagua*. He got stung when he picked it up to inspect it. He was tempted to crush a tomato fruit to squelch the pain. But he needed the *bibijagua* to continue to cooperate with him so he ignored the pain and moved the gourd closer to the church.

He went back to the swamp and found a hollow reed. He silently approached the cellar window. "Auntie!" he hissed. Thankfully, she wasn't asleep. She came to the window immediately. He handed her the reed and the stoppered gourd. He passed several of the tomato fruits in through the small window.

She understood what they were for but didn't understand what he wanted her to do with the gourd and reed. He explained.

"The gourd is full of *mabi*. Dribble some of it across the floor, in a straight line, from the window to the door. Put the reed under the door and blow as much *mabi* as you can, as far as you can, into the next room. After that, crush the tomato fruits on yourself and on both sides of the trail of *mabi*. Let me know when you're ready."

She left the window. Felipe ran back to the nest of the *bibijagua*. He crushed the rest of the tomato fruits and rubbed himself liberally with juice, then picked up the tree branch he'd left lying nearby and began ripping apart the nest. He scooped water from the nearby pond and sloshed it over the site. He kicked it apart some more and wet it again. The *bibijagua* scrambled furiously, seemingly in chaos. But many of them found the scent of the aphids and began following it toward the church.

Felipe dropped the stick, squeezed the last tomato onto his hands and picked up the gourd now teeming with thousands of *bibijagua*. He returned to the window. "Auntie? Are you ready?"

While he was gone she had followed his instructions to the letter, trailing the *mabi* across the floor of her tiny cell to the barred door. She had managed to use the reed to blow much of the sticky liquid far under the door into the room of the sleeping fat woman. She had scrubbed most of the floor on both sides of the trail with juice from the tomato fruits. When she was finished she had stripped off her coarse black robe and crushed and rubbed the remainder of the tomato fruits all over herself. She was standing at the window. "Yes. I'm ready."

"Step to the side," he said and, as one brave *bibijagua* overcame his revulsion of tomato and stung the back of Felipe's hand, he tossed through the small opening the gourd packed with 10,000 angry, hungry fire ants.

***

He was awakened at dawn as his fellow stable hands began preparing for the trip to Havana. After so little sleep Felipe quickly roused himself, dumped a bucket of water over his head and set to work.

The horse crew was small. Most of Cortes' men had opted for the ships. Walking any distance was too much like labor. Even some of the stable lads had found excuses to sneak on board ships leaving Felipe, Pedro, and two other stable hands under the command of Avila to drive the horses to Havana. They were joined by only Bartolome the miner and Ortiz the musician.

There were now thirteen horses. With Ortiz the musician and Bartolome the miner it should have been easy – seven riders, six of them leading a second horse. But of course it wasn't that simple. Ortiz and Bartolome couldn't be trusted even to stay in the saddle let alone lead another horse. And one of the other stable lads, an awkward young man of eighteen, had apparently stayed in Trinidad not to help with the horses but because he was in love. He spent the first hour on the trail crying for a girl named Maria. He finally got off his mount and walked away from the group, heading back to town, leaving a stable lad named Juan, Felipe, Pedro and Avila to look after all the horses.

Avila took charge of the riding lessons. He allowed only one of the non-horsemen to ride at a time. And he rode right beside the hapless fumbler.

"No! Heels back! Lean forward." He lashed his quirt across the thigh of the ungainly Ortiz who instantly moved his feet further back along Isabella's swollen sides.

"And stop yanking on the rein!" Avila continued. "It is not a church bell. You are confusing the horse. You only pull it when you want to stop. You can hold her mane if you need a handle."

"This horse hates me," Ortiz grumbled.

"Isabella is the most forgiving horse in the whole herd."

"If I don't hold the rein tightly I'll fall off. Again. Or she'll run off."

"If she runs off it will be because you are a bigger burden than her own foal. Balance! Balance your weight on the stirrups. Don't just sit there like a bag of onions. Yes I know, it takes muscles you don't have. We will build them out of the lard you carry around on your butt."

Pedro rode at the front of the string, a bell tied to his saddle. Avila and (currently) Ortiz were riding behind him. Nine other horses strung out after them following the bell. Juan strolled along, keeping the horses moving if any chose to stop for too long. Bartolome couldn't decide if he was insulted by having to walk or grateful not to be dealing with Avila's riding lessons. He walked alone, trying to avoid stepping in something.

Felipe rode Majesty. He knew the obstinate stallion, left to his own devices, would refuse to follow Pedro's bell. If he got loose he'd probably head back to the stable in Trinidad.

Felipe turned in the saddle to peer back. But even the church's tall steeple had disappeared from sight. The only hint of the town was a column of smoke rising through the still air. Probably just a cooking fire, he thought. Surely the old woman hadn't set the church on fire. Just as well. If word got out what he'd done…

***

The rest of that night's activities had gone by in a blur. He'd lain on the grass outside Ana's window, his ear pressed to the opening, waiting for a sign that the fire ants were having the effect he had hoped for. It seemed like ages that the fat woman continued to snore. Then, an abrupt snort.

"Wha…?" Came from the other side of the door.

He waited some more. A few minutes later he was rewarded with a loud shriek, followed by banging, as the woman tried stomping on the fire ants. Another yell as she got bit again. Then a light flashed under the door as the woman struck steel to flint. Soon the glow under the door evened out as the woman got a candle going. If she saw the trail of sap…

"Aaug!" She yelled. "Mother of God!" as she got bit again. Felipe heard the latch as she headed out her door. That was the signal he was waiting for. He ran to the corner and peeked around. Sure enough, the woman was running for the creek. He raced up to the door she'd left ajar and entered a dark hallway. He began preparing a story in case she came back quickly. 'I heard you scream, I thought you needed help'... She didn't come.

As Ana had said there was a steep stairway just inside the door leading down to the cellar. He ran down the steps and surveyed the cellar. Musty boxes and termite-riddled furniture filled most of the space. Three doors opened off the central space. One of them was open and dimly lit by a candle. He quickly went to that doorway. The room looked as if it was alive as the candle flickered and guttered over the thousands of scuttling ants trying to lick up all the aphid *mabi*, looking for anywhere to tunnel down to build their new home. He slid back the heavy bar on the door at the back of the room and had to duck as Ana swung a fist at what she guessed was the fat woman.

"It's me," Felipe said.

"Thank God!" she said. "Let's get out of here."

At the top of the stairs she started to head for the familiar back door but he stopped her.

"The fat woman is out there. This way."

"But – she has my cross!"

"Let her keep it. It isn't Christian anyway."

They turned the other way and eased quietly down a plain hallway past several closed doors. The sound of someone snoring came faintly through one of them – presumably the fat Father. They glided silently past his door. The hallway ended at heavy red drapes. Pulling them aside, Felipe and Ana found themselves in the nave of the church but behind the Altar. Ana crossed herself but seemed confused by the rough, unfinished lumber revealed on the altar's back side.

They passed silently through the rail. They walked up the aisle between the pews, past the font to the tall front doors. The doors were shut for the night with a massive bar through hoops that were nearly even with the top of Felipe's head. He reached up and pushed on the end of the bar but it didn't budge. Ana added her weight, pulling on the handle in the bar's middle and it slid back with a groan. Felipe looked anxiously toward the back of the church, sure that the noise would awaken the fat, snoring priest. But no one came.

***

"Why did you help me?"

"I had to. Señor Cortes did the same thing to us. Right now my father is in the jail in Santiago. If he is still alive. I couldn't let Señor Cortes get away with doing the same thing again."

She kissed the top of his head. "Thank you. But now I don't know what to do. If I go back to my Antonio, they will just come for me again."

"You won't be going back to Señor Alaminos for quite some time," Felipe answered. They were out of sight of the church. As they walked, Ana and Felipe rubbed more tomato juice on their fire ant stings and the pain vanished. They headed toward a different part of the same creek that the fat woman from the church had run to, to rinse off the residue from the tomato juice. The fat woman would be there longer – water alone wouldn't do much for her stings. When she got back to her room in the cellar and found it overrun with fire ants, what would she do then? Would she try to burn them out as the town of Santiago had done? If she did she might burn down the church. But if she didn't Sunday mass at the church would be a memorable affair. Felipe found he didn't care.

"My Antonio will be worried about me! I need to get home."

"I'm afraid you'll have to forget about your home. Señor Alaminos is no longer there anyway. Señor Cortes used you to force him to join the expedition. He is on a ship headed for Havana."

"Then I will go to Havana!"

"No, Auntie. If you show up there, you will be taken again. Cortes is quite determined that your husband go on the expedition."

"Then what am I to do?" she wailed.

"Auntie, please don't cry," Felipe was near tears himself. He hated to see her in anguish. But he knew there was only one safe course.

"My mother's people will take you in," he said. "They fled to the mountains when the disease began." Smallpox had begun taking its toll on the natives. "Head toward Santiago. When you come to the river of three waterfalls turn upstream. You will find them near the headwaters. When Señor Alaminos and I return to Cuba, I will come find you."

She shook her head sadly. "I hope I see you again, I do. And I will go find your family. But I know I will never see my Antonio again. I was never really his wife. I was just his Cuban wife. If he is back at sea he will never return."

CHAPTER THIRTEEN

January, 1519

The herd clattered into the village of Havana a week later. Their trip had been moderately successful: They'd acquired thirty more men, one of whom owned a decent horse.

Havana was even newer and rougher than Trinidad, barely a half dozen buildings strung haphazardly around the mouth of the Mayabeque River. The trail that Felipe, Pedro and the others had traveled had been barely recognizable in places. At times it was only Felipe's tracking skills that kept them on course. But over the last couple days the trail expanded to a path, then to a road. The trickle of other travelers became a steady stream of farmers taking their goods to market. As word had spread about Cortes' mission everyone was hoping to cash in.

Ortiz and Bartolome, while they had finally learned to ride a horse at a gallop without falling off, couldn't abandon the group fast enough when the first tavern came into view. Juan followed suit, as did nearly everyone else. Felipe, Pedro and Avila shouting, whistling and whip-cracking pushed the horses on through the town and across the waist-deep river to an empty corral. When the last horse was penned Avila left as well. Pedro and Felipe set to work making sure the horses had bedding, water and feed. When they were finally free to survey the town they discovered the mood was uneasy. And they quickly found out why.

Cortes was overdue.

They had spent eight days moving the horses overland. Most of the ships had arrived before them. But *Concepcion* was missing. She should have been able to make the trip from Trinidad to Havana in three or four days. There were no significant harbors in between. But even if they'd stopped at a fishing village somewhere the longest they'd have taken was a week. Had they encountered bad weather? Gotten into a chase trying to capture a ship? Lost a mast? Lost the ship…

In Cortes' absence a significant oversight appeared: He hadn't appointed a second-in-command.

***

The town had not been designed for the entertainment of young boys. Felipe wandered past a tavern from which wafted a song being sung by a group of drunks, a song whose lyrics he had no business listening to. A few doors away, a brawl spilled from another tavern out into the street right in front of him, causing him to jump into the mud to avoid the grappling men and the shouting, laughing group placing wagers on the fighters. On the other side of the street he looked in the window of a small market but, since he had no money, nothing there interested him.

He headed down to the harbor and surveyed the small fleet of ships moored there. He became puzzled by what he saw. A gun crew heaved and strained at a gun slung between two rowboats. The boats alternately grounded and bobbed in the surf, bouncing the mass of iron up and down like a fishing cork as the crew tried to heave it ashore where three other guns already sat – guns that they had so recently been wrestling with to move them in the other direction at Trinidad. Looking out to the harbor Felipe saw that other ships were likewise engaged in transporting the guns to shore.

"Excuse me, Señor," he approached a well-dressed junior ship's officer, a boy no older than himself, who had come ashore with the gun crew. The lad was standing to one side, trying to avoid getting wet, watching the progress of the gun crew and occasionally yelling unnecessary commands, slashing at the sailors' legs with a short piece of rope. "Why are they unloading the guns?"

The other boy turned and looked Felipe up and down and sneered at him.

"How dare you address me, *peón*! I am *Rodrigo Hidalgo de Martinez*. Get back to your business, Indian! This is no concern of yours." He puffed his chest and stood taller in an effort to show his exalted status.

Felipe knew what racism was, had indeed felt its sting before. But something was changing. As he got further and further from his home, and in the absence of his father and the other father-figures in his life, he was growing more independent. And with that came a need he was barely conscious of: to stand up for himself, a need to take action against bullies. Like the other boy, Felipe adjusted his posture, lifting himself above the image created by his only item of clothing, the ragged cut-off tunic he'd been wearing since he left his home.

In Greek he rattled off, "As Paul said to the Romans: 'Who are you to judge your brother? We all shall stand before the judgment seat of God.'"

"What did you say?"

"I was merely introducing myself, *Señor*," Felipe replied, making the honorific sound like an insult. "I am *Don Felipe Ferrer y Mendoza*, fourth duke of *Arjona*. Kindly remember that in future. Now, answer my question: Why are they off-loading the guns?"

58

Suitably chastened, the overdressed ship's boy replied, "My apologies, Don Felipe. Father, I mean Captain Martinez, ordered the ship unloaded. He did not like its balance on the trip here. Mostly, however, it is to keep the men occupied I think, Señor."

"But why are *all* the ships sending their guns ashore?"

Rodrigo looked around furtively, and lowered his voice. "Cortes is overdue and no one knows what to do. My father decided on his own to unload our ship and the other captains are following suit."

"Is your father in charge, then?"

"No one is in charge," Rodrigo whispered. "Velasquez' man Diego de Ordas is ordering everyone around, but most are ignoring him. He said no to the gun exercises. He said it would be a waste of gunpowder! But then Mesa, the master gunner, told him he knows how to make powder. He has offered five maravedis per ton for guano and sulfur, and a maravedi per ton for finely ground charcoal, and the farmers are bringing it."

Felipe couldn't imagine how bat droppings could be turned into gunpowder. But he didn't want to display his ignorance to Rodrigo. He simply nodded and Rodrigo continued gossiping.

"So de Ordas decided his soldiers need armor. The town was stuffed with bales of cotton when we arrived. Everyone in town saw our sails before we got here and believed we were the cotton merchants. De Ordas purchased the entire crop and hired locals to make up a hundred thick cotton tunics. So then the other captains ordered cotton armor for their men. Seems like a waste of time to me."

"Actually," Felipe said. "I've heard it is quite effective against the native weapons we'll be seeing."

Rodrigo's mouth fell open. "You're a soldier?"

"No," Felipe said. "I'm a horseman." And he walked away. He wondered whether the armor-making would include padding for Majesty and the other horses.

Further along the shore, where a small creek curved between rounded boulders before entering the harbor a group of women were washing clothes and spreading them out on the rocks to dry. Felipe noticed a girl a year or two younger than himself, crying silently and staring out to sea as she angrily beat a pile of white soggy fabric against a rock.

Felipe touched the girl's shoulder but she just glared at him and snapped, "*Xe!*"

One of the Taino women stopped chattering to the others and called out to him. "You won't get anything out of her, little brother. She's stupid. She can't say anything sensible. Only gibberish. She just cries all the time."

In Spanish Felipe quietly replied, "It's okay. I won't hurt you. I'm sorry I don't understand you." The girl just looked at him blankly. "Do you speak Spanish?"

"*Ma tin na'atik.*"

He turned back to the washing women.

"Where did she come from, Aunties?"

The first one who had spoken, who introduced herself as Brizuela, replied, "She was captured by my master on the Grijalva expedition to the west. She just got here. He gave her to me to help with the housework. But she's not much help."

The girl had gone back to pounding on the laundry. Felipe touched her shoulder again to get her attention. He pointed to his chest. "My name is Felipe. Felipe." Then he pointed to the girl. "What's your name?"

She looked at him for a moment. Then she wiped her eyes and pointed at herself. "Slave," she said.

Felipe smiled and shook his head. "No," he said. "That's not your name. Name... Felipe," he said again. "Auntie?" he called to Brizuela. "Would you please point to yourself and say your name?" The woman just waved him off and continued her work. "Please, Auntie? And the others as well?"

The girl looked from Felipe to the washing women as one after the other they pointed to themselves and said, "Brizuela," "Casiguaya," "Tinema," "Habanaguanexa." The women all laughed and splashed water at the last one, who had named herself the queen of Havana. Felipe again pointed to himself and said "Felipe," and pointed to the girl, who finally understood.

"*In ka'aba'e Abí,*" she said. "Abí."

"Abí," Felipe said. "Aunties," he called to the washing women in Spanish, "Allow me to introduce Abí." The women all waved and said 'Hello, Abí,' mostly in Spanish.

"Auntie," Felipe called again to Brizuela. "If I can teach her Spanish she'll be more help to you, yes?"

"She'd be more help if she could understand Taino."

"As you said," Felipe replied, "she's too stupid to learn Taino. But I think I can teach her Spanish, if that's okay with you." Felipe felt bad about calling Abí stupid but a plan was beginning to germinate in his mind.

Brizuela knew quite a bit of Spanish. She could see the advantage of being able to communicate with the girl – Abí was just as good a name as any, she supposed – instead of simply pointing at things and beating her when she didn't comply. "Fine. Waste your time if you wish. But she's probably too stupid even to learn Spanish."

"Thank you Auntie." Felipe began speaking to Abí quietly but quickly, helping her finish the laundry while describing what he was doing in Spanish.

"This is water. This is a rock. This is laundry. That is the ocean. Now tell me your words..." After all the clothing was spread out to dry on the

60

rocks, he took her hand. "Hand, arm, finger, head..." As she repeated the words, he led her away from the women.

They spent the rest of the day roaming the town and its surroundings. Abí flinched every time a gun fired and Felipe would have had to drag her to get close to one. He did, however, persuade her to wade across the river with him to inspect the horses.

At first she thought they were deer or elk. When Felipe clucked to Majesty and he came over to the fence for a treat, she quickly backed away.

"It's okay. He won't hurt you." Even if she'd understood him she didn't believe him.

"You eat?" she asked.

"Horses?" He laughed. "No! We ride them. Ride." He tried to pantomime what riding was but she wasn't getting it.

Climbing to the top rail, Felipe took a handful of Majesty's mane and sprang aboard. Abí screamed and backed away, certain her new friend was about to be eaten.

"*Kim-se'e! Kim-se'e!*"

Felipe had no intention of killing Majesty. But he couldn't resist showing off so he trotted Majesty around the corral, his arms out like a bird's wings, holding on with his knees. Abí could only stare in amazement. Not only had she never seen a horse before, she'd never seen – or even thought about – a human riding an animal.

***

By the time the laundry had dried and they had collected it and returned to the house Brizuela kept, Abí was able to say, "Good night Felipe. Tomorrow morning, yes?"

After clearing it with Brizuela, he arranged to meet her the next day. After morning stables he ran to her house and helped her complete her morning chores, keeping up a running monologue of what he was doing and encouraging her to repeat everything he said and teach him her words for the same tasks.

Ten days later, when Cortes finally arrived, Abí's Spanish was improving. It wasn't nearly good enough for her to interpret, but that wasn't the point.

Felipe was nearly fluent in Mayan.

CHAPTER FOURTEEN

Cortes was furious.

He so wanted to blame Alaminos but he couldn't. Before the incident the pilot had been up nearly thirty hours straight. They were close to their destination, only about ten leagues from Havana's harbor. Cortes (secretly) wanted to be seen, not only by *Concepcion's* crew but by the men already ashore, piloting the ship into harbor himself to build the confidence of his followers. So he'd sent Alaminos below to sleep.

Alaminos had tried to warn him that *La Jardines*, a complex mass of hundreds of small islets guarding the approach to Havana, was tricky. But Cortes didn't listen. After all it was daylight, the weather was fine and visibility was perfect. He'd put a man in the chains at the bow to throw a lead weight on a line far in front of the ship to sound the depth of the water. Nothing could go wrong.

And he'd run *Concepcion* aground.

She had shuddered a couple times as if trying to free herself. The masts whipped like a pine forest in a storm. The main yard broke loose and spun around the mast before dangling from one end, the other end stopping just short of impaling the deck. Then all motion died away and she settled and became as unmoving as solid ground.

The ship's boats that had been towing behind were drawn up and filled with sailors. Using an anchor cable as a tow line they rowed with all their might to try to pull her free, but it was like trying to tow an island. They tried again at high tide, hoping that would lift her free, but she remained glued to the sea floor. A crewman who could swim was lowered over the side. He dove to the bottom on both sides then reported to Cortes: The ship had grounded easily on a mud bank, fortunately, not coral. The hull was undamaged as far as he could see. But the mud bank ran nearly the full length of the keel and the suction was enormous.

Cortes ordered the ship lightened. Using the ships boats they'd ferried everything – guns, gunpowder, spare sails and spars, food and other stores– to one of the nearby islets. They emptied the fresh water into the sea and ferried the empty water butts ashore. Still the mud held. They ran a long line from a block at the top of the mainmast to an anchor lodged as far out amidships as the cable would reach. They attached the other end of the line to the capstan. The crew trudged round and round the capstan, winching the line tighter and tighter, hauling the ship almost onto her beam ends. Then they removed the push bars and stepped back. The master hit the pawl with a mallet. The capstan blurred as it unwound and the ship swung back upright. When she still didn't float the anchor was raised and ferried far out to the opposite side and dropped and the process was repeated. And finally, with the next high tide, she floated free. They maneuvered her to deeper water and began the arduous task of reloading all the supplies.

The nameless islet had no streams or springs. The men had to slake their thirst by sticking their faces into puddles left by the last rain. They'd rigged a sail to catch rainwater and direct it into one of the water butts but it was less than half full when they loaded it back aboard and set out again. By the time they reached Havana nearly twenty-four hours later they were parched.

Rowboats and barques scuttled out to the arriving ship. Cortes waved the first one over and was down the side into it before *Concepcion*'s anchor had even settled into the sand on the bottom of Havana's small harbor. A crowd of men and officers met him as he stepped ashore – most expressing their relief that he was safe. But he also detected that some were less than pleased to see him.

He waved them to silence, looked around quickly and pointed to the square. "Gather your men there. I'll be along after I present my compliments to the alcalde."

"He has orders to arrest you," one of the men called.

"Let me worry about that. Make way."

A young man Cortes reckoned could be no more than eighteen refused to be dissuaded. He was adorned in a too-large burgundy velvet coat with Velasquez' coat of arms embroidered into the left breast. He stepped forward, barring Cortes' way and unrolled a piece of parchment. He began reading in a loud voice that would have been more effective if it hadn't cracked on some of the more difficult words.

"By order of Don Diego Velasquez de Cuellar, Governor of Cuba, you are hereby placed under..."

With his focus on the words on the parchment in front of his face he failed to see the sword Cortes drew. Faster than he could blink he was suddenly holding half of the parchment in each hand. A gold button on his right sleeve hung on by a thread for a moment then fell toward the surf. Cortes caught it in his left hand and examined it. Solid gold. Interesting. He tossed it to the youth who caught it and stared at it as if he had never seen it before.

"*Jóven*," Cortes spoke, not wanting to dignify the infant with the title Señor, "You have two choices," he said. "You can return to Don Velasquez and report your failure. And explain how you damaged his coat." The crowd laughed. "Or, you can use those gold buttons to outfit yourself as a *conquistador*, and join us on the greatest expedition the world has ever seen!"

Without waiting for an answer Cortes pushed through the crowd and headed for the mayor's office.

***

Felipe had watched the ship arrive with mixed feelings. He'd been enjoying his independence. Furthermore, part of him wished the man who had imprisoned his father on trumped-up charges was dead.

But Felipe knew that no one was going to release his father without orders from Cortes. If Cortes died, so would Felipe's father. So he needed Cortes to stay alive. At least long enough for Felipe to enact his plan for his father's release. He was realistic enough to know that Cortes would never take a boy seriously. That was why he'd allied himself with Alaminos.

After Cortes left the beach Felipe closely watched the other boats, waiting for Alaminos to come ashore. What to tell him? He wanted to relieve Alaminos of the worry he must be feeling about Ana. And Felipe wanted the praise and approval he would surely get from Alaminos if he told him the story of his daring rescue of Ana from the lecherous Father. On the other hand, if he told him where to find Ana Alaminos might abandon Cortes and run back to her, despite what she believed.

For now, Alaminos was in the same circumstance as Felipe. Being an adult Alaminos would eventually be able to reason persuasively with Cortes for both Ana's release and, as long as he felt indebted to Felipe, for the release of Felipe's father. To save his father, then, Felipe needed Alaminos to be his partner.

***

Alaminos saw Felipe standing on the shore. He jumped over the gunwale, waded through the waist-deep water and grabbed Felipe's shoulders.

"Were you able to save my Ana? Is she here?"

"She's safe, have no fear. But it would not have been safe to bring her here."

"Where is she? What did you do?" Alaminos demanded. "How do you know she is alright? Is she staying at the church? Is that greasy father keeping his hands off her?" He crossed himself, either as a prayer for his Ana or as an instant repentance for the slander against the priest.

"She's safe, I promise you. I spoke with her. I gave her food. I made sure she is out of reach of the priest."

"How can that be? Where is she?"

Felipe looked away for a moment. "You will have to trust me. The father is not going to touch her."

"How do you know? What did you do?"

"The church has many workers," he said vaguely. "Vendors coming and going. Taino gardeners, laundresses and cooks. And Spaniards can't tell one Taino from another. Do not worry about where Ana is. She'll be surrounded by Taino. She will be fine."

Alaminos wanted more details, but Felipe was determined not to give them to him. He didn't want Alaminos to leave the expedition.

"Now," Felipe said, "I need a favor from you in return."

Alaminos looked at him suspiciously. "What?"

"It is a small favor, I promise. But it is very important to me. And Señor Cortes is more likely to listen to me if I have your support."

***

Felipe stood in front of the ornately carved desk in the house Cortes had commandeered and made into his recruiting office. To say it was the best house in the village of Havana wasn't saying much. The desk, on the other hand, was impressive. It was a massive piece of oak, blackened with age. It had clearly been built centuries ago for an important family by a Spanish craftsman, not cobbled together from local wood. In fact, it looked like it could sail itself back to Spain if someone merely added a mast and a rudder to it.

Felipe tore his gaze away from the ancient wood and looked up, and up, to meet the intense gaze of the towering Cortes. He'd wanted Cortes' undivided attention. Thanks to Alaminos introduction he now had it. For the first time in his life Felipe understood the importance of clothing. He was acutely aware of the rag of a tunic that surrounded his waist, contrasted with Cortes' burgundy velvet doublet and starched white ruffled collar.

"So," Cortes prompted. "Señor Alaminos tells me you have a business proposition for me."

Felipe cleared his throat and tried to stand taller. "I do. The people of the Yucatán speak a language called Mayan. It has some similarities to my native tongue, Taino." There was actually no connection between Mayan and Taino but Felipe was still convinced that Cortes should not know about his facility with languages. "I've succeeded in learning some of it."

"Well, thank you for letting me know. That could prove useful."

"I wish to renegotiate the terms of our contract."

Cortes raised an eyebrow. "Indeed?" One corner of his mouth lifted and Felipe knew he was struggling not to laugh at the small, rag-wrapped barefoot boy standing before him.

"Yes. I…" The enormity of what he was asking almost overwhelmed him but he rushed on. "The expedition will require an interpreter. I wish to be the official expedition interpreter rather than merely Majesty's groom."

"What will become of Majesty?" Cortes asked.

"I can do both."

"Well, that is very generous of you…"

"For a fee."

At last, Cortes understood why Felipe had wanted this official meeting rather than merely broaching the subject at the corral. The priest, Diaz, was sitting in the corner with a quill and paper, waiting for instructions to record necessary details of transactions.

"A fee, you say? Well there's no question that an interpreter would be convenient, possibly even save lives." Felipe hadn't even thought of that argument.

"Yes, sir! Disagreements and fights with the local people could be avoided." Cortes saw that shift in Felipe's eyes he'd noticed before as the boy accessed his memory. "'For if the trumpet gives an indistinct sound, who will prepare for battle?' Paul's first letter to the Corinthians." How, Cortes wondered again, could this child remember so many bible verses? Fortunately for Felipe, Cortes didn't think to wonder how he knew those verses in Spanish when the bible was always quoted in Latin.

"You mentioned a fee…"

Here was his moment. Felipe looked him in the eye. "Send a paper to Santiago absolving my father of his debt and ordering his freedom. Majesty will become yours, free and clear, and I will serve as your interpreter for the rest of the expedition."

Majesty was already his as far as Cortes was concerned. The horse would die of old age before Ferrer's debt was repaid. As to an interpreter…

Cortes called to a soldier sitting just outside the door. "Lares! Pass the word for Melchior, immediately." The soldier hurried off. Cortes turned his attention back to Felipe. "Please sit down, sir. This should only take a moment." Felipe knew Cortes was toying with him, calling him "Sir." But he didn't know what was going on. After a few moments Abí peeked in the door and saw him.

"*Hola*, Felipe," she called, then switched to Mayan. "Guess what? I heard someone else speaking my language!"

This announcement filled Felipe with dread. He stood but before he could decide what to do, Lares returned with a stranger, presumably the person Melchior that Cortes had summoned.

"*Peeksik, k'as paal, Tabasco!*" Melchior said, kicking Abí out of his way.

"*Kala'an ku'ruch!*" she replied. She was probably right, Felipe thought; he might not be a cockroach but he certainly smelled like he was drunk.

Spying Cortes, Melchior drew himself up in the doorway. Before he entered, though, he had one last shot at Abí. Nodding toward Cortes he said in

66

Mayan, "This is the man who killed your father. I saw him! He cut his heart out and laughed. He has probably brought you here to cut yours out, too."

"Quiet," Cortes said. "Now, Felipe, allow me to introduce to you Señor Melchior. He is a slave brought back by Cordoba. He has managed to learn some Spanish since his capture and I have acquired him for our expedition. *He* will be serving as our interpreter. Melchior," Cortes said, addressing the man directly, "please allow me to introduce to you Señor Felipe. He wishes to take your job."

Melchior froze, confused, wondering who Señor Felipe was. Looking around, he could see no one except for the scruffy child. He finally decided Cortes was having some fun at his expense. He bowed deeply to Felipe and said, in Mayan, "Your mother is a crocodile."

Felipe smiled and bowed and replied in the same tongue. "Yes, she was. And she ate for breakfast the dog that gave birth to you."

Melchior was shocked, stunned to silence. Aside from a few rude words his Spanish captors had picked up he'd heard no Mayan in nearly two years. Now suddenly he was confronted with two children who were fluent in it. The girl he'd paid no attention to but he peered more closely at the boy. The Spanish might be fooled, but this child wasn't from his land.

"How do you speak my language?"

"Any idiot can speak your language," Felipe replied. "The proof is standing in front of me."

Enraged, Melchior swung a sinewy right arm, intending to pummel the disrespectful child into oblivion but Felipe easily dodged it. As he suspected, the man was drunk.

"Enough!" demanded Cortes. Melchior froze and did his best to stand at attention. "You have presented me with a quandary, Felipe. On the one hand, you clearly do command at least enough of the tongue of Yucatán to insult the natives. I don't expect to have too much need for that."

"Surely you are not entrusting your enterprise to this, this... drunken fool?" Felipe cried.

"His drunkenness is no concern of yours." He turned to Melchior. "If you ever prove to be drunk when I need you to translate, however, I will have you chained to the mouth of a cannon until you sober up. And if we happen to need the cannon in the meantime, I will not waste the time to remove your chains. Do you understand?" Melchior blanched. He understood but his Spanish had fled. He simply nodded.

"Good." Cortes turned back to Felipe. "Thank you for bringing your skill to my attention. It may prove beneficial to have a second translator. However, as you see, your skill is not so rare as to force me to cancel your father's debt. Suppose we agree to an increase to five maravedis a week?"

"Five maravedis a day."

Cortes glared at him. "No. The most I will agree to is three maravedis per day."

Felipe thought about it. In his heart he knew it was the best he was going to be able to do. His father would remain in jail. But at least the debt would be settled faster. He nodded.

"Fine," Cortes said. "Three it is. But only on those days when you are serving as a translator. Now go check on the horses. We leave soon."

Felipe knew Cortes would want the last word. "Agreed." He turned to Diaz. "And please write down today as one of the days I served as translator."

***

"You were very brave to stand up to him, Felipe," Abí told him later.

"It does not need bravery to stand up to a drunk," he replied. "What does *tabasco* mean?"

"That cockroach is from Campeche. My people are Tabasco, from across the river. Our side is much nicer, and the Campeche are jealous. Campeche and Tabasco usually get along, but not always. Some, like that cockroach, only like to get drunk and fight."

"What river?"

Abí just shrugged. "The river where gold comes down from the mountains," she said. "It is a big river, very big. With steep cliffs on both sides. His people usually stay on their side and we stay on ours. Our side gets more gold. To cross requires a canoe and strong paddlers. To cross without a canoe a person needs to go very far upstream. When your people, the Spanish with the floating houses, came up the river they fought against Cockroach's people and he became a slave. When the Spanish came back later they came to our side of the river. That was when they killed my father and took me away. My mother and my grandmother must think I am dead."

"You will see your mother and grandmother again, Abí. I promise."

CHAPTER FIFTEEN

February, 1519

Felipe warned Alaminos about the approaching weather. Alaminos looked at the clear blue sky, skeptical. "I don't see any sign of it," he said. Then he shrugged and turned his palms upward. "But even if you're right there's nothing I can do. We must do as we are told. He says we go, we go."

***

Two days after Felipe's promotion to some-time translator rumors had spread of Velasquez leading an army to Havana to personally arrest Cortes. Whether true or not, Cortes decided it was time to get under way. He assembled all his soldiers and sailors. They gathered on the wide dry dusty space that served as an outdoor market on Sundays and a makeshift parade ground as needed, just across the river from the corral. Cortes waded across the river, climbed to the top rail of the fence and turned to address them so that his voice was amplified by the expanse of water. Felipe wondered if he was purposely copying Jesus' speaking technique.

"Men," Cortes began. "I hold out to you a glorious prize. But it is to be won by incessant toil. Great things are achieved only by great exertions. Glory was never the reward of sloth. If I have labored hard and staked my all on this undertaking, it is for the love of that renown which is the noblest recompense of man." Some of the men shifted and murmured, and Felipe knew what they were thinking: renown was not what they'd signed up for; they wanted gold.

Cortes knew it too. "But, if any among you covet riches more, be but true to me, as I will be true to you and to the occasion and I will make you masters of such wealth as our countrymen have never dreamed of!"

Hats were thrown in the air, and the cheering drowned out Cortes' oratory for a moment. When the hubbub quieted, he continued. "You are few in number, but strong in resolution; and, if this does not falter, doubt not but that the Almighty, who has never deserted the Spaniard in his contest with the uncivilized infidel, will shield you, though encompassed by a cloud of enemies; for your cause is a just cause, and you are to fight under the banner of the Cross. Go forward, then, with alacrity and confidence, and carry to a glorious issue the work so auspiciously begun."

More cheering. No doubt history would end the record of his speech there, thought Felipe, rather than with his actual conclusion: "You've had all the women and drink you're going to get for awhile. Now, let us concentrate on getting these ships loaded."

***

Water casks were filled, food stores topped up, powder checked. Once again the horses had been driven into the water and made to swim out to the ships and lifted aboard in slings. Once again Majesty behaved as if he'd completely forgotten the process and was about to die.

A priest came to bless the fleet. Spanish superstition kept him from going onboard any of the ships – even though Felipe had seen Diaz already onboard *Concepcion* wearing sailor's clothes – so he had to content himself with a hastily arranged mass from the shore, vaguely gesturing out toward the ocean. About a quarter of the sailors took a knee in a group to receive a blessing as the young priest butchered the Latin phrases. None but Cortes and Diaz – and Felipe – knew enough Latin to recognize his mistakes.

The armada now consisted of eleven ships: *Concepcion*, one hundred tons; *Santiago* and *La Trinidad*, each seventy tons; *Santa Maria de los Remedios*, fifty tons; and eight more that were too small to ship even a single horse. There were a total of sixteen horses, 110 trained sailors and 553 soldiers. All the ships had more Indians than Spaniards but no one had bothered to count them – there could have been a thousand or more altogether.

To Alaminos the blue skies and high, wispy clouds didn't seem any different than any other day in the Indies. But he'd come to respect Felipe's knowledge about anything pertaining to Cuba so he'd recommended that all the ships be prepared for severe weather. Light canvas was stowed and storm canvas raised, sheets were doubled, worn stays were replaced. Alaminos had himself rowed around the fleet looking at everything with a critical eye, giving orders as if he were an admiral. Some of the masters grumbled that he was overstepping his position but, as the signs of approaching foul weather continued to increase, their grudging tolerance turned to genuine respect.

Once they cleared the west end of the island the sea developed a long uneasy swell from the south that convinced Alaminos that the resourceful young native boy had been right. The awkward motion was a new experience for Felipe, quite different from the easy cruise from Santiago to Trinidad. Within the hour he lost his appetite, and an hour after that the sailors were teasing him for 'feeding the fishes.'

70

Pedro had come to be recognized as the most knowledgeable horseman in the fleet so when a stallion on the *Remedios* became ill Pedro was called for. Since Estefan had simply tied up Isabella and left, Felipe was left alone to care for all six horses on *Concepcion*.

Even though it meant more work, he'd been counting on just such an occurrence. He sprang to the feed bin and quickly lifted out several bundles of the dry corn stalks. "Abí, are you okay?"

The girl rose, shaking dust out of her long, black hair. "Are we there already?" she asked.

"No," Felipe replied in Mayan. "I understand it may take a week, perhaps two. You certainly cannot spend the whole trip in the corn bin. We need to make you look like a ship's boy."

"I'm a girl!"

"I know, little sister. But we don't want anyone else to know. There aren't any other girls on board. So you're going to have to look like a boy. Put this on." He handed her a small *pantalon* he'd begged off the ladies doing the washing in the creek after his embarrassment in front of Cortes. They'd been happy to comply but he'd been too busy to figure out what to do with the perplexing garment.

For all the time Abí had spent washing them she'd never worn a pantalon either. Felipe had at least seen men put them on but now he wished he'd paid more attention.

"No," he said as Abí held the pantalon to her waist like an apron and started tying the legs together behind her. "I think you put your feet in and then pull it up your legs." She promptly put both her feet into one of the legs, effectively locking her legs together with the waist pooled around her feet. "How can anyone move in this thing?" She pulled the garment back off and tried putting it on over her head.

Eventually they got her into the pantalon and cinched it around her waist. Felipe next took out his knife. Because of the incident with Bernardo the jailer Felipe never wore the knife openly. On the cruise from Santiago to Trinidad he had decided the walking stick was too cumbersome. He'd discarded the longer piece of the staff and kept just the short part with his name carved in it that sheathed the knife blade. He'd braided corn leaves and wrapped the braids above and below his name on the stick and on the handle of the knife He now kept it strapped to his back like a small, crude quiver.

"I'm sorry," he said, and began slicing off her long hair. While his own hair reached past his shoulders, he'd noticed that most of the ship's boys wore their hair chopped short.

Abí didn't seem to mind, but she was curious. "What's wrong with my hair?" she asked.

"Nothing at all. But if we want you to look like a boy, 'Nature itself teaches, for a man to have long hair is a shame; for a woman, long hair is her glory.' Paul's first letter to the Corinthians." She looked at him blankly. He tried again. "Girls naturally have longer hair than boys. Sailors seeing you with short hair will assume you're a boy and ignore you. But with your pretty face and long hair, they might look twice. And we don't want them to look twice."

"You think I'm pretty?"

***

"Have you seen Abí?" Felipe had asked Brizuela casually the day before.

Brizuela had looked up from pounding washing at the creek. It was about three hours after sunrise. "No child. I thought she was with you." She had looked around to see if Abí was elsewhere among the women working on laundry. "She's not here. Where could she be?"

"Perhaps at the garden. I'll check there," Felipe had said. He knew precisely where Abí was but he wanted to create as much confusion about her disappearance as possible.

Felipe hated slavery as much as his father did. He knew there were scriptures that slave-owners used to justify it. He didn't know how to refute those scriptures. Furthermore, stealing was clearly wrong. And Brizuela's masters – and all of Spanish society – considered Abí to be Brizuela's property; so taking her away from Brizuela was stealing. Felipe couldn't explain the contradiction; He just knew in his heart that keeping the young girl as a slave was a greater wrong. Abí had been stolen from her family. The expedition was going back to somewhere near where her family lived, or at least to where there were people who spoke her language. Therefore Felipe saw it as right that he do everything in his power to return her to her family.

After transporting Majesty to the ship in the small hours and getting him settled in just as dawn was breaking he'd caught a ride back to shore. Abí had met him on the beach, eager to spend another day with her new friend and distraught that he was leaving her. "Will you return soon?" she'd asked. "I don't have anyone else here to talk to."

"Do you want to go back to your people?" he'd asked her.

"Yes! I miss my mama so much!" Tears began to leak from her eyes. "Can you take me to her?"

"If that is what you want I will try. But you must do exactly as I say." He'd taken her with him to drag an oxcart to the temporary corral from which the horses had already been removed. He instructed her to lie down at the bottom of the cart and he covered her with cornstalks and dragged the cart by himself to the beach. An eager boatman came to the cart immediately but seeing no adult with the load he was worried he wouldn't be able to collect for his services. Felipe had tried using his '*I am Don Felipe*' voice to convince the boatman to accept his signature but to no avail. He dug through his bat-wing bag and found a wood carving he'd made of Majesty and offered that as payment. The boatman was clearly delighted with it. But he pretended to be concerned it wasn't enough.

"I'll do all the loading myself," Felipe said to sweeten the deal. "Why don't you go get yourself a drink and come back when it is loaded." The boatman agreed to the suggestion and headed off to the nearest tavern. Felipe reckoned it was possible he wouldn't return, and that would serve his purposes just fine.

"Abí, quickly," he said. "Into the boat." She crawled out from under the dusty sheaves and jumped into the bottom of the boat. Felipe got busy covering her with corn stalks. When the boat was loaded the boatman, as expected, was nowhere to be seen. So Felipe rowed the boat himself out to where *Concepcion* lay at anchor. He'd never rowed a boat before and his path from the beach to the ship wandered. But he was very strong for his age and he finally mastered it.

When they reached the side of the ship he again appeared to lose control of the boat and purposely pulled up near the rudder, too far back to unload. The sailors onboard began shouting at him to pull further forward. But their view into the boat was blocked by the overhang of the gallery protruding from the captain's cabin.

"Quickly, Abí. Up the side," he said. She climbed out of the corn stalks. He boosted her up until she could grasp some of the gingerbread on the side of the ornate balcony. "Don't go into that area," he said. "The captain lives there. Work your way forward." She looked at him confused. "That way," he said, pointing. "Climb in through whatever small opening you can and find someplace to hide. In a few hours it will get quiet after the sailors eat, when they take a siesta. When that happens come find me. Majesty is on the main deck." Confusion appeared on her face again. "On the level that has no roof." He pointed up. "Just in front of this part with the fancy decorations." She nodded and began climbing. Felipe quickly rowed over to where the sailors were waiting to help him with his load of corn.

He let them pull up the corn, returned the boat to the beach, and began spreading confusion about Abí's whereabouts. Just before his last trip to *Concepcion* he'd casually bumped into Brizuela again as she returned from the market. He'd told her he had just left Abí talking to a young girl whose family had come to town hoping to sell charcoal, too late for the expedition. He felt bad about lying to Brizuela, but he didn't want her to entertain the possibility that Abí might be stowing away on the expedition and raise an alarm. Better to let her wonder whether Abí had joined the imaginary charcoal family.

In any case they were scheduled to weigh anchor on the next high tide, just after midnight. If Brizuela figured out the truth after that, it wouldn't matter.

***

He'd congratulated himself for pulling off a neat trick. But now, her question about whether she was pretty flummoxed him. He felt his face flush red. "Well, you're prettier than I am at any rate. All I meant was we want you to be invisible. Now, help me water the horses." He showed her where the water cask was and how to fill a bucket and she pitched in.

The seas worsened. The sky darkened. Sailors ran past taking down the last of the canvas. Majesty managed to kick down the panel closing the front of his stall, intent on running – somewhere. Felipe grabbed a handful of oats and jumped in front of him.

"Easy, boy," he said softly. "Where do you think your going?" He held out the oats with one hand and held the panel closed with the other. "Abí," he said. "Hand me some rope." The girl, wide-eyed, didn't want to get any closer to the stallion than absolutely necessary. But she circled wide around boy and horse to a coil of rope hanging from a peg, took it down and tossed it to Felipe. He caught it with one hand, quickly sliced a hunk off it and wound it several times around the cracked gate and the side panel to which the gate would no longer bolt. Majesty calmed down as he munched on the oats and Felipe worked.

When he finished he turned to see Abí wide-eyed, crowded as far back as she could get into a corner near the feed bin. "None of the men helped," she said.

"It wasn't their job. Besides, Majesty could have hurt them."

"He could have hurt you!" she wailed. She ran to him and hugged him fiercely.

"Majesty would never hurt me," he said. He awkwardly patted her head. "I'm fine."

"You're my only friend," she said. "If anything happens to you, I don't know what will happen to me."

"Nothing's going to happen to me," Felipe said. But as the ship rose to another wave and his stomach flopped again he wasn't so sure.

74

CHAPTER SIXTEEN

White water raged all around them. The scream of the wind was unrelenting. As the light faded, no one moved about the deck unless they absolutely had to. Those who did kept at least one hand firmly grasping a lifeline. One man was lost overboard and there was no thought of trying to go back to save him. The ship could not have altered her course.

Sundown merely meant a complete loss of what little light there had been. Before the light had gone completely Felipe took a lantern below to the galley and had the cook light its candle from a coal. He got there just in time. The cook followed him on deck and pitched the galley fire over the side.

The shrieking of the storm, if anything, intensified as the night wore on. Most of the crew gradually came to the conclusion that God was against them, that the ship would be lost, but no one seemed to have the energy to fight the realization.

Felipe's headache and nausea had completely cleared. Focusing on Isabella's predicament had driven all other thoughts from his consciousness. The mare's distress was clearly not illness. She had apparently decided that the storm was a perfect time to give birth. Delivering a foal was something he'd seen his father do a couple times – though, admittedly, never in circumstances like these – and he was determined to wring every single detail he possibly could from his memory.

Now, in the feeble light of the lantern he could see that Isabella was becoming more agitated, pawing at the straw as if looking for something. Felipe knew she needed to lie down. Fortunately, Pedro had thought to have an extra stall constructed – seven stalls for six horses. Every day, the first horse was moved to the empty stall while its stall was cleaned; then the next horse was moved to the clean stall, and so on. When Majesty had broken the gate Felipe had thought of moving him to the empty stall. But since he'd calmed it made more sense to leave him where he was.

The extra stall he'd come to think of as stall number one was on the far end of the line from Majesty. In stall number two beside it was a bay mare called Catalina. Isabella was next to her in stall number three, and she needed more room. Even with the storm raging, Felipe had no choice but to remodel.

He bent down to the ring bolt in the deck and unpinned the partition that divided stall one from stall two. With Abí's help he lifted the partition out of the way. No doubt it was his imagination, but the bay seemed pleased about the extra room. Well, don't get used to it, he thought. Next he needed to swap the bay with Isabella. He led out Catalina and held out the lead to Abí.

He'd seen her feed and water the mares with no problems. He believed she could hold the bay's lead for a moment while he moved Isabella. Just as he unlatched the gate to stall number three to take Isabella out, he felt the ship rising to another huge wave.

"Hold on tight," he yelled to Abí . When she put both hands on the lead rope he yelled, "No! I meant…" He didn't have time to finish. He meant, Hold on to something. Abí thought he meant hold on to the mare. When Catalina, instinctively bracing against the roll, raised her head she lifted Abí's feet from the deck. She couldn't hold on. The lead was jerked from her hands and she tumbled to the deck just as a wave broke over the bow and a waist-high wall of water swept the length of the ship. Abí disappeared in the churning water.

Felipe forgot about Isabella and the bay and dove to the deck to grab Abí. Flailing around blindly in the foam, his hand brushed her leg and he grabbed on tight. His other hand found a rope, and he prayed it was attached to something. It was, and after what seemed forever the water drained and Abí became visible, half of her hanging out through the lifelines that Alaminos had had installed along the edge of the deck in preparation for the storm. Felipe pulled her back aboard. She turned and clung fiercely to his neck while coughing and retching water over his shoulder.

"You're okay," he said, pounding on her back. When she was breathing more or less normally he said, "Let's take care of the horses." Isabella was still standing in her stall, focused now more on her internal struggles than the storm.

But the bay mare, Catalina, was missing.

***

What to do first? Search for Catalina or secure Isabella? His mind raced. If the bay had been washed overboard there was nothing he could do about it. If she hadn't she could not have gone far. He led Isabella to the newly widened stall. She circled once then lay down on the bed of corn husks.

"Don't do anything. She's fine," he told Abí as the ship's bow began to ride up the back of another colossal wave. "Just find something solid and hang on tight."

Before he'd even finished the instructions he heard a sailor calling "*Mostengo! Mostengo!*" and he grabbed the rest of the coil of rope and raced forward.

Two sailors stood on the deck, each holding tightly to a line with one hand and waving the other. The bay stood with her back to the bow, wanting to run back toward her stall but put off by the waving sailors. She reared and lashed her front hooves out at the menace. One of the sailors drew back from the threat and immediately lost his footing. The bay, ignoring the steep and rising angle of the deck decided this was her opportunity and she bolted. The sailors scrambled out of the way of the large animal.

Felipe sprinted forward. As he ran he formed a loop in the rope. He tossed it over her head as she came within range. But it didn't slow her down and his small body wasn't enough to stop her. She just dragged him. He snubbed the loose end around a taut cable holding up one of the masts as she dragged him past it and that slowed her down. Then the next wave crashed over them. The mare lost her footing and slid aft on her haunches, legs flailing uselessly in the air. Felipe released the rope from the cable stay and jumped nimbly over the flying hooves, landing on the side of her neck with his mouth near her ear.

"You're fine, my darling. Everything is fine. I'm here," Felipe cooed. The bay mare began to calm, her eyes getting a little less wide. "You're a good girl, Catalina, you're fine. Good girl. Everything is fine I'll take care of you." What remained of her halter dangled uselessly from her neck. He passed a loop of the rope over her nose to form a makeshift halter and cinched it firmly. "Come on, I'll take care of you." He slid to the deck and stood in front of the mare. "Come," he said again more firmly, tugging on the rope. She stood awkwardly, swaying as the deck swooped again. She tried to move her head but Felipe held the rope firmly. "No. Focus on me. I have food. You're fine. Look at me. Come this way." Felipe pulled on the rope and the mare took a tentative step, then another. Felipe led her back to stall three and closed the gate across in front of her nose. As she thrust her nose into the feed bag Felipe went to the tack crate and found a new halter. He tied one end of a new lead onto her halter and the other end to the gate. Then he slipped in beside her and threaded the sling under her belly and retied it to the partition. When the ship rose again the mare stiffened. But when she felt Felipe's hand patting her neck she mostly ignored the ship's motion.

With that problem solved, it was time to check on Isabella and Abí. As he headed over to Isabella's stall he was surprised to see her back on her feet. Abí was on her knees, ignoring the storm, cradling a small furry bundle. She looked up at Felipe.

"I'm keeping her," she said.

***

By dawn, the storm had lost most of its fury. The waves were still very large but not the life-threatening monsters of the night before. They no longer poured over the rails like demented waterfalls. Things were starting to dry out. The captain had ordered some sails aloft and the ship leapt ahead in the strong winds. The sailors moved about with enthusiasm as if embarrassed about their fears of the previous night.

Felipe hadn't bothered to argue with Abí the night before. He thanked her for her help and suggested she get some sleep, hoping she'd forget about her claims by morning. That hope was dashed when she climbed out of the feed bin and rushed to Isabella's stall.

After she'd gone to bed he'd thoroughly inspected Isabella and her new addition. Both were fine, neither of them any the worse for wear for their nighttime ordeal. Both were eating. If he didn't know better he'd have sworn Isabella wore an air of pride and smug satisfaction. The baby was unlike any he'd ever seen. He'd heard there was a pinto stud at a ranch on the north side of Cuba. Clearly that was where Señor Sedeño had taken Isabella when he objected to Majesty's stud fee. But this foal was the first evidence Felipe had that multicolored horses were not simply a myth.

The new horse had long legs, an Arab nose and a short tail, all features he'd seen on other horses. What was different was the coloration: white face and stockings, the body a medium brown. Its hindquarters looked as if someone had draped a black-spotted white blanket over them.

Abí slid between the rails and dropped to her knees to hug the new foal. "Isn't she the prettiest creature you've ever seen, Felipe? I'm thinking of calling her 'Señorita.' Is that a good name? I like the word. What do you think I should call her? I wanted to call her 'Abí' but that might be confusing. What do you think about Señorita"?

"Well, there are several problems with that, Abí."

"Like what? Are you thinking of a different name?"

"That, yes; but there are bigger problems." He paused. He hated to disappoint her. But she needed to understand before she went too far down this road. She looked at him expectantly. Now she was paying attention.

"What problems?"

"First, she's a He. The foal is a colt, not a filly. He'll grow up to be a fine stallion."

"Oh." She stepped back and cocked her head, taking a new look at the multicolored colt. Her experience with Majesty made her question whether she could trust this animal that was going to grow into a stallion. Then she shrugged, dropped to her knees and hugged him. "I don't care. I'll make sure he grows up nice. He'll like me. And he's still the prettiest horse I've ever seen. I'll just have to come up with a boy's name. How about 'Felipe'?"

"I don't think so."

"Well I'll think of something. But you said there are other problems. What else?"

"The main thing is… Abí, he's not your horse. He's not my horse. Right now he belongs to Isabella. But Isabella belongs to Señor Sedeño. Therefore the colt belongs to Señor Sedeño. We can't claim him just because we were here for his birth."

"Oh." Her lower lip began to quiver, then a tear rolled down her cheek. It tore at Felipe's heart and he was afraid he might start crying himself. That would never do. He had to think of something.

"Um, I have an idea. I don't think Señor Sedeño would object to you naming his colt, as long as we come up with a good name. He doesn't seem to care about horses much. He hasn't been around to see Isabella once since the storm started and probably won't be until we are back on land."

This news brought a smile to the young girl's face. She immediately began trying out different names.

"What do you call a horse that looks like this?" she asked.

"I've never seen one before. But I've heard of them. In Spanish it would be called 'pinto,' painted. In Taino – but we have no horses, so no words for horses. His colors would be called 'pu-yu.'"

"Puyu. Hey Puyu." The colt seemed to be too interested in his next meal to respond to Abí's call. "I don't think he wants to be called that. He looks like he has a cloud over his rump. What about – what is the word for the *chich-iik* we just went through?"

"Spanish is '*tormenta*.' Taino is 'hurricane.'"

"Hurricane! I like 'Hurricane.'" She turned to the colt. "Hurricane! Do you like that name?" The colt actually turned from Isabella for a moment and nudged his forehead against Abí's chest. "I think he likes it. Hurricane! Do you want to be called Hurricane?" She turned to Felipe. "Do you think Señor Sedeño will approve?"

Felipe really didn't think Señor Sedeño would care. "We'll convince him."

CHAPTER SEVENTEEN

The fleet was gone.

Concepcion was alone on the vast brilliant blue expanse of sea. The other ten ships, assuming they had survived the hurricane, had been scattered to the four corners of the compass. Alaminos wasn't going to go looking for them. Cortes had instructed the captains to stay within sight of the flagship but Alaminos had known that might not be possible. So he'd given the captains clear directions for finding their destination on their own. If all else failed, all a captain had to do was to sail west from wherever they were and they'd find the coast of Yucatán, then turn north until they spotted a large island. Hopefully they would converge on roughly the same spot.

"Who's this, then?" Estefan had reappeared when the hurricane was over, and he was peering into the enlarged stall holding Isabella, Hurricane and Abí. Felipe wasn't sure if his question was about Hurricane or Abí. He decided to cover all possibilities.

"Yes. Isabella foaled last night in the midst of the storm. Since you weren't here I convinced this cabin boy, er, Pablo, to help me. He's been a great help. The colt's name is Hurricane."

"What makes you think you have the right to name a colt from my mare?"

"She is not your mare. She belongs to Señor Sedeño. If your claim to Isabella is based on your taking care of her, I think you lost that right when you were nowhere to be found when you were most needed."

"I've heard you call Majesty your horse," Estefan whined. "More than once!"

"That's because Majesty *is* my horse. Cortes is holding him as collateral against a loan to my father. My father sent me along to see that our property is well taken care of. In any case," Felipe continued, "Pablo and I were here, doing your job, when the colt was born. And we decided to name him Hurricane."

"Well, we'll just see what Señor Sedeño says about that." He turned and looked over the other stalls. His eye fell on the hasty repair Felipe had done on the gate across the front of Majesty's stall. "Sloppy. Why is this done up like this?"

"Because," Felipe explained patiently, "Majesty broke it during the hurricane. When you weren't here. I had to mend it quickly. I've already spoken to the carpenter about it and he has it on his list to take care of after more urgent repairs."

"Shoddy work. Won't hold that stallion. Get it fixed." Then he marched off as if he had pressing business elsewhere. Felipe was happy to see him go, even if he was only going in search of another bottle.

About noon of the day after the hurricane the lookout reported a ship on the horizon. It had no sails aloft and was dead in the water. They overhauled it rapidly. It was *Remedios*. She had been badly damaged by the storm. Felipe, standing at the rail of *Concepcion*, could see nothing but a confused tangle of ropes and broken wood where her quarterdeck should have been. He hoped the horses – and Pedro! – weren't buried under it.

The mizzen mast – a short mast at the stern that supported a lateen, angular, sail – had fallen, crushing everything on the quarterdeck and some of the captain's quarters beneath it. Had the captain been in his quarters he would no doubt have been killed. Instead, he'd been on deck at the time, having just ordered the lowering of the lateen…not soon enough, as it turned out. A falling block broke his arm and knocked him senseless. With him out of action the rest of the crew was just beginning to repair the damage.

Cortes immediately called for a boat to be lowered and had himself and the carpenter rowed across. Within an hour the boat was making its way back with an extra person on board.

The relief Felipe experienced when Pedro's friendly face rose into view above the rail was overwhelming. He hadn't realized just how much the care of the six – now seven – horses had been weighing on his young shoulders.

"Pedro! Welcome back!" He ran to the older man and threw his arms around his waist. Pedro tousled the boy's hair.

"You seem to have grown in three days. How did you do that?" he asked.

"We have a new-"

"About time you returned." Estefan had miraculously appeared, drawn up from the bowels of the ship by the noise on deck. "Left me with far too much to do, you did, and too few hands to do it."

Tears threatened to spring to Felipe's eyes. He opened his mouth to defend himself, but it wasn't necessary. Pedro said all that was needed.

"I knew I could trust Felipe to take care of everything in my absence." He turned his back on Estefan and headed for the stalls. "So," he continued to Felipe, as if Estefan wasn't there. "Tell me your news."

"Isabella foaled!" Pedro stopped and cocked his head to one side, his eyes narrowing.

"How did that go?" he asked gently.

"No problems," Felipe replied. "She did most of the work. And a cabin boy named Pablo has been a big help."

Pedro surveyed the new stall arrangement. He looked closely at each horse in turn. He ran his hand over the rope holding Majesty's stall shut. "You've done an amazing job, young horseman," he said. Felipe beamed. Pedro noticed Hurricane's spindly legs below Isabella's belly. And the small bare feet standing beside the colt. "And that must be Pablo. Pablo! Come introduce yourself!" No response. Pedro cocked an eyebrow at Felipe.

In Mayan Felipe called to Abí. "Abí! Come say hello to Pedro. I told him your name is Pablo."

Pedro had heard Felipe and Abí speaking in Mayan for the past couple weeks so he was immediately suspicious. When Abí shyly stepped out from behind Isabella's rump his suspicions were confirmed. He looked at Felipe, who was doing his best to keep a straight face, and back to Abí. He took in her pantalon and her chopped hair. Then he nodded his head once and sighed. "I hope you know what you're doing," he said to Felipe. Then, to Abí, "Pleased to make your acquaintance, Pablo. Thank you for your hard work. I hope you will continue to assist us."

***

"LAND!"

The cry from the lookout reinvigorated the whole crew. After inspecting *Remedios* Cortes and the carpenter had decided that she needed too much work to try to accomplish the repairs at sea. Her rudder was gone and the upper gudgeon – a heavy wooden circle upon which the rudder pintle pivoted – was shattered.

Instead of repairs a boat crew rowed a line across from *Concepcion*. The light line was attached to a heavier cable on *Remedios*. *Concepcion's* crew manned the capstan, reeling in the lighter line until the cable had been drawn all the way across. They made it fast to the stern bitts and *Remedios* was taken in tow.

The tow made travel almost as uncomfortable as the rough water had. Often, *Concepcion* would be speeding down the face of a wave just as *Remedios* would be slowed by a different wave, jerking on the tow line. Then *Remedios* would run just as *Concepcion* slowed. The cable length was altered several times trying to get both ships into a rhythm, but the wave timing simply wasn't consistent enough. The jerky motion continually threw everyone off balance and the cry of "Land" was a welcome relief.

When the lookout spotted land Felipe and Abí ran to the rail and peered where everyone was looking. Eventually a mountaintop became visible in the distance. "Is this your land?" Felipe asked.

They watched for a long time as the land drew closer. Finally, Abí turned away. "No. That's *Kutzumal*. My land is further that way." She pointed to the west and then continued. "This is an island. I was here once. They have a stone god that talks."

"Idols do not speak."

"This one does. People come to ask him questions."

This was news to Felipe. What came to his mind instantly, as if he could see it in front of him, was the passage from book five of the Psalms. "Feet have they, but they walk not: neither do they speak with their mouths. They that make them will become like them." He didn't bother quoting it to Abí as he normally did but it made him wonder. If this idol could speak, that would mean that what his father had taught him from the Bible was wrong.

He was still pondering it when they dropped anchor in the harbor on the west side of Kutzumal. They were the last to arrive.

CHAPTER EIGHTEEN

"What were you thinking?" Cortes berated Alvarado, loudly, in front of the entire crew.

He had already had Alvarado's pilot, a man named Triana, clapped in irons for failing to obey the specific directions he'd given that the fleet must stay together. He couldn't put Alvarado in irons without destroying the man's authority. But he wasn't going to allow the indiscretion to slide.

"We need these people's help and support. We can buy their gold for a few glass beads; we can convert them to Christ. They will give us – give us! – everything we need to resupply our ships. If we steal from them and make them enemies, do you expect them to convert? Do you think they will help us water and victual our ships?"

Alvarado hung his head and did not reply. When his and the other ships had arrived two days earlier, instead of waiting for Cortes they had dropped anchor and gone ashore. Seeing the large fleet, the locals fled. Alvarado and the other captains commandeered the empty houses. The crew had scooped up the gold trinkets the natives had placed on and around their idols, and anything else that caught their eye. They also caught and slaughtered several of the local fowl. A sailor said they looked like a bird he'd seen once on a voyage to Turkey, so the birds were called turkeys.

They had also captured three of the locals, a woman and two children, planning to keep them as slaves. Cortes had the three brought forward and he called for Melchior and Felipe. Abí stood in the crowd, trying to stay close to Felipe but also trying to stay invisible.

"Tell them," Cortes said, "that my men acted rashly. They did not have permission to take these things. And tell them that they have the apologies of His Catholic Majesty, King Charles."

"He says," Melchior said, "He is a great man, a king. He is angry at men who work for him."

Felipe spoke up in Mayan. "He said he *represents* the king of Spain, and he – how do I say apologize, sorry?" Melchior didn't answer, but although Felipe was looking at him, he was really speaking loudly enough for Abí' to hear him.

She whispered "*Ma'taali'teeni'*" just loudly enough for Felipe to hear.

"He apologizes for his men stealing from you," Felipe finished. Melchior glared at him, but Felipe stood his ground.

Cortes continued. "I am returning to them all that was stolen. I cannot return the turkeys that were eaten but I wish to pay for them." He turned to a man nearby who was holding a small wooden chest. "Show them the bells and beads and let them take what they want. I think one of either one for each bird would be sufficient."

Melchior stepped over to the chest and pulled out a tiny bell and a glass bead. He shook the bell so that it tinkled. The Indian children laughed delightedly at the sound and the woman visibly relaxed. Melchior held out one in each hand and said, "He offers you these for the things that were taken."

Felipe interjected. "He offers you these for the *birds* that were eaten. All your other things," he gestured to the pile of gold, clay figurines and embroidered fabrics on the ground in front of Alvarado, "are returned to you."

The woman came forward tentatively. One of her children took the bell from Melchior's hand and shook it and they laughed again, their mother joining them this time. Felipe reached into the chest and handed each of them two bells. He then counted out forty beads for the forty slaughtered turkeys and handed those over as well.

"Tell them to take a message to their chief," Cortes went on. "'We mean them no harm. We wish to be their friends.' Send them on their way."

"Great king is friends of your chief. Tell him to come," translated Melchior. Felipe decided that was close enough.

"The chief is my husband," the woman replied to Felipe, ignoring Melchior and Cortes. "He has never met your king. But he will be grateful for our safe return. I will tell him the *Castilanos* released us unharmed."

"'Castilanos'? How do you know that word?" Felipe asked.

Cortes, too, had picked up on the word. "What did she say?"

Felipe repeated his question. The woman replied. "The people of the west come here on pilgrimage to *Ixchel*. They tell of two men with beards who live among them. Over there," she gestured westward toward Yucatán. "About two days. *Castilanos* is the word these men call themselves. Am I saying it wrong?"

"No, no," Felipe assured her. "You are saying it just fine." He turned to Cortes. "She says there are Castilians in Yucatán, two of them!"

"Find out all you can about them. We must send for them at once!"

***

By the time the natives began filtering back to their village from the jungle their houses had been vacated and, as far as possible, the belongings restored to their rightful places. Cortes paid particular attention to returning the gold ornaments to the odd-shaped cross and the idol that stood on top of a small pyramid-shaped platform. The platform stood to one side of a vast, stone-paved square in the center of the town. On the west end of the plaza was a stone temple, the largest building in the village. Diaz, who had changed back into priestly garments now that he was back on land, railed against the pollution of the cross. He hated seeing it standing next to the pagan god of the locals. He did so in Spanish, apparently for the benefit of any of the soldiers or sailors who were standing around since the inhabitants didn't understand it.

"It doesn't look like any cross I've seen before," commented Cortes. "Perhaps it means something different to them."

"How could it?" asked the priest. "The cross is the cross. We know Saint Thomas preached in India to bring the light of the savior to these benighted people. Who knows how far he traveled? Perhaps he reached all the way to India's east coast and even to these islands."

Cortes said only, "Hmm..." and continued to study the intricate carvings on the stone cross as the priest prattled on about the saint's supposed travel to India in the first century. He scratched at a portion of the stone with a fingernail. "That looks like a bird. And that is definitely a snake. Not the kind of thing Thomas would have taught them, I wouldn't think."

"Of course not! They have perverted it over the centuries since Saint Thomas gave it to them." The priest was quite confident.

A sailor tossed a chain of gold beads at the foot of the idol and then crossed himself without seeming to be aware of the contradiction.

"Sorry. It's not very good gold anyway," the sailor said to no one in particular. "It's mostly copper. I thought this place was supposed to have whole buildings of solid gold!" The clay idol beside the stone cross, no taller than Felipe, depicted a squatting, large-headed man with snakes growing out of his hair and an ear of corn in each hand. As darkness approached the natives drifted off to their dinner fires. They had already grown accustomed to the strange visitors in their midst and, as Cortes had predicted, some of them traded gold for glass beads.

At sunrise the next morning Melchior began calling loudly for the natives to assemble.

Cortes waited patiently until most of the natives had returned to the square, where they sat on the ground facing the idol platform. Cortes then placed a statue of Mary on the platform on the other side of their idol, so that the clay man was flanked by both Mary and the cross. The natives looked curiously at this new idol. Then Cortes nodded to the priest. Diaz stepped up next to the idol of Mary, pulled out a piece of paper and began to read loudly, in Latin. As the priest read Felipe was shocked at what he heard. He expected to hear something about Jesus dying for their sins, or about Mary, or at least about Thomas. Instead, he heard:

"The lord God appointed Saint Peter as the first head of the only true church, the Holy Roman Church. His Holiness Pope Alexander the Sixth, as Saint Peter's lawful successor, ceded all these lands to His Majesty King

Ferdinand the Second of Spain in the Treaty of Tordesillas of Seven June, the year of our Lord 1494. Pope Leo the Tenth, as Pope Alexander's lawful successor, and His Majesty, the Holy Roman Emperor, King Charles the Fifth of Spain, have renewed this agreement.

"Therefore, know ye by these presents: By your presentation of yourselves for baptism without delay and your unswerving devotion to the true cross and to the virgin Mary, Mother of God, and by your paying the required tribute, you will be acknowledged as loyal subjects of His Majesty King Charles. If you refuse to get baptized, if you continue to worship pagan idols, or if you do not pay the required tribute you will be viewed as enemies of Spain and the Holy Roman Church and will be subject to the penalties thereof, namely, slavery or death, and may God have mercy on your souls."

Diaz then turned the paper over, and read the other side aloud in Spanish, apparently for the benefit of the soldiers and sailors standing around. Felipe noted the differences, and wondered what they meant.

"By order of His Majesty King Charles V, we claim these lands for Spain and declare all persons herein to be subjects of His Majesty.

"The Lord God created all men from Adam and Eve, so that you and we may be brothers. By accepting the True Cross and the Virgin Mary as the only path to salvation, and getting baptized, you inherit the rights of Indian subjects of His Majesty and may come under the protection of the Spanish Crown. Your friends will be our friends, and your enemies will be our enemies. God save the King."

Felipe was confounded by the announcement. Obviously the Spanish members of the expedition understood the last reading, but the natives would have understood neither. Did Diaz think they understood Latin? Of course not. So, was there something in the Latin that Diaz didn't want the sailors to hear? Perhaps the part about slavery? No; most of the men knew that collecting slaves was part of the mission. So it must be the part about paying tribute. He knew the word from Paul's letter to the Romans, the part about the higher powers: "Render therefore to all their dues: tribute to whom tribute is due; honor to whom honor is due."

Was Cortes one of the "higher powers"? Felipe assumed he was. The king certainly was. But did the pope have the right to give an entire part of the world – apparently the entire New World – to King Charles, and require that they pay him tribute? That was too difficult a question for Felipe's young mind to deal with.

But the fact that the words had been secreted in a Latin document that no one was expected to understand made him suspicious. The Indians continued to sit and chat, most of them ignoring the priest Diaz, some appearing to try to absorb what he was saying, some stood, looking like they were about to wander off. Felipe saw several of them look to an older man with a tattooed face and colorful feathers protruding from large holes in his earlobes. Perhaps he was a chief.

"Excuse me, Uncle," Felipe began in Mayan. Several of the Indians stopped to look at him. "Would you like me to translate what he is saying?"

"Felipe!" Cortes called.

"Yes, sir?"

"Come here, I need you."

Felipe immediately went to Cortes, who didn't appear to be doing anything. Cortes told him, "I'll tell you when and what to translate. For now, leave it to others."

Diaz conferred quietly with Melchior for a moment. Melchior then stepped up onto the stone platform and addressed the natives in Mayan.

"This man is a priest of the Castilano religion. He wants you to worship this god," he pointed to the image of Mary, "and he wants to sprinkle water on your heads and give you something to eat. If you do as he asks, you become part of the Castilano religion, and the Castilanos will protect you from your enemies. If you don't do as he asks, you will be enemies of the Castilanos. They may decide to kill you."

Felipe didn't think that was right, but, again, he held his tongue. This was not a new concept to him. His father had taught him about the Spanish forcing Jews to convert or be killed. Father had explained to him that when Jesus said to make disciples, he didn't mean *make* people become Christians. He meant to teach them and let them decide whether to become disciples. But his father had also taught him not to contradict adults.

Felipe was still a boy. They must know what they are doing, he decided. Cortes didn't seem to need him for anything, so after assuring him that he wouldn't translate until asked to, he eased over near the natives to listen. The Indians began to discuss the instructions among themselves, and he heard snippets of their conversations. Some felt it made sense to worship the lady image to keep the Castilanos happy. Others felt their gods might strike them with lightning if they worshipped a different god. The chief had disappeared.

Finally, an old woman said, "These people have strange customs, and a strange language. Perhaps Mary is the name in their language for Ixchel. I have lived a long life. If Ixchel doesn't like me worshipping the Mary lady image, she can strike me dead."

With that, the old woman went over to the image of Mary and got down on her knees. She bowed until her forehead was touching the dust, calling out, "Great Ixchel, mother of the gods, goddess of the moon and the sea. Please forgive these ignorant Castilano heathens for making such a bad image of you." When she straightened, Diaz was standing in front of her. When she started to stand, he put his hand on her shoulder, keeping her on her knees, and dribbled water on her head, intoning, "*In nomine Patris et Filii et*

Spiritus Sancti." When she held out her hand to take the wafer he slapped her hand away, which confused her. Then he stuck out his tongue and pointed to it. She got the idea and stuck out her tongue and he laid the wafer on it. She chewed on it a minute, grinned broadly and rubbed her belly. As soon as Diaz moved on, she spit it out.

She turned to the others. "See? No lightning. But the Castilanos are terrible cooks."

CHAPTER NINETEEN

Some of the other natives got baptized. Most didn't. Cortes noticed many of them heading up to the top of the mountain. He'd heard there was another altar up there with more idols, and he wanted to see if they were going to blatantly defy the order to stop worshipping their idols, so he followed them. Felipe wanted to check on Abí, but his curiosity got the best of him and he went along. He jogged quickly past Cortes. He got a few sidelong glances from the Indians – they weren't sure whether he was Indian or Spanish, and he decided this might be a time for discretion. He melted into the jungle cover and eased silently up to the clearing at the top of the island.

The altar there was a pyramid about three stories tall, larger than any building Felipe had ever seen. It had an immense clay god on a platform near the top. The god was painted brightly in orange and turquoise. The head featured a bright yellow parrot's beak.

And it was speaking.

"Woe unto any who join the Castilanos! Woe to any who let the Castilanos pour water on their heads! Woe to any who bow to the lady goddess of the Castilanos!"

Just as it finished speaking, Cortes strode into the clearing. The natives were all bowing before the god, but Cortes stood erect, facing it defiantly.

"What is your name, god?" he called in Spanish. When the god remained silent, he repeated the question in Latin.

After a pause the god spoke again. "Woe to any who join the Castilanos! Woe to any who let the Castilanos pour water..."

Cortes interrupted. "If you are a god, you should be able to understand my question, regardless of what language I speak. Tell me your name, god."

While this was going on, Felipe had slipped through the jungle and begun exploring the other side of the tall pyramid. Most people would not have seen the well-hidden door cut into the side, but Felipe was following a faint trail which led him to a blank wall. When he pushed on it, the door swung silently inward. The voice of the god came to him, sounding decidedly less godlike and more human. He crept through the door and up a steep flight of stairs. As he peeked over the top step, he saw the Mayan man with the feathers in his pierced earlobes that he'd seen in the village, the one that he had assumed was a chief. Felipe now understood he was a priest. And he was tricking his followers.

***

Cortes continued to stand in the clearing before the pyramid and taunt the parrot-beaked god.

"Answer me, god! You should know my language. Why can't you tell me your name?" No response. Cortes wanted to show the simple people that they were being fooled, but they couldn't understand him anymore than the god could. He wished he'd brought Melchior. He looked around for Felipe to translate his conversation with the god, but he couldn't find him.

What the people heard was, "Woe unto any who join the Castilanos! Woe to any who let the Castilanos – OW!" Even Cortes understood that something had changed.

There came a hollow thunk from the mouth of the god, then: "What are you... OW! Get out of... OW! Stop that!" Then silence.

Then came a much higher, child's voice that Cortes immediately recognized, even though he didn't know the Mayan words. "I am the god Felipe! But I am not a god, and neither is this man who hides inside this false god and pretends to speak as a god! The true God would not fool you! The true God who made earth and heaven has told you not to make idols, not to worship them, and not to listen to them."

Then spotting Cortes through the small mouth hole of the god, Felipe switched to Spanish. "Señor Cortes! It's me, Felipe!" In case Cortes hadn't already figured that out. "The priest was pretending to be this god the Indians call *Itzamna*. They call this place *Ka'na Nah*. There's an echoey room inside this god that makes your voice loud! It will take a few men, but we can pretty easily knock it down and show the people that it's a fake!"

Cortes simply nodded and waved for Felipe to rejoin him. When he came running up red-faced and grinning a few moments later, Cortes asked, "What did you do to the priest?"

"Who? Oh! Well I, um, I threw some stones at him." What he had actually done was to use his sling to send several stones flying very precisely at the man's ear.

"Did you injure him? We can't afford to make the natives angry." Showing they'd been duped by their fake god was one thing. Wounding or killing a high-ranking member of their tribe was quite another.

"No. Just stung him a bit. He ran off."

"Good. Run back to the village and send up half a dozen of the men. We'll expose this fraud to the people and see how they react."

"Yes, sir!" And Felipe sprinted off down the mountain.

When he returned, Cortes was nearly alone. A few natives sat on the grass at his feet, but most had gone about their business. Cortes hadn't been able to keep them there for the show he wished to put on. But Felipe had thought of that. In addition to bringing six sailors, he'd called out to the crowd in Mayan, "Come to *Ka'na Nah*! Come see *Itzamna*! Come quickly! See if he can protect himself from the Castilanos!"

As a consequence, about a hundred Indians followed Felipe and the six sailors up the mountain to where Cortes waited.

"We'll need some levers," Cortes said. The sailors rooted around in the underbrush and found several fallen branches and small trees. "Now," Cortes said. "Come with me."

Cortes, Felipe and the sailors climbed the stone stairs of the pyramid, straight up to the face of the *Itzamna* god. At Cortes' direction, they jammed their levers into the nearly invisible mortar line where the clay god met the stone of the pyramid, and pried up and sideways several times. The god barely moved. They then attacked the mortar joint on the opposite side and pried the god back the other way, and gained more movement, but not much.

"I have an idea," Felipe said. The men stopped and looked at him. "What if we went around behind it?"

He led them around the pyramid and showed them the hidden door. There was only room for three of them inside, but they squeezed in. They put their backs against the inside of the clay god-statue, and their feet against the solid stone of the pyramid. One of the men called "Heave!" and they all pushed mightily. "Heave!" and they pushed again, and it moved a bit more.

Then, as the natives watched, *Itzamna* slowly slid forward, leaned over, and appeared to bow to them for the briefest of moments. Then it toppled forward and began rolling down the steps of the pyramid. It picked up speed, began bouncing, and finally shattered, leaving nothing but a pile of clay fragments. And the natives, who had at first been nervously drawing back just to get out of its path, screamed and turned and ran.

***

"Felipe," Cortes called.

They were heading back down the mountain, and Felipe had started to run ahead. He was feeling bad about leaving Abí alone all day. He stopped and turned and ran back to Cortes.

"Yes, sir?"

Cortes flipped a gold *real* up into the air. Felipe watched it spinning toward him and grabbed it out of the air. "Thank you, sir." Then he stopped walking and waited for Cortes to close the distance. He handed the coin back to him. "Please apply it to my father's debt." Cortes smiled – Felipe couldn't recall the man smiling at him before – and accepted the coin back and nodded.

"I will. You did a good thing, for me and for these ignorant people," Cortes said. "You have my thanks. I have another job for you, if you'll do it."

"Certainly, sir."

"Before our expedition there were rumors of lost Spaniards living among these heathen – possibly as many as six. We now know for certain from the natives that there are at least two gentlemen, living quite near here, in conditions we can only imagine. I wish to send letters to these two men. Melchior tells me that natives in a canoe can reach Yucatán from here in an hour or two, and can march inland to where these two men are being held in less than two days."

Felipe had begun conversing with the Yucatán pilgrims in hopes of finding some from Abí's village, and he had quickly discovered the same information about Spaniards living there. One story said they were slaves. Another said they lived as kings. Since Spaniards lived all over his native Cuba, he hadn't realized that news of Spaniards in Yucatán was important. Now, he felt guilty about not reporting the news to Cortes earlier. He wasn't sure why Cortes was telling him this now, so he just waited.

Cortes continued. "I don't entirely trust the natives to deliver my letters and report back. Melchior has offered to go with the natives to translate. But I'm afraid if I send him I'll never see him again. I'd like you to go with them. Your Indian seems to be nearly as good as Melchior's, and obviously your Spanish is considerably better."

"I – um," Felipe didn't know how to answer. A million thoughts raced through his head at once. From the top of the island he had seen the coast of Yucatán. How big was it? What part of it was Abí's country? Would he be near there? Should he take Abí along? How could he possibly do that? All he could think to ask was, "Who will take care of Majesty?"

"Others can take care of Majesty. I can't imagine you would pass up an opportunity to earn translator wages?"

"No! Of course, I'm happy to help. Let me just go and check..."

"Fine, fine. You're not leaving this hour. Make whatever arrangements you need to make. Find some natives with a boat who are willing to make the trip and take you along and recover the Spaniards if possible, and then bring them and you back here. I should think a week would be sufficient. We'll say eight days. Don't offer them much; they highly value the beads and bells. Come find me about midday. I will have letters for you to carry to the lost Spaniards."

"Yes, sir."

He went to the ship to tell Abí what was happening.

"No! Don't go! If you go to the wrong tribe they might kill you!"

"I will go with men from a trusted tribe who will guarantee my safety."

"Well, take me with you."

"I can't. I can't explain bringing you along. I couldn't explain to Señor Cortes that I want a ship's boy to accompany me. I'll be back in eight days." He did his best to hide from her his fear that he would not be back in eight days, nor in eight years.

"What am I supposed to do in the meantime?" That was a good question.

"Take care of Hurricane. Do what Pedro tells you. Stay out of the way. Start counting – eight days. But if you see people from your part of the world don't wait for me. Leave a message for me with Pedro and let them take you home."

***

"Noble Sirs: I left Cuba with a fleet of eleven ships and 500 Spaniards, and laid up at Kutzumal, whence I write this letter. Those of the island have assured me that there are in the country men with beards and resembling us in all things. They are unable to give or tell me other indications, but from these I conjecture and hold certain that you are Spaniards.

I and these gentlemen who go with me to discover and settle these lands urge that within six days from receiving this you come to us, without making further delay or excuse. This messenger has payment that you may use as you see fit to affect your ransom if needed, or reward your rescuers if that is the more appropriate description of your plight. I shall send a brigantine to the northern tip of Yucatán with instructions to wait until you arrive, or until eight days have passed from today."

Felipe stood under a piece of sailcloth that had been set up as an awning, in front of the sea chest Cortes was using as a desk, waiting for him to finish writing. Behind him stood four Mayan men Felipe had found who had a canoe. They had paddled over from Yucatán. They had easily agreed to be hired to conduct him to the ones they called Castilanos and bring him back. One of them claimed that he knew one of the missing Castilano men personally.

Cortes handed two copies of the letter to Felipe. Felipe glanced at them briefly then began to roll them up. "I suspect you can read, can you not?" Cortes inquired.

Felipe couldn't deny such a direct question. "Yes, sir," he nodded.

"Read it, then."

Felipe read the Spanish writing quickly then nodded again. "What payment, sir?"

"Perhaps you should ask these gentlemen to wait in the courtyard."

94

Felipe pointed to some stone benches in the shade on the other side of the courtyard and suggested the men wait for him there. When they left Cortes handed Felipe a small leather bag.

"Don't dump it out," Cortes advised, with a glance at the Mayan men. Felipe peeked inside the bag and saw a large handful of glass beads and copper bells and a small bundle of steel needles. "The clappers of the bells are wrapped with straw to prevent them ringing, so the natives won't know what you are carrying," Cortes said.

Felipe was glad Cortes had thought of that. For the first time, the enormity of the task he was about to take on struck him. He was a child, going to a strange new world, in a canoe full of strangers – grown men! People whose language he had just learned, whose habits and customs he didn't know. For all he knew they might hit him over the head and take the bag of trinkets the minute they were out of sight of the island!

"If you'll allow me, sir." Without waiting for a response Felipe took the bag of trinkets and placed eight piles of trinkets on Cortes' temporary desk, carefully counting two beads and one bell in each of the first four piles, and then eight beads and four bells in each of the other four piles. Then he opened his bat-wing bag. He cinched the leather bag tightly and stuffed it far down into his bat-wing bag. He then turned and raised an arm and whistled like he was calling Majesty and got the attention of the four waiting Mayan men. The men came back over to Felipe and Cortes and squatted on the ground in the shade of the sail.

Felipe held up the rolled up letters and pointed at the first four piles. "My chief has agreed," he said in Mayan, "to give you each this payment to transport this letter, and me, to the Castilanos on Yucután."

While they were still digesting how they had suddenly become so rich Felipe scooped up the four larger piles and handed them to Cortes. "Hold these a moment, please, sir." Reverting back to Mayan he explained. "The second payment," he said, pointing to Cortes' hand, "you will receive only when you bring me and the Castilanos back here in eight days."

They all stared at Cortes' closed hand. "What if the Castilanos do not want to come?" asked one of the Mayan men, an older man who clearly was the leader.

"As long as you take me to meet them and bring me back safely you will receive your reward." He told Cortes what he'd just said and Cortes nodded and said, "I agree. They will be paid."

The older man nodded once and held out his hand. Felipe put two beads and a bell in it. When one of the other men held out his hand, the older man slapped it away and kept his own hand out. Felipe gave him the payments for all the other men. He pushed the beads and bells into the waistband of his loincloth. Then he took his long thick braid of hair and wrapped it in an elaborate bun. He took the letters from Felipe's hand, rolled them up and tucked them into his hair. "Best way to keep dry," he said. "Let's go."

CHAPTER TWENTY

The men sang as they paddled. The song seemed to keep them all paddling in the same rhythm. Felipe had asked some polite questions, carefully, because he did not know what their customs were. They gladly told him about their trip. The wife of one of them had borne no children in the three years they had been married. So the men had brought her to Kutzumal to petition the fertility goddess Ixmal for help. The leader, whose name Felipe learned was Chimalatl, had left his wife with her as a chaperone. He joked about hoping Ixmal knew which was which, as he already had four sons and three daughters and didn't need any more. They asked about his family and Felipe told them his mother had died before producing any brothers or sisters. He didn't tell them about Cortes cheating and imprisoning his father. He needed them to trust Cortes.

The conversation drifted to crops and the weather. They liked the word 'hurricane.' It had produced only some much-needed rain where they lived, no devastating wind. From his seat in the bottom of the canoe the waves looked huge, but Felipe knew it was a fairly calm day so he simply relaxed and trusted the frail-looking craft; he even slept for awhile. And it seemed only moments later that the man in the front of the canoe jumped into waist-deep water and drew it onto a tiny patch of beach. Felipe barely got his feet wet as he stepped out.

They were not in a bay. The narrow beach faced directly onto the sea. It was only just broad enough to accept the full length of the canoe at its widest point and it disappeared completely a stone's throw in either direction. Its upper edge was walled by an unwelcoming cliff face. Looking up, Felipe could just make out the top of the cliff, perhaps as high as two palm trees. Dragging the canoe as close to the cliff as they could the men left it there and quickly began climbing. If the whole coast looked like this, Felipe could now understand why Cortes hadn't sent one of the ships to bring back the Spaniards.

In the few moments that Felipe had stood looking around the Mayans had completely disappeared. He went to where he'd seen them last and made out a series of rocky steps and handholds. He quickly made his way up the face of the cliff. At the top, although the vegetation was similar to what he'd seen on Kutzumal, this land seemed to be as flat as a plaza in every direction. Turning and looking back out to the east, he couldn't see the island through the haze on the ocean. When he turned to face inland the four Mayan men were nowhere in sight. That didn't worry him; he simply followed their footprints. Shortly he heard them whispering, and then a slight splash of water.

Another step and he had to grab a branch to keep from toppling over the edge of a large hole in the ground. Now he could hear them speaking quietly to each other. The footprints he was following led to the top of a ladder. At the bottom of the ladder the four men were on a small sandy ledge beside a crystal clear pool of water almost completely hidden by the jungle. An intense blue, it looked as if it ran clear to the center of the earth.

"Why are you whispering?" Felipe asked them.

"Ah! You found us," said Chimalatl quietly, looking up. "They were afraid you would be lost."

That wasn't it. Felipe wasn't sure what was going on. "What is this place?"

"Keep your voice down," Chimalatl replied. He pointed to the ladder. "Come, drink."

Instead of clambering down the ladder, Felipe launched himself off the edge of the hole and dove smoothly into the water. He immediately regretted it: the water was colder than anything he had ever experienced in his life. He returned quickly to the surface and found that his leg muscles didn't want to respond properly to his instructions to kick. He managed to thrash his way over close to where the men were and one of them extended a branch, which he grabbed to pull himself, dripping and shuddering, out of the water. His skin was covered with goose bumps and his teeth were chattering.

"Ai! That is cold!"

"Shh! Keep your voice down!" the men all urged. But they were having a hard time keeping their laughter quiet. Felipe shook himself like a dog and squatted beside the men and waited. Gradually, the sun warmed him back up to normal temperature. Then he resumed his questioning.

"Why did you think I was lost? And if you thought I was lost, why didn't you come looking for me?"

"How did you find us?" Chimalatl countered.

"Anyone could find you. You left a trail."

"Are you Mayan?" one of the men asked. The three men, other than Chimalatl, might have been triplets, to Felipe's eyes. Their foreheads were all flattened and sloped backwards. Their eyes were crossed. Their hair was cut straight across the bottom like someone had placed a bowl on their heads. They had large wooden plugs in holes in their ear lobes and gold rings hanging from their noses.

Chimalatl, on the other hand, had none of those features. His hair had never been cut. His eyes focused normally and his forehead hadn't been flattened. Three broad blue stripes were tattooed down the left side of his face

98

from his hairline to his chin. His lower lip had been pierced for a gold ring but it wasn't stretched. One of his front teeth had a jewel embedded in it.

He explained the reason for their questions. "You speak our language. But not properly; and you don't have any markings."

"No, I am not Mayan."

"But you are not Castilano, are you?"

"Why do you say that?"

"You sound different. You smell different. And the Castilanos are not so good at following a trail."

Now Felipe understood. They weren't trying to lose him. They were simply trying to figure out who this brown child was who spoke their language but wasn't Mayan but didn't look like a Castilano, either.

"I am Taino. I am an Indian, like you but from an island called Cuba, far that way." He pointed east. "In calm weather you could paddle your canoe there in about five or six days, though I wouldn't recommend it."

"What does 'Indian' mean?"

"It is what the Castilanos call us, the people like you and me who were here before they came."

"You were here before they came?"

"My mother was."

"So they have only come recently. Where did they come from?"

"These men and these ships came here from Cuba. But before that, they came to Cuba from a place called Spain, far across the sea. It would take you three months of hard paddling in your canoe to reach there, with no land in sight the entire time." The looks they gave him at this news told him they did not believe him.

"No one could make such a trip," Chimalatl declared. "You are trying to deceive us." He shook his head. "You cannot drink from the ocean. Do they not drink water?"

"That is why they have such large ships, so they can carry enough water for such a long trip. Did you see our ships arrive, with the white cloth overhead? The cloth catches the wind, and the wind pushes the ships without having to paddle."

Chimalatl just shook his head. Rigging a sail to a canoe was one thing. But moving such a large vessel without paddling was ridiculous. He changed the subject. "How do you speak our language?"

"A friend, taken by the Castilanos as a slave, taught me."

Chimalatl looked at him sharply. "Is he one of my people?"

"I don't know. She is from a place called Tabasco. Are you from Tabasco?"

Chimalatl lost interest. One female slave more or less was of no concern. "No, they are across the big river. There are many of us. There are not as many Tabasco. You said she is a slave. Are you a slave? Why are you with the Castilanos?"

That was a tricky question. Clearly, they didn't consider the Spanish enemies, exactly, but they didn't trust them either. He decided to tread carefully. "I owe a debt to the chief, Señor Cortes. I am working it off."

That seemed to satisfy his curiosity, and the questions stopped. Now it was his turn. "What is this place?" He gestured to the blue pool of water.

"It is called a *cenote* – water underground. This whole land is flat. The water does not run down in streams as it does on Kutzumal. The sun god, *Kinich-Ahau*, once dried up all the rivers, so the water god *Chaac* hid the streams underground, in the rock. We had to dig to find it."

"There is only one God. He is not a human. He made both the sun and the water. Why would the sun fight with the water?"

Chimalatl shrugged. "Gods fight. Who knows why? The god you are describing is *Uracan*, the creator."

"If he created the sun and the water, he must be greater than both of them. He would not argue and fight with other beings. Humans do that. The creator is the only God."

"What do you call him?"

Felipe hesitated. His father had taught him the name but had warned him not to use it in front of Spanish speakers, particularly priests. On the other hand, these were not Spanish speakers or even Christians. And they believed in many gods. If he told them 'Lord', they would say, 'lord of what?' If he told them people customarily didn't use God's name they would want to know why. And Felipe didn't know why.

So he answered. "*Iehova.*"

Brows furled, the Mayans tried out the word. "Never heard of him," Chimalatl replied quietly.

"Why are we whispering?"

"Because, this is not our cenote. It belongs to the *Xelha*. We are *Itza*. The Xelha don't like us using their water."

"Perhaps we should leave then, before they find us?"

"Yes, that would be best. Fill your belly with the cold water. We have a long walk."

CHAPTER TWENTY ONE

They walked west in silence for hours. When they got hungry, they approached a tree with shiny, dark green pear-shaped fruits hanging from it. Chimalatl pointed at one of the men and told him to climb.

"I climbed the last time," the man complained.

Felipe took his sling from his bat-wing bag, found a rock, and hurled it. One of the fruits fell and he caught it. He tried to peel it but found the skin was tough.

"Avocado," one of his guides said. "Do you have this fruit where you come from?"

"I've never seen one before." He didn't want to pull his knife. Maybe if he knocked it against the tree trunk it would split and he could slurp the juice? He tried that and the fruit split, filling his hand with buttery goo. The men laughed at his ignorance and Felipe laughed along with them, licking his hand. He was surprised to find a huge, hard smooth pit inside the fruit, as big as a mango seed but easier to separate from the fruit.

By now one of the men had climbed up and knocked down a couple more, and they used their stone knives to split the tough skin. Not to be outdone, Felipe took out his sling and flipped the avocado pit at a high-hanging fruit, knocking it loose. He caught it before it hit the ground and handed it to the man wielding the knife to be split.

"Do that again," Chimalatl said. Felipe obligingly picked up one of the pits dropped by the others and slung it and another avocado fell to the ground.

Chimalatl took out his own sling, fired a pit into the tree and hit nothing but leaves. Then the others did likewise. Some of their attempts managed to strike a fruit but they weren't able to knock any loose.

"You have to aim at where they attach to the branch," Felipe said as he fired three stones in quick succession. Soon they were all noisily sucking the smooth pulp from the dark-green armored fruits.

"Can the Castilanos all do that, with their slings?"

"No, they don't have slings. They have other weapons."

"What weapons?"

Felipe thought about how to describe arquebuses and crossbows but gave up. "Bad weapons. Hopefully, you will never find out."

Just as they were about to press on, Chimalatl quickly waved them to silence. Felipe melted into the brush as the others did. Moving nothing but his eyes he scanned around, trying to find the threat that had alerted Chimalatl.

He gradually discerned the panting of a large animal about ten paces to his left. Then he picked up a whiff of an acrid urine smell. Finally, his eyes made out movement where there should have been none in the still jungle as the big cat swiveled its spotted head, looking for the source of the noise it thought it had heard or the scent it thought it had smelled.

After what seemed an eternity, the cat apparently decided its next meal wasn't hiding nearby and it moved on, one padded foot barely whispering on the grass, then another, then silence. The Indians rose. "Jaguar," said Chimalatl. He touched his fingertips to the dirt and then raised them to his lips. Felipe assumed it was some sort of superstition but Chimalatl explained. "Thank you for leaving us alone. I kiss the ground you walked on." To Felipe he said, "I'm glad we didn't have to defend ourselves from him with slings and stones."

Felipe eyed the stone-pointed spears they were carrying. "Why would you not simply use your spears?"

"It is forbidden! We might kill him. Only kings or priests are permitted to kill jaguar. He is a great god."

Felipe shook his head but said nothing.

***

The rest of the day was uneventful. They travelled from cenote to cenote so they didn't need to carry water. The jungle provided food when they were hungry. At nightfall they climbed into the crotches of large trees and slept high above the trail.

They returned to the trail before first light. When the sun came up the four Mayans stopped and turned to face it, bowing their heads and mumbling words Felipe couldn't completely make out - something about asking the sun to be kind to them. He kept silent and waited for them to finish. Chimalatl then led them off the path to another hidden cenote. By now Felipe knew better than to jump in and he climbed down the ancient stone steps with the others. After drinking deeply, he dipped some of the icy water from it to wash his face. After the break they got back on the trail. Felipe snagged a scaly fruit to eat as they marched.

"You can't eat that!" Chimalatl objected.

"Why not?" Felipe asked. "Is it sacred?"

"No, but I think it is poisonous. There are many other things to eat."

Felipe borrowed a stone knife from one of his guides and split the fruit open. He used the point of the glassy black stone blade to dig the small black seeds out of the white flesh. Then he wolfed down half of the sugar apple and offered the other half to the man whose knife he'd borrowed. The man shook his head and backed away. Felipe wiped the knife on some leaves and handed it back to the man. "Keep it," the man said, as if it was contaminated. "I'll get it back when you die."

Felipe just grinned. "Thank you." He examined his new knife. Though he'd never seen this type of stone before he'd read in the Latin dictionary of a black glass-like stone found near volcanoes called obsidian. The chunk of obsidian was about as long as his thumb. One end of it was embedded in a piece of hardwood, held in place with a leathery thong that looked like sinew or gut from an animal. He wondered briefly if he would have had the skill to make one if he hadn't managed to retrieve his Toledo steel knife from Bernardo. He stuck the knife under the strap that held his bag.

"When you see that I don't get sick," he said, gulping down the rest of the sugar apple, "perhaps you'll change your mind." He grabbed several more of the fruits and deposited them in his bat-wing bag.

About midmorning there was a subtle change. The trail underfoot gradually widened and its surface was no longer dirt. It was flat and smooth and paved solidly from side to side with stone, just like the stone paving in the plaza of the town on Kutzumal. It looked very old and the vegetation was encroaching from both sides. But the even, well-worn paving was clearly visible. His father had told him about the paved streets in Salamanca but he'd found it hard to imagine, as there were no paved roads anywhere in Cuba. Even experiencing the wide paved plaza in the town on Kutzumal hadn't really prepared him for this. He could understand villagers getting together and spending a month finding and setting smooth stones to make that courtyard. But a road could go on for leagues. It would need hundreds of people, thousands of people even, and it would take them years upon years to build such a thing.

Who were these people?

***

A few hours later they began to encounter others. Many, many others. Felipe began to realize that this was not a small tribe like his mother's people had been when Velasquez arrived on Cuba. And they weren't living a simple life of fishing, picking papayas from the jungle, weaving hammocks and building thatched huts that had to be replaced every few years. This was much more permanent. There were enormous, arrow-straight square fields as far as the eye could see with neat rows of maize, squash and beans. There was a complex system of small canals feeding smaller ditches delivering water to rows of crops in measured amounts. Young boys removed or replaced small logs to direct the flow of the water where it was needed.

"If your water is all underground," Felipe asked, pointing to a canal, "where did all this water come from?"

Chimalatl responded. "The rain god Chaac drops it from the sky. We capture as much as we can and store it in *chultunes*. When we need it, we lift it out of the chultunes and pour it into the canals to water crops."

He pointed off to the left where Felipe now understood what he was looking at. A woman stood near the short end of a long pole that pivoted atop a tall, three-legged stand. The pole had a large stone weight attached to the short end. When she added her weight to the pole, a clay jar on the other end, bigger than Felipe, rose from a hole in the ground. The hole must open to the chultune, the reservoir Chimalatl spoke of. She swung the pole through half a circle and lowered the jar on a dirt ramp that tipped the jar over and its contents emptied into a canal.

Still further along the road Felipe began to smell smoke. Soon he saw a vast hazy cloud of it rising. It looked as if the whole land was on fire. The dried leaves and stalks of a previous crop were being burned. Felipe had noticed near his home that the ground seemed more lush a year or so after lightning caused a fire. But it had never occurred to him to purposely set the land on fire. The land in Cuba produced food so easily no one went to such extraordinary lengths. As they got closer, he could see the low flames beneath the pall of smoke. A line of dozens of men and women moved along slowly near the flames, making sure the dead plants were completely burned.

As they passed people on the road Chimalatl and the other three exchanged greetings and sometimes introduced Felipe, who also greeted the strangers in Mayan. Some of them regarded him with curiosity but most ignored him once they realized he spoke their language. He was hardly remarkable; just one more half-naked young boy in a crowd. When an old woman noticed his slight accent she asked Chimalatl, "Is he your slave? Why do you introduce your slave?"

"No," Chimalatl replied. "He is not a slave. He is an emissary from a far-off king." The old woman squinted at Felipe, then shrugged and shook her head. "What kind of a king uses children as messengers?" She went on her way without waiting for an answer.

Just before the sun went down they entered a vast stone city. Felipe had never seen or even imagined such an imposing complex. Even when he had tried to imagine Salamanca from his father's descriptions the word pictures hadn't prepared him for anything as enormous as this. Buildings of chiseled stone, five and six stories tall, stood next to smaller stone houses. Everything looked as permanent as the earth itself. There were no thatch or mud huts. Steep-sided angular temples and pyramids – and altars with dark red stains that didn't bear thinking too much about – bordered stone courtyards that would have held the entire village of Santiago. And more people than Felipe had ever seen together in one place.

Hundreds of market stalls sold everything imaginable. Smoke rose from some offering cooked meat. They stopped at a stall with something that smelled wonderful, rolled up in a corn husk it had been cooked in. Chimalatl told Felipe they were called tamales and ordered one for Felipe and two each for himself and the other three men. He pulled from his waistband a small fragment of the sharp black obsidian stone similar to the knife that had been given to Felipe. He finally learned what the stone was called here: *Itzli*. The vendor wanted more. The other three men had watched closely to make sure Chimalatl didn't trade away the glass beads or bells he also carried in his loincloth. Chimalatl and the tamale vendor haggled, a second smaller piece of obsidian joined the first, and the deal was done.

Felipe watched the others eat first – he wasn't sure how to eat it – then unrolled the corn husk and devoured the contents. It seemed to be corn meal, with which he was familiar, wrapped around some sort of meat he couldn't identify, and some spices. It was gone too quickly, and he wished for more. He looked around to see what other new delicacies awaited him. Chimalatl could tell the boy was still hungry, but they moved on – this vendor was too expensive.

They came to an intersection where a wide avenue crossed their path. One of the younger Mayan men took his leave and headed down that street toward his home. Soon the other two left them, and Chimalatl and Felipe walked on alone.

They passed a pen that held several hundred turkeys. Another held dogs being fed avocados. Market stalls offered every sort of pottery, from small intricate cups to huge water jars, and some displayed rows of clay masks and dolls, mostly looking to Felipe like images of their gods. More sellers offered jewelry in silver and gold, feathers, and dozens and dozens of varieties of fruits and vegetables. At Chimalatl's request a vendor deftly impaled two mangoes on short sticks and peeled and carved them so that they resembled pineapple tops. He handed a stick each to Chimalatl and Felipe and they continued down the street, munching as they walked. There hadn't been any bartering or exchange; perhaps the man knew Chimalatl.

They came to a stall that had fabric in a brighter shade of red than Felipe had ever dreamed. He exclaimed at the sight and touched the vibrant cloth. "How is this possible?" he asked. "Is it made from parrot feathers? Or do you have a plant that I don't know about?"

"Actually," Chimalatl explained, "the dye comes from a bug."

"A bug!" Felipe studied the man's face to see if he was teasing him. He didn't appear to be. "Can you show me?"

The stall owner, an old wrinkled woman with gray hair and a toothless grin had noticed Felipe's enthusiasm. But she didn't seem to be able to speak. She waved the boy over to her side and pointed toward the ground. There Felipe saw a small cage, barely large enough for even a chicken, made of woven pine needles. Peering closely through the tiny openings between the needles he saw hundreds of dull red beetles, smaller than melon seeds, busily crawling all over a hunk of gray-green cactus. The old woman reached into the cage and brought out one of the beetles on the tip of a gnarled finger. She crushed the bug between her thumb and finger and both became as red as blood. She grabbed Felipe's face and pinched it and laughed, leaving horizontal red lines on his cheeks. He smiled and bowed his head and thanked her for the demonstration. As she continued to hold her hand out he realized she expected to be compensated for the demonstration. He looked at Chimalatl, who had suddenly become fascinated with a vendor on the other side of the alley. He thought of the obsidian knife given to him by his Mayan travel companion who was afraid of the sugar apple – but certainly that was far too much to give the old woman for the red markings on his face. What else could he offer? He reluctantly reached into his bat-wing bag and felt for the small leather bag. Without taking it out he fumbled the mouth of it open and withdrew a blue glass bead and handed it to her. She shouted excitedly at this marvel, though no comprehensible words came out. She stood and started waving her neighboring vendors over to see her amazing treasure.

Out of the corner of his eye he saw that Chimalatl had not missed the transaction. He was looking thoughtfully at Felipe's bag. Apparently it hadn't occurred to him before now that Felipe might be a source of even more of the glass beads. Felipe was glad that Chimalatl and the other men hadn't known about the beads he carried when he was alone with them in the jungle.

"Come on," Chimalatl said. "I will be honored to have you spend the night in my humble home. And tomorrow we will go see Lord Taxmar and his Castilano."

CHAPTER TWENTY TWO

With the news of possible Spaniards on Yucatán, what Cortes had intended to be only a quick stop at Kutzumal became an extended stay. Cortes ordered the water butts to be ferried ashore for refilling and a corral and stable for the horses.

Pedro had found that, in the absence of Felipe, even the simplest tasks became difficult. Old Estefan the drunk, naturally, was already ashore and could be counted on only to remain invisible until the ship sailed. This left Pedro to unload the horses with only the assistance of the girl he had to remember to call Pablo. She was a hard worker and determined to be helpful but she knew very little about horses. And she adamantly refused to go near Majesty.

She had, however, been a priceless help with the foal, Hurricane. The two had become closely attached. She mimicked the colts neighs and nickers and gait. She could be seen running delightedly around the cramped deck, and even exploring below decks, making neighing noises and jumping over obstacles with Hurricane right behind her. Isabella neighed loudly whenever the colt was too long out of her sight.

When it came time to drive the horses over the side for the swim ashore Isabella balked. It took Pedro by surprise. He was expecting to have problems from Majesty, not Isabella. But the colt was afraid of this new maneuver and was hiding behind his mother. And Isabella didn't trust that her colt would follow her over the side so she wouldn't budge. It was at this critical juncture that 'Pablo' justified her presence, in Pedro's view.

Abí approached the colt and put her arms around it, whispering in its ear. She then spoke to Isabella in a language Pedro didn't understand. Isabella visibly calmed. The girl started running and Hurricane ran after her, loving the game. They circled the deck one time. Then Abí ran and jumped through the gap in the railing, into the warm turquoise waters below, and Hurricane went right with her. Isabella, perhaps out of concern for her colt, jumped immediately after them.

Which was a good thing since Abí didn't know how to swim. She grabbed a handful of Isabella's mane and floated along the mare's left side. Hurricane confidently swam on his mother's right side, and the threesome made it to shore.

***

Cortes could be found each morning on his knees before the statue of the Virgin Mary they'd set up in the village. He ran the beads of his rosary through his fingers one by one and loudly recited the memorized words. He didn't command any of the men to join him but a few did. None stayed as long as Cortes did, however. He stayed on his knees until the stones were cutting off his circulation, praying for the conversion of the natives, praying for the success of his mission, even praying for forgiveness of the activities he was certain some of his men had engaged in the night before.

There was a reason for the show of piety. It had little to do with respect for God. His crew was divided into two camps. One camp included all those who were his enthusiastic supporters; or at least, those whose greed convinced them that Cortes' success meant success for them. Cortes' morning prayers added to their conviction that God would surely bless their devout leader and make them all rich.

The other camp consisted of followers of Governor Velasquez. They were counting on Cortes' failure. They too believed that God had ordained that Spain should conquer these lands but they were convinced God would never use a reprobate like Cortes to do it. While Cortes was not given to foul language and hated it in others, he was not averse to gambling or drinking. And his attraction to young ladies was legendary. He had already found a local woman to share his bed despite having a wife in Santiago.

So the followers of Velasquez hedged their bets. They had come along on this expedition on the off-chance that Cortes might make them rich, that they might stumble across enough slaves or gold to make the trip profitable.

But Cortes knew they were really waiting for the opportunity to return to Velasquez gleeful with the news of Cortes' failure, hoping Velasquez would reward their loyalty. Cortes' daily devotions perplexed them. Perhaps they had misjudged him. His constant prayers for the conversion of the Indians reminded them that Cortes was carefully fulfilling the letter of Velasquez's orders; that these Indians weren't slaves – yet.

So Cortes knelt until his knees screamed for relief. Cortes didn't really believe that repeating these words would have any effect on the outcome of his endeavor. But he believed that being seen to do it might have an effect on the men of both camps that he knew he was going to desperately need to fight for him.

***

Chimalatl's home was anything but humble. It featured its own private outdoor courtyard with a bubbling fountain. Felipe wondered about the running water. But he suspected the answer would involve a lot of slave labor so he kept his silence. Inside, the house consisted of two rooms –

another luxury. Most of the houses they'd passed were a single room, even though most of the families seemed to be as large or larger than Chimalatl's.

Felipe was introduced to several of Chimalatl's children who had been left in the care of a trusted slave girl while their parents had made the trip to Kutzumal. They stared at this strange visitor. One of the younger ones, a girl about three or four, approached and poked at him. An infant seemed to be captivated by his bat-wing bag. They were not surprised at his command of their language; instead, they were confused as to why he didn't speak it perfectly. And they asked if he was their cousin.

This last remark was prompted by his looks. They were pleased to meet someone who, like themselves, 'looked funny.' He didn't have the flattened forehead or crossed eyes most of their friends had. Chimalatl explained that recently, for about the last twenty years or so, it had become fashionable for mothers to strap a board to the foreheads of newborns to push back the soft bones of the skull as they grew. Additionally, the board featured a bead suspended between the baby's eyes. As the baby focused on it during his first few months of seeing the world, his eyes became crossed.

Chimalatl didn't like it. He felt that, while he couldn't say one way or the other whether the gods were honored by it, it certainly didn't honor his children; and he wasn't going to allow his children to be deformed just to please a fickle god who might decide to change the fashion before these children had even reached adulthood. Then he turned to the children, in a gruff growl they had apparently heard many times before and said, "But none of you will repeat that opinion outside of this home, or I will throw you into the sacred cenote myself!"

The children laughed at their father's pretend-threat. One of his children, a chubby boy about Felipe's age named Kabil, offered to share his sleeping pallet with Felipe and they all went off to bed.

When day dawned in the city the three Mayan companions arrived at Chimalatl's house. Felipe hadn't heard any arrangements being made and he wondered how they knew to meet. Then, as they were about to step outside, the three men stopped and held their hands out to Chimalatl. He tried telling them the treasure was well hidden, but they were adamant. Grudgingly, he handed each one a copper bell and a glass bead.

"The agreement was two beads," one of them complained. Chimalatl struck the man's head with the back of his hand. "The agreement was with me, for eight beads and four bells. How I choose to distribute them is for me to decide. If it wasn't for me, how many beads would you have, eh? None. Be thankful you have one. I have mouths to feed."

Apparently his conscience got the better of him, however. When they stopped at a tamale vendor for breakfast Chimalatl bought a dozen tamales for the group and paid for them with one of the beads.

As Felipe followed the others through the city something struck him: many of the old stone structures were shrouded in vines, as if the jungle was trying to take back the space that had been taken from it. Looking at one that was being worked on, Felipe realized that it wasn't a case of the city being actively eaten by the jungle. No, it was more as if the city had already been eaten, and the present inhabitants were trying to undo the damage. There were no new structures being built. The buildings being used seemed to be just as old as the buildings covered in vines. In fact, Felipe now realized, the 'hills' they had passed on the outskirts of the city the evening before were not, in fact, hills – they were overgrown pyramids. In some places the paving stones in the streets were pushed up by tree roots. But he also saw crews of slaves at work on some of the broader streets, pulling the stones up, hacking at the roots, and resetting the stones.

He asked his travelling companions about what he was seeing.

"This place is *Yaxunah*. It is the largest city in the land of the Itza."

"Eetsaw?"

"It is what we are called. The Itza abandoned the land two hundred and seventy years ago and moved far away, when the sun god Kinich-Ahau defeated Chaac and stopped the rains. Eighty years ago, when my grandfather's father, *Ah Xupan*, was just a boy, he went hunting with some friends and they travelled very far. They eventually found this place and realized where they were, that it was the home of the ancients. It was obvious that Chaac had once again triumphed over Kinich-Ahau. My grandfather's father and his friends convinced the tribe they should come back and live here again."

Felipe finally worked up the nerve to ask Chimalatl, "Why are your markings, um, different, from these men?"

Chimalatl puffed up proudly, just a bit, at the question. "Tattoos are for warriors. In my time," he said, "we didn't cut our ears, we got tattooed. And not just to look like everyone else. No. A soldier only got a tattoo, or later an earplug, when he killed or captured enemies in battle." He pointed to his tattoos. "Each one of these stripes represents a battle. Look," he said, inviting Felipe to peer closely at his stripes. Felipe now saw that each stripe had several segments. "The longer the stripe, the more captives taken. These young ones, they get the ear piercings and the lip piercings and the nose piercings just to look pretty."

"So then, Great Chimalatl," the one who hadn't managed to father any children asked with a grin, "Why do you wear a ring in your lip?"

"Because on a warrior, on me you young fool, it looks good!" They all laughed good-naturedly.

They had continued to walk as they talked, and Felipe now was staring at a magnificent, partially overgrown castle.

"The legend says this was the royal home of *Hunac Ceel*," Chimalatl said.

"No it wasn't," replied one of the younger men. "I heard that was at *Chichen*."

Chimalatl gave the man a withering look. "Most educated people know it was here," he said, daring anyone to contradict him. He turned back to Felipe. "Chichen Itza was important to the story, but it was not where this happened."

"Hunac Ceel? I don't know who that is." Felipe said.

Chimalatl looked at him as if he had said he didn't know what the sun was. Then he patiently explained. "Three hundred and seven years ago, *Hunac Ceel Cauich* was a slave of the old ones. No one knows where he came from. He was sacrificed to Chaac in the sacred cenote here in the city. But he survived. By the way, don't try that stunt, here, jumping into the cenote. You will not survive. The sides are sheer and slick and there are no handholds."

"How did he survive?"

"Some say he flew out. Others, that the gods allowed him to breathe underwater, and he swam underground to another cenote and climbed out there. Anyway," Chimalatl continued, "the old ones believed that anyone who survived being thrown into the cenote became a true prophet. Hunac Ceel prophesied that Chaac would bring the rains that year – which he did. But he also prophesied that he himself would become king of the Itsa. He went to Chichen Itza to wait – back then, Chichen Itza was as big or even bigger than Yaxunah. When the rains came as prophesied, the king grew worried and sent his son to Chichen Itza to kill Hunac Ceel. Hunac Ceel killed the son instead. He then brought his head here, to the king's castle. He walked right in; no guards tried to stop him. He walked in and killed the king and declared himself king, fulfilling his own prophecy."

"But then the city was abandoned thirty seven years later. Your Chaac seems very fickle."

"When people are thirsty, sometimes they forget about gods. And heroes. Anyway, it is just a story."

As they approached the gate of the castle Felipe paused, his hands resting on the giant vine-covered stone walls, and closed his eyes. "What are you stopping for?" Chimalatl inquired. Had Felipe suddenly decided to pray to his God? "This is our destination, right here." He pointed to the gate. Large guards with painted bodies and elaborate feather headdresses stood in front of the gate. Each held a long spear with a large obsidian head. The guards recognized Chimalatl and greeted him. He merely said, "I bring a messenger for Lord Taxmar." They glanced at Felipe, nodded and let them pass.

"Is this Lord Taxmar going to help us find the Castilanos?" Felipe asked quietly.

"One of the Castilanos should be here," Chimalatl replied. "He is one of Lord Taxmar's slaves."

CHAPTER TWENTY THREE

Lord Taxmar and his wives, children, courtiers and servants occupied only a small portion of the castle. Most of it was un-restored. The travelers walked a well-worn hallway through the gloom to an open-air courtyard. Taking it all in, Felipe's assessment was that it would have been uncomfortably hot when it was new and open to the sun. But the jungle that had so recently covered it had been trimmed back carefully, just enough to allow the breezes to come in but leaving enough vegetation to provide shade. In addition, a pool in the center of the courtyard had a fountain. Water sprayed far into the air, falling as a fine mist, and that also helped to cool the air. Several children played in the water. About a dozen adults sat on stone benches, some watching the children, but with an attitude of waiting for something to happen. Another two dozen sat on the ground.

One man was not sitting on a simple bench. His seat could only be what Felipe had read about but never seen: a throne. This had to be Lord Taxmar. A slave girl knelt before him with a gold platter of fruit resting on her head. Another slave stood behind him slowly waving a fan made of parrot feathers.

On the ground beside the girl with the fruit platter sat a man wearing only a loincloth, like the others. His skin was nearly as brown as the others. His dark hair was long and well-groomed. Unlike any of the others, it was interspersed with gray. He also, unlike any Mayan Felipe had seen so far, had a beard. A Spaniard! Felipe almost ran to him, but Chimalatl gave him a warning look and he froze.

The Spaniard was reading from a small book. And Lord Taxmar and his attendants were all laughing at him.

"So, Saint Aguilar, who is the saint of the day?" asked Taxmar.

The Spaniard closed the book and addressed the crowd. From his bearing it appeared that this scene had happened many times before. Though the question was in Mayan, the chief stumbled through the Latin pronunciation of 'Saint Aguilar.' Felipe wondered how the chief had learned those words.

"Today is the day of Saint Luca Casali", the Spaniard replied.

The Mayan court all responded, vaguely in unison, with a very bad version of what Felipe deduced was supposed to be Latin for "All hail Saint Luca Casali!" and laughed at each others' results. The Spaniard waited.

Taxmar then asked, "And what were the amazing exploits of Saint Loka?"

"Saint Luca Casali," the Spaniard replied, "was the abbot – the spiritual teacher – of a group of monks…"

While he was speaking, Felipe flashed on a breviary his father had borrowed from the village priest a couple years ago. Felipe had read it in a day and, without thinking about it, had memorized it. He was now able to call back to his mind the passage about Saint Luca Casali: Born in Nicosia, educated by the abbot of the Saint Philip monastery in Agira. When he realized his vision was fading he memorized the gospels and the psalms. He was appointed against his will as Abbot of Agira. One day, while travelling to Nicosia with his students a young monk decided to play a prank on him and told him a crowd was following them waiting for Casali to preach a sermon. Casali turned and blindly preached a sermon to an empty field of stones. When he finished, according to the students, the stones cried out "Amen!"

Felipe had at first been amazed at all the miracles the breviary had described. But later, when his father had brought home a book about all the popes – virtually all of whom were "saints" – some awkward conversations had ensued. He'd asked his father how these men could be "saints" or even popes when they clearly disobeyed God's words in the Bible? His father had replied, "The Church is The Church, and there is no other path to God at present. The Church would have you believe that, for that reason alone, it is The Way and must have God's approval. But what did Jesus say? Is there only one way?"

Felipe had answered promptly from his memory. "No, there are two: 'Enter by the narrow gate; for broad is the gate and wide the road that leads to destruction, and many are they who go in by it. Whereas narrow is the gate and constricted the road to life, and only a small number find it.'"

"Would you say The Church is few, or many?"

"Many. So is The Church on the wide road to Hell?"

"No, no. You can't make that judgment. But does The Church seem to you like a narrow gate, a constricted road?"

"No."

"So there must be some other narrow gate, some other constricted road. But for right now, The Church tolerates no other." Miguel Ferrer briefly replayed in his mind the angry Cardinal Cisneros in Salamanca warning him about the Inquisition.

"But," his father had continued, "the Bible is God's word. He has protected it even when The Church has tried to change it or destroy it. So even though we are members of The Church, when The Church and the Bible conflict always trust the Bible. Just don't say so out loud or The Church might send you to meet God sooner than you want to."

Felipe snapped back to the present as the crowd lost interest in the Spaniard and began drifting away. Felipe began to approach the Spaniard, but Chimalatl stopped him again. Turning, Felipe realized Chimalatl wasn't looking at the Spaniard or at him. Felipe followed his gaze. Lord Taxmar had spotted the visitors and was approaching them. Chimalatl bowed his head to Taxmar and Felipe did the same. Then Chimalatl reached up to the knot in his hair and withdrew Cortes' letters to the Spaniards and handed it to Taxmar.

"My lord," Chimalatl said. "I bring you greetings from the chief of the Castilanos on Kutzumal. He has sent a message about your Castilano slave."

Taxmar looked at the piece of paper, turning it one way and then the other, then handed it back. "This makes no sense to me. Can you tell me what it means?"

Chimalatl stared hard at the black squiggles as if the intensity of his gaze would force them to give up their meaning. Then he shrugged and handed it to Felipe.

"My lord," Felipe suggested to Taxmar. "Perhaps it means something to the Castilano."

"Who is this waif?" Taxmar asked Chimalatl. Chimalatl nodded at Felipe.

Felipe replied, "My lord, I am Don Felipe Ferrer y Mendoza, fourth duke of Arjona. I bring you greetings from His Excellency Captain General Don Hernando Cortes de Monroy y Pizzaro, Alcalde of Santiago and, er, chief of the Castilanos on Kutzumal." He'd caught himself at the last moment. He didn't think it would be wise to tell Taxmar that one of Cortes' titles was head of an expedition with orders to conquer and convert or enslave the Yucatán.

Taxmar looked him up and down for a moment. "If you are the best emissary the Castilanos can send I guess we don't need to worry about them. Go." Taxmar waved them toward the Spaniard. "Saint Aguilar!" he called over his shoulder as he walked away. "You have visitors!"

Felipe took the letter and approached the bearded man still seated on the ground. "Señor?" he said in Spanish. "Am I correct in assuming you are Spanish?"

The bearded man stared up at him as if he were an apparition. He tried to speak but no words came out. Finally he managed: "*Dios? Santa Maria?*"

Felipe hadn't realized it but the sun was directly behind him, creating a halo behind his head and throwing his face into darkness. He squatted beside the man. "No, Señor. My name is Felipe. I have a letter for you." He held out the piece of paper and the man took it.

He looked at it uncomprehendingly, his brow knitted in concentration. He couldn't make sense of it. He had been speaking Mayan for so long he'd forgotten Spanish. He vaguely remembered some of the words Felipe spoke, he recognized some of the shapes on the paper but couldn't remember how to say them, either. He pointed to himself. *"Sevilla,"* he said.

"Is that your name, Señor, *Sevilla*? Or is it Aguilar? There is a city by the name Seville in Spain. Are you from that city?"

"Sevilla," the bearded man said again.

Suddenly Felipe had an idea. The man's knowledge of saints... He switched to Latin. "Sir, my name is Felipe, and I have a message for you. I have been sent to help you to return to your people. Am I correct that you are from Seville, or is that your name?"

Instantly, the look on the man's face changed. "Jesus, Mary and all the saints! You have been sent from Heaven! Tell me your name – did you say Felipe? Are you Saint Felipe? Are you named for Saint Felipe? Saint Felipe, apostle of Christ, May the First, is this May First? No. Perhaps you are Felipe the Evangelizer, the baptizer of the Ethiopian? No, he was not a saint. But perhaps he was and we don't know it? Isn't this March second? Saint Luca Casali's Day? Are you Saint Luca Casali?" He paused in his rambling long enough for Felipe to speak again.

"No, sir, I am not a saint. And today is not March second. It is March first, Saint Pietro Ernandez..."

"Yes! You are Saint Pietro Ernandez, I knew it right away! The gift of tongues. That is how you speak Latin and Spanish and Mayan!"

"No, sir. I am not a saint. I am a boy named Felipe. My father is a horse rancher in Cuba. He named me Felipe because it means lover of horses. And you are named...?"

"Ah, I thought I told you. I am Brother *Jeronimo de Sevilla*. Yes. No. Jeronimo de Aguilar. And I am *from* Seville. Yes, that's right."

"I am pleased to meet you, Señor Aguilar," Felipe responded in Spanish. "And are you able to read what is written on this letter?" Felipe offered the letter to Aguilar again.

"What? No. I – No," he continued in Latin. "It is all jumbled. Whoever wrote that needs to work on his Latin. It makes no sense. And it is fuzzy."

"It is not Latin, sir. It is Spanish. Would you like to try again?"

"No, no. Just read it to me." Felipe began to read the Spanish. "No, no. In Latin, boy, in Latin."

Felipe read him Cortes' letter, translating to Latin as he went. *"Noble Sirs: I left Cuba with a fleet of eleven ships and 500 Spaniards, and laid up at Kutzumal..."*

Aguilar interrupted. "He says 'sirs,' as if he is addressing many. And I don't know this Kutzumal."

"He says 'sirs' because we do not know how many of you there are among the Mayans. Kutzumal is a small island off the coast a few days march from here."

116

"Oh! I see. Yes. I am not familiar with Kutzumal. I am a slave, after all. I go where my Lord requires. I have been only a few leagues from this place. And even then I was burdened down with such a load I was in no position to take note of the geography. Yes, that's right, isn't it?" Felipe wasn't sure how to answer so he addressed the other question instead.

"Are there more Spaniards here besides you?"

"What? Yes, of course! Well, not many, not anymore. There were six of us but some were eaten. But we escaped, Guerrero and I, yes. Then Taxmar caught us. But he doesn't eat people so we were safe, except we were slaves."

"So there is another Spaniard here named Guerrero?"

"No, of course not. There is only me. If Guerrero were still here I would not have forgotten how to speak Spanish, would I? No. He gave Guerrero to another chief, Lord *Xpatal* of *Chatamal*."

"Is that near here?" Felipe asked.

"Yes, no. Not far. I'm not sure. I have been only a few leagues from this place," Aguilar repeated. "And even then I was…"

"So Guerrero is more than a few leagues away?" Felipe interrupted. "Do you know how many leagues?" Felipe was unfamiliar with how far a league was but he thought he'd heard a soldier say something about marching seven leagues in a day.

"I don't know. Perhaps a day, a few days? Yes, two days, there and back. We must ask Lord Taxmar to send runners, right away."

Felipe began to get worried. He hadn't looked far enough ahead. He had reasoned that two days to reach the lost Spaniards meant two days to get back. He'd assumed he would be back with the expedition, with Abí and Pedro and Majesty, in four or perhaps five days. But now he was looking at more days lost collecting another Spaniard some days away.

On the other hand, if another Spaniard was nearby, even a few days away, he couldn't simply be abandoned. Somehow he needed to make sure Aguilar saw the urgency of the situation.

"Please, sir," he said. "Allow me to read the rest of the letter." He began to translate the rest of the Spanish into Latin for the monk: *I and these gentlemen who go with me to discover and settle these lands urge that within six days from receiving this you come to us, without making further delay or excuse.*" He looked intently into the slightly vacant eyes of the sun-baked monk. "Señor Cortes said six days because these men," he pointed to Chimalatl and his companions, "they said you were two days from us. And this is the third day already since we left. But we must be at the rendezvous in six days, or we will miss the ships. And if we miss them, you will never get back to Spain, to *Sevilla*." And I will never get back to Cuba and my father, Felipe thought.

"Six days?" Aguilar said. "Six days. See? Plenty of time. God made the world in six days, yes. We must send for Guerrero."

CHAPTER TWENTY FOUR

Hurricane was growing rapidly. He spent most of his time either running with Abí or eating. Isabella neighed loudly if Hurricane and Abí got too far away.

Abí helped Pedro feed and water the horses every morning and evening in the temporary corral the sailors had knocked together – really just a line of boards and rope strung from tree to tree and attached to a stone building on one side. When it was time to run Abí didn't bother to use the gate. She had found a gap in the boards where she could simply lift the rope and Hurricane would duck under it.

After everything on the ships was repaired, tested and properly stowed there was no reason to keep the sailors on board, except for the anchor watch. Life ashore had quickly fallen into the routine of sailors on friendly shores everywhere. Eating and drinking, rising late and staying up late, music and dancing and gambling. Cortes appeared to frown on the dancing. But as long as the men didn't harm the natives or each other he was content to let them be. And, as he had predicted, most of the gold of the place was soon in the hands of the Spaniards, traded for a handful of trinkets.

***

Aguilar refused to go looking for the great man. Only when Taxmar decided to reappear would they be able to present their requests, to ransom Aguilar and to send a message to Guerrero.

Felipe had discussed it with the still addled Aguilar. "Sir. Please note Don Cortes' words in the letter. *'Ransom if needed, or reward your rescuers if that is the more appropriate description.'* So is it ransom or reward? Do we try to buy you from Lord Taxmar, or do we simply thank him for his hospitality and reward him?"

"Hmmm. That is a good question, young man. Ransom or reward? Jesus is our ransom. In some other context is he also termed a reward? 'He is the rewarder of those who seeketh him,' I remember that…"

"Sir, please concentrate. We are not talking about Jesus. We are talking about how to approach Lord Taxmar. Does he consider you a slave to be purchased? Or would he more likely be flattered by a reward for your rescue?"

"Oh! Yes, I see. Well, he is certainly a vain man. And extremely wealthy. One slave more or less, even one he finds entertaining as he does me, would not particularly matter to him. But offering him a reward rather than a payment, painting him as a hero, especially if you give him something rare, yes, along with the thanks of a grateful Spanish nation for saving one of their own, or some other such fluff, yes, that is more likely to win him over. That paints him as a hero, do you see?" Felipe nodded. "So, what reward can you offer him?"

"Let me show you. Am I free to leave the castle and come back?" Felipe asked. "I mean, if I leave, will the guards let me back in?"

"Oh dear, I have no idea. They would prevent me from leaving, I'm sure. At least, I believe they would if I were to try. Actually, I've never tried. When Lord Taxmar saved me from those others who ate... well, I was so grateful. I never bothered..."

"Don't worry about it. I'll ask Chimalatl. Wait here."

Felipe approached Chimalatl and the other three Mayans, who seemed perfectly content to sit in the shade and wait.

"I need to leave the castle for a moment. Will the guards let me back in?"

Chimalatl rose from the shady spot on the ground where he was waiting. "They will if I'm with you. Where are we going?"

Felipe just gestured for him to follow and headed back to the street. "Where are we going?" Chimalatl said again. He knew Felipe didn't know anyone here. Did he need something from the market? But they went only a few steps and Felipe stopped in front of the same spot on the wall where he had paused on the way into the castle, when Chimalatl had thought he was praying. Felipe slid his hand behind a large, gnarled vine and withdrew a small leather bag.

"I'm sorry," Felipe said. "I didn't know who we were meeting, or how we would be received. I was afraid someone would search me and find the payment I've been authorized to give to secure Aguilar's release from Taxmar." He fished in the bag and retrieved eight more beads. "Please share this payment with the others. I am giving all the rest of this up for Aguilar. But I will see to it that Señor Cortes gives you twice that much for safely returning Aguilar and me."

They went back into the castle. The guards looked at them curiously but didn't slow them down. Chimalatl rejoined his companions and Felipe returned to Aguilar. Aguilar was staring intently at Cortes' letter, still trying to make sense of the Spanish.

"Good sir! Saint Felipe! How kind of you to... No, no, not Saint Felipe, just Felipe, lover of horses. Where did you go? I was beginning to think I had imagined you."

Felipe took the letter from Aguilar's hand and laid it flat on the paving. He opened the small leather bag and poured its contents onto the letter, using one hand to shield it from the view of the others in the courtyard. Aguilar looked at him uncomprehendingly.

"Beads? Copper bells? Needles? Is this the reward you plan to offer Taxmar? These are practically worthless! What on earth are we supposed to do with these? I thought you would have gold *reales*, or silver, or at least some of those new copper coins, marva-something..."

"Sir, the Mayans we have encountered so far don't seem to place much value on gold or silver. Copper, yes, but not as coins. And I understand there is a shortage of the copper maravedis anyway, so our expedition has none. But in my experience the Mayans do seem to highly value these glass beads, since they have no glass but obsidian; and they also seem very pleased with the copper bells. And I know they have no steel needles such as these. Don't you think that Lord Taxmar would be proud to be the owner of the only such items on all of Yucatán?"

"Ah! Yes, I see! Yes, that makes sense." Aguilar picked up one of the copper bells and shook it. It made no sound. He frowned and shook it again, then dropped it and picked up another. "These don't work! What good –"

Felipe took the bell from his hand, reached into it and removed the piece of dried grass that had been wound around the clapper and handed it back. "I didn't want them making noise during my trip here," he said.

"Ah! I see. Certainly, very wise, yes." He shook the bell vigorously again, and this time the tinkling sound rang out across the courtyard. A dozen heads jerked up at the sound. Many of the Mayans started over to discover the source of it. Felipe quickly picked up the paper and used it to funnel the treasure back into the leather bag.

"What is this?" several asked, as Aguilar continued to rattle the bell. "Well," he began in Mayan," this is called a, that is, it is a," He returned to Latin. "Oh dear, I don't know how to say "bell" in Mayan. I've never seen one, so I've never needed to know how to say it. What do I say?"

Felipe told the crowd in Mayan, "It is a gift for my Lord Taxmar. In our country it is called a 'bell.' We attach great importance to them, for signaling, and for music." Several of them had been reaching for it until he said it was for Lord Taxmar. Hands were immediately drawn back.

The bell's sound had an additional effect: Lord Taxmar himself, followed by his entourage, strode back into the courtyard. "What did I hear?" he asked.

Aguilar started to speak, but Felipe said, "Let me," and took the bell from him. "My Lord Taxmar. The king of the Castilanos, His Excellency Holy Roman Emperor Charles the Fifth, king of Spain and Germany, Lord of the West Indies and the Main Ocean Sea, sends you his most humble greetings. He has heard about your valiant exploits and he praises you for rescuing his most valued servant, Aguilar. He has sent me, your humble servant, to reward your gallant efforts with these lowly trinkets. He hopes you will accept these small gifts. He also requests that you accept his hand in friendship, one sovereign to another." Aguilar was looking at Felipe with a new-found respect. Some of the old Spanish titles drifted back into his memory. It had not occurred to him that the poorly dressed child messenger might actually be someone important. Felipe had read the king's full name on one of the recruiting posters Cortes had posted and of course he remembered it. He had purposely skipped over the details about 'king of Sicily, Corsica, Jerusalem, Hapsburg, Holland…'

He handed the bell to Taxmar. It jingled slightly in the transaction. Taxmar looked at it curiously and jingled it again, then more vigorously. He laughed loudly and jingled and jingled the new toy. *"Tetzilakatl!"* he shouted. *"Tetzilakatl!* The ancients had these! I have read about them. I even saw an old one hanging from the belt of my brother, Xpatal, when last we met. Oh, but his does not sing like this one!" He shook his new bell again, and laughed delightedly.

"Ahem, yes, My Lord Taxmar," Aguilar began. "You mentioned the chief Xpatal. We wanted to discuss him with you. You recall that the other Castilano, Guerrero, that you sold, er, traded… that is to say, that you graciously agreed to Xpatal becoming the protector of Señor Guerrero. We would like to send a message to Señor Guerrero advising him that the Castilanos are here to provide us with transport back to our home."

Taxmar frowned. He had been well compensated for the slave Guerrero. If he asked to have him returned, Xpatal would want payment. "Are you planning to give him a tetzilakatl?"

"Well, there are several…" Aguilar started, but Felipe interrupted him. He could see that it was important to Taxmar to be the sole owner of any bells.

"We have some other trinkets, my lord," Felipe said. "None so valuable as the bells, the tetzilakatl. Allow us to give them to you. Then you may decide whether you wish to share something with Xpatal." Aguilar smiled and nodded at Felipe's diplomacy.

"Show me," Taxmar demanded. He turned on his heel and walked to his throne and sat. The entourage followed. Felipe and Aguilar approached the throne. Felipe laid the letter on the footstool and, as he'd done before, poured the contents of the leather bag onto it. The entourage gasped with delight and began excitedly buzzing among themselves at the sight of the glittering pile of beads and bells. Taxmar waved them to silence and leaned forward, poking through the pile with a finger. He picked up another bell, but no sound came from it. Felipe immediately stepped forward and said, "Allow me." He removed the packing. "We encountered a fierce beast on the way here. It seemed prudent to make no sound."

Taxmar nodded as if it was his own sage advice. He separated the rest of the bells from the pile – there were more than a dozen all together. His finger encountered the needles, and he yelped and drew it back. Leaning forward again he carefully picked up the packet of four needles. "What are these?"

"Needles," Aguilar supplied. "They are for…"

"I know a needle when I see one," Taxmar replied impatiently. "But how are they so small? What are they made of?"

Felipe didn't try to explain steelmaking; he simply said that in the country of the Castilanos was a much harder metal than silver or gold. Taxmar, embarrassed by his flinching from the needle-stick to his finger, pinched the flesh on the bridge of his nose and drove a needle through it, leaving it sticking out from both sides just below eye-level. The entourage laughed and clapped. Felipe thought, but didn't say, that Taxmar would probably remove it the first time he tried to drink something from a cup.

"What is your name again, child?"

"Just call me Felipe."

"We will not give tetzilakatl to Xpatal. Nor any needles." He turned to the entourage. "Let us say, half of the round jewels to Xpatal," pointing to the glass beads. "The rest of them we will add to the treasury." Felipe wondered how many of them would actually make it to the treasury and how many would end up in the hands of the entourage. Cortes had made him cynical.

"We shall send all these things to Xpatal as his reward for helping the Castilano." He addressed himself to Aguilar. "Write your message. I will have messengers take it immediately. But," he said, "I cannot insist that he return him. I can only suggest it. He is a chief, he can do as he sees fit."

A boy a year or two older than Felipe stepped forward and casually took one of the beads for himself. No one tried to stop him.

"Ox-Ha-té, you are stealing from the national treasury."

"Sorry, Father," said Ox-Ha-té, who didn't seem sorry at all and did not offer to return the bead he'd taken.

"Ox-Ha-té, this is – what was it? Oh, yes: Felipe. He is the distinguished ambassador of the king of the Castilanos. He has come to collect Aguilar. You should learn about the Castilanos from him while he is here."

***

Ox-Ha-té had no interest in learning about the Castilanos from Felipe and he wandered away. He was older than Felipe and nearly a head taller. He couldn't imagine that the smaller, younger Felipe had anything to teach him.

Aguilar quickly organized some paper-like material and some quills and ink. He explained to Felipe that when the Mayans had learned he could write they'd happily provided the supplies he needed. But when they couldn't read the Latin words they quickly lost interest. The Mayans wrote too, using what looked to Felipe like pictures, in multiple colors. They viewed Aguilar's writing as child-like, primitive.

"Guerrero does not read Latin," Aguilar explained. "Well, honestly, I don't know that he reads Spanish either. But we have to try." Aguilar dictated the letter to Felipe in Latin and Felipe translated it to Spanish and wrote it down:

"Señor Guerrero. Greetings! Glory to God, the Spanish have arrived and we are saved! Come to me without delay at Taxmar's castle, where an emissary is waiting to conduct us back into the arms of our brethren. Your fellow servant in Christ, Jeronimo de Aguilar."

Aguilar then asked one of Lord Taxmar's court people to write the same message in Mayan. Both papers were handed to a pair of messengers.

Felipe wanted to go with the messengers to make sure there was no delay. But he mostly wanted to have something to do to keep himself occupied, rather than simply waiting and worrying whether Guerrero would arrive in time. But Aguilar dismissed the idea.

"You would simply slow them down, do you see? Yes. These men are professional runners. That is all they do. They carry messages to and from Lord Taxmar. They would lose their heads if they delayed. They can travel ten leagues, some of them twelve leagues, in a day."

"How far is a league?"

"Take a few long steps," Aguilar instructed, "as long as you can." Felipe walked quickly in a circle around Aguilar, stretching his stride as far as he could. "Yes, as I thought, small steps. So: a league is five thousand varas, and a vara is longer than one of your steps. Perhaps not quite as long as two of your steps. You see? You would slow them down."

Felipe had to admit that he would, indeed, slow them down.

While they had been writing their letters Taxmar had dictated a third letter to Xpatal using one of his Mayan scribes. He explained that he agreed with the unusual request of his advisor Aguilar; that the king of the Castilanos had indeed sent an emissary to beg for the return of his lost subjects. He glossed over the fact that the 'emissary' looked like a street urchin. He carefully gave Xpatal the proper respect, explaining the gift of strange-colored beads from the king of the Castilanos, and asking the man whether he would consider releasing the Castilano in his employ so that he could be allowed to return to his people.

Taxmar's message was added to those Aguilar and Felipe had already entrusted to the pair of messengers. The three letters went into their hair. The small leather pouch containing a greatly diminished pile of glass beads went into the belt of one of the runners and the young men set off.

Now, all that could be done was to wait.

CHAPTER TWENTY FIVE

The wait was crushing. The words of Cortes' letter, "*northern tip of Yucatán*" and "*until eight days have passed from today,*" kept running feverishly around and around in Felipe's head. Three days had passed. Why had Cortes given him so little time? Why hadn't he, Felipe, realized there could be delays? Why hadn't he asked for more time? If they were not back at Kutzumal in three days or, failing that, at the cape on the north of Yucatán within five days, Felipe would never see his father again.

To take his mind off his worries he decided to see if he could help Aguilar reclaim his lost Spanish. He asked Aguilar to tell him, in Spanish, how he had come to be a slave of the Mayans.

"Oh my, yes, well: I was living in..."

"*En español, por favor.*"

"Oh yes, right." Aguilar continued, in Spanish, as Felipe had asked. "I was living in, I don't know, Darien? Is that right?" Felipe had never heard of it but he nodded to encourage the monk to continue. "Yes, Darien. It is far south of here. It had been a native fishing village until Balboa brought in many Spaniards to find gold. A vile place. Everyone immoral, everyone fighting. I tried to remind them of their obligations to the Church but they seemed to believe that they had left God behind in Spain, do you see?"

Felipe corrected a few places where he had slipped back into Latin then encouraged him to go on.

"After a year I realized I was not welcome and I took passage on a, um, a big boat, ship..."

"A caravel."

"Yes! Yes, a caravel, back to Santo Domingo. There were sixteen of us. No. Plus two women, so eighteen of us. The caravel struck a, something, something underwater, and sank very quickly. I was lucky to survive. Eleven of us, twelve? I don't know. Let us say eleven of us managed to climb into the ship – no the small boat of the ship. Yes. We had no oars, no water, no food. But we could see land. One of the sailors said he thought it was Jamaica. We all paddled with our hands, paddled and paddled. But we couldn't get to it. The river, no, the um, current! Yes, the current took us, swept us away from the land. By the time we ran ashore in Yucatán, only eight of us were left. Some of the natives found us, gave us water and food. But they put us in boxes. No. Cages. Yes. One by one they either ate or sacrificed the others, all except me and Guerrero the soldier. We were too skinny, do you see? They were fattening us up. But we were inventive, Guerrero and I. We chewed on the vines they had used to lash the branches together to make the cage, when they were not looking. Chewed our way out like, oh, how do you call it? Badgers! Yes! Chewed like badgers."

Felipe had no idea what a badger was, but Aguilar seemed very pleased to have remembered the word for the animal.

"Chewed like badgers, yes. In the night, when they all slept, drunk on their *pulque*, we pulled some of the bars loose and made our escape."

"That is an amazing story. How did you end up a slave to Taxmar?"

"Well the four of us…"

"Four?"

"Yes, four. Were we four? Yes. Oh! Yes, we were four, not down to two, not yet. Yes, four of us were not eaten. We were too skinny to eat. The four of us slipped away in the night. But there are many people in Yucatán, many, many people. And we could not stay concealed. Guerrero tried, I think we tried his patience, because he was a soldier, do you see? And we were not. He tried to help us take care, but we kept making mistakes, and finally we were captured again by people who sold us to Taxmar."

"Do you remember what happened to the other two?"

"Who? What other two? Oh! Yes, the other two Spaniards, I see. Yes, the one was, let me think, Gonzales, something like that? Do you know him? No? And the other was a woman, I'm sure I don't remember her name. Anyway, Lord Taxmar does not eat people…"

He had reverted to Mayan again at the mention of Taxmar. *"En Español, por favor."*

"What? Oh, yes. Spanish, indeed. Lord Taxmar does not eat men, does not let his people eat men. He put us to work carrying water. Huge, heavy jars of water. Guerrero did fine with it but the rest of us, we couldn't keep it up. Gonzales and the woman were too sick. They died." He stopped the story and crossed himself. "Guerrero knew we wouldn't last. Lord Taxmar was preparing for war with a tribe to the south, the Xelha. Do you know them?"

"I was told they are not friendly," Felipe said.

"Yes, not friendly at all, indeed. Anyway, by this time I had managed to learn some of the language. I told Chimalatl that Guerrero and I were great warriors, that we knew how to defeat the Xelha. Of course, I had no idea how to defeat them, but I assumed Guerrero would know, being Spanish, and he could tell me what I needed to know, do you see?"

"So you fought the Xelha?"

"Yes! Well, no, not me. I am a man of God. But with my help, Guerrero was able to give Taxmar's warriors directions for winning a battle the Spanish way. We flanked, no. Flanked? Yes? Is that a word? I don't know. Anyway, we maneuvered around in ways the Xelha didn't understand, had never seen, and we defeated them. So Taxmar made us his personal servants. Yes. Guerrero and I. He gave us both wives. Guerrero had babies and began to learn Mayan customs. But I wasn't having it. I was horrified. I told Taxmar about my vow. He laughed. He sent women to my bed every night, for weeks. I sent them all away." He stopped himself, realizing this was not something to discuss with a child.

"Anyway, let us just say he found my vows amusing. When he couldn't break me he admitted me to his inner circle, as an advisor. I think he values my advice, but he always acts as if I am a fool. I tell them stories about horses, and guns, and wheels – can you imagine, they draw circles for their calendars, but they have never built a wheeled cart? And they wouldn't even build one after I described it! One of their artists tried to carve a horse based on my description. But Lord Taxmar laughed when he saw it. Sometimes when he has to travel he leaves me in charge of his wives."

"How did Guerrero end up with Xpatal?"

"Oh! Yes, well, Lord Taxmar owed him a debt. I don't know what. Xpatal sent a message that he needed help fighting an enemy that came in *nah maaxí baab*, so Taxmar sent – Oh!" He stopped.

Felipe prompted. "He sent Guerrero to help him fight? What? What does *nah maaxí baab* mean? Who were they fighting?"

Aguilar lowered his voice almost to a whisper. "Were there Spanish ships off the coast before now? Perhaps… two years ago?"

Felipe realized what he was implying. He knew that Grijalva's expedition had just returned, so it couldn't have been that. But he also knew that there had been an expedition about two years ago led by Cordoba – a mission that had been an utter failure. They had been overwhelmed by the natives. Many of the Spaniards had died and Cordoba had later died of the numerous wounds that had been inflicted on him by the Mayans. "I can't say for certain," Felipe told Aguilar. "I am only a child."

"Well, *nah maaxí baab* means 'house that floats'… I didn't think about it at the time. But I think it must have been a reference to Spanish ships."

Aguilar was devastated that his friend and fellow Spaniard, Guerrero, had possibly helped the Mayans kill Spaniards. Felipe simply said, "Your Spanish is much improved. This has been a long lesson. You must be tired. I will come see you again tomorrow."

***

On day four, with no demands on his time other than Spanish lessons for Aguilar and still trying to distract himself from the thought of being left behind by Cortes, he accepted the offer of Chimalatl's son, Kabil, to show him around for the day.

There was a pot of something brewing over a fire in the back yard. It was light brown and thin, like soup. Actually, it looked like muddy water. But it smelled wonderful! Felipe asked about it.

"It is called xocolatl," Kabil said.

"Shoclatl," Felipe tried out the new word.

"Xocolatl. It comes from those," Kabil pointed to some broken, bright yellow husks on the ground that looked a bit like squash except the flesh was bright white. Felipe picked one up. The smell of the flesh was faint, but it was similar to the wonderful aroma coming from the pot. He sampled some of the raw flesh. It was a bit slimy but it tasted very much like the wonderful smell.

"Don't eat that!" Kabil said.

"Why not?"

Kabil shrugged. "I don't know. I suppose you can. No one does. The pods are just the home for the seeds." He pointed to a row of dark brown, nearly black, seeds on a shelf attached to the wall of the house, each one nearly as big as an avocado pit. "First they have to dry there for a few days. Then we roast them and grind them up. Then we boil the ground-up seeds to make xocolatl."

"It smells good." Felipe was disappointed. He was hungry, and he was hoping there was more in the soup pot than just some ground-up seeds.

Kabil dipped a clay cup into the pot and handed it to Felipe. "Be careful, it is hot," he advised.

Felipe realized it was not soup but a drink. Who ever heard of drinking something hot? He put it to his lips and slurped; and immediately burned his tongue. He grimaced, and Kabil laughed.

"I told you it was hot!"

"You did. I should have waited." He blew across the top of the cup several times and took a smaller sip. "Um, it is very bitter. Is it supposed to be?"

"Baby. Here, let me sweeten it like we do for babies." He took a clay pot down off a shelf and removed the lid. He stuck a pudgy finger in it and withdrew it coated in honey. He dripped honey into Felipe's xocolatl, then licked his finger. "Try it now."

Felipe took another sip and quickly realized why they went to all the trouble with roasting and grinding the seeds. "That tastes wonderful!" he said. "Is there something we can eat?"

"We don't usually eat in the morning. That is for peasants. Xocolatl is for royals and others of the first class. My father is one of Lord Taxmar's most important advisers so we have xocolatl for our first meal of the day. Finish it, and we can go. If you are still hungry we'll get something in the market."

***

They went to a very tall pyramid first, on the north side of the city where Felipe hadn't been yet. Kabil challenged Felipe to a foot race to the top. Felipe did very well, considering that the steps had certainly not been designed for boys to run up. In light of how precise everything else was, Felipe was surprised to find that each of the steps was a slightly different height and just slightly slanted. He quickly found that the apparent irregularity of them actually had a pattern, and after that he was able to keep up with Kabil. In fact, he had to slow down so as not to embarrass his host.

The closer they got to the top, the more the steps were covered in a tar-black stain. At the top was an idol and an altar. The altar was completely black, stained with what was undeniably blood from sacrificial victims. Felipe shook his head, and Kabil noticed.

"What?"

"Why do you..." Felipe paused to try to choose more tactful words. Cortes had reminded him that his job was to make peace not stir up trouble. "So much blood," he said instead. "Does it bother you?"

Kabil shrugged. "The gods require it. If we want their blessing we must appease them."

"But what about the lives?"

"Whose lives?"

"All the victims!" Felipe realized he was not cut out to be a peacemaker.

"What about them?" Kabil seemed genuinely puzzled at this line of questioning. "They are slaves. The gods decide who lives and who dies. If a person is a slave, the best use his life can have is to pour his blood out to a god."

The conversation wasn't going anywhere. Felipe turned away and took in the view. From here, atop a pyramid, it was easy to see the other pyramids, laid out in a pattern of four rows of three. He could also see that the surrounding country was, just as he had originally concluded, remarkably flat. To the south he could see a smudge in the sky where fields were being burned. To the northwest, barely discernable, was another group of pyramids. He hoped that was where Guerrero was located, so that he or at least the runners would soon be on their way back.

He looked over the city. The order was amazing. The streets were all straight. The buildings formed straight lines. The precision of the pyramids was astounding. Here was evidence that these people were disciplined, organized in a way that his Taino people, or even the Spanish people on Cuba, were not.

Was this what was meant by civilization? He had always heard Indians described with terms such as savage and pagan. In the eyes of most Spaniards, Indians were lowly and uneducated. He'd seen how Spaniards often looked right through him, as if he wasn't truly a person. They no doubt felt the same way about Mayans. In the Spanish mind, did civilization mean Christianity? Or did it mean European? If Christianity was a necessary component of civilization, then of course the Mayans were not civilized. Cortes' mission was to conquer lands for the king of Spain, to conquer the uncivilized masses. Felipe had heard some of Cortes' men referring to themselves as "conquistadors." What was the justification for doing that? According to the declaration the priest Diaz had read to the uncomprehending people, the pope had decreed the conquest to spread Christianity. But his father had told Felipe that Jesus' command to make disciples didn't mean "make" them, by force.

On the other hand, did these amazing buildings make them civilized? Didn't all the killing, all the bloodthirsty gods, didn't that prove they were uncivilized and deserving of whatever Cortes brought? The pope, and hence Cortes, believed that these Mayans could be enslaved for refusing to get baptized into the Church, that they weren't entitled to freedom because, after all, they weren't civilized. And civilization stemmed from Christianity.

It was confusing.

His questions had gotten Kabil thinking, too. It was Kabil's turn for questions. "Why are you bothered by the blood? Do your people not bleed?"

"Of course my people bleed. All people bleed. That is my point: people are people even if they are slaves."

"No, no," Kabil replied. "People are people. Slaves are slaves."

"Why are they slaves? How did they become slaves?"

"The gods decreed it. Some were born as slaves. Others were captured in battle."

"What about you? What if the gods decreed that you be a slave? What if you were born a slave?"

Kabil scoffed. "I'm of the first class!"

"What if you were taken captive in a battle?"

"If the gods allow that to happen, then I will be a slave. But they will not allow that to happen. I am nobility."

"So nobility never get captured?"

That stopped Kabil for a moment. "Sometimes, it is true. But not if you are well-trained. Not if the gods are with you."

"And if you are not as well trained," Felipe said, poking Kabil's round belly, "if you don't work hard to learn to fight, if you drink too much xocolatl, if the 'gods' are not with you, then some priest on the other side of the battle could someday lead you to the top of a pyramid like this one and cut your heart out to please his god."

Kabil was clearly uncomfortable with that thought. "So, do the Castilanos not have battles?"

Now it was Felipe's turn to squirm. "They do, yes. And they kill people in battle, and they capture people in battle. And yes, those people are slaves. But they do not kill slaves to please God. In fact, God would be displeased with them if they killed slaves. Instead, slaves are put to work in fields. They are given food and places to sleep."

Kabil just shook his head. "And one day those slaves will rise up and slaughter their masters! No. It is best to sacrifice those taken in battle. But we do it in a way that pleases the gods. And the slaves don't mind. They are honored to be used in that way. Being sacrificed to the gods means that they go on to a higher order in the afterlife. But if they were killed in battle, they would simply go to the underworld, and no one wants to go there."

"I don't think we will ever agree. I'm still hungry. Can we go get something to eat?"

***

After some tamales in the market, which Kabil paid for with an obsidian chip, he asked Felipe, "Do you have *Pitz* where you come from?"

"I don't know what that is."

"Pitz. The ball game."

"I'm sorry, I don't know what a ball game is."

Kabil looked around and spotted a young boy in front of a house, bouncing a ball. "A ball. Round, covered in *chicle*, like that," he pointed. "For games."

Felipe watched as the young boy, who couldn't have been more than five or six, threw a round object that looked like a cannon ball against a stone wall and caught it when it bounced back to him. Felipe laughed, delighted. "How does he do that?"

"He isn't doing it. The ball is." Kabil walked over to the child and caught the ball as it rebounded. The young boy wasn't happy about giving up his ball, and started crying. Kabil just shushed him and tossed the ball to Felipe. Felipe caught it. He'd never felt anything like it. It was perfectly round like a cannon ball but it was light. The only thing Felipe could compare it to was a gourd; when he squeezed it, it gave slightly and then bounced back. He wondered if that was why it returned to the young boy who was throwing it at the wall. He threw it at the wall himself and the ball came right back at him, and he caught it again. He tossed it back to the child, who caught it easily and instantly stopped crying. "Thank you for sharing your ball with me. I have never seen one before."

"When I grow up I'm going to be a great Pitz player, like *Muluc*," the little boy replied.

As they walked away Felipe asked Kabil, "Who is Muluc?"

131

"He is a great Pitz player. Perhaps one of the best ever. Follow me." He led Felipe to the western part of the city, in the shadow of the largest pyramid. They rounded a corner and went through an opening only a bit wider than a door and suddenly they were standing in a wide, grass-covered alley with blank, smooth stone walls on both sides, going straight up. There were Mayan words Felipe couldn't read carved into the stone walls. Kabil pointed at one of the inscriptions and said, "That's Muluc."

Studying the carvings, Felipe saw Muluc's symbol in several places. The walls stretched upward. They were taller than he could have reached even if he'd been standing on his father's shoulders. At the top of the vertical portion the walls angled sharply outward in a series of steps. Midway down the length of the alley, on both sides, just below the top of the vertical part of the wall, two large stone rings with intricate carvings on them jutted out over the alley. Felipe judged the inside of each of the rings to be slightly larger than his head. The slanted wall above the rings had no steps. It was smooth and steep.

"This is the Pitz court," Kabil explained. "It is one hundred *b'i-xi* long."

"I'm sorry, I don't know the word *b'i-xi.*"

Kabil took an exaggerated step. "As far as a tall man can step," he explained.

"Ah! The Spanish say *vara.*"

Kabil continued. "So the court is one hundred *varas* long and twenty varas wide. The goals are four varas above the court." He picked up two small rocks and tossed one of them through the center of the circular rock goal. Then he tossed the other one to Felipe. As Felipe started to throw it, Kabil interrupted him. "Wait: There is only one rule in Pitz. You can't use your hands."

"How am I supposed to…" he stopped and thought for a moment. "Only my hands are forbidden? I can use anything else?"

"Right. Just not your hands."

Felipe dropped the rock and kicked it just before it hit the ground. It sailed in a high, curved arc and struck the inside of the rock circle, bouncing out the other side. "Easy," he said.

"Yes, easy." Kabil was impressed, but he didn't want this foreigner to know it. "Easy for now – with no one trying to stop you, no one trying to take the ball away from you."

"If the other player is my size, I think I could get past him pretty easily. And if he can't use his hands either, he can't take the ball away from me."

"There are usually several players on each team."

"Oh, I see," Felipe thought about that. "Yes, that would make it harder."

Kabil continued his description. "You can use your foot, your knee, hip, elbow, shoulder, even your head."

Felipe laughed at the idea of trying to knock a ball through the hoop with his head. "I'd have a very sore head!"

"Well, remember it is a ball, not a rock. Most of the balls are hollow. I heard they used to be made from the skull of a slave. Now they are made by sewing two baskets together and coating them with *chicle*."

"We don't have chicle where I come from," Felipe admitted.

"It is sap from a tree. It is very sticky, but when it dries, it is springy, and once you bounce it a few times, it picks up some dust and it isn't sticky anymore. But," Kabil explained," Pitz balls can be very heavy. Some use a very small basket with a very thick coating of chicle. Some are even solid chicle. That is why the players wear head pads. And elbow pads and knee pads."

"How many players on each team? And how do they decide whose turn it is?"

"Teams can start with as many players as they like, as long as there are equal numbers of players on both sides. But if a player is hurt or killed, the team must go on without him. And they do not take turns. It is a battle. If the other team has the ball, your team does whatever it has to do to take it from them; you try to keep them too far away from the goal to take a shot, and you try to block them if they do get close enough to take a shot."

"I suppose one goal is for one team, and the other is for the other team?"

"No. Well, sometimes teams may decide that at the beginning. But most games a goal is a goal, through either hoop."

"How many times must you get the ball through the hole to win?"

"Twice."

"Just twice?"

"It is a very hard game," Kabil answered defensively. "Sometimes, no one has scored when the sun goes down. When that happens, the game starts again the next day, and goes until one team scores twice."

"Are there prizes? Do they get gold or obsidian, or something?"

Kabil casually said, "The captain of the winning team usually wins the head of the captain of the losing team. The rest of the players on the losing team become the slaves of the winning team. Muluc has twenty-one skulls, and nearly two hundred slaves."

CHAPTER TWENTY SIX

They passed through the ball court and came out on the opposite end. It opened into the plaza of the sacred cenote. The cenotes Felipe had visited in the jungle had not prepared him for this. Those watering holes all had irregular, steep sides with a trail or a ladder down one side and lush vegetation surrounding them. In some cases the cenotes had had vertical sides most of the way around, but then had a steep overgrown slope going down to the water in one place. In the cenotes that didn't have any sloped sides previous visitors had carved steps into the stone for access.

By contrast, this cenote was square, with vertical rock walls on all sides. Much labor had gone into making it a special place. The light gray paving stones of the large plaza stretched out from the cenote's east, north and south sides. There was a protective railing of carved black stone surrounding it on those three sides. The top of the railing was rounded and smooth. It was supported by intricately carved black basalt pillars set about a handbreadth apart.

The west side of the cenote had no railing. The steps of a pyramid began at the edge of the cenote and rose steeply to an altar at the top. A person on these east steps of the pyramid would have to be careful not to lose their balance or they would tumble right into the water. The builders' plan was obvious: Anything that was dropped or poured out on the altar at the top of the pyramid would run down the steps unimpeded and land in the cenote.

The plaza had some vendors and some artisans but not the crush of the market. Children played. A small child approached the cenote and threw something into it. But when he took a step closer to the open side his mother quickly scooped him up and moved him to a safer distance. Kabil led Felipe up to the railing and they both leaned over and looked down. The hand rail was in the middle of his chest. The water, about ten varas down, was green, not the cold turquoise-blue of the other cenotes he had seen. The cenote could have held the whole house he had slept in the night before. The irregular vertical sides of the water hole had no ladders, no steps. A few bushes had found footholds in cracks in the upper half of the northern face where the sun reached for part of the day.

The people of Yaxunah did not take water out of this cenote. They only threw things into it. Kabil tossed in a piece of obsidian and mumbled something from memory. A chilly breeze rose to Felipe's face, bringing with it a stagnant smell.

"BA'AX KA WA'ALIK!" he called, and the echo rang hollowly back to him from the hole and rolled over the crowd in the plaza. No one was surprised. Children always delighted in shouting Hello to the god of the cenote. Kabil just shook his head.

"Baby," he mumbled.

Felipe spent another moment taking it all in. Then they pushed on to inspect the rest of the plaza. Felipe could see why Chimalatl had warned him not to try jumping into the sacred cenote. There really was no way out.

***

Around the corner of the pyramid from the cenote, about midway along the pyramid's northern side, was a single Pitz hoop. Smaller than the ones at the official Pitz court, it jutted out at an awkward angle from the pyramid, about twelve steps up from the plaza. The hoop was carved from some heavy tropical wood rather than stone and attached to a portable wooden base. Felipe guessed it was removed when religious ceremonies happened but otherwise remained semi-attached to the steps, held in place only by its own weight. A large scrum of teen-age boys was in the plaza beneath it, fighting over a ball. One of them connected with a kick and the ball soared up the steps. It landed wide of the hoop and began bouncing back down the steps. No one chased it. The steps beneath the hoop were off limits. The players had to wait for the ball to drop back to the pavement. On its last bounce before landing, one of the boys dove forward, careful not to touch the steps, and used his head to send the ball straight up. When it came back down again a tall boy Felipe recognized grabbed the ball with his hands and stood still. Some of the other players began to object, but then the game stopped as the other boys deferred to the larger boy: Taxmar's son, Ox-Ha-té.

"Look who it is," he sneered. "The mama's boy and the king of the Castilanos." He bowed deeply, mockingly to Felipe.

"I am not a mama's boy!" Kabil objected. "And Felipe didn't claim to be a king. He is an emissary from the great king of the Castilanos. I am showing him around. He had never seen a ball before today."

"He is a liar," Ox-Ha-té sneered. "If this ragged boy is the best emissary the king of the Castilanos can find, he cannot be much of a king."

Felipe recited in Hebrew, "As Solomon said, 'Better is a poor but wise child than a rich but stupid king.'"

"What did you say to me?"

"I was simply offering my credentials. I was not given this assignment because of my looks. I was chosen because I can speak your language, as well as Aguilar's. If my appearance offends you, I apologize. But it would be as big a mistake to decide anything about the Castilanos based on your opinion of me as it is to form an opinion of me based on my clothing."

135

"It is not just my opinion. It is also my father's. He wanted you to believe he was taken in by your trinkets. He is not stupid. And neither am I!" As Ox-Ha-té said this, he dropped the ball and kicked it straight at Felipe's face.

Felipe instinctively raised a hand to deflect it. At the last possible instant, he remembered not to touch it with his hand. In a flash he dropped his hand and raised his shoulder, turning his face away. The ball slammed into his shoulder and glanced upward, striking his ear before flying off at an angle. His ear stung and his shoulder throbbed but he had obeyed the rule, even as Ox-Ha-té started a new game.

"My team!" Ox-Ha-té called. "Amun, Tohal and Xuman." Two tall boys and a smaller one joined him. "You two," he pointed at two others. "You and the mama's boy will join the Castilano king. He can be the captain," Ox-Ha-té added with a smirk. Somehow he'd gotten control of the ball again and stood with one foot resting on it. The other boys sat down on the steps to watch the game. The two boys Ox-Ha-té had designated to 'help' the opposing team didn't seem too enthusiastic.

"Wait!" Kabil called. "We did not agree to that!"

"We can do this," Felipe said. He sprinted straight at Ox-Ha-té, hoping to knock the ball loose from his foot.

"Oh, one more thing," Ox-Ha-té said, almost as an afterthought. "The losing captain will tempt Chaac." Then he drew back his foot and fired the ball toward a teammate who was closer to the hoop.

Felipe did not know what 'tempting Chaac' meant, but it clearly terrified Kabil. Felipe put it out of his mind. There was no more time for discussion. He dove in front of the ball just as it began to soar upward, deflecting it to one of the boys assigned to his team. The ball bounced off the boy, who did nothing to control it, and Amun, one of the tall boys on Ox-Ha-té's team, flipped it up with his foot and caught and balanced it on his head. Felipe had never imagined anyone having such a skill. Amun bounced it up a few times, dropped it to his foot and kicked it back up to his head, dropped it to a shoulder and back to his head again. Felipe got so absorbed in the delightful show he almost forgot he was supposed to get the ball away from the boy. Just as he charged forward, Amun headed the ball over to the shorter of his teammates, who stopped it with his chest then began bouncing it off one knee and then the other. When Felipe ran towards him, he bounced it back to Amun.

Through it all, Kabil stood, flat-footed, looking from one boy to the other but not moving toward either of them. "Kabil!" Felipe called. "Stay with him!" he pointed toward the boy Amun was playing catch with. Felipe's plan was for each of them to stick with one of the players instead of trying to run after the ball.

The plan had no chance. Kabil knew it from experience. Just as Felipe and Kabil got close enough to cover both boys, Amun flicked it to Ox-Ha-té.

Fortunately, the two boys who had been assigned to Kabil's team decided it would be more fun to play than to simply stand around. When Ox-Ha-té fired the ball toward the hoop, one of the smaller boys stepped in front of it. It bounced off his chest and fell to the ground. Before he could get control of it, however, Ox-Ha-té plowed into the smaller boy and sent him sprawling. Ox-Ha-té stood for a moment with his foot on the ball, defying any of the other boys to try to take control of the ball from him. He drew back his foot to kick the ball but then paused, almost as an afterthought.

"This is One," he said, and fired the ball perfectly toward the hoop. He was right. The ball sailed through the hoop, striking the steps on the far side. It bounced up once, then began dribbling lightly down the steps.

Kabil surprised everyone. Fatalistically perhaps, he had decided Ox-Ha-té's shot would succeed and he had placed himself perfectly to catch the rebound. When the ball bounced back to the pavement, Kabil was right there to stop it. With no one near him, he was able to take his time aiming, and he sailed the ball back up to the hoop. It struck the back edge of the hoop, twirled around the edge, and dropped from the other side.

"Yes!" Kabil whooped, raising both arms and dancing in a circle. "Now we are even!"

Ox-Ha-té had been running toward him and, even though the ball was long gone, he didn't even slow down. He powered into Kabil's back, slamming him to the ground. Kabil's face bounced off the pavement and he lay there, bleeding and crying. Ox-Ha-té stalked away without a backward glance. "Mama's boy," he called.

From instinct, Felipe ran toward Kabil, intending to help him up. But another instinct quickly kicked in. He knew that if he focused on Kabil, the other team would score an easy victory. Even though he didn't know what 'tempting Chaac' meant, he knew he didn't want to do it. So instead, he kept his gaze intently on Kabil and continued running toward him but in his mind he was seeing what Ox-Ha-té and his teammates would do. Just as he drew even with Ox-Ha-té he quickly darted to his left. He knew as if he could read the boy's thoughts that Ox-Ha-té planned to slam a fist into him as he ran past, and he was right. The fist sailed through empty air. Ox-Ha-té was thrown off balance. Temporarily out of Ox-Ha-té's vision, Felipe dropped to the pavement and wrapped his legs around the larger boy's ankle. Ox-Ha-té's body continued to rotate. His arms flew up and waved wildly, trying to recover his balance. Then, reminding Felipe of that time his father had chopped down a mahogany tree, Ox-Ha-té tipped straight forward. Unable to get his hands in front of him in time to arrest his fall he did the same damage to his own face that he'd just inflicted on Kabil.

Unlike Kabil, Ox-Ha-té jumped quickly to his feet and looked around for Felipe. But Felipe had already scrambled out of reach. He knew Ox-Ha-té was now feeling murderous. He would have to stay out of the older boy's way for the rest of the game.

Amazingly, Amun and the rest of Ox-Ha-té's team were stunned. They had never seen anyone take down their captain. While they had been watching the fighting between Kabil and Ox-Ha-té and Felipe, the smallest boy on Felipe's team had gotten control of the ball. He seemed relieved when he saw that Felipe was available and quickly kicked the ball over. It was coming too high. With an eye on Ox-Ha-té and the other on the ball, Felipe bent forward and allowed the ball to strike the top of his head, sending it straight up. As it began to descend again Felipe could see that Ox-Ha-té would arrive before the ball would reach his feet. He knew that, having never practiced the move, he had no chance to put the ball through the hoop with his head. He only trusted his aim with a kick. So he didn't wait for the ball to reach ground level. He flipped backward. Before his shoulders hit the ground he'd brought his legs up above his head, his right foot connected with the ball and he sent it cleanly through the hoop.

He quickly regained his feet before Ox-Ha-té could attack him. He needn't have worried. Ox-Ha-té stood frozen, the color draining from his face.

Kabil came puffing up, wiping his bloody nose on his arm, and pounded Felipe on the back. "We did it!" he said. He turned to Ox-Ha-té. "I believe you said the losing captain would walk the rail?"

CHAPTER TWENTY SEVEN

Felipe could tell Ox-Ha-té desperately wanted a way out. He could almost see him weighing his options. He could bluster about being the chief's son and claim he was exempt. But the other boys would make up an insulting name for him as he had done for Kabil. He could simply run away. But none of the boys would ever be seen with him again if he did that.

Felipe found out what "tempting Chaac" meant. Apparently the boys spoke of walking the black protective rail around the cenote as 'tempting Chaac.' They had often spoken of it. Some of the older ones had occasionally climbed up on the railing and balanced there, even taking a few steps. Legend had it that it had been done, but none of the current crop of boys had ever done it; it was always a cousin that none of them knew; or someone from their older brothers' generation; someone known only by reputation but never met. This mysterious 'someone else' had supposedly walked the rail successfully, tempting the god of the cenote, Chaac. The legend claimed that tempting Chaac, walking the rail, properly, meant climbing up from the pyramid end onto the protective hand rail that surrounded three sides of the cenote; then walking on the top of the smooth, rounded stone railing the length of one side, directly away from the pyramid; rounding the first corner and walking the length of the rail protecting the east side of the cenote; then around the final corner and walking back to the pyramid steps before jumping back to the ground. The myth stated that if you slipped off and fell to the paving, you had to go back to the beginning and start over.

And, of course, if you fell off the other way you landed in the cenote. And there was no way out of it. You were sacrificed to Chaac.

"I was only joking," Ox-Ha-té said.

"No you weren't," Kabil replied. "You made Xo-tli walk it last year."

"Yes, and you told your mama," Ox-Ha-té sneered. "And she came and grabbed Xo-tli off the rail."

"She caught him when he slipped. If she hadn't he would be dead now." Kabil turned to Felipe and explained, "After that, our parents told us we must never walk the rail."

"Exactly. My father will be angry if I do this," Ox-Ha-té said.

"So, daddy's boy, are you going to go back on your agreement?" Kabil taunted.

Ox-Ha-té glared at him. "I can do it with my eyes closed."

Felipe tried to talk him out of it. "Don't risk your life. I understand you were only joking."

"No, he wasn't," Kabil jumped in. "Do you really think he would have said he was joking if we had lost, as he thought we would? No; he would insist that you, the captain, walk the rail." Ox-Ha-té said nothing. He was standing on the first step of the pyramid. In front of him, just one long step up, was the beginning of the southern protective rail. He stared at it intently, as if it were an enemy he was commanding to surrender. His forehead was coated in small beads of sweat that Felipe knew had nothing to do with the sun.

"Don't do it," Felipe said again, just as Ox-Ha-té blew out a breath and stepped up on the railing. His arms flailed for a moment then stilled. He grinned, lifted his chin, and stepped forward. He walked to the corner slowly, casually, as easily as if he were walking across the plaza. One by one, as people saw what was happening, the plaza grew silent and everyone began to gather quietly near the railing. Felipe was surprised by the silence – he would have expected adults to yell at the boy to come down. But no one wanted to be the cause of Ox-Ha-té losing his concentration and his footing.

At the corner, the railing butted into a square corner post. Its top flared to a platform half a handbreadth above the rail. Ox-Ha-té easily stepped up to it, one foot then the other, and turned to his right. He seemed to become conscious of the crowd for the first time. He gave them a wave and a grin. "I am Ox-Ha-té, son of Taxmar," he told them. "Chaac will not dare take me!" And he put his right foot down onto the long eastern handrail.

Before he even completed stepping down with his left foot, his right foot slipped to the outside and his body tumbled into the cenote.

Felipe was stunned. Between one breath and the next, Ox-Ha-té vanished. He expected screams and cries from the crowd, but there were none. Quiet gasps of shock were all the sounds they emitted, then they all fell prostrate, bowing toward the cenote.

"We can save him!" Felipe yelled. No one even looked at him. Kabil touched his shoulder.

"It is the will of the gods," Kabil said.

"No, it isn't. It was one foolish boy. And he shouldn't die for that." Felipe checked that his bat-wing bag was tightly sealed. Then he dove over the railing into the murky water.

***

He was surprised at how warm it was. The air trapped in the bat-wing bag brought him quickly to the surface. He could see Ox-Ha-té floundering just a body-length away, striking at the water as if it were an opposing ball player. The boy clearly didn't know how to swim.

140

"Ox-Ha-té," he called, and was ignored. "Ox-Ha-té!" he said, louder. Ox-Ha-té turned his head wildly, trying to figure out who was calling him. He spotted Felipe.

"Help! Help me!"

"I will. Just calm down," Felipe said. "Look. Watch." He demonstrated how he was moving his hands back and forth to keep his head above water. "Move like this."

Ox-Ha-té's movements became a little more orderly, and he managed to keep his head above the smelly water for a longer period of time. Then his nose slipped back under and he surged back to the surface, wild-eyed, flailing in all directions at once. Felipe reminded him again to control his hands and slowly the older boy calmed.

Felipe swam to the side of the cenote. As he'd been warned, the walls were shear and vertical. But he remembered that there were some bushes growing from the rock face on the north side. He looked up to get his bearings. He was closest to the southeast corner of the cenote. He began swimming toward the north side.

"Wait! Don't leave me!" Ox-Ha-té called.

"I'm not. I'm getting us out of here." He demonstrated again how to swim. "Do this. Move your arms like this, kick your feet and swim toward me."

Ox-Ha-té had no skill at swimming but he continued to thrash and gradually moved toward Felipe. As he did so, Felipe back-stroked away. "Wait! Come back!" Ox-Ha-té yelled.

"I'm not going anywhere. Just keep calm, keep breathing, keep moving toward me. You'll be fine. We'll get out of this," Felipe said, though he had no idea how. He kept moving away because he knew, instinctively, that if Ox-Ha-té reached him he'd grab him. And Felipe knew that if he did that they would both drown.

By the time they reached the northwest corner of the rock pit Ox-Ha-té was exhausted. His nose dipped below the surface again. He came up coughing and sputtering, thrashing the surface wildly. Felipe talked calmly to him, again, explaining once again how to move his arms and legs to keep himself afloat. He also wriggled out of the belt of the bat-wing bag and pushed it toward Ox-Ha-té. Ox-Ha-té grabbed it. He tried to put all his weight on it and promptly sank out of sight. When he resurfaced again, shaking his head and spluttering, Felipe instructed, "It won't hold you up. It will only make swimming a bit easier. Just pull the belt over your head and put the bag under your chin. And stop fighting the water: just float."

Felipe quickly scanned the rock face and finally saw what he was hoping for. A little more than an arm's length above the water, the smooth rock surface was cracked. He pulled his father's Toledo steel knife from the

141

sheath strapped to his back. Extending his arm as high as he could reach, the crack in the rock was still a few handbreadths too far.

He allowed himself to relax and sink into the water. As he began to rise again he kicked strongly, lifting his head, shoulders and arms out of the water and drove the knife at the crack. It didn't penetrate. The knife scraped uselessly on the rock and nearly tore from his grasp as he slid back down into the water.

Felipe forced himself to relax. He floated on his back, scanning and re-scanning the rocky trap. But his first instinct had been right. If they were going to get out, this was their only chance. He looked up and memorized the crack in the rock face. He blew out all the air in his lungs and allowed himself to sink below the surface of the water. Then with both hands and both legs he drove himself upward through the water, kicking his body as high out of the water as he could, and again drove the knife at the rock. Half the blade penetrated the crack and lodged there firmly. Felipe held on. From the knees up his whole body was out of the filthy water.

He turned to beckon Ox-Ha-té, but he needn't have bothered. Ox-Ha-té saw him half out of the water and scrambled up the smaller boy's body as if it were a ladder. He stepped on Felipe's fingers wrapped around the handle of the knife, but still Felipe held on. Ox-Ha-té stretched upward for the nearest bush, but it was beyond his reach. In frustration he yelled at Chaac, "I am Ox-Ha-té, son of Taxmar! I refuse to die in this despicable place. Let me go!"

Felipe could see he was getting ready to jump upward toward the bush that was just out of reach and he stopped him. "If you miss, you will fall back into the water. And I won't be able to pull you out again. My arm is too tired."

Ox-Ha-té stood still and looked down at Felipe. "Sorry. What do you suggest?"

"Take the bag from around your neck. The belt is very strong. See if you can snag the bush with the belt."

Ox-Ha-té quickly took the bat-wing bag and its belt off his neck. He swung the bag upward and caught the fist-sized trunk of the bush on the first try. He started to pull himself up.

"Wait," Felipe said. Ox-Ha-té wasn't going to wait for long, but he paused just long enough for Felipe to wrap his left hand around Ox-Ha-té's ankle. With his right hand Felipe pulled upward on the knife. It took a couple of tries but finally the knife gave up its hold on the crack in the rock. Felipe returned it to its sheath to free up both hands. He then climbed up over Ox-Ha-té, treating him as a ladder as the older boy had done to him. When he had a foot on the bush he found that another bush was within reach of his hand. He grabbed it and turned and extended his free hand down to Ox-Ha-té. He pulled Ox-Ha-té up until the older boy was firmly grasping a couple bushes of his own.

Between cracks in the rocks and strong bushes they managed to get within a couple varas of the top. But then they were stuck. The rock was smooth; no cracks, no bushes. They looked back and forth trying to find some way forward but every hand grip seemed to be below them, or too far out of reach to the right or left. Felipe wanted to cry with frustration.

"Perhaps if we go down a bit and work our way to the left," he said, though he knew there was no better path over there. Then a rope hit him in the face.

***

"Tell me: Is your silver knife a gift from your gods? I've never seen one like it." The group of boys strolled slowly, walking back toward the castle. Everyone stood aside and stared as they passed.

"It is not a gift from God," Felipe answered Ox-Ha-té. "It is just a knife, made of a very strong metal. It was a gift from my father and it is very important to me. I hope you can forget you saw it. But remember it if you think about fighting the Castilanos. They have many such knives. And many other weapons you have never seen. You will not win such a battle. I do not wish to lose your friendship."

"That sounds like a prophecy. Do you know the story of Hunac Ceel?"

"About him supposedly becoming a prophet when he survived the cenote? Yes."

"Just between you and me: I don't feel like a prophet. Do you?"

Before Felipe could respond, a pregnant woman came running up and stopped in the street in front of the boys, dropping to her knees and bowing.

"Please! Prophesy… am I going to have a girl or a boy?"

"We are not-" Felipe began, but Ox-Ha-té stopped him.

"It will be the one you are hoping for," he said. The woman jumped up and hugged him.

"Thank you, prophet! Thank you!" She ran off, telling her friends, "A girl! I'm going to have a girl!"

Felipe looked at Ox-Ha-té, puzzled. "I thought you said you don't feel like a prophet. Have you changed your mind?"

"It seemed like the decent thing to say. If she has a girl she will tell all her neighbors that I am a true prophet."

"What if she has a boy?"

"If she has a boy, she will be so delighted she will decide that was what she wanted all along."

"Is it important?" Felipe asked. Ox-Ha-té gave him the look that let him know he'd missed something, then patiently explained. "Girls are never sacrificed. Only boys and men."

143

Felipe just shook his head. "Promise me, when you are king, you will change these practices. Killing all these people does not honor God."

"I will carefully consider it. But I won't be king. I am the second son. I can promise your safety, certainly. It would be very bad luck to harm someone who saved my life."

Felipe stopped. "Has there been a threat to my life?"

Ox-Ha-té hesitated before replying. "My father smiles and nods, but he doesn't listen. He believes you are bad luck," he said. "This is now the third time the Castilanos have come. He is worried. Father believes he must find a way to show your god the power of our gods. I fear he plans to do that by humiliating you. Or worse." Ox-Ha-té glanced at Felipe to see how he was taking this information but Felipe didn't react. "Father is wrong," Ox-Ha-té continued. "You saved my life. Your god *is* stronger."

Kabil and the other boys tagged along behind as Ox-Ha-té and Felipe talked. But it was clear to all that the group had a new order. Felipe was the new leader; Ox-Ha-té, the former bully, now trying to gain his approval. And the rest of them were somewhere below that status.

Kabil had watched dumbstruck as Felipe dove into the water. No one ever went into the sacred cenote voluntarily. While the rest of the people knelt with their foreheads to the ground, praying to Chaac, Kabil stepped over to the rail and watched Felipe calm Ox-Ha-té and then watched the two of them move through the water to the far side of the cenote. When Felipe appeared to rise magically from the water with Ox-Ha-té right behind him, Kabil knew Chaac was not accepting the sacrifice of the two boys, that there would be no penalty for helping them. In fact, they might now be prophets! It would be wrong *not* to help them. That was when he'd run quickly to a market stall and grabbed a rope, pulling down the stall in the process. When the stall owner yelled threats, Amun and a couple other boys had held him back while Kabil and the rest of the ball players ran quickly back to the railing. They tied the rope on to a spot above where Felipe and Ox-Ha-té were struggling to climb and tossed it down.

When Felipe and Ox-Ha-té climbed over the railing, dripping and exhausted, the people who had been imploring Chaac to accept their sacrifice began bowing instead to the boys and imploring them to tell the future.

Felipe was reminded of a quote from Paul and quickly translated it into Mayan: "Do not do that! We are humans, having the same infirmities as you." He showed them his thigh, where a rock had gouged it and left a trail of blood. Then he opened his right hand, which was still bleeding from hanging onto the knife supporting both his and Ox-Ha-té's weight. "There is no god in that cenote. There is only very dirty water."

144

CHAPTER TWENTY EIGHT

Experience had taught Cortes the truth of Jerome's words: *fac et aliquid operis, ut semper te diabolus inveniat occupatum.* For those who are idle, the devil finds work. He was determined the devil would find no idle hands among his crew.

Guns were brought ashore and exercised, cleaned and exercised again. The noise of the guns stunned the natives and chased away the swallows Cortes had discovered were the actual *kutzus* for which the island was named, not the local tribe. Not that it mattered. He had renamed the island Santa Cruz after the holy cross he had had the carpenter build to replace the pagan crosses that littered the island.

He had set crews to work scrubbing the stones around the altar in the plaza and the pyramid at the top of the hill, trying to remove the stains. When that failed, he had the men whitewash the blood-soaked stones.

There was a large supply of whitewash. The locals mixed quicklime and chalk to paint their houses. But they also used lime without the chalk to make a type of flat corn cake Cortes had never tasted but instantly loved. His men, too, were far more enthusiastic about them than the cassava bread they'd brought. In Cuba, corn was only ever eaten fresh. Dried corn was considered inedible, only good for horses. But the Mayans soaked the dried corn in the watered down whitewash, ground it into a paste and cooked thin, flat cakes of it on a griddle. His men had dubbed the little cakes *tortillas*. Cortes requested several barrels of the tortillas for each ship and paid for them with a handful of glass beads and needles.

Every man was also required to spend an hour a day practicing with the crossbows. There weren't as many crossbows as there were men, so they took turns. The crossbows fired short arrows called bolts – a wooden shaft not much longer than from the tip of a man's thumb to the tip of his outstretched little finger, but fatter than an arrow – with a heavy iron head on one end and three small feathers on the other. A log wall had been constructed behind the thatch targets to stop errant bolts. After each session the bolts were carefully retrieved and counted. When the number came up short – which it invariably did – the ground beyond the log wall was scoured for the missing bolts, usually with little success.

Naturally, a young Mayan boy finally found one of the missing bolts the Castilanos had failed to collect. He gave it to his father, who instantly became the richest person on the island. Enormous amounts of goods were offered for the small arrow, to no avail. Its new owner sliced off the feathers and honed one side of the iron arrowhead on a rock until it was razor sharp. He added a hand grip and wore the device in a crocodile leather scabbard on his belt, like a knife.

Melchior the translator overheard the conversations about the new knife and the offers that were made for it, and he realized he was sitting on a fortune. He knew where to find hundreds of crossbow bolts.

***

All the idols and temples on the island had been torn down except for one. The main temple on the west end of the village plaza had been turned into a center of operations. It was a large, stone single-story building with a flat timber roof. It had two wide doorways, facing east and west, and two smaller doorways on the north and south ends. Above the east-facing door, opening onto the plaza, was the sail that had been erected as a canopy marking Cortes' center of operations, shading Cortes' chair and the sea chest he used as a desk. Two guards stood watch at the temple door behind Cortes' chair all day. When Cortes wasn't off planting crosses on top of pagan altars or tending to other expedition business he could be found sitting there reading reports from the captains or dictating orders to be written by Diaz, who sat on the ground using a flat stone for a writing surface. When neither man was there the chest and chair were hauled inside and the door was bolted.

On the opposite side of the building a corral had been built, and it connected by way of the wide western door to a large room in the temple that had been subdivided into stalls. If Cortes believed that turning their temple into a barn would convince the natives that their gods were false he was wrong. It only served to reinforce their belief that the horses were gods.

The door on the south side of the temple accessed a room where the cannons were stored, as well as other valuables, such as the Indian trade goods of beads, needles and bells. It also held the barrels of ingredients that the gunners hauled down to the beach everyday – far away from everyone else – to grind and mix into gunpowder to replace what had been used in gunnery practice. Guards went with them to discourage any Indians who took too close an interest in the recipe. When they left, the guards bolted the room from the inside and exited by the north door. Melchior thought about getting in there to pilfer some of the beads but quickly put the thought out of his head. He was afraid of the gunpowder.

It was the other door, the door on the north side of the temple, that interested Melchior. He had already discovered that there was no way to open the south door from outside. He had also inspected the horse room – no one had tried to stop him, there were no guards. But that room didn't have any doorways into the rest of the building. As for the east door, he wasn't going to

146

attempt to get past Cortes himself. And he assumed that the guards on that door were especially chosen for their loyalty to the chief.

His goal was the north room. That room had a fireplace with a chimney. It wasn't actually a fireplace. It had been used for burnt offerings of some sort. But it was similar to a fireplace and was easily turned into a forge. Cortes had put the blacksmiths there. The blacksmiths had objected that they would be much more comfortable outdoors, and could easily build a forge, but Cortes insisted: They were to do their work out of the view of the Mayans. The natives could only listen to the Clang clank! Clang clank! that emanated from the room and wonder what sort of ceremony was being performed for what sort of god.

The blacksmith room was where the smaller guns and the crossbows were stored. It was also where several barrels of finished crossbow bolts were kept.

The door to this room had two guards posted at all times. Cortes knew that his whole campaign could be endangered by pilfering and petty theft. He had planned this expedition meticulously. The beads, bells and needles were for trade. The iron was for war. Everything he'd learned about the Mayans told him they did not have iron. The Spanish had thousands of bolts, and they had blacksmiths to make more. But Cortes knew that the sharp, iron tools were a major advantage he had over the natives and he was determined to keep them out of the hands of these potential enemies for as long as possible.

***

Melchior strolled toward the blacksmith room and greeted the guards like he was their best friend. They knew who he was. He'd spent the previous day talking to them, bringing them water, papayas and tortillas. He sat on the ground and kept up a running chatter they could barely understand. He told them he wanted to improve his Spanish. When the new guards came on the old shift introduced him to the new shift, as he had hoped. He wandered away, came back with more tortillas and a bottle of sherry. He'd found it while digging through the belongings of other soldiers Cortes was keeping busy with one whitewash project or another. When one of the night guards had stepped away to relieve himself in the nearby bushes Melchior had asked the other to let him just step in to the blacksmiths' forge, still hot from the day's work, to warm the tortillas. The guard had politely but firmly refused.

When that guard had stepped away to take care of similar business Melchior had tried out the same request on the other guard, with the same result: Cortes would have them whipped if they let anyone into the room. It made no sense to Melchior: Why should Cortes care if Mayans saw the forge? Why should he care about some rusty iron, piles of which had been free for the taking in Cuba?

147

But here he was again. "Morning, Melchior. What have you got for us today?"

He handed each of them a packet of tortillas then casually mentioned, "Ask smith to warm for you." They agreed that was a good idea. Melchior offered to take the tortillas inside to the smith, but no. One guard took the tortillas inside, while the other stayed outside with Melchior.

This was getting him nowhere. With a wave, he walked away. He would have to find another way to get into the blacksmith room.

***

Abí was getting worried.

Felipe had said he would be back in eight days. She had been counting carefully. It was now day seven. What if he didn't come back? She had no other friends. Pedro had been nice enough. He had politely continued to pretend that she was a boy named Pablo. If any of the men looked at her for too long, Pedro could be counted on to say, "Pablo! More water for Isabella, please." Then he would wink at her.

The other grooms had slung hammocks to sleep in, in between and above the heads of the horses. She didn't want to sleep with all the snoring, smelly men. And she was afraid that during the night, whether from going outside to squat or crying out during a bad dream, somehow one of them might figure out that she was a girl.

Watching the men thread the ropes of their hammocks over the beams gave her an idea. The building had no solid roof. The roof beams rested on the stone walls, and thick layers of Palm fronds had been laid across the beams. When the roof leaked, more fronds were added. The practice had been going on for years and the thatch was almost as thick as Abí was tall. She found, when she crawled up there, that she was able to push the packed, dry thatch this way and that and worm her way into a snug little nest above the snoring men.

As she lay in her nest on night seven, worrying about Felipe another worry, far more urgent, materialized. Something was moving through the thatch.

***

This building was constructed similarly to those where Melchior was from. He knew there was nothing but thatch above the stone walls and wooden beams. If he could get into the building anywhere, he could worm his way through the thatch, over the walls and down to where the bolts were.

He wasn't going to try to sneak in past all the sleeping horsemen at night. And he didn't like or trust the horses. Instead, he watched for a time

148

during the day when the horses were being exercised outside. Then he crawled up and burrowed into the thatch and waited, unmoving, for nightfall. Well after the grooms had bedded down for the night and their hammocks had stopped squeaking and their snoring was consistent, he made his move. He eased back down to the bottom of the thatch and worked his way from rafter to rafter until he reached the central wall. He pushed up on the thatch just enough to get over the wall onto the rafters above the blacksmith's room. He could feel the heat rising from the banked fires of the forge. Careful not to loosen any of the thatch, he dropped silently to the floor and began scouting for one of the barrels that held the bolts.

***

Half an hour later Melchior's mission was accomplished. It would have gone much quicker, but he hadn't thought ahead about how to get back up to the rafters. It was important that the blacksmith not know about the nighttime visit; Melchior planned to return in the future. He knew that if the blacksmith suspected an intruder new safeguards would be put in place.

Standing on a barrel, he could barely touch a rafter. He could place a chest on top of the barrel but if he left it there, the blacksmith would know. How could he get the chest back to its original position after he was up? He finally worked it out. There was a piece of rope lying in a messy pile on the floor. Standing on the chest balanced on top of the barrel he poked the rope over a rafter and tied it off. Then he climbed back down and returned the chest to its proper place. He pulled himself up the rope, then untied it and tossed it back as close as possible to its original position. He then slowly eased back from rafter to rafter, through the thatch to the stable side of the building. Carefully selecting a spot away from the unpredictable animals he hung for a moment from a rafter, then dropped lightly, quietly, to the floor.

And suddenly the place lit up as the shutters were thrown open on several lanterns and their candlelight flooded the room.

"Your thatch seems to be infested with rats, Pedro," said Alaminos. When Abí had heard someone moving through the thatch she had awakened Pedro to tell him about it. She hadn't been able to imagine why anyone would do such a thing but Pedro knew instantly. He was reasonably sure this warranted waking someone in authority. Pedro didn't have the courage to wake Cortes. But he'd seen Felipe speaking easily with Alaminos the navigator, and he felt that he could wake him.

Melchior tried to run but the stable hands had strong muscles and quick reflexes from dealing with horses. Melchior instantly found himself being pressed against the cold, stone floor with half a dozen hands holding him down. He looked around wildly, and his eyes fell on Abí, who immediately cowered behind Pedro.

"You! You did this!" he shouted in Mayan. Pedro was the only one there who wasn't puzzled by Melchior's screaming at 'Pablo'.

"Settle down," Alaminos said. "Get me some rope."

Pedro handed him a long lead rope. Alaminos handed it to one of the stable hands holding Melchior on the floor. "Tie his hands securely and bring him. If you don't walk properly, Melchior," he told the translator, "I'm sure these men will be happy to also tie your feet and carry you."

"I did nothing! I was only looking for a warm place to sleep!"

Alaminos began patting the man's shirt, then his pantalon, which made a noticeable clinking sound. The ten crossbow bolts he'd taken were quickly discovered tucked beneath his belt.

"We don't need to wake the Captain," Alaminos said to Pedro. He pointed at the prisoner. "Bring him and come with me."

They led Melchior, still protesting his innocence, around the corner of the former temple to where the soldiers were standing guard in front of the closed door to the blacksmith's shop. The soldiers appeared asleep on their feet but they quickly snapped to attention when they saw the crowd approaching.

The stable hands dropped Melchior in a heap at the feet of the guards.

"This comes under your responsibility, I would think," Alaminos said. "This man was caught thieving from the blacksmith shop." He placed the ten bolts in the hands of one of the guards. "See that these get returned in the morning, and see that this one," he poked a booted toe into Melchior's side, "is still here in the morning for Captain-General Cortes to deal with. Don't fall asleep."

"Yes, sir. No, sir, we won't!"

***

Cortes was in a foul mood. He had made it clear to one and all, both in his fleet and among the pagans: the penalty for theft, no matter how small the item, was death by hanging. He had had Melchior announce it in no uncertain terms to the natives. Perhaps the message hadn't been clear. The penalty had to be enforced. The first Mayan caught – the same old woman who had stepped up to receive the communion wafer – had stolen a leather rein from the stable when the horses were out. She had been caught wearing it as a belt. Cortes didn't want to hang an old woman. He wanted the locals as allies. He'd had her whipped with the leather rein instead.

She'd suffered the beating silently, stoically, while the other native women looking on had wailed and made cuts in their scalps with pieces of seashell, so that blood ran down over their faces. When the whipping was over and her hands were cut free from the palm tree she straightened her bent, bleeding back, patted the hand of the Sargento who had wielded the leather,

150

then walked over to the priest. She closed her eyes and stuck out her tongue, waiting for him to place a communion wafer on it. The flustered Diaz pulled a piece of tortilla from a pocket of his robe and placed it on her tongue. As he made a sign of the cross over her head, she grinned and smacked her lips.

Cortes had had Melchior repeat the warning while he stood beside him scowling at the audience. The next day, however, a Mayan man was caught rifling through the chest in an officer's tent while the soldiers were practicing a close order drill on the beach. Cortes had had that man hanged. Standing in front of the man's twisting body Cortes had again had Melchior repeat the warning against theft.

What was he supposed to do about Melchior? Cortes fumed. He couldn't ignore the infraction. But he needed Melchior alive. What if Felipe didn't bring back one of the lost Spaniards, or what if those men hadn't learned Mayan? What if Felipe himself didn't return?

"Thank you, Señor, for alerting me to this," he said to Alaminos. "And thank you, Pedro, for bringing this to our attention. You can go back to work now." He tossed a small gold coin to Pedro, who touched his forehead and left. Alaminos took his leave as well.

Cortes sat, looking down at Melchior. His hands were still tied. The blacksmith shop guards had very enthusiastically trussed up his legs as well, drawing his feet back toward the back of his head and running a line from his ankles to his throat. His legs had fallen asleep, but every time he tried to straighten them, the rope choked him. He whimpered, hoping Cortes might take pity on him.

Grudgingly, Cortes decided Melchior would have to be kept alive. But he would be taught a lesson.

CHAPTER TWENTY NINE

The news about the two boys surviving the cenote travelled swiftly, reaching the castle before the boys did.

And, as such news does, it expanded as it travelled.

***

That morning, Taxmar had instructed Ox-Ha-té to befriend Felipe and bring him back to the castle. "We have much to learn from the Castilanos," he had said.

Ox-Ha-té had rolled his eyes and shook his head at his father's instructions. He hadn't cared; he couldn't be bothered. He'd had no intention of befriending the foreigner who was younger than he and anyway, the boy dressed like the poorest farmer in the kingdom. Of course all that changed in the cenote. But Taxmar didn't know about that.

Taxmar was desperate to save his people from an attack he knew was coming from the Castilanos. He needed to awaken the gods to this threat. So his plan had been that when Ox-Ha-té brought Felipe to the castle he would have him seized and sacrificed, perhaps along with Aguilar as well, to appease the gods.

The news about the cenote changed all that. Stories of the boys sprouting wings and flying out of the cenote could be dismissed. But there were also several stories about prophecies – some of which were said to have already come true.

Taxmar's concern now was the rest of the Hunac Ceel legend.

***

As the day wore on, the boys one by one went to their respective homes until only Kabil, Ox-Ha-té and Felipe were left.

"Come on, Felipe. Let's go home. Supper will be waiting," Kabil said.

"No," Ox-Ha-té said. "You can go if you wish. But I need Felipe to stay with me."

"Why?" both boys asked at once.

"My father will have heard by now. Do you remember the legend? Father is probably thinking that I plan to try to assassinate him. And if he believes that, he might be arranging to have me killed to save himself."

"What? Why would he do that?" Kabil asked. But Felipe understood it.

"He may believe this is all a play being acted out by his gods, that he has no choice."

"Exactly. We have to think of a way to stop it."

"I know a way," Felipe said. "To change the legend, we need to create a new legend."

A short time later, the guards at the entrance to the castle saw a sight they were not prepared for.

Felipe strode purposefully toward the guards, holding a rope in his hand. The other end of the rope was tied around the neck of Ox-Ha-té. Kabil brought up the rear. He wasn't part of the plan. He was simply curious to see if it would work.

"Stand aside," Felipe ordered. "I have an important message for Lord Taxmar." When the guards didn't move he added, "A prophecy."

When the guards still hesitated, Ox-Ha-té spoke up. "You can see that I am no threat to my father. But if you do not move, I may be a threat to you. Perhaps a prophecy about your wife," he said to one. "Or your son," he said to the other. They looked at each other. They were wavering, torn between the orders from their chief and their fears about a prophecy. Felipe spoke up. He began reciting, in Hebrew:

"E'sher 'iysh halak 'etsah rash' ámad derek chatta…"

The guards quickly moved out of the way.

"What did you say to them?" Ox-Ha-té asked quietly.

"'Happy is the man who does not stand in the way of sinners.'"

The sight of the two boys walking into the courtyard – the younger, smaller Felipe leading the son of their lord like an animal on a rope – induced a shocked silence in all present. Even Lord Taxmar was at a loss for words.

"Father," Ox-Ha-té spoke up quickly. "Felipe saved my life. I fell into the sacred cenote," he continued, "and Felipe jumped in and pulled me out. It is their custom that his life is now sacred and that I am now his slave. It would bring evil on our kingdom if any harm were to befall him."

"What? That is impossible! You are not a slave! You are the son of a king. After your brother, you are the next in line…Aguilar! Aguilar… Tell me the truth: is this a custom of the Castilanos?"

Felipe didn't trust Aguilar to be quick-witted enough to play along. He needed to give him direction. Looking upward as if he were seeing one of the gods, he loudly chanted in monotone Latin, "Our very lives, yours and mine, depend on you confirming this supposed custom. Do not let on that you understand what I am saying."

153

"I'm sorry, my lord, I wasn't paying attention. What were you saying? Custom? Oh, yes. The slave custom. Yes, quite so. I assumed it was common knowledge. If you save someone's life, they become your slave. Most parts of the world observe this custom. It is quite well known. The Hindoos..."

Taxmar waved him to silence. Staring fiercely at Felipe he demanded, "What did you say? Don't lie to me."

"I can tell you what he said, Father," Ox-Ha-té said.

"You cannot. You know only our language."

"But I can. Since coming out of the cenote, I have noticed I have several new abilities. And it seems I can understand strange utterances."

Felipe wondered where he was going with this. The boys had planned the charade with the rope primarily for the purpose of throwing Taxmar off balance. They assumed he was preparing for the possibility of his son coming to the castle to murder him and take over the kingship as Hunac Ceel had done in the legend. So they came up with the idea of presenting Taxmar with the sight of a very submissive and non-threatening Ox-Ha-té. Felipe had thrown in the bit about Ox-Ha-té being his slave with the intention of offering to trade Ox-Ha-té's freedom for his own. But Ox-Ha-té was heading off in a new direction.

"The words are from the gods. They speak of a dark menace threatening our land. My new master Felipe is the one who keeps the dark menace in check. Without him to control it, the dark menace will destroy us. His life must be preserved.

"The words further tell me," Ox-Ha-té continued, "that my life is sacred also. The gods have designated me to be the one who will end the dark menace. I will stay alive as long as the dark menace exists. My life will end when it no longer threatens our people."

Felipe had no idea what Ox-Ha-té was talking about. They had not discussed any of this. But the people in the courtyard were all mesmerized by the words. The message had the desired effect. Taxmar sat down heavily on his throne.

"So be it," he said. "The gods have spoken." To Felipe he said, "What must I pay you to buy my son out from slavery to you? I have much gold. Name any amount; it will be yours."

"I do not want your gold, my lord. Nor do I believe in slavery. So how could I sell a slave? All I want in exchange for Ox-Ha-té's freedom is my own freedom; mine and Aguilar's, and Guerrero's if he's joining us-"

"He isn't," Aguilar informed him. "The runners arrived just before you did."

"Fine," Felipe continued. "Freedom for myself and Aguilar, and an escort back to Kutzumal. That is all we require in exchange for Ox-Ha-té's freedom."

"You shall have it."

***

Felipe, Ox-Ha-té and Kabil were walking back to Kabil's house in the dark. It had been an eventful day.

"So, what is it like to be a prophet?" Kabil wanted to know.

"We're not prophets. We are the same people we were this morning," Felipe answered.

"But, the gods spoke through you! I heard it. And Ox-Ha-té: if you're not a prophet, how do you explain that you understood the language of the gods when they spoke through Felipe?"

"The gods did not speak through me. I speak several languages. You know that. I told you, that was why I was sent here. But I have a question," Felipe said, turning to Ox-Ha-té. "What was all that about a dark menace?"

"I have no idea. I was just making stuff up. Sounded pretty scary, didn't it?"

***

Chimalatl had wanted to bring Aguilar home so that they could leave directly from his home in the morning but Taxmar had refused. He said he would have a message for Felipe to take back to the king of the Castilanos.

Felipe, Aguilar, Chimalatl and his three companions stood in the courtyard of the castle in the chill pre-dawn air drinking xocolatl, waiting for the chief to get up. Kabil had said he wanted to come, too. But Felipe was sure he would slow them down so he had slid out of bed quietly as Kabil slept.

As the first light began to show in the courtyard Taxmar made his appearance wearing a robe dyed the brilliant scarlet color Felipe had seen at the market. Ox-Ha-té was at his side, rubbing his eyes. The two boys grinned at each other, acknowledging their bond.

"I did not properly thank you yesterday for saving my son's life," Taxmar said. "The sight of my son, a prince, on a leash…" Taxmar shook his head. He beckoned Felipe to follow him and stepped away to a dark corner of the courtyard. "I want you to have this." He pulled his bright red garment off over his head and dropped it over Felipe's head. It was extremely heavy, and far too long to move easily in. It clinked a bit as it shifted, in a way fabric alone did not.

"You are far too kind, my lord. This is too grand a gift for me."

"There is no gift grand enough to express my thanks. Please accept it. And tell your holy emperor King Charles of the Spain-germy that I am like

155

his brother even though I am across the sea. And I will extend my open hand to him when he arrives."

"I will convey that message the moment I am in his presence."

"But my welcome extends only to the king," Taxmar continued. "I believe that the ways of the Castilanos will bring harm to my people. You must tell your chief on Kutzumal, if he is contemplating bringing his army to my land, that they will not be welcome here. You must never return here. If you do, you and all your companions will be sacrificed to the gods."

"I understand. I will tell my chief."

***

They travelled due east, back the way they had come. Chimalatl set a swift pace. Aguilar could not keep up. Even Felipe was struggling. He had taken off the fine red robe and stuffed it into his bat-wing bag. The bag swung heavily, banging into his hip with every step.

Felipe had explained the dilemma to Chimalatl before they set out. They had been gone from Kutzumal for five days. Their orders were to either be on the cape at the northern tip of Yucatán on day six, or back on Kutzumal on day eight.

"Neither one is possible. Why are Castilanos in such a hurry?"

"It is not my place to question. But it is two days back to Kutzumal. Which means we would not get there until day seven. I don't know how many days it would be to the cape. You must know."

"I do. That's why I said neither is possible. The cape is four days. If it was just you, perhaps we could do it in three. But with him," he pointed a thumb at Aguilar, "Never. Four might not even be possible. Kutzumal is closest… two days. We may not even make it in two. But we can try."

Felipe dropped back to Aguilar.

"Did you say that Señor Guerrero sent a message?"

"He did, yes," Aguilar puffed. He stopped to talk, but Felipe urged him on. He spoke in gasps as they moved.

"He said," (puff) "he doesn't believe," (puff) "he would be accepted back in," (puff) "civilization." He went on for several steps before trying to speak again. "He has tattoos," (puff) "on his face," (puff) "and piercings in his lips," (puff) "and ears. He also," (puff) "has a wife and three children." (puff) "But I don't think that's the real reason."

Felipe didn't want to encourage him to talk anymore, but Aguilar pressed on anyway. "I think," (puff) "the real reason is," (puff) "he fought against," (puff) "the Spanish when they came last year."

"Save your breath for now, sir," Felipe said. "Perhaps we can talk more tonight."

156

There was no more talking the rest of the day. And when they camped for the night both Aguilar and Felipe fell asleep almost immediately. The next day was harder. Aguilar's legs were cramped and his feet blistered. Felipe had red welts around his hips from they weight of the treasure in the bat-wing bag.

They pushed on grimly, trying desperately to get back to Kutzumal before the Spanish fleet left them behind.

They didn't make it.

CHAPTER THIRTY

Cortes ordered the ships prepared for sea. The guns were back aboard. Kegs upon kegs of gunpowder and salted turkey meat and casks of water, and dozens of baskets and barrels of tortillas, were ferried out to the ships in the harbor.

Melchior, in chains, was rowed out to the flagship. His back was raw from the forty lashes Cortes had sentenced him to. The whipping had been delivered enthusiastically by two of the soldiers he had pretended to befriend who had been guarding the blacksmith shop. They took turns laying on the lash, each egging the other on with taunts of how they'd been duped by the thief.

Last aboard were the horses. Majesty almost mutinied, as usual, but Pedro finally managed to get him in hand. Isabella, too, was a problem, but for a different reason. She refused to go without her foal, and Hurricane was nowhere to be seen. 'Pablo' had disappeared with the colt.

Abí wasn't gone long. Hurricane's hunger, and his instinct to answer his mother's insistent calls, caused him to head back to the beach where Estefan was trying to force Isabella into the water, and Abí came right behind him. She didn't want to be left on Kutzumal; she would only end up as a slave to the locals, to be sold to the next tribe to visit. But she was searching frantically for any way to delay the ships from sailing without her friend Felipe.

***

Felipe, Chimalatl and the others reached the beached canoe well after dark on the second travel day. There was no moon but even if there had been, they needed to rest before attempting to cross to the island. Reluctantly, he agreed with the decision to try to get some sleep and paddle across at first light.

Before the sun rose the next morning Felipe was on the beach, straining to see the island he knew was there, hidden by the mist rising off the sea. The four Mayans soon joined him. He went back up the trail and found Aguilar, awake but looking anxiously at the steep climb down to the beach. "I don't think I can do that," he said.

"I'll guide you. You'll be fine."

It took nearly half an hour, Felipe standing below the friar, guiding each foot onto a solid step then encouraging him to step down again. When they finally assembled on the beach it was fully light. They could see the top of Kutzumal through the rapidly clearing fog.

When they had paddled a few leagues from the shore they finally spotted a sail. It was not in the harbor at Kutzumal.

It was on the horizon, to the north, sailing away.

***

Abí's heart sank as she heard the anchor cable being cable aboard. She had been all over the ship, looking for some legitimate reason for it not to sail. She had found a little water sloshing in the bilges and thought that might be the answer. She had run to Pedro to tell him the ship was sinking, that it wasn't safe to put out to sea.

He'd simply tousled her hair. "There is always a little water in the bilge, Pablo. It seeps in through the cracks. There might be a little more leakage than usual; I understand this ship scraped the bottom in Cuba. But we survived a hurricane! It can't be too bad. When it gets too deep the sailors will pump it out, don't worry."

She wasn't worried about the ship sinking. She was worried about never seeing Felipe again. She made another inspection, this time armed with the knowledge that this ship had been damaged recently. She looked for any hint of dampness higher than the bilge.

And she found some.

***

Chimalatl and the men stopped rowing. They all turned and stared at the small sail. Felipe stood up in the canoe and frantically waved his arms at the retreating ship.

"Lord, please make them see us," Aguilar prayed.

The three Mayans accompanying Chimalatl looked from him to their passengers and back. They weren't sure what to do now.

"Keep rowing. We need to get to Kutzumal in any case." They all began digging their paddles into the water and the canoe drove forward again.

Felipe stared at the scrap of sail, willing it to turn. It was too far away to see clearly. Was it changing shape? Or was it just getting smaller? He thought of his father, rotting in Bernardo's jail. Would he ever see him again?

***

Abí was far below the waterline. She found a small but steady drizzle of water oozing in below a small board that had been nailed to the inside of the hull as some sort of repair. She tried pulling the board loose but her fingers were not strong enough. She went and found a metal bar and came back and tried prying the repair loose with the bar. It didn't budge.

She finally went and got Hurricane. The young colt was untrained and certainly no work animal. But they had been all over the ship together. She had taught him to navigate the almost ladder-steep gangways between decks with her help. If she could teach him that, she could teach him to do what she needed now. He was stronger than she was, and she had an idea.

She positioned him with his hindquarters against the repair in the hull.

"Kick!" she said. He nuzzled her shoulder. "Kick!" she said again, with the same result. Holding his halter with one hand she picked up the iron bar she'd been using as a lever and tapped his rump with it. He tried to step forward, but she blocked his path. "Kick!" she said again. He was now confused. She tied his halter to a post and stepped to his rear. She tapped his rump again. "Kick!" she said. He tried to turn to see her but he couldn't. "Kick!" she tapped his rump again and he lashed out with his hind feet at the annoyance touching his rump.

"Good! Again: Kick!"

She repeated the lesson - tapped him again, said "Kick" and he kicked again, and she told him, "Good boy!" He did it again.

The fourth time he kicked the board it came loose.

She pried it away with the iron bar. Behind it was, not the ocean, but gray metal. The outside of the ship's hull was lined with lead. She didn't know what it was, but she struck it with the iron bar anyway.

The bar went through the gray metal as if it was a tortilla. A torrent of water jetted in, knocking Abí down. Coughing and choking, she floundered up from the water as it started to fill the hold.

Isabella neighed for her son and Hurricane ran off. Abí ran as well, sopping wet, certain that she had condemned the ship, and everyone on it, to death.

***

Felipe stared at the scrap of sail until his eyes watered. Finally, he was certain his mind was not playing tricks on him: the sail was definitely getting bigger. The ship had turned back. Felipe pounded on Aguilar's shoulders and yelled for joy.

CHAPTER THIRTY ONE

After a hectic two days the fleet was once again at sea. Horses – and everything else – had had to be offloaded again on Kutzumal to repair the ship. Seawater-soaked tortillas were ferried ashore and swapped for fresh ones. The ship was careened on the beach to expose the hole in the bottom. The carpenter and his crew had carefully salvaged the lead sheeting on the hull and torn out a large patch of timber around the hole that was all found to be infested with worms.

"It's a good thing she leaked when she did," Abí overheard the carpenter tell Cortes. "If we had been further to sea when this let go, we'd all have gone for a swim." So perhaps she hadn't almost sunk the ship. Perhaps she had saved everyone.

Aged timbers were pulled from the roof of the temple, and paid for with beads. The carpenter's mates sawed them to fit and pinned them in place with wooden dowels. The blacksmiths reshaped the lead into new sheets that were nailed over the fresh wood. Then the ship had been refloated and reloaded, ending with the water butts, fresh tortillas, and finally the horses.

When they'd seen the ship turn, the four Mayans were nearly as relieved as Felipe and Aguilar. They could now count on their reward. They began digging their paddles into the water with renewed vigor toward the sailing ship until they realized it wasn't heading for them. It was heading back to Kutzumal. They quickly altered course.

Before they'd reached the island, the initial euphoria wore off. Felipe had told Aguilar, in Latin, "We must do what we can to discourage Señor Cortes from attacking Yucatán."

"I don't see why. They are blood-thirsty heathens – present company excluded. They have been on their best behavior for you. But I saw them at their worst, yes, and believe you me, if they will not come to Christ they should be wiped off the map!"

"But you and I both owe our lives to Taxmar," Felipe said. He was thinking as much of Ox-Ha-té as Taxmar. He also had in mind Chimalatl and Kabil and the other Mayans he'd met. He didn't want to see any of them attacked by the Spanish.

Now that he was free, however, Aguilar was not feeling nearly as charitable toward his captors. "Our lives would never have been in peril in the first place had it not been for Taxmar and his people. The devil take them!" As he said the last, however, he seemed to realize it was not a proper attitude for a man of God. "In any event, it is the decision of your chief, Señor Cortes, may God bless him. I can't imagine he will seek direction from me."

"That is why I'm bringing this up. He likely *will* seek your direction. The translator he has now is, well, not a nice man. Not reliable."

"I thought you were his translator."

"I am a child. I happen to have a little Mayan. He certainly does not look to me for guidance."

"But you speak Latin!"

"Only what my father taught me. And Señor Cortes doesn't know about this. To him, I am simply an Indian child, barely worth acknowledging. And I am happy with that relationship. I would rather he not find out I know Latin. It would disturb him."

"I see," Aguilar said. But he really didn't see at all. "Well, I can see that he will need a counselor, yes. Someone who is not merely fluent in the language but familiar with the customs. Yes indeed, I can see that."

"You owe it to Señor Cortes and his men to give him the best advice you can. Which I'm sure you will do. We also," he added, "owe a debt of gratitude to these men." He gestured to the four Mayans vigorously rowing the canoe.

"What would you suggest I tell Cortes, then?"

"You can tell him truthfully that there is little gold in Yucatán. And what there is came from elsewhere."

"True, yes that's true. I saw no gold mining, only farming. And building. And their disgusting religion-"

"You can also tell him honestly," Felipe interrupted him to get him off that thought, "that there are hundreds of thousands of well-armed Mayan warriors on Yucatán."

"Also true. Although, if he asks me, I have to tell him their arms are primitive in comparison to Spanish arms."

"And you must tell him about Señor Guerrero."

Aguilar eyed him suspiciously. "Tell him what about Señor Guerrero?"

"You need to tell him about Señor Guerrero helping the Mayans fight against the Spanish."

"No! I will not sully the man's reputation. He saved my life! More than once! No," Aguilar shook his head. "I will not be party to that. I will say only that he chose to stay because of his wife and children."

Felipe sighed. Was this what it felt like to grow up? As a child, he didn't expect to get his own way. He simply did as he was told by whatever adult was speaking to him. He had always assumed they knew best. But now, he felt like he was seeing a bigger picture. Yet he was having to try to convince someone else – an adult – who simply refused to consider all the facts.

"Sparing Guerrero's reputation will have an enormous cost. If Señor Cortes attempts to conquer the Yucatán and the people there are prepared for the battle by Guerrero, the attack could cost the lives of many of Señor Cortes' men, perhaps all of them. Your fellow Spaniards." And with them would go any chance of returning to his father, Felipe thought.

"I don't care," Aguilar said. "I won't ruin the man's name."

"Certainly you care. I'm sure you don't want anyone to die."

"In the cause of Christianity there are always martyrs." Aguilar insisted.

"Here's an idea, then," Felipe tried a different tack. "Suppose you were simply to tell Señor Cortes about Guerrero's facial tattoos and pierced lips and ears?"

"Yes! Yes, I can do that. That could be seen, by a reasonable person, as merely an attempt to be assimilated into local culture, yes. No one could fault him for that. And it would be a fitting explanation for his, er, reluctant abandoning of his dear homeland, yes, I like that: 'reluctant abandoning.' That's true. That sounds more like he was torn; that he truly wanted to remain a Spanish gentleman but was forced to 'reluctantly abandon his dear homeland…'"

He was still muttering the words to himself when the canoe had grounded on Kutzumal. Spaniards with swords had been there to meet them. All they saw was a canoe full of Indians. Felipe spoke up. "Please tell Señor Cortes the mission was a success. The lost Spaniard has been found."

"Why did you not bring him here, then?" asked one of the soldiers.

"Please tell them who you are, Señor Aguilar, in Spanish."

"Oh! My. Yes. Well, I am, yes, I am Jeronimo de Aguilar, a friar of the Franciscan order, of Seville," he said in his rusty Spanish. "And I am glad to welcome you. I mean glad to be home. Well, to be here. Yes, here with my brethren."

The soldier's eyes widened as he realized the brown, wrinkled man wearing nothing but a loincloth was actually a Spaniard. "Señor Cortes will be happy to see you." The soldier looked at Felipe again, finally figuring out that he was part of the expedition and not one of the Mayans. "You know where his quarters are, don't you?"

Felipe led the group back to the plaza where Cortes was sitting near the fountain, waiting for his canopy to be erected. He stood when he saw Felipe.

"No luck?"

"Señor Cortes, may I present Señor Jeronimo Aguilar, a Franciscan friar and late advisor to the court of Lord Taxmar, king of Yaxunah."

Cortes was taken aback by the sight of the half-naked man standing beside Felipe. Aguilar pulled his breviary from his belt.

163

"I believe it is Tuesday, March ninth, yes? Am I right? Saint Pacian's day, Bishop of Barcelona."

Cortes stood in shock for a moment, but quickly recovered. He whipped the cloak off his back and wrapped it around Aguilar. "Good sir! We are so pleased at your escape. You must tell me all about it."

***

Aguilar, as he'd warned, refused to say a bad word about Guerrero. When Cortes finally sent the man off with a servant to get him properly groomed and dressed as a Spaniard, Felipe stepped forward with Chimalatl. Cortes praised and thanked the man, through Felipe, and paid him a handsome reward of beads, bells and needles. He then dismissed them and began to walk away.

"Sir," Felipe called after him, and Cortes stopped and came back. "What now?"

"Did Señor Aguilar tell you about Guerrero?"

"You mean *Señor* Guerrero, don't you? The Spanish gentleman who had to give up his homeland to stay alive?"

"Yes, sir. Sorry, sir. Did he tell you about the tattoos on his face?"

Now he had Cortes' full attention. "He did. Why?"

Felipe turned to Chimalatl. "Please tell my chief about the tattoos on your face."

Chimalatl explained, with Felipe interpreting, how each tattoo represented a battle and the length of each line represented how many warriors he'd captured. Though Chimalatl didn't mention it, Felipe added the detail that the captured warriors were later sacrificed to Mayan gods.

"Sir, the tattoos on Guerrero's face" – Felipe purposely skipped the *Señor* again. "He got those tattoos for fighting against the Spanish. He taught the Mayans how to defeat Spanish tactics."

Cortes eyes narrowed at this piece of news. "This one," he said, pointing to Chimalatl, "has seen our horses, has seen our troops riding them. Ask him if Guerrero taught him how to defend against men on horses."

Felipe translated the question and Chimalatl's answer.

"He said Guerrero taught them to form up back to back in a tight bunch with their spears pointing outward."

Cortes nodded thoughtfully. "Ask him if the natives of Yucatán would have shared this information with others, other Indians not from Yucatán."

Felipe translated the question, then the answer. Chimalatl shrugged. "Our back is to the river. It is a very large river."

164

CHAPTER THIRTY TWO

They skipped Yucatán.

Ten days after leaving Kutzumal, having sailed north, then west, then south around Yucatán they spotted the large river that Grijalva had named for himself, separating the Yucatán peninsula (they now knew it was not an island) from a new, unexplored land. The dropped anchor in the harbor formed by the mouth of the river.

Abí was literally jumping up and down. "This is my land! This is Tabasco! I'm home!" She hugged Felipe's neck. "Can I go now?" She stopped herself. "I can't take Hurricane, can I? And I will probably never see you again." She began to tear up.

"I said I would get you home to your people and you are here. You are free to go to them or stay with me, with us."

But that turned out to be easier said than done. A small landing party was put together consisting of only Cortes, Alaminos, Aguilar, Melchior and a dozen soldiers armed with arquebuses and crossbows. Felipe was back to his position as a groom. Cortes certainly had no need for a third interpreter.

Before the boats had gotten out of the shadow of the ship hundreds of canoes bearing thousands of Mayans bore down quickly on the explorers.

Cortes held up his hand in a calming gesture and spoke. His words, translated by either Melchior or Aguilar, seemed to have no effect. The gestures of the natives made it clear they were not welcoming the visitors. Felipe saw movement in the boats and realized Cortes had ordered the men to arm themselves. When the natives continued to shake their fists and spears, Cortes pointed to one of his men and said something. Felipe saw a puff of smoke and then heard the boom of an arquebus being fired. The effect on the Mayans was profound. Fists and spears were lowered. Cortes spoke again. After a pause while his words were translated a few more words were spoken. Then the native canoes turned away and the boats returned to the ship.

After the men were back aboard Felipe sought out Aguilar.

"He told them," Aguilar said, "that he only wanted to talk to them. He said that he wished to trade for wood and water, no more. But they recognized the markings on Melchior. They said they are a people called Tabascans. But they said Melchior's people – Taxmar's people, I suppose one could say, actually – had come across the river and chastised them for trading with the Castilanos the last time, and that they had no interest in trading again. They were surprised Melchior was helping us. Of course, Melchior did not translate that. But I informed the Captain. Señor Cortes had me tell them 'in no uncertain terms,' he said, that he would come to their city tomorrow to speak with them. They said no. He said he will be coming anyway, that his intentions were peaceful. But that he was coming whether they agreed to it or not. He repeated that he does not want war but he will come into their city to talk and if they insist on war, it will not go well for them. He is very brave."

"Yes." Felipe realized with a start that he meant it. Even though Cortes was his enemy who had falsely imprisoned his father, he admired the man's courage.

***

Before sundown, the ships were re-positioned so that the guns of each could protect the other. The flagship was placed furthest upstream, starboard side on to the flow of the Rio Grijalva. A kedge anchor had been dropped from the stern to hold it in that position. Releasing that cable would allow the ship to spin quickly, to alter the aim of her guns. Behind it in a line abreast were the three next larger ships. The other eight small ships formed a rough circle around the armada. At daybreak the officers appointed a skeleton watch crew for each ship with instructions to shoot any canoe that approached within gun range. Everyone else – over four hundred Spaniards and twice that many Taino – was ferried ashore.

"You will take two hundred men inland," Cortes said to Avila as they formed up. He pointed to the southwest. "Head that way a league or so, then turn toward me. I will take the rest of the men in the boats this way," he pointed up the Grijalva, "until I discover their city. Alaminos says it is about a league upstream." Alaminos nodded but didn't say anything. "Hopefully we can come at the city from two different directions, so that if they choose to fight we can squeeze them between us. I will take Aguilar and Melchior with me. Felipe will go with you."

Turning to Felipe he said, "I'm still hoping to avoid fighting these people. Do not antagonize them. Assure any you meet that we come in peace, that we are only looking to purchase water and wood. But if they decide to fight, get to the rear and let the men fight."

All the horses had been brought ashore except Isabella and Hurricane. Avila was mounted on the black stallion El Arriero. Felipe would be riding Majesty, partly to give him more authority should he need to speak to any Mayans, and partly because only he, Cortes and Avila could ride Majesty – the stallion would tolerate no other riders. Felipe was delighted that he would be riding beside his hero, Alonso de Avila the great horseman.

In addition to the horses they had landed the armor, crossbows, arquebuses and four of the falconets – the lighter field guns that fired a half

166

pound charge. While in Kutzumal, two-wheeled carriages had been constructed for these guns to make them more maneuverable on land. On a fair surface a falconet carriage could be drawn by a single horse or a few men. Four of the horses where hitched to them. Two others were hitched to a wagon loaded with shot and powder.

The two hundred men assigned to Avila were organized into companies. Avila and Felipe would ride at the head of the first. Officers rode the remaining horses and formed rallying points for each company. The throng was quickly formed up into marching order.

Felipe looked over the crowd of men and boys accompanying them. He saw Pedro give him a nod and, in his shadow, Abí was trying her best to look like a man instead of a scared little girl.

Earlier, when she had climbed down into a boat between Felipe and Pedro in the pre-dawn darkness, Cortes had addressed her for the first time in her life. "Are you scared, boy? Maybe you should stay on board with the watch crew."

She opened her mouth, but fear of the great man stole her voice. Felipe spoke up. "I'll keep an eye on him, sir."

***

Half a league inland from the mouth of the river Cortes' crew spotted a beach. The expedition had a total of twenty five boats, but they'd left a boat with each ship so the watch crews could reach each other if necessary. This left Cortes with fourteen boats of varying sizes. Each was so packed with men there was barely enough room for the sailors to row.

Beyond the beach they could see a stout wooden wall with a gate set into it. The tops of stone buildings poked above the wall. As they watched, the gate was slammed shut.

"We need to get through that gate. Forget the beach. See if you can pull ashore anywhere along here," Cortes ordered. Where he pointed, the trees reached down to and even over the water on the edge of the river. The sailor at the helm pulled the tiller over and pointed their boat directly at the tree-lined shore downstream of the beach. The other thirteen boats followed suit. Before they got within ten varas of shore, however, hundreds of arrows arched out of the sky. One bounced off Cortes' armor. Another buried itself in the thigh of the soldier sitting next to him. The man stared at it for a moment, then pulled it out with a grunt.

"Huh." The man held it up for Cortes to see. "No arrowhead."

Cortes looked over the side. The water was less than waist deep. "Into the water!" he called. "Keep the boats between us and the shore!"

Several more men were wounded. Cortes ordered an arquebus fired. Birds flew up and natives screamed at the unfamiliar, stunning noise. But there was no indication that any natives had been hit. After a moment of quiet, the arrows started again.

"Fire all the arquebuses!"

This time they saw a native fall from a tree branch and plop into the shallow water and the wailing of the enemy became non-stop.

"Push for shore. Crossbowmen! Fire!"

Two dozen bolts flew into the trees and another group of Mayans began wailing. But still the arrows continued to fly back.

A Spaniard took an arrow in the chest in spite of his cotton armor, which was quickly soaked with blood. Others lifted him and rolled him into the bottom of a boat. The Spaniards continued to push the boats toward shore. The Mayan warriors continued to fall back toward their wall. As the Spaniards stepped onto land the arquebusiers were able to reload. Cortes looked down and realized he'd lost a shoe in the mud.

Seeing a rearguard of warriors midway between their position and the gate in the wooden wall, Cortes pointed and called, "*Santiago* and at 'em!"

The Spanish soldiers who had crossbows fired. The rest waved their swords and charged. The Mayans fell back toward the gate and it opened barely wide enough for them to squeeze through single file. Before they could get it bolted again, however, a huge Spaniard, one of the blacksmiths, drove his sword through the opening. The Mayan who was pulling on the gate screamed and fell backward. The blacksmith stuck his foot into the gap and continued to stab his sword through the small opening. He was quickly joined by others, and the gate was pried open. Several men in the first wave went down under a hail of native arrows but more were right behind them. The Mayan warriors abandoned the gate and fell back to the nearest houses.

Wounded Spaniards were dragged unceremoniously outside the gate and left to fend for themselves. The rest of the Spanish continued to press forward, driving the Mayans back from house to house. When they reached the central plaza, they saw the Mayan army just disappearing into the buildings on the far side of the expanse.

"I should have brought dogs," Cortes said to no one. He estimated that a hundred or more of his men were wounded, some of them seriously. Perhaps some had even died. Charging across the open square to attack the Mayans barricaded in the buildings on the far side would cost him more men. It could even end his expedition before it started.

***

Felipe had enjoyed riding beside Avila. He imagined himself as an equal, or at least a lieutenant, of the handsome man. He allowed himself to daydream for a moment, wondering what it would be like to ride Majesty into battle, troops looking up to him for leadership, marveling at his bravery.

Avila woke him from his reverie. "Ask her were the town is." He was pointing to an old woman carrying a water jar who had stopped to stare at the men and horses.

They had ridden up the beach to find solid ground. They had quickly hacked a path for the guns through the hedge that edged the beach and found themselves in a bean field. Crossing the field they saw natives in the distance moving away but none up close. Forty men had quickly hoisted the guns across a small irrigation ditch where they found a dirt path wide enough for the gun carriages, running past more fields. They followed it for a while. But now it seemed to be bending away from the direction Cortes had gone.

"Good day, grandmother," Felipe called. "Can you tell me please, does this road lead to the town?"

The old woman turned when she heard her language being spoken. But on seeing the men on horses she dropped her clay jar, which shattered on a rock. She shouted a warning to others Felipe couldn't see, and quickly ran away along the path.

Abí came up on Felipe's left side and waved to get his attention. She didn't want to get too close to Majesty. "This path leads only to a corn field," she murmured in Mayan. "You should have gone to the left just after the bean field. Felipe?"

"Thank you, 'Pablo,'" he replied in Spanish. "What is it?"

"You won't harm my family, will you?"

Before he could respond, they heard the faint boom of the arquebuses far to their left.

"Come on!" shouted Avila. He wheeled El Arriero and headed quickly toward the sound of the guns.

"I won't hurt your family, Abí. But if you can, you should find them and warn them to keep their heads down." Then he called to Avila. "Wait! Back this way! There is a path we missed." Without waiting for Avila to acknowledge, he turned Majesty and rode back through the troops to the border of the field and turned to the right onto a narrow footpath. The officers looked from Felipe to Avila, trying to decide which to follow. Avila quickly angled across to join Felipe and the other officers turned back and ordered their companies to about face.

The horses pulling the falconets and wagons were unhitched. Soldiers grabbed the pull bars and manhandled the carriages back facing the other direction. The horses were re-hitched and their handlers began driving them as quickly as they could after the men.

Avila raced ahead. The track ended at a high wooden wall. When Felipe caught up with Avila he had reined to a stop in front of a stout gate and dismounted. He pushed on the gate, but it didn't budge. He climbed back aboard El Arriero and then jumped up and stood on the saddle, reaching up toward the top of the wall. It was just beyond his reach.

"Felipe, climb up here. I'll boost you up."

Felipe stood up on Majesty's back and lightly jumped over to El Arriero's back. Before he'd even steadied himself, Avila caught him and in one smooth motion tossed him toward the top of the wall. Felipe was not expecting the move but his reflexes were quick. He caught the top of the wall, pulled himself up and straddled it. He stopped and looked back at Avila. "Now what?"

"Can you see the inside of the gate?"

Felipe hung upside down and looked. There was a bar set in thick wooden hoops holding the gate shut. He pulled himself back up.

"Just a moment," he told Avila. He dropped to the ground inside the gate and pulled the bar out of its hoops. He swung the gate open and whistled. Majesty came to him as Avila and the others rode through. The foot soldiers were slower catching up. In several places they'd had to chop at the bushes on both sides of the path to get the guns and supplies through.

There was no one inside the wall. There were no Mayans visible at all. Avila assigned the first soldiers who arrived to keep the gate open until the guns and ammunition arrived. As the rest trickled in he organized scouts to search the city. They could guess the general direction they needed to go from the battle sounds but the city was a maze. And then the noise that had been coming from the far side of the city fell silent.

***

There was a large tree in the middle of the plaza. Cortes pointed to it and gave orders to his men.

"That will be our anchor. Search these houses," he said, pointing behind them. "Make sure there are none of the enemy behind us. Drag out everything you can carry. We're going to build a movable barricade and work our way to that tree. From there, the Indians will be in range."

His men began kicking in the doors of the houses on their side of the plaza and tossing tables, beds and doors into the street. The houses were all empty, all looking as if the inhabitants had left in a hurry. When they had enough wood for all of them to crouch behind, they began sliding the barricade forward across the plaza. Shortly before they reached the tree arrows began thunking into upended beds, doors and tabletops.

Cortes quickly turned to Aguilar – Melchior had disappeared – and told him, "Tell them, again, we do not wish to harm them. We wish to talk to them."

Aguilar repeated the speech he had shouted before, repeating the same message over and over: "Stop shooting at us, and we will stop shooting at you." His voice rose frantically as an arrow struck near his head.

When another arrow found its way through the junk pile into the chest of one of his men Cortes ordered his arquebusiers and crossbowmen to all fire at once. Across the plaza the wailing arose again as a Mayan warrior fell. The arrows stopped. Cortes ordered everyone to reload quickly. Then he stood up and called to the Indian warriors to come meet him peacefully under the tree. Aguilar, crouched behind a bed frame, shouted the translation. In answer, an arrow struck Cortes' armor.

"Keep the barricade anchored by the tree on the left. Pivot the rest of it forward," Cortes said. He pointed to four men clad in steel armor. "You men. Take arquebuses to the right end of the line. Only fire one at a time, and wait until you have something to shoot at. Keep the Indians from turning our flank."

Something Felipe had said about the motives of the Mayans came back to him. Cortes put it together with their wailing when one of their own was struck, their use of arrows without arrowheads. The Indians weren't trying to kill his men; in fact, they were trying *not* to kill them.

What they wanted was to capture his men alive and use them later as sacrifices. He could use that information to his advantage.

"No more volleys," he said to the crossbowmen. "Wait for orders from the Sargentos. Sargentos, listen," he continued. "Don't waste any more bolts. Use only the most skilled crossbowmen. Pick your targets one at a time. They have us outnumbered ten to one but they hate losing a single man. You notice their wailing? If we want to see Spain again, we need to give the Indians more to wail about."

***

The scouts Avila had sent searched street by street and sketched maps of the city. The gunners prepared the falconets. The rest of the men found shade and flopped down, awaiting orders. No other Mayans appeared.

"Felipe." Avila had been looking at his young assistant. "It doesn't look like there is going to be anyone for you to practice your translation on. You should probably stay here when we advance."

Felipe was perfectly happy with that decision. He had no desire to be a soldier. Having come to know Abí, he certainly didn't want to be put in a position to have to fight some of her relatives. He was glad Ox-Ha-té, Chimalatl and Kabil were on the other side of the river.

He watched as the scouts filtered back to the square, reporting and showing their maps to Avila. After the last one returned orders were given, the men formed up into their companies and marched out down a narrow opening in the far left corner of the plaza. Two men who had injured themselves hauling the guns over the rough terrain stayed behind. They found some shade under one of the trees that bordered a small fountain gurgling in

171

the plaza. Felipe and Majesty joined them. Soon, the injured men were snoring. Felipe sat on the ground, his chin resting on the short stone border of the fountain. Majesty began chewing leaves from one of the trees. He found them quite tasty. He didn't even react when the noise of the arquebuses came again from across the city.

As Felipe sat quietly watching the street down which Avila had led his men a movement caught his eye. A band of about two hundred Mayans crept silently out of an alley to his right and headed up the street where Avila and his men had gone.

The surprise attack force was about to be surprised.

***

Cortes was growing concerned, though his men saw nothing but confidence in his demeanor. They continued their war of attrition, targeting with deadly accuracy any Mayan who grew too bold or careless. But bolts for the crossbows were running out. The crossbowmen had taken to collecting the arrows that lay scattered all over the square and chopping them short enough to fit the crossbows. Unfortunately, they were no more effective against the Mayans than they had been against the Spaniards.

The arquebuses, too, were low on supplies. The last few reloads had been with small stones rather than lead balls. They had enough powder for perhaps ten more rounds each. After that, the Mayans would realize they were no threat and they would charge. Cortes knew his hundred or so steel swords were no match for a thousand obsidian-headed spears.

***

Without a moment's hesitation Felipe grabbed Majesty's rein from the ground and vaulted into the saddle. He kicked him in the ribs and aimed him toward the narrow street where the Mayans were trying to sneak up on Avila.

As soon as they entered the stone-lined alley, the clattering of Majesty's hooves echoed back to him, making a racket he had no way to hide. But Felipe knew the Mayans had never heard that noise before and might be surprised by it. He added to the din by whistling and shouting "Avila! Avila! Behind you!"

The street turned sharply to the right and Felipe and Majesty barreled around it. They slammed full speed into a Mayan warrior, knocking him into another. Majesty kicked out at a third, sending him flying. Felipe continued to shout and whistle. When an arrow flew past his ear he tucked is head tight against Majesty's neck and put his feet straight behind him, making it impossible to distinguish between child and beast. And he pushed Majesty faster and faster.

Majesty jumped over a dozen warriors who were huddling on the ground, kicked another, stepped on another then screamed and reared. Felipe hung on like he had grown there. The rest of the Mayans fell to the ground and bowed toward the huge animal, trembling in fear.

As Felipe leapt past the last of them, Avila and his men came into sight around the next corner. Alerted by Felipe's yelling and whistling they had retraced their steps and were now perfectly placed to repel the Mayan surprise attack, which quickly fell apart.

"Sanchez," Avila called. "Take your company back to the plaza. Deal with any Mayans you see and protect the two injured men there." To Felipe he said, "Thank you for the warning. You had better stick with us. But stay at the rear, out of the way."

"Yes, Señor."

The arquebuses had fallen silent. Led by the wails and chants of the Mayans and the occasional shouts of their Spanish companions they found their way through the confusing streets. As they entered the main plaza from the west they were met by a sight: They were looking at the backs of nearly a thousand Mayan warriors, screaming and waving spears in the air, bearing down on Cortes' embattled company near the big tree.

"Cavalry! Forward!" At the command the officers on horseback moved to the front. Majesty started to go with them and Felipe had to hold him back. Many of the war horses neighed excitedly and the Mayans stopped and turned at this unfamiliar sound. They began pointing, trembling and screaming. Many of them dropped to the ground, bowing toward the horses. Either they thought the horses were gods or they were imploring their gods to protect them from this fearsome sight.

Avila led his horsemen at a trot to his left, not aiming directly at the Mayans but trying to edge them back, creating a separation between them and the Spanish barricade. The Mayans obligingly drew away. He moved slowly, giving his gunner time to aim the falconet. When he estimated the gap to be sufficient, he raised his right hand and halted the advance. "Back!" he called, and the horsemen backed their horses slowly toward the barricade. The Mayans were confused by the apparent retreat. But before they could decide whether this was good news or bad the falconet roared, cutting a swath through the packed Mayan army.

CHAPTER THIRTY THREE

"Avila says you saved his life."

"No, sir. I'm sure he would have been fine."

"According to him," Cortes continued, "You charged through a mass of armed Mayan warriors screaming like a demon loosed from Hell itself and alerted him to the surprise attack."

Felipe blushed and ducked his head. "I didn't think."

"No, you didn't. Avila is a trained soldier. He could have dealt with the threat at his back. You risked your life. Needlessly. One Indian more or less means nothing to me; but you also risked Majesty's life. The horses will be the success or failure of this mission. All our lives might depend on them. Think next time." And the great man stalked off without another word.

**

When the falconet had roared, mowing down so many of the packed warriors, those Mayans still standing froze. After a moment of shock from both the incomprehensible noise and the devastation, they dropped everything and ran. By the time the falconet was reloaded there was no enemy to fire it at.

"Get help for our wounded," Cortes said. He turned to Avila. "What is the butcher's bill?"

"No one killed, sir. I had a couple small injuries from moving the guns, and a few more when we encountered the enemy, but none serious."

Cortes nodded and walked away.

The rest of the day was spent in feverish activity. There were nearly a hundred injured Spaniards. The seriously wounded were ferried back to the ships. The boats returned loaded with supplies. All the heavy guns, shot, gunpowder and foodstuffs were brought ashore. By sunset the plaza was stuffed with crates and barrels. The ships were nearly empty.

The city wasn't designed to be defended by cannon but that was quickly remedied. Holes were chopped in the wooden wall just large enough for the muzzles of the cannons sitting at ground level. The buildings closest to the courtyard were quickly ransacked by Spaniards hoping for gold, though little was found. Flocks of turkeys were found, and herds of tame deer, which the men turned into a hearty dinner. But there were no people.

Just before the light faded completely a delegation of natives came slowly out of the trees. When the Spanish guards challenged them they dropped to their knees with their hands stretched out wide to their sides.

"They are asking for permission to collect their dead and wounded." Felipe had been nearby walking Majesty toward the river when he heard the guards' challenge, and he stopped to translate. A messenger was sent to Cortes. The answer he sent back was curt. 'Agreed. But tell them I want to see their chief at daybreak tomorrow.'

A company of Spanish soldiers escorted the Mayan delegation as they picked up their fallen comrades, wailing loudly every time they found one dead. The wailing was nerve-wracking and the Spaniards were relieved when silence finally descended.

The next morning, three Mayans wearing bright cloaks of parrot feathers, with ten warriors behind them, approached the guards manning the gates of the city. The guards barred the warriors but admitted the men dressed in feathers once they dropped their obsidian-studded clubs. They escorted the men to the plaza. The three men trembled and knelt. They pulled small gold chains from somewhere inside their cloaks and held these out, quickly reciting something that Aguilar started to translate.

"They claim this is all the gold they have. They want us to take it and leave." Cortes waved him to silence.

"We found more gold than this in one temple. There are four more waiting to be searched. If you left that much behind, we know you took much more with you." The three Mayan men simply sat and stared at the ground as Aguilar translated.

Cortes, Diaz and Aguilar were standing near the huge Ceiba tree in the courtyard. Felipe sat on the ground nearby. He was still smarting from the tongue-lashing he'd received from Cortes and would rather have been somewhere else. But Aguilar had asked him to stay close in case he struggled with translating the proceedings.

Cortes stared at the three emissaries crouched before him and shook his head. "These are not chiefs," he said. "Not high chiefs at any rate."

He stepped over to the tree. He pulled his sword and slashed wickedly at it, three times. He'd formed an odd-looking cross with two horizontal crossbars, the lower one longer than the upper. Felipe wasn't sure if he'd meant to produce the odd cross or if he simply hadn't been happy with the first slash and decided to make a deeper one. Regardless, it had the desired effect on the Mayans: First, clearly, they could see that this man was angry. And either he was extremely strong or he was wielding a miraculous weapon. They had never seen a sword that could slice through wood that easily. They also, Felipe knew, considered the Ceiba tree sacred, a link between heaven and the underworld. And they were wondering why the angry man who slashed it hadn't fallen down dead.

"I told you," Cortes said, "I would only speak to the chiefs. You dishonor me by sending fools. You fools," he continued as Aguilar translated rapidly, "will take this message back to your chiefs. I only wanted water and wood. There was no need for this bloodshed. You started this battle." He pointed a threatening finger at the three trembling, kneeling men. He didn't wait for Aguilar to finish interpreting; he just spoke over him. "We came to be your friends. You have forced us to be your conquerors. Fine. Consider yourselves conquered. I claim this land in the name of King Charles and name it New Spain. You will submit to our cross and the Blessed Virgin, and pay tribute to our sovereign." He nodded to Diaz, who stepped forward and loudly, quickly read The Proclamation.

Aguilar hadn't heard The Proclamation before but it didn't surprise him. He was quite pleased with the idea of bringing the thousands, possibly even millions, of the pagan bloodthirsty Mayans to Christ if at all possible. He didn't bother trying to keep up with translating the details of the actual proclamation. He simply told the natives that God had condemned them to the wrath of hellfire and their only salvation lay in accepting the religion of the Castilanos and placing themselves at the mercy of King Charles.

When Aguilar finished speaking Cortes spoke again. "You are now under the protection of the Spanish sovereign, King Charles. Your enemies are our enemies. But you will tell your chiefs, the real chiefs, that they must come here tomorrow morning and submit to me, in person. If they do not, if they resist, I will put every man, woman and child in your land to the sword."

But Cortes knew they would not submit.

CHAPTER THIRTY FOUR

The town– a city actually, with more than ten thousand houses –the natives called Potonchan. It was now a ghost town. It had been stripped of most of its valuables by the Spaniards. The stone idols, many of them looking a lot like crosses, had all been torn down and broken up. All the gold found was loaded into government strong boxes chained together and watched over by the most trusted guards. Of course, at least as much gold found its way into secret folds, pockets, and seams within the soldiers' uniforms.

Potonchan was situated with its east side protected by the river. West were fields of crops. To the north some trails ran a short distance through a dense, swampy jungle to the sea. Cortes had placed guards atop the walls to keep an eye in all directions. As the sun rose on their fourth day in Tabasco the guards looking south could see, on the far edge of a plain the locals called Centla, a dust cloud indicating some activity. It was only a hint; they could see no details. But they sent word to Cortes.

Cortes stared out at the dust. He knew an army was coming. He could, probably, defend this city. At least for a time. But going on defense would not accomplish his goal. No reinforcements were coming. To reach his goal he had to move forward. He had no desire to repeat the fight of the other day, destroying Mayans one at a time or even wholesale. While only one of his men had died so far from taking the city of Potonchan, dozens were out of action. By sheer numbers, the Mayans would eventually wear them down and wipe them out.

No. Fighting to hang onto a city he didn't want was not an option. His army's advantage would be on the plain.

Melchior's tunic had been found hanging from a tree limb. Cortes thought about the consequences of that. The Mayans chased away by Avila's counter-attack would have told stories about the roaring falconet and about the horses. They may or may not have been believed. But backed up by Melchior, their stories about horses and a loud roaring monster that killed in an instant, even if not fully understood, would nevertheless be valuable information if they chose to act on it. If he had lost the element of surprise he may well have lost the battle before it began.

The deadline Cortes had set came and went. No chiefs arrived. They didn't send any messengers. That the chiefs hadn't come was all the proof Cortes needed that surprise was not going to be on his side.

"Felipe."

"Yes, sir?" Felipe needed to get back into Cortes' good graces. After his chores were done he sat within earshot of Cortes' tent in case he was needed.

"Saddle Majesty and bring him."

"Yes, sir."

When he returned, Cortes was giving orders to two men. Felipe recognized one of them as Alvarado, the captain who had been chastised for stealing from the natives on Kutzumal.

"Take one hundred men apiece, on foot. Go south in two parties along the edges of the plain. Alaminos says the plain is about half a league broad. If you encounter any serious resistance, don't hesitate to use the arquebuses. If either of you hear shots, cut across quickly so as to support the other and take the enemy from two sides."

The men left. Cortes turned to mount Majesty. "What's this?" Most of the horses had steel armor, but there simply wasn't enough to go around, so Cortes had insisted that what there was be given to others. Besides, Majesty refused to tolerate the steel *chanfron*, the horse version of a helmet. But Felipe had gotten a glimpse of the violence that accompanied a battle. So he'd spent the day before with a needle and thread, fashioning a thick covering for Majesty from several spare sets of cotton armor. Majesty now sported an odd-looking quilted cotton pad that covered his neck, chest, and hindquarters.

"I am trying to protect him, sir, as you ordered."

Cortes walked around Majesty, looking him over. The quilt would do nothing for his image, but he appreciated the boy's efforts to protect the horse. "Very good," he said, and mounted. He rode through the city, giving orders for everything to be packed and moved out onto the plain. Then he rode out onto the plain himself to scout out where he wanted to prepare for battle.

In an hour he was back. He gave orders to the Sargentos, and the expedition's supplies began to be moved. Cortes had found a place where a small creek ran from west to east across the plain, arcing shallowly like a crescent moon from the hills on the west and emptying into the river on the east. The ground dipped down to the creek on both sides, and the small depression would give his men cover. He directed the large guns to be evenly spaced in the middle of the line. The falconets on their carriages were divided between the flanks. If as he suspected a large Mayan force was marching north up the plain, they would be within gun range before they knew the Spanish were there.

Still on Majesty he ordered his cavalry to mount up. Avila was on El Arriero. Sedeño was on Isabella, and she seemed to enjoy being back to work. She was moving like a youngster. Felipe had to hold on to Hurricane to prevent him joining his mother.

Cortes realized all his most seasoned officers were with him on horseback, leaving the battle line in the hands of less experienced men, so he made a change. He ordered a tall, lean man with a receding hairline off his gray mare. "Ordas, I need you to take charge of the line," Cortes told the man. He scanned the men waiting in the battle formation and saw a familiar face. "Lares! What are you doing?"

"Gun captain, sir!"

"You're a horseman. You're with me. Take Ordas' mare. Alaminos!" Cortes had spied the navigator sitting on the supply wagon. "We don't need a navigator now. We're here! Take charge of Lares' gun." Alaminos tossed a casual salute to the Captain General, stepped forward to the gun carriage and tightened the fasteners of his armor.

As Cortes was giving these instructions, they all heard the distant booming of arquebuses half a league to the south. The noise seemed to be coming from the right hand side of the plain. Majesty's ears pricked up.

Cortes pointed the opposite direction, to the trees separating the plain from the river and ordered. "Avila! Lead the cavalry. Get them out of sight over there and wait for me. Sargento!" he called to no one in particular. A Sargento who didn't look much older than Felipe ran up to him and saluted. "My compliments to the gunnery officer on our right and ask him to take two falconets to the assistance of our people."

"Yes, sir," the young man answered. "Where, sir?"

"How would I know?" He pointed vaguely toward the south and west. "Tell him to follow the noise! Go!"

The Sargento ran off quickly toward the west end of the line. Shortly after, two dozen Spaniards ran forward from the Spanish line dragging two gun carriages. The falconets bounced over the uneven ground like children's toys. Another group ran behind them, hauling a cart loaded with supplies.

Cortes turned Majesty and rode, alone, southward through the middle of the Centla plain.

***

"Have you ever been in a war before?" Felipe asked Pedro, who had come up to stand beside him and stare to the south.

"No. And we are not in one now," Pedro replied. "You and I will be back there." He gestured toward the wagons parked close to the city behind them. "We are not soldiers. Our job is to take care of horses. Since the horses are being used, we have nothing to do at the moment but watch this young one," he said, pointing to Hurricane. "But that does not make us soldiers."

Felipe nodded and the two turned and slowly walked along behind the line of guns, leading the colt, stopping from time to time when Hurricane stopped to investigate something in the grass. Except for the threat posed by the dust cloud to the south it was a beautiful day.

"What happened to your friend Pablo?" Pedro asked.

179

"I haven't seen her, er, him, since the first day we came ashore. I think – I hope – she found her family."

Cortes came galloping up on Majesty and reined to a stop. He dropped the rein at Felipe's feet. Majesty was blowing a bit. Felipe handed Hurricane's lead to Pedro and grabbed a nearby bucket. Since the guns hadn't been fired yet, the water in the bucket, ready for wetting the gun rammers, was still clean. He set the bucket in front of Majesty's nose and the stallion drank thirstily.

"Ordas!" Cortes called.

"Here, sir!" The man hurried over.

"They are coming in a phalanx about a hundred men across, right up the middle of the plain," Cortes told him. "They are less than half a league away. They will probably stay in that formation only until the first shot from the guns. After that, if they turn and run, forget the guns and chase after them. If they don't run, expect them to split and try to get around your flanks. If that happens try to force them back to the center. Watch for us over there." He turned and pointed to the trees where he'd sent the cavalry. "We are going to wait until they are all here, do you understand? You will have to hold them off until all of them are massed in front of the guns. Then the cavalry will hit them from their flank."

"How many, sir?"

Cortes shook his head. "All of them." Felipe had never seen the man show any fear. But he seemed less sure of himself now. "Thousands. Perhaps ten thousand. Perhaps more. But," he interrupted himself, remembering that others were overhearing him, "they have never seen guns, or horses, or Toledo steel! Their shields are wood, and ours are iron! And they have never seen Spanish resolve. They fight battles like they are playing *Escondite* – all they need is a blindfold! They are not accustomed to seeing their companions die beside them. So we will show them something, yes?"

"Yes!" several men nearby called back.

"*Santiago!*" he called, invoking James, the patron saint of Spain.

"Santiago!" the men replied, and others took up the chant, until the whole line was chanting "Santiago! Santiago!" Then he vaulted onto Majesty's back and galloped off toward the trees where he had sent the other horsemen.

***

A rumbling like a clap of thunder told of the firing of the first falconet. Felipe imagined he could hear the wailing of Mayan warriors. And he subconsciously began counting. Before he reached one hundred, the second Falconet roared.

"Too soon," he muttered.

"What?" Pedro asked.

"The second falconet fired too soon. The first one is not reloaded yet. If the..." Before he could say more, they both heard the higher cracks of arquebuses. Ordas climbed to the top of the rise in front of the battle line and stared south, watching the dust cloud grow. He walked a hundred paces forward of the line and turned and looked back. When he returned he ordered the five heavy guns moved. Two were dragged lower. Two were run forward a couple paces. Ordas wanted their snouts to just poke above the tall grass of the plain. He walked out again and looked back. When he returned he was satisfied. "Everyone down. Lie down! No one stands until I order it."

Pedro tapped Felipe on the shoulder and the two turned and led Hurricane back to their position behind one of the baggage carts. Ordas continued standing in the center, on the top of the rise that hid the battle line, as if offering himself as a target. He knew the natives had no weapons that could reach him. He simply wanted to give them a point to fix on, to draw them into a tighter formation.

Felipe wasn't imagining it now – he could hear singing and chanting coming from the valley plain in front of the guns. Ordas continued to stand on the hilltop, occasionally pacing a few steps one way, then the other. Then he reached up and closed the visor on his helmet just before arrows began falling around him, some of them bouncing off his armor. He stood a moment longer, then turned and slowly walked back toward the line. "Gunners!" he called. "Fire!"

Felipe had heard the guns fire before. But this time the conjoined sound that rolled back over him was a physical assault. Five flames shot out from the cannons. The grass in front of the cannons was scorched and flattened. Five iron balls flew waist high through the enemy lines, killing and maiming hundreds of the Mayan warriors. The frightening roar was unlike anything the natives had ever heard before. It was a hundred times worse than the most terrible thunder storm any of them had ever experienced. And they always associated thunder with their gods being angry. They could only conclude that their gods must be about to destroy them. Stunned and deafened, many of them dropped to the ground, holding their heads from the pain in their ears. Others looked up to the sky, pleading for their lives.

"Arquebusiers, ready!" Ordas called. "Forward! Don't shoot until ordered. Just to the top of the rise here. That's good. Don't fire yet. Let's wait for their charge."

He wasn't at all sure there would be a charge. Many of the Indians were still rolling around on the ground, wailing, calling out to their gods, covering their ears. But some of them were recovering, shaking their spears and swords. Some began firing arrows and slinging stones again.

"Shields up!"

A cloud of stones and arrows began arching through the sky and raining down on the area, invisible to the Mayans, where the Spaniards were crouched below the rise. Ordas stretched the interval as far as he could, trying to buy the gunners time to reload. When it was clear the Mayans were recovering and beginning to move forward again he called, "Arquebusiers: Fire!" The arquebuses were spaced out evenly along the gun line. When they fired in unison, the noise was loud but not nearly as fearsome as the initial firing of the guns. The Mayans flinched but didn't panic. Nevertheless, the twenty shots plowed furrows through the Mayan ranks and the Indians who saw compatriots fall beside them stopped running forward and began wailing for the loss of their fellows.

"Crossbowmen! Fire, and keep firing!" Dozens of bolts began finding their marks in the Mayan ranks. The brightly painted quilted padding of the foot soldiers and the parrot feathers festooning the chiefs offered little protection from the crossbow bolts.

The Mayans were discovering that their enemy had no regard for the fighting practices they had followed for centuries. Standing tall, making yourself look as big and fearsome as possible, challenging an enemy whose warriors were also standing, confronting you, looking for someone to take you on man to man; these strategies now were nothing more than an invitation to be killed. They needed to learn new methods and they needed to learn them quickly.

The Mayans who had dropped to mourn a comrade or to pray to their gods had survived the worst of the onslaught. "Down! Lie down!" they called to their companions. Some of them grabbed handfuls of dust and tossed it into the air to further obscure their positions. Others quickly copied them.

Ordas suddenly had no enemy to aim at. "Gunners! Lower your muzzles! Now. Move!" Men jumped to knock wedges out from under cannon barrels. Before they were even lined up again Ordas commanded "Fire when ready!" The guns boomed out again, in ones and twos, sending iron five-pound balls skimming and bouncing through the grass. Burning wadding flew from the barrels and started fires in the grass in front of some of the guns. The white smoke from the grass fires mixed with the dirty gray gun smoke from the cannons and the arquebuses. Added to the dust thrown up by the Mayans, visibility dropped to zero.

Ordas was in a quandary. Where was the cavalry? What if he fired blindly into the smoke just as the cavalry charged into the smoke from the other side? He looked around and his gaze fell on Felipe and Pedro. "You!" Felipe started to step forward. "No, not you, boy. You!" Pedro ran to him. He handed him a yellow flag on a stick. "Run to that end of the line," he said, pointing toward the river. "Get past the smoke and look for the cavalry. I need to know where they are. If you see them getting close to the range of the guns, wave that flag and I'll suspend firing. Go!" Pedro ran off to the west.

In his haste to reload, one of the men on Alaminos' crew kicked over the water bucket and it rolled empty practically to Felipe's feet. Felipe picked it up and filled it from the small creek that ran behind their position and ran it back to Alaminos.

"Thank you, Felipe." To his crew Alaminos said, "All of you: The work is only going to get hotter. Get a drink now while it is still clean."

Immediately, the next gun crew over called. "Boy! Water!" Soon he was running back and forth from the creek to the soldiers at the guns, water slopping over his feet as he ran.

"Load shot!" Ordas called. He didn't specify who should load with shot. Some of the faster arquebusiers had already reloaded with lead balls. The rest interrupted their reloading process and dumped gravel and nails – shot – down their bell-shaped barrels instead of a ball. They rammed down rag wads to hold it in place. "Crossbowmen! Reload but hold fire! Arquebusiers! Hold fire! Gunners! Load with shot and hold fire! Hold until you can see what you are shooting at!"

Felipe recognized most of the commands but not enough to grasp the tactics. What he did understand, however, was the urgency in Ordas' tone. Surely Cortes' cavalry should have been here by now? He scanned the left end of the line, looking for the yellow flag but didn't see it. And Pedro had not returned. Felipe worked his way back to Alaminos.

Suddenly the stones of the slingers stopped falling. The blood-curdling war cries rose in volume. Waving their obsidian-studded war clubs and shaking their spears thousands upon thousands of Indians materialized out of the smoke. Their hair was plastered flat and painted glossy black. Some of them had red and white stripes running down their cheeks. Others wore headdresses designed to make them look like parrots, frogs, or jaguars. Some wore quilted armor, others wore only paint. From the brief explanation of Chimalatl, Felipe thought he knew from the markings which ones were experienced warriors and which were youngsters engaged in their first battle. But it hardly mattered. There seemed to be a thousand charging toward each gun.

And Felipe thought he saw a face he recognized.

CHAPTER THIRTY FIVE

If Chimalatl had gotten back to Lord Taxmar quickly, perhaps he could have prevented it. Perhaps he could have influenced Taxmar's thinking. Chimalatl was wise and Taxmar had always trusted his counsel. But Chimalatl wasn't there. He and his men were taking their time bringing their wives home from Kutzumal.

After Felipe and Aguilar left, Ox-Ha-té's father, Lord Taxmar, king of the Yucatán city of Yaxunah, began to have second thoughts about letting Felipe go. It was true that he also missed the daily entertainment from Saint Aguilar the Castilano, but he could live without that. It nagged at him that he had given up Felipe.

He had promised the gods he would sacrifice Felipe. Then, overcome with gratitude for the boy's saving his son's life, he had reneged on that promise. And things had begun to go wrong as soon as the child prophet left. One of his wives suddenly fell ill and died. Then his oldest son, the next in line to be king, suffered the same fate. Now the younger boy Ox-Ha-té was next in line to be king.

Taxmar became obsessed with the idea that Felipe was the key. It was the status of the boys as prophets. Seeing his son on a leash in the hand of the Castilano had shaken him. Ox-Ha-té's cryptic prophecy about a black menace haunted him. Taxmar became convinced that his son had to rise up against his new master and throw off that leash, or the Mayans were doomed to be enslaved to the Castilanos.

And no one but Ox-Ha-té could defeat Felipe, he was sure of it. He could send ten thousand warriors against him and the boy would defeat them as surely as he had defeated Chaac. But Ox-Ha-té had also defeated Chaac by climbing alive from the cenote. So Ox-Ha-té could defeat Felipe.

Where would he be now? By now they would have left Yucatán in their floating houses. Felipe had assured him he would do his best to convince his chief to avoid Yucatán. Apparently he had done so. If the Castilanos had attacked anywhere in Yucatán Taxmar would have heard of it. Perhaps they had gone home? But if that were true, this feeling of dread would have left him.

No. They had to be attacking his brothers on the other side of the river. He would send an army to find them. If they weren't at Potonchan, the army would continue west until they found them.

And at the head of the army, Lord Taxmar would place young Ox-Ha-té, a boy of only fourteen summers. Go across the river and support your brothers in Potonchan against the Castilanos, he told him. For the salvation of your people you must find Felipe and bring him back here alive. If he will come, bring him. If he will not, kill him. Do this and you will be king. Fail, and you will live your life as a slave.

Felipe's death would be the salvation of his people. But if Felipe continued alive, Lord Taxmar was sure, he would somehow bring the end of the Mayan world.

***

The cavalry had gotten bogged down.

Cortes had led them into the trees that bordered the river. They picked their way south through the jungle, keeping out of sight of the Indian army off to their right marching north on the plain. They couldn't see them but they could hear them singing, screaming, chanting and dancing. It seemed to take an incredibly long time for them to pass. The sixteen horsemen rode quietly, single file, slashing at vines and swatting mosquitoes. Majesty threw his head up and Cortes, knowing he was about to bugle their presence, yanked sharply on the rein. Majesty snorted, but his neck relaxed and he settled back to plodding forward.

When he finally judged that the bulk of the Mayan force was past Cortes turned right and started leading the horsemen back to the plain. That was when they realized they had cut themselves off.

At first, the ground was just soft. But the further they pushed west, the muddier and wetter it got. The plain was so close – it looked like they were not more than thirty paces from it. But those thirty paces were a swamp. Forward through the swamp, or retrace their steps to more solid ground? Cortes made the decision: They pushed forward.

The water got deeper. Fortunately, it came no higher than Majesty's chest. Another dozen steps and it began to drop. Soon they were back to a light brown, knee-deep mud that coated the horses and riders in white as it dried. Finally, after what seemed an eternity, they were back on solid ground. But they were far behind the Mayans.

***

The Spanish army was facing a mass of humanity unlike any they'd ever seen before.

"Fire!" Ordas ordered. The five cannons roared, mowing giant paths through the Indians. Again, Mayans fell dead, injured, or just terrified. Thousands wailed and fell to the ground, covering their ears. But more pushed forward. When they were almost close enough to touch the cannons the points of pikes, lances and halberds suddenly sprang up at an angle, the butts firmly planted in the ground, creating a wicked fence to protect the Spanish line. Arquebuses and crossbows fired, taking down a hundred more, and the Mayans fell back. But still those in the rear pressed forward.

"Reload!" Soldiers pulled their swords and slashed threateningly as the hoards pressed in, keeping a clear space for the gunners who feverishly swabbed and poured, rammed and loaded the guns.

"Ready!"

And then Hurricane whinnied.

When the Mayan stones and arrows were falling, Felipe had taken Hurricane and crawled under a wagon. But when the sky cleared of missiles his curiosity had gotten the better of him. He and the horse had crawled out to see better.

"Wait!" Felipe screamed. Ordas heard him and turned quickly to look, thinking that perhaps some of the Indians had gotten behind them. But that wasn't it. Hurricane had smelled his mother, Felipe was sure of it. He waved both arms. "Cavalry! The cavalry is coming!"

"Hold Fire!" Ordas called. There was a pause in the fighting. The Mayans, too, seemed to sense that something had changed. Perhaps they heard something or smelled something. Perhaps it was simply that the throng that had been pressing them forward was no longer pressing. Then Felipe felt the slight tremble under his bare feet, and he knew instinctively it was something the Mayans had never experienced before.

Sure enough, the native warriors were glancing down. Felipe heard some of them say, "Earthquake!" Then the Mayan warriors at the rear started screaming.

***

The survivors of the battle in the city of Potonchan a few days before had told stories of the horses. Never having seen horses before, however, their stories were not accurate. A few described them as large hornless deer, with armor. Some of those most terrified by them tended to compress the details of the horses with those of the cannons. They told tales of roaring, fire-breathing monsters as tall as houses, monsters that shook the ground when they ran.

Melchior wasn't much help. He was terrified of horses. The others saw the fear in his eyes even as he tried to tell them that the horses and guns didn't matter – that there were only a few Castilanos, and that the Mayans outnumbered the invaders by a hundred to one. But being from the tribe on the Yucatán side of the river, his advice was met with skepticism. In the end, the Mayans had decided that, no matter what monsters the newcomers had, they were a tiny nuisance and could easily be overwhelmed.

The roaring of the guns had been shocking. It had begun to convince the non-believers that there might be something to the stories about the strangers. But those who survived the initial onslaught of the guns regained their confidence. There were, after all, thousands upon thousands of warriors, and only a handful of the interlopers. The stories about fire-breathing beasts were simply not true.

But feeling the ground shake beneath them brought back all the fear of the fireside stories of the night before. Hearing the hoof beats as the sixteen horses charged into their ranks from behind caused even the most seasoned warriors to quail. How could the enemy be in two places at once? And when they finally saw the tall, metallic-skinned creatures sporting long silver swords and surrounded in white halos as the drying, caked mud disintegrated into dust, it was too much. Hundreds, then thousands of terrified natives screamed, dropped their weapons, and ran.

They weren't particular where they ran. Many of them ran straight ahead, away from the horses, straight onto the pikes and lances of the Spanish line. Those who kept their wits and their weapons fought the Spaniards. But they were no longer fighting to capture Castilanos, or even to kill them. Their motivation now was simply to get past the Spanish battle line and away from the dreaded horses.

Others ran west, away from the river, away from both the horses and the battle line. But a running man cannot outrun a horse for long. This was the type of fighting Cortes had had his cavalry practice over and over. And now they were in their element.

***

The face Felipe had thought he had seen was Ox-Ha-té. He saw him again now. His first instinct was to raise a hand to wave at the boy who had bullied him, the boy with whom he had bonded after pulling him out of the cenote.

But the look on Ox-Ha-té's face now told a different story. In just the short time they'd been apart, Ox-Ha-té had changed from a boy to a young man – a man intent on getting to Felipe. What he would do when he reached him was unknown. But his face told a grim story.

Felipe didn't flinch. He stood and faced the older boy. A Spanish soldier swung his sword at him and Ox-Ha-té dodged it as easily as Felipe had seen him move on the ball court, swinging his shield around, knocking the Spaniard to the ground and continuing to press forward, intent on his quarry.

Over his shoulder Felipe saw a rider appear, slashing through the massed Mayan throng. Horse and rider were both ghostly white. Some of the Spaniards pointed and began calling "Santiago! Santiago!" as if the long dead disciple had appeared to fight with the Spanish. Felipe understood the confusion: the Spanish herd included no white horses. But he quickly saw through the foolishness of the supposed miracle, as he recognized Majesty and Cortes under the coating of white mud. Cortes lowered his lance and rode directly toward Ox-Ha-té's unprotected back.

"No!" Felipe sprinted forward. But Ox-Ha-té had already sensed the horse behind him. Unlike so many of his comrades, he didn't try to run. He turned on his heel and dropped to the ground, and thrust his obsidian-tipped spear up into Majesty's chest.

"NO!" Felipe screamed. Majesty screamed, too, and reared impossibly high, dumping Cortes unceremoniously onto the ground before falling half on top of him.

Felipe was in shock, staring at the scene. Ox-Ha-té looked at the horse and rider on the ground, then looked back at Felipe, and made up his mind. He turned toward Felipe, to finish his mission.

He never saw Alaminos.

Alaminos had turned from the fighting behind his gun when he heard Majesty scream. He already had a halberd in his hand, and Ox-Ha-té was a threat. The halberd swept through the air and buried itself in Ox-Ha-té's side. The boy who thought he was a man crumpled to the ground.

"The dark menace was white," Felipe heard him say. Felipe ran to Majesty, who was trying to stand. "Easy, boy," he said, tears streaming down his face. "Take it easy, you'll be okay."

"Get him off me," Cortes commanded. "Now! Move him!"

Alaminos grabbed Cortes under the arms. Felipe persuaded Majesty to roll a bit and Alaminos pulled the Captain-General free. Majesty flopped back down, and Felipe patted him. "Good boy." Through his tears, Felipe saw a blurry shadow behind Alaminos, raising a spear. In an instant, Felipe reached around to his back and his Toledo knife flashed through the air, burying itself in the arm raising the spear.

Kabil dropped the spear and stared stupidly at the knife protruding from his bicep. Before the pain had even registered, however, Cortes' sword ended his life.

Felipe's brain stopped. He couldn't make sense of what he was seeing. Majesty injured, Kabil dead, Ox-Ha-té dead or dying. What was Kabil even doing here? Apparently he'd followed Ox-Ha-té into battle. But why was Ox-Ha-té here?

But none of that mattered. He had to save Majesty. He turned back and dropped to his knees beside the stricken horse and placed a soothing hand on his neck.

And a sling stone fell out of the sky, struck his head, and the world went dark.

CHAPTER THIRTY SIX

He woke in the dark, in a house. He tried to sit up and his head throbbed. He groaned and flopped back down again.

"So, you decided to live, did you?" Alaminos dropped a cold wet rag on his face and Felipe held it to the large, tender lump on the top of his head.

"What happened?"

"One of the Indians flung one last rock, and you tried to catch it."

Suddenly Felipe remembered, and he sat up straight in spite of the pain. "Majesty!"

"Just calm yourself, boy. You need to focus your attention on mending."

"Where is Majesty? Who's taking care of him? I have to go see him!"

Alaminos came over and firmly pressed Felipe back onto the bed. "There is nothing you can do for Majesty now."

"Where is he?"

"Well I don't imagine anyone moved him. He's probably lying where he was the last time you saw him. What are you planning to do – bury a horse all by yourself?"

Tears ran down Felipe's face. "He's dead, then?"

"Boy, we had a bit of a fight on our hands. We couldn't just stop and begin caring for a horse. All I had time to do with you was toss you into that supply cart you were supposed to stay under."

"Tell me what happened."

Not much to tell. The Indians ran. The cavalry chased them."

"No, before that. What happened to Ox-Ha-té and Kabil? Were they really there, or did I dream that?"

"I don't know who those people are."

"The one who stabbed Majesty. And the one who was about to stab..."

"The other one who was planning to stick me? You saved my life, by the way, throwing your knife like that. That's two I owe you. I cleaned up your knife. It's over there." He pointed to a table across the room.

"So I killed them."

"No," Alaminos said patiently. "You didn't kill anybody. The one that stabbed Majesty, the one that I punctured, was probably picked up and patched up by the Indians when they went out to collect their wounded. The other one, the one you saved me from, well, you didn't kill him, either. You just slowed him down. Cortes finished him off. I grant you he was little, and I don't know what they were thinking sending a child like him into battle. But he would have killed me just as certain as if he was a grown man. I don't think the Captain-General is going to lose any sleep over him. Anyway, after that the Captain took El Arriero from Avila and he and the cavalry chased the Indians south for a while. They finally stopped running and threw down their weapons. They started bowing and calling out gibberish. Aguilar was sent for. He said they wanted peace. Cortes told them to send their chiefs, and to bring lots of gold. So tomorrow we should all be rich."

"That was this afternoon?"

"You're missing a day. Yesterday was spent patching up the wounded and mixing more gunpowder and fixing whatever broke."

"Where are we now?"

"We're about a league south of where we were yesterday. We're in a smaller town here called Centla – I guess it was the town's name, not the name of that plain we were on, but we didn't know. Anyway, the locals ran off. We moved in. The Captain-General ordered the ships completely unloaded and everything moved here. He's kept the sailors busy bringing boatloads up-river – pretty much everything that wasn't nailed down. Which makes me wonder."

Felipe stood. The room spun for a bit. But he hung on until it settled down. "I have to go find Majesty."

"When you're well. First you eat, then you sleep some more, then we'll see."

***

Alaminos had learned that Felipe was resourceful and determined. He dragged a chair over in front of the door and slept in it to prevent the boy from going out in the dark to search for Majesty. But Felipe had slept the clock around and he was wide awake. When Alaminos went out to relieve himself, Felipe slipped out the door.

He followed his nose and ears to the horses. A temporary corral had been set up by running a rope from tree to tree. Most of the horses were dozing on their feet, some were lying down, but he knew instinctively that none of them was Majesty. Nevertheless he slipped under the rope and peered closely at each of the dark horses just to make sure. Majesty wasn't there. He headed north.

The sky was just thinking about turning gray when he arrived at the spot where the battle had been. At least he believed it was the spot. Half the plain had burned. The dead and wounded had been collected on both sides. Dropped weapons had been collected. The ground was a morass of boot prints, hoof prints and drag marks. The only landmarks he was sure of were the pairs of deep grooves worn in the ground where each of the guns had recoiled. About three paces to the left of the center gun was where he remembered Majesty falling. There were a lot of dark patches where people had bled. Felipe imagined that one of those marks might have been where Majesty had bled. But Majesty wasn't there.

When he returned to Centla he started looking for Cortes, but Pedro intercepted him. "Ah! There you are. How's your head? Come with me. We have horses to tend."

"Have you seen Majesty?"

"I'm sorry, little one. I thought you knew. He was hurt in the battle, the same time you were."

"Yes I know, but where is he now? I just went to where the battle happened, but he is not there."

"I don't know. I didn't see him. I was busy tending other horses that got cut. Maybe he got up on his own and ran off." Pedro thought it more likely, but did not say, that Majesty had probably limped off somewhere and died. "I assure you, he is not with the other horses."

"I need to find Cortes."

Pedro looked at him, hard. "*Señor* Cortes is too busy for you. You need to wait."

"I need to see him now. He killed my horse."

Pedro placed a hand firmly on his arm. "Listen to me, boy. Two soldiers died in that battle. Nearly a hundred were wounded. Señor Cortes has all of them weighing on his mind. He does not need to deal with unfounded accusations from a child. You don't even know what happened to Majesty. Now come along. Stop this nonsense. We have horses that need looking after."

Reluctantly, Felipe followed Pedro to the corral. Seeing it in daylight his heart immediately went out to the horses. Some of them had been brushed but some had not. All except Hurricane looked exhausted. Several had cuts. Hurricane, Felipe noticed, was nursing from a mare that was due to foal in a few weeks rather than from his mother.

"Here," Pedro pointed. "Take care of Isabella."

Dried sweat coated both Isabella's sides. Her mane and tail were tangled and full of dried leaves and dust. She had a rag, stiff with dried blood, tied roughly over an ugly gash that started on one foreleg and ran across her chest. Felipe eased the crude bandage away to examine it. Then he straightened and patted her shoulder.

"There's nothing you can do for her," old Estefan chose this moment to appear. "I already looked at that. She's comfortable enough for now but it's not going to heal right. Won't never heal at all. That leg's hot and it's already starting to swell. She should be put out of her misery."

Felipe turned on him angrily, waving a finger under his nose. "You keep away from her! She'll be fine if you leave her to me. We're not losing any more horses!"

Estefan shrank back from the boy's anger. "Fine," he said. "You take care of her." He turned to leave. "But don't blame me when her leg rots and falls off," he mumbled. And he walked away.

"You're going to be just fine, girl." Felipe patted her neck. "Let me get you fixed up." He spotted a patch of aloe out in the sunlight. He sliced off several of the fat leaves and cut away the spines and outer skin. Isabella's skin quivered when he placed the cool slime from inside the leaves against her wound but she showed no other reaction. He bound the poultice in place with a clean cloth as she munched on some grass. Then he set to work on her coat, tail and mane.

***

Felipe was still determined to speak to Cortes but, thanks to Pedro and working with Isabella, he had calmed down and could think more clearly. He set off to determine the best place and time to confront Cortes, rehearsing in his head how he could politely ask about Majesty.

Cortes' tent had been set up as his headquarters in the form of a *mirador* – the back and both sides down, the entire front open and staked up to form an awning. The shaded front of the tent was facing the plain and the tent's back was almost touching the jungle. Felipe could see the folding stool and the trunk he used as a desk. Currently, Diaz was seated on the ground opposite the stool, using the top of the trunk to write something.

Cortes wasn't in the tent. He was standing in the clearing in front of his tent, speaking through Aguilar. "What is it with you people?" He spoke loudly. Before him, prone in the grass, lay a dozen Mayans dressed in rags. Their faces were painted black and their noses practically touched the ground. They had brought an offering: twenty slave girls, seated on the grass nearby, each carrying a gold chain and a clay cup full of red, green and pale blue gems.

"I said I wanted to see the chiefs – the chiefs, do you understand? Not beggars," Cortes said as Aguilar translated. "The chiefs will come tomorrow morning, one hour after dawn." Aguilar knew from experience they didn't use hours, so he pointed to a fork in a nearby tree on the east side of the clearing.

"When the sun crosses that branch, no later," Aguilar said.

"And each chief will bring a handful of gold, do you understand? One handful per chief!" Then he turned on his heel and went back to his tent.

"He is a brave, devout man," Aguilar tried to explain to the Mayan emissaries. "But the Castilanos have a disease that can only be cured by gold."

As if to emphasize the point, Diaz showed up just then with a sack and started taking the gold and gems from the women. The emissaries bowed and quickly left.

One of the slaves, a short woman of about thirty with a shaved head, spoke up as she rose from the ground. "We understand the thirst for gold. The *Mexica* have the same disease."

"The Mexica?" Aguilar asked.

Another young woman stood. She was tall and striking. Felipe decided she was prettier even than Anacoana, perhaps almost as pretty as his mother had been. Her glossy black hair had not been cut or shaved. Unlike the other women who wore nothing but short skirts of palm fronds, the tall woman had a brightly dyed wrap of woven cotton hanging from her shoulders to her knees. "*They* call us Mexica," she said. "We call ourselves Aztec."

"I don't understand," Aguilar said. "Aren't you all Mayans?"

"I am not Mayan," she replied scornfully. "I am Malinalli. I am the firstborn daughter of a chief of the Aztecs. I should have become chief after him. But when he died the elders said I was too young. My mother remarried. When she had a son she sold me to these," she looked disdainfully at her fellow slaves, "these people, so her son could be chief. And now they are selling me to you."

"No, no, goodness me, not sold," Aguilar was flustered by this beautiful, powerful woman. "You have been, that is, yes, you are being graciously given the opportunity to accept, er, that is…" he finally ran out of words.

Felipe, who had been standing and listening, took up the conversation. "Excuse me, elder sister. Can you explain more about the Aztec people? You speak differently than these others. Do you also have a different language?"

Malinalli looked down at the handsome boy. He had lighter skin than the Mayans, but darker than the Castilanos. And he spoke to her respectfully, in a manner no one had in years. She dipped her head politely and answered. "My native language is called Nahuatl. I only learned their language five years ago."

And that one," Felipe pointed to the short Mayan lady who had made the remark about the Mexica having the gold disease. "Am I correct that her people do not like your people?"

"My people are the lords of these people. They pay tribute to us," she replied. At that, the short Mayan woman swung a fist at the tall girl. It never connected. Malinalli swiftly leaned to one side. As the fist sailed past her head, she pushed on the back of the woman's shoulder. The woman tripped over Malinalli's foot and sprawled to the ground. The Aztec girl fiercely growled something neither Felipe nor Aguilar understood. The older woman may not have understood it either but she stayed on the ground.

Malinalli continued as if she had not been interrupted. "The Aztecs, my people, conquered this land in the time of my grandparents. They built a city on a lake in the mountains, where the sun sets, at a place called *Mexico*. It is the greatest city in the world. The gods have decreed that…"

"What's going on?" Cortes had noticed the fight between the beautiful Aztec girl and the Mayan woman. Or perhaps he had simply noticed the beautiful girl.

"My lord," Aguilar said. "May I introduce Miss Malinch, that is to say, Marnal…"

"Malinalli," Felipe put in.

"Yes, Malinalli. She and these others are part of the gift to us, or to you, rather, from the Mayans. But she claims she is not Mayan, or that her people are not Mayan, but I never heard of…"

Cortes turned to Felipe. "Did you understand this the same way? Are there two different peoples in these lands who fight each other?"

"Yes, sir. She says her people are called Aztecs. They have a different language. They live up in the mountains west of here. It appears they may have conquered the Mayans and force them to pay tribute. The Mayans are not happy about it."

Cortes nodded thoughtfully, and walked away. Then he came back and addressed Aguilar.

"Does she speak the language of these Aztecs?"

"Why yes! Yes she does. She was just saying…"

"And this is a language you do not speak?"

"No, I'm sorry, I don't." Aguilar said.

Cortes nodded again. "Deliver these women to the officers. Make sure they understand they are slaves, and that fighting and talking back will be severely punished. This one," he pointed at Malinalli. "This one especially: make sure she understands obedience. Then bring her to me."

Felipe's heart sank as he watched Cortes walk away. He knew Cortes well enough by now to know what he was thinking. And he knew Cortes' plan would only take him still further from his father.

CHAPTER THIRTY SEVEN

"There are different tribes of Mayans. They don't get along. The Aztecs play on their petty differences to get them to fight with each other. They fight each other mainly with the object of taking captives. And it is all so that they can send the captives as slaves, to pay their tribute to the Aztecs."

Cortes and Diaz were talking inside the tent and Felipe was listening outside the back wall. The sun had just gone down. Cortes had spent the afternoon with Diaz, Aguilar, and Malinalli. Aguilar had been sent away, and now Cortes was summing up what he'd learned.

"Which tells us what?" asked Diaz.

"The Aztecs need the slaves for their blasphemous sacrifices. But they also need the goods the Mayans produce, their crops. They could use the slaves to grow their own crops but they don't. They sacrifice them and *buy* the Mayan goods, with gold. If they are paying gold for food, they must have an abundance of it. Mines. The mines, the source of the gold, are up the mountain, in Aztec land, this Mexico."

They were speaking in Latin, because Cortes still didn't trust that the beautiful girl didn't understand Spanish.

And Felipe was listening because he had learned not to trust Cortes.

When Felipe thought about how he had almost begun to admire Cortes, he was disgusted with himself. What had completed his transformation was the conversation that afternoon.

***

When Aguilar had left Cortes' tent, Felipe had decided it was the right time to approach Cortes about Majesty.

"Sir?"

"Ah! Felipe. Good timing. My other interpreter has stepped away and I wish to continue my conversation with this delightful girl."

"Yes, sir. Um, sir? Before that: I need to know what happened to Majesty."

"Majesty? Oh! My horse. You know as much as I do. One of the Indians stabbed him. Probably still lying where he fell, I imagine."

"He's not. I looked."

"Well, how should I know? What am I supposed to do about a dead horse?"

"So then: will you release my father?"

Cortes stopped, dumbstruck. "Your father? Who on earth? What does your..." Then he remembered; remembered where and how he had acquired Majesty, and how he had come to know Felipe.

"Your father," Cortes sneered, "if I recall correctly, is in prison for failure to pay a debt. I don't see how one dead horse would change that. I will be riding El Arriero from now on, but I'm sure your services as a groom will continue to be needed."

"You took Majesty as collateral, sir, and now you cannot return him. The law, in the book of Exodus, requires that you either cancel the debt or repay my father fourfold the value of the collateral."

Cortes glared at Felipe. Felipe held his gaze and refused to look away. Cortes didn't remember reading any such thing in the Bible. Yet Felipe had demonstrated before that his knowledge of the Bible was encyclopedic. And while Cortes wasn't bound by biblical law he did recognize Spanish law, which was even stricter about caring for livestock held as collateral. Cortes pondered for a moment, then smiled.

"Felipe, I certainly owe a great debt to your family. You're right: It is not proper that I have enjoyed my victories on the back of your father's property while your father still languishes in prison. Diaz, write this down."

Cortes then dictated to Diaz: "Write the usual, 'To his majesty, etc,' and a copy to be forwarded to Velasquez in Santiago." Then he switched to Latin: "'The prisoner, Miguel Ferrer, having failed to repay what the court decreed for the assault on my person, has been living on the kindness of the government too long. Being unable to repay his debt and restore his place in Society, he is to be executed immediately and his estate sold at auction.'"

Felipe kept his face perfectly blank, giving no hint that he understood the death sentence just handed down on his father. He watched intently as Diaz scribbled on a scrap of paper.

Cortes reverted back to Spanish. "Write that out in fine, Father Diaz, on parchment, two copies, and prepare them for my signature and seal." He smiled at Felipe. "Court documents must be in Latin, and I'm afraid I don't write it well. That's what I have Diaz for. What it says is simply that your father's debt is paid in full and all charges against him are dropped. His time in prison will come to an end and his little farm will be restored to its rightful owner. I will see that the order is on the next ship to leave here. And I will personally pay my respects to your father the moment I return to Cuba. Now, if there is nothing else?"

"No," Felipe's voice squeaked, but he controlled it. "No, sir. Thank you, sir."

***

196

What had been a weight on Felipe's shoulders before was now a burden that threatened to crush him. He had to find a way to get back to Cuba and free his father. He would do whatever it took to make that happen. And that was why he continued to listen outside Cortes' tent.

"Speaking of the good Governor, Velasquez," Cortes asked. "What do you hear from his acolytes in our midst?"

"I heard the confessions of many of them today. Several of them are having second thoughts since the battle. Alaminos, for example, begged God's forgiveness for his not believing in you. He says now he is convinced God made you leader of this enterprise. Others too seem pleased about the progress we've made. They are assuming this new colony is simply an expansion of the Cuban territory of that abominable puppet Velasquez."

Cortes snorted. "They are pleased about the gold they've managed to pilfer."

"True. They don't seem to understand the significance of the mark you carved in the tree in Potonchan and the proclamation making it a province of our worthy sovereign."

"I'm glad they are content."

Diaz frowned. "You shouldn't be. Most of them are still loyal to Velasquez. As you pointed out, many have filled their own pockets with loot. Between their stolen gold and their legal shares in your venture, they have already seen a substantial return on their investment. They are happy to have been tested in battle and survived and now they believe it is time to return to Cuba."

Felipe couldn't follow the politics and his mind wandered. That afternoon, when the scheming priest Diaz had left Cortes' tent, Felipe had discreetly followed. He discovered the house Diaz had commandeered to be his temporary home, chapel and confessional. When Diaz left again, Felipe slipped in and found the two fine parchment copies of the death sentence. One was complete, ready for Cortes' signature. The other was about half finished. He studied them closely, memorizing every curl, slant and loop of the priest's handwriting. Then he found the priest's box of supplies and helped himself to three blank parchments, a quill, a block of red sealing wax and a small, unopened bottle of gum arabic. He had tucked the treasures into his bag and slipped out.

***

"...plan to keep them from going back to Cuba too soon?" At the mention of Cuba Felipe's attention snapped back to the present and now he didn't know what Cortes and Diaz were talking about.

"Perhaps if I order a snap inspection, or a strip search," Cortes said.

"That would not be wise. I think you would find that your own faithful followers enriched themselves just as much as Velasquez's sycophants did. Soldiers always feel they are entitled to loot."

"Perhaps just the ringleaders of the Velasquez party, then. If I hang a couple of them I'm sure the rest will find a new enthusiasm to follow me to the gold."

Diaz pondered that for a moment. "Allow me to suggest, rather than hanging them, we can put them to a better use."

"Go on."

"If we were to search their belongings quietly, without a fuss, then confront them privately and *threaten* them with hanging, I'm sure they would be glad of an opportunity to switch their allegiance and become your enthusiastic supporters."

Felipe struggled to keep up with what Diaz was suggesting.

"I see," Cortes said. "So, the ringleaders among Velasquez's men suddenly have a change of heart. They encourage the others to back me when I suggest we press our attack inland."

"More than that," Diaz explained. "We spoke earlier of the fate of this new colony. There are two different paths to governorship. Asking Velasquez to appoint you…"

"That will never happen. And even if he did, I would still be his vassal."

"I agree. The other way," he said, "works like this: Suppose a group of men, independent of any influence from you, of course, decided to plant the Spanish flag and claim this land as a *new colony* of Spain? They might call it Vera Cruz, since we have encountered so many false crosses. They would create a council and elect officials. Suppose they came to you and requested you to become the governor of this new colony?"

"The king might see that as disloyalty to Velasquez. Why would he agree to what amounts to insubordination in his ranks?"

"Yes, he might see it that way. It is a gamble. But if the Vera Cruz Council directly petitioned *the king* to recognize this as a new colony? If *they* told the king they had asked you to be their governor? What if your letter to the king acknowledges that their venture will not succeed without proper leadership? And you therefore advise *the king* that you have reluctantly submitted your letter of resignation to Velasquez and accepted their appointment to be their new governor. I can write out your resignation letter and attach it to the Council's request."

"Hmm. The king might see it as sidestepping the chain of command. What would be the benefit to him?"

"He will gladly accept your proposal if you send along with it *all* of his share of the expedition's gold. You might attach to it what is owed to Velasquez and ask the king to forward it to the governor. The king surely knows that, if his share passes through Velasquez's hands, a much smaller portion would find its way to Spain."

Cortes laughed. "And doing it that way, no doubt a portion of Velasquez's gold will stick to the king's fingers instead of the other way around. That would truly be just."

"By the time we sail back to Cuba a few months from now, Velasquez will have received your appointment letter from the king. When you step ashore in Santiago Velasquez will have no choice but to honor you as a dignitary, a Governor of another colony, an equal, rather than treating you as his errant messenger."

Cortes was silent for so long Felipe started to worry that the two men had left the tent. Then Cortes finally spoke.

"Yes. It is a good plan. Except for one thing."

"What is that?"

"I'm never going back to Cuba."

CHAPTER THIRTY EIGHT

Cortes had come for Felipe before dawn. He'd only just fallen asleep, having spent most of the night at Alaminos' table, carefully writing out two Latin documents on his valuable parchment. Alaminos hadn't come home all night. Felipe had held a piece of slate above the candle to collect soot and mixed it with the gum arabic he'd gotten from Diaz's room. He had worked out the wording by writing on the stone of the hearth with a piece of charcoal. Fortunately, he'd cleaned it when he was finished, so there was no writing there when Cortes showed up. As he drew each letter in ink on the parchment, slowly and carefully, he hadn't made any uncorrectable errors and the third parchment that he had 'borrowed' from Diaz hadn't been needed.

The version of the letter he'd written made it clear that Don Miguel Ferrer y Mendoza de Arjona had been unjustly imprisoned, that his debt was paid in full and he was to be freed at once and his estate and good name restored to him. As an afterthought, Felipe added, "As compensation for his wrongful arrest, the deed for one hundred caballerias of the Cortes estate is to be transferred to Don Ferrer's estate." One hundred Caballerias would measure about two leagues square – not worth quite as much as Majesty, especially with no way to work it, but it was better than nothing. And if Cortes meant it when he said he was never returning to Cuba, the land would go to waste anyway.

Felipe had been careful to copy not only Diaz's handwriting but also his phrasing. At a glance, the documents were very similar to the originals.

Now all that was needed was to somehow substitute it for Diaz's version, so that Cortes' signature and seal ended up on Felipe's version.

"I have a job for you," Cortes said. He turned on his heel and walked out, leaving the door open. Felipe scrambled to throw on his tunic and bag and strap on his knife. He hurried out the door, rubbing the sleep from his eyes.

"Yes, sir?"

"Follow me." Cortes marched away, Felipe hurrying to keep up. They entered the jungle behind Cortes tent and Felipe's heart caught in his throat. Had Cortes somehow determined that Felipe had been back there spying on him? Had someone seen him? Cortes cast about in a circle, finally settling on an opening beneath a nut tree, not even a pace away from the tent. "Here should do."

"Do?"

"That mare that dropped a foal a few weeks ago."

"Isabella?"

"Yes, Isabella. She should be back in heat by now. Yes? Good. Bring her here. Don't let any of the Indians see you. And keep her quiet. That's important, do you understand? No noise, either from you or the mare."

"Quiet. Yes sir. What are we doing?"

"We're putting on a little show for the Mayan chiefs. If they ever decide to show up." With that, he hurried off.

Felipe ran to the corral. Isabella was looking much better. Her eyes were bright, and there was very little heat in her right foreleg when he ran his hands down it. He replaced the aloe and bound it on with a fresh cloth. Then he untied her lead from the rope that served as the corral, held the rope up and led her under it. He watched her move as he led her to the spot Cortes had assigned him. She seemed happy to munch on the nuts that had fallen from the tree, and Felipe settled to the ground to wait.

***

Eight Mayan chiefs came shortly before midday. They were dressed brilliantly in bird feather cloaks and tall headdresses. Behind them came a retinue of nearly a hundred slaves, bearing roasted turkey, fruit, flowers, fabrics, and gold. Felipe, peeking through the small hole in the back of Cortes tent, watched the spectacle. One of the Spanish officers met the chiefs and called for Spanish slaves to come relieve the Mayans of their gifts. The chiefs bowed low to the officer, but he did not return their bow. Cortes was nowhere to be seen.

Then Felipe heard Cortes call from a distance away. The officer and the chiefs turned. Felipe looked where they were looking and saw Cortes waving them over. The officer led the chiefs over to where Cortes and Aguilar stood next to one of the five-pounder cannon and its gun captain. Felipe couldn't hear what was said but it didn't matter. Cortes nodded to the gunner and took a step away from the gun. Felipe saw the gun recoil before the enormous boom! reached him. He heard the ball whine as it sailed away from the town out over the jungle.

The Mayan Chiefs all fell to the ground and bowed to the gun. Cortes stood beside the gun, arms crossed, glowering, so that it looked as if they were imploring him. Which, perhaps, they were.

After that, Cortes became the genial host. He touched the shoulder of one of the chiefs, encouraging them to stand and follow him away from the gun. He led them to his tent.

They all seated themselves on the ground. Cortes sat on his camp stool. The officer who had initially greeted the chiefs – Felipe didn't know his name – served out pewter cups of sherry. The chiefs sniffed it and looked

201

suspiciously at Cortes. He raised his cup to them and drained it. The chiefs tasted the sherry, decided they liked it and gulped it down, loudly smacking their lips, laughing and talking.

"They are quite pleased with the sherry, sir," Felipe heard Aguilar say.

"As they should be. I have only four more kegs. No, don't translate that. Tell them one of our horses demands an audience with them."

"Sir?"

"Just tell them exactly that." Aguilar translated the odd message. Cortes gave no other explanation. But Felipe peeked through the hole in the back of the tent and saw Avila leading El Arriero out toward the meadow in front of the open side of the tent. Isabella got a whiff of the stallion and she raised and cocked her head. Felipe stood beside her head and patted her nose to keep her quiet, as instructed.

A few steps closer and El Arriero got Isabella's scent. He stared intently, straight into Cortes' tent, as if his eyes could bore holes straight through it to the space behind, where Isabella was. His ears came forward. He pawed the ground and began tossing his head. Avila held on firmly. El Arriero neighed loudly and jerked his head up, twisting right and left, nearly lifting Avila off his feet. He let out a bit of the lead and the stallion reared up and whinnied again, and again.

Felipe almost laughed at the drama, but he caught himself – Cortes had told him to keep quiet.

The chiefs were terror-stricken. They screamed and chattered incoherently. Several of them dropped their cups. They all fell on their faces, begging the horse to spare their lives, apologizing to it for whatever offense they had committed. Even Aguilar, who clearly wasn't in on the scheme, seemed terrified. The horse seemed to be looking directly at him.

Cortes subtly nodded at Avila, and he led El Arriero away. "His name is El Arriero and, as you can see, he is angry." When Aguilar translated this, the Mayans all spoke at once.

"One at a time, if you please," Aguilar said. "Sir, the gist of it seems to be that they are frightened out of their wits and wish to know what they can do to please the horse."

"El Arriero is not just angry at you," Cortes continued. "He is angry at me for sitting and drinking with you. He is a war horse. All he wants is to fight my enemies. I will explain to him, as I explained to you, that there is no need for you to be my enemies." He paused to let Aguilar catch up. "This is now the third time I have explained to you, you are not my enemy. You are subjects, whether you agree or not, of King Charles of Spain. If you agree, you have a powerful ally. Your land is his new land. We will call it New Spain. If you disagree, we will be just as powerful an enemy."

Some of the chiefs had regained enough composure to ask questions. "How did we become subjects of Spain? We are Mayans. Our king-"

Isabella chose that moment to drop a load of horse apples and Felipe decided it would be best to get her back to the corral before she gave the game away.

***

Back at the house he found Alaminos nursing a hangover from the night before. While sherry might be scarce, the conquistadors had found that nearly every house in the abandoned town of Centla had clay jars of *pulque*, fermented cactus juice. And one of the buildings the soldiers had entered had turned out to be an entire storehouse of the stuff.

Felipe filled in Alaminos on what he'd heard and seen, hoping Alaminos could make sense of it.

"Won't work," Alaminos said.

"What won't work?"

"The Captain-General's plan."

"You understand what Cortes is planning? Explain it to me."

"Velasquez revoked the permission for this expedition before we even left Cuba. That makes Cortes basically a mutineer. He knows when he goes back Velasquez will want to hang him. So he figures the way to make Velasquez happy is to return with gold – lots of gold. He thinks he has figured out that the gold in this country is all inland, somewhere just a little ways off, up in the mountains. Hike up the hill a few days, fire off a few rounds from the cannon, scare the natives with the horses, and we're all rich."

"What's wrong with his plan?"

"A couple things: First, we're already rich. Any man here who didn't snap up more than five years' wages in loot simply wasn't trying. There's gold all over the place. Look," he pointed to a mask hanging on the wall that looked like a gleaming, bug-eyed frog. "Gold. Not pure, but worth more than Majesty. It has some sort of jewels for eyes, and they're probably worth more than the gold. Take it. I've already got as much as I can carry."

"No thank you. I do not steal."

"It's not stealing. It's looting."

"Still. In any case, why does their having gold mean Señor Cortes' plan will not work? If they continue the expedition they will have more gold!"

Alaminos sighed. "For many of these men, this expedition was an investment. They have already had a good return on their investment. All they want now is to go back to Cuba, to their wives and children, brag about their battle and spend their riches."

"But Cortes is in charge, is he not? If he orders them to stay, they must stay."

"It isn't that simple. Think about all the stuff needed for this expedition, from ships to horses to gunpowder to bread. If Cortes could have afforded to pay for all those things entirely, himself, out of his own pocket, then yes, they would all be his soldiers, employees, or slaves and they would have to do whatever he says. And looting this gold frog," he stepped over and took the gold frog down from the wall and laid it on the table, "would be stealing from Cortes. But he didn't have the money to pay for this whole expedition. So, many of these men are not employees or slaves. They are investors."

"I guess I don't understand what 'investors' means."

"To get the money to buy ships and powder and everything else, Cortes approached other wealthy men. Men like Isabella's owner, Sedeño. He says to Sedeño, 'Give me your ship and the forty tons of food you have on board, bring your horse, and when we are finished I'll give you five percent of all the gold we find."

Alaminos pulled his knife and carved a small piece off the gold frog. "That will be your profit for using your money for the trip, Señor Sedeño." He proceeded to slice more pieces off the frog. "And Señor blacksmith, for your services, that is your piece; and Señor Alvarado, that's yours for the men and guns you brought, and Señor Martinez, that is your share for the bread and soldiers you brought,' and so on." The frog was getting smaller as the slices piled up in front of Felipe.

"Don't forget," Alaminos continued. "Cortes didn't simply come here on his own. He is not a pirate. He came with the king's blessing – in the form of permission from Velasquez." Alaminos chopped the head off the frog. "The king gets one fifth of all the profit. Of course, in this case, Velasquez expects the king's money to come to him first, and he will figure out a way to enrich himself from that share before sending on a much smaller 'fifth' to the king." He dug the two gems out of the gold eye sockets of the frog and put them in his belt, then pushed the eyeless frog-head to Felipe. "Your one-fifth, Your Highness."

"That would be stealing!"

"Of course. Happens all the time. Cortes sold more and more shares." Alaminos cut the body of the frog in half. One half he trimmed into smaller and smaller slices, and he pushed these across the table toward Felipe. "But he made sure to keep a good-sized share for himself." He picked up the lump that remained of the body of the frog and put it in his belt. "The wealthiest men on Cuba are friends of Velasquez. Most of them invested in this expedition. Many of them, like Sedeño, came along on this trip to protect their investment."

Felipe looked at the remains of the gold frog on the table. "Is that legal?"

"Perfectly legal."

"So why does this mean Señor Cortes' plan will not work?"

"Because he will be outvoted. He is technically in charge; but he is indebted to them. If they decide they have had enough of battle and wish to return home while they still can with their illegal loot and their legal shares, there is nothing he can do to stop them. And there is an added bonus: If they renounce Cortes as a mutineer when they get back to Cuba, he gets no share." Alaminos pulled the lump of gold from his belt and added it back to the sliced-up frog. "They all end up dividing a larger frog. Believe me, his plan won't work. We'll all be home in a month. If Cortes doesn't agree, they will sail away anyway and leave him here." Felipe wasn't happy at this news, and Alaminos could tell. "What's wrong? Don't you want to go home?"

"I want that more than anything. But Cortes has already written an order to execute my father."

CHAPTER THIRTY NINE

"FALL OUT!" The sun wasn't up yet but Felipe and Alaminos woke to a Sargento pounding on the door, yelling. "Fall out for battle drill! Fall out!"

Felipe rose from the hearth where he'd slept, donned his knife, belt and bag and headed for the door. Alaminos was still lying in the bed. "Come on, Señor Alaminos." Felipe shook his shoulder and the man growled and rolled over. "Come on, sir. We are being ordered to assemble."

Alaminos sat up and rubbed his eyes. "We're not soldiers. Why do we have to practice?" But he got up and dressed, carefully checking all the hidden pockets in his tunic and breeches and cape.

"Do you think we are going home now?"

"I think we're probably going to exercise the guns. Then I think Cortes is going to give a speech to convince the men of how much gold waits just over the horizon. And then the men are going to rebel. That's what I think is going to happen. But," he grinned. "It's always good practice to take everything with you when you are in the army, because you never know. Besides, this army is full of thieves. If I leave something here it will be gone when we get back. You're lucky you don't have anything." Felipe carefully avoided reaching to his bag to make sure the special gift from Taxmar was still there. Better to continue to be seen as a poor waif. He patted his knife, though.

When they stepped outside they found the Sargentos had been busy. Nearly all the soldiers and sailors were heading for the plain in front of Cortes' tent. Some of them had had the same thought as Alaminos: don't leave anything of value in the temporary quarters. Others had stumbled out instantly, only half-dressed.

Cortes was on El Arriero, riding slowly in a large circle around the plain. The Sargentos yelled and pushed the men until they formed a semi-organized battalion, following Cortes. He made three large laps in the field. By the time an hour had passed, the men were loosening up, and most of the native *pulque* had been sweated out of them. When Cortes arrived back in front of his tent, he stopped and turned the horse and faced the men.

Uncharacteristically, he smiled. "It has come to my attention," he began, "that some of you may have heard of a city of gold up in the mountains and wish to press on until we capture it."

The gathered soldiers and sailors began to murmur among themselves. A few even cheered. Cortes let them go for a moment before nodding to a sargento, who bellowed, "Silence in the ranks!"

"I was not taking a vote. I was merely explaining. A group of men came to me last night, claiming to represent most of you. They informed me that they have decided to declare this place a colony of Spain. They have formed a colony council. They are calling it Veracruz. And they would like me to accept the position of Governor..."

Felipe's spirits soared. Alaminos was wrong. Cortes was not going back to Cuba. He was going to send his messages somehow, but he was going to stay here. That meant that if Felipe could substitute his forged letter for the death sentence letter Cortes would not be in Cuba to contradict it.

Felipe quietly eased away from the grassy area and drifted into the jungle. At the back of Cortes tent, he peeked through the hole in the fabric to make sure Diaz was not there. Then he pulled his knife and made a small slit at the bottom, and wiggled inside. Staying low, keeping the trunk between himself and the hundreds of eyes of the men facing his direction, he started carefully searching.

There was a small pile of parchment documents resting on top of the trunk. A quill, a dish of ink and a dark red block of hard sealing wax sat beside a lit candle. There were two leather-bound strongboxes on the floor. One was closed and had red wax seals on its latches. The other was open. Peeking inside, Felipe saw several gold bars and more parchments, each folded into thirds and sealed. Keeping the propped open lid of the box between himself and the grassy parade ground he grabbed all of the documents and lay down on the floor. He squeezed each one, careful not to break the seal – just opening it enough so that he could peek in from the side to read a portion of the text. They all appeared to be addressed to the king. A couple of them were lists. One seemed to be the colony declaration Cortes had referred to. On the fourth one, he spied the name "Miguel Ferrer." He pulled it out, and put the rest of the stack back in the chest. He broke the seal and scanned it. It read exactly as he remembered. And Cortes had signed it.

He withdrew his forged documents from inside his tunic. He had folded his into thirds in exactly the manner as other papers he'd seen on Cortes' desk. The documents waiting to be signed, however, were still flat. He knew there was no way to un-crease his forgery. So he picked up the documents still waiting for signatures, creased them all in thirds and opened them again. Now his forgeries looked the same as the rest. He added his to the stack, tucked the genuine death sentence parchment into his tunic and eased out of the tent the way he had come. He circled through the jungle and rejoined Alaminos.

Cortes was saying, "I want you to know how proud I am of all of you for your accomplishments so far and I recognize what a sacrifice it will represent for those of you who wish to remain here and conquer this land for our king."

Murmuring arose again, and Cortes raised a hand to quell it. When it died away, he continued. "I know it is not the will of all of you. Having watched you fight the other day, however, I can say with confidence that none of you would be happy to abandon your fellows and go home for the sake of personal safety and comfort, when glory and riches lie in the other direction."

A cheer rose at that, though it wasn't shared by the majority. Cortes continued. "Accepting the assignment as Governor of this new land, however, would require me to step down from the post I have been assigned to by Governor Velasquez. That is not something I take lightly. So I propose to go-"

Cortes was interrupted at this point by Diaz, who stepped up to him and handed him a note. Cortes scanned the note then called to the sargento. He leaned down to him and gave him the note and some instructions.

The sargento called out, "Form two companies! If your name is called, form up on my left! If not, move to the right!" He then conferred with the other sargentos, and they went through the ranks calling out names and pushing men left or right. They ignored Felipe and Alaminos.

"What's happening?" Felipe asked Alaminos.

"Your guess is as good as mine. The names being called are all Velasquez men, though."

Once the two groups were clearly defined, Cortes called out, "Right company! You're dismissed. Left company! About face! We'll be marching north. Sargento, as soon as Father Diaz is done, take them double-time back to the battlefield and wait for me there." Diaz was walking past the troops, tossing holy water over their heads and making the sign of the cross.

"Yes, sir," the sargento replied.

"I'm going after them," Felipe said to Alaminos. "I need to know what he's planning to do."

"I'm going back to bed. You can tell me about it later."

But Cortes had other plans. He rode up to them. "Señor Alaminos."

Alaminos tossed off a casual salute. "Yes, sir?"

I have a mission for you. I hope you are carrying everything you wish to take."

"Yes sir. I'm ready to go wherever you send me."

"Good." Cortes turned in his saddle and pointed toward his tent. "Do you see those two strongboxes? I need you to bring them. They are very heavy. Felipe, fetch a horse. Bring the boxes to me on the beach."

"The beach, sir?"

"Yes. The beach closest to the ships."

"Yes, sir."

Alaminos headed for the tent, and Felipe walked beside him. "The seal," he said quietly.

"What?"

"He forgot to finish with the seal."

"How do you know that?"

"Never mind. He'll thank you. Catch him before he leaves. Tell him he forgot to finish signing and sealing." Then Felipe ran to get Alaminos a horse.

***

Before Felipe got to the corral he saw Pedro riding toward him on a plodding mare ironically called Lightning by the grooms. When Pedro saw him he yelled, "*Mostengo! Mostengo!* Some of the horses are loose! Come quickly and help."

"I can't," Felipe replied. "I am on a mission for Señor Cortes. In fact, I'm afraid I need to take your horse."

Pedro gawked at him. "But... the horses! We must collect the horses. Hurricane is missing. Isabella, two other mares. We must get them back. We cannot let the Indians get the horses."

"I understand. But would you disobey Señor Cortes? Please, Pedro. Please. I must take your horse."

Pedro shrugged and stepped down from Lightning. She was an old barren gray with a white face and stockings. Felipe knew she was easy to ride but very slow. Still, she was better than nothing.

As Felipe hopped on her back he asked Pedro, "How did they get away?"

"No one knows. We were short-handed this morning because of the drill. We didn't notice some of them were missing until the sun was well up."

"I'm sorry, Pedro. I'd help if I could, but I have to go. I hope you find them. Goodbye, my friend. Thank you for everything you taught me."

"You sound like I will never see you again."

"We'll see." Felipe couldn't imagine that Cortes would willingly give up so many of his men, even if they were supporters of Governor Velasquez. But he was marching them to the beach. If he was putting them on board a ship bound for Cuba, Felipe would do whatever he had to do to stow away.

When he got back to the parade ground, Alaminos was alone, the two boxes at his feet. Felipe noted that both boxes now had red splotches of wax on them.

"What took you so long?" Alaminos complained.

"Did he sign the documents?"

"Yes. Diaz stopped him before he left. Signed and sealed. El Arriero wasn't happy about being used as a writing desk. Now, help me get these aboard this beast. If I keep him waiting..."

Felipe tried to lift one of the boxes but it was way too much for him. Between them, they managed to lift a box to the top of a log. Felipe looped a piece of rope through the handles and tossed it to the other side of Lightning. Alaminos caught it and pulled, cinching the heavy load to the mare. Then Felipe walked her in a circle to get her other side next to the log and they repeated the operation.

"I guess I'm walking to the beach," Alaminos complained. He clucked his tongue and tugged on the rein, but Lightning refused to move.

Felipe got in front of her and held out some grass and talked sweetly to her, walking backwards. She stretched her neck out toward him with a little more enthusiasm. He tugged harder on the rein, and she grudgingly moved sluggishly forward. He encouraged her some more, trotting backwards in front of her, and she kept moving.

"I guess you're going to have to come along," Alaminos said. "But it's two leagues to the beach, you can't walk backwards the whole way." The young man never ceased to amaze him. It was like he spoke to horses. Felipe moved along easily, even though Alaminos could tell that his bag, the "bat-wing bag" that never left his side, slammed heavily against him with each step. Alaminos had no doubt he could run every step of the two leagues if need be, even carrying whatever treasure the boy had managed to loot.

***

They actually arrived at the beach at the same time the army did. Cortes had not marched them directly there. Instead, he took them back to the battle line. He had stopped there and given them another lecture about bravery and sacrifice. Then they'd marched back through the empty streets of Potonchan and he stopped them again in front of the Ceiba tree where they had withstood the initial onslaught of the Mayans – the tree where he had carved the mark of King Charles – and he explained to them what it signified. Then he allowed them to break ranks to scavenge some lunch. The men were surprised – it was as if he were giving them permission to steal whatever they could carry. When they returned to the square, their pockets loaded down, Cortes formed them up again. But he marched them, not back to camp as they expected, but further north.

When the men came huffing up to the beach they were exhausted, as Cortes intended, and they flopped down on the sand.

Then Cortes told them the real reason for the march.

"You men are here," he said, "because your names are on this list." He waved the piece of paper they'd all seen Diaz hand to him earlier. "This list was made by Father Diaz, accompanied by two sargentos. While you were on the parade ground this morning they searched your rooms. And in your rooms," he paused to let his message sink in, "they found loot you failed to turn in." Several of the men began to object loudly. But Cortes had prepared for this and a sargento stepped up on each side of him, pointing arquebuses at the throng on the sand. They quieted back down.

"You could be hanged as thieves. If I had you all searched right now, how many of you would I have to hang? But I'm not going to do that. I don't need thieves. I don't need any of Velasquez's self-serving boot-lickers. What I do need are men I can count on. I need men such as I saw the other day on the battlefield, men who can stand up to the worst the Indians can serve up, and take it, and beat them anyway. So: we are all here to give you a choice. I'm not going to hang you. The ships are right there. You can sail home to Cuba if you wish."

Felipe looked at the ships anchored in the harbor formed by the mouth of the Grijalva River, seeing them as his hope to return to Cuba and his father. No doubt the men were also seeing them as a lifeline, though they no doubt were weighing them against the experience they had just had, of picking up loot so easily.

Felipe noticed that ten of the ships were very close together, practically touching. He was sure they had been further apart when they had anchored originally. Only one was anchored separately, far from the rest; Sedeño's caravel *San Lazaro*.

"I had a report," Cortes continued, "that some of the ships have become infested with wood-worm. I sent the carpenter this morning to do a more thorough inspection to make certain they are seaworthy. I wouldn't want you to sink on your way home to Cuba. I expect his report momentarily."

Even as he said it, Felipe and Alaminos saw a rowboat pull away from the massed ships and head for shore. Before it arrived, however, something else caught everyone's attention: Smoke began rising from one of the ships. And then another…

"Fire!" Several of the men called at once. They jumped to their feet, as if there were something, anything, they could do about it from this distance.

Everything about a ship is highly flammable. The wood is dry. It is coated with tar and pitch and varnish. The seams are stuffed with old, dry rope soaked in tar. The flames greedily ate at the partitions, sails, spars and rigging, jumping from ship to ship until it seemed as if another sun was being born in the bay. The popping and crackling noises that carried to them over the water sounded festive. But the sight of the burning ships was as shocking and disheartening to the men on the beach as an icy downpour.

By the time the carpenter and his crew rowed ashore, the flames were already subsiding. One of the hulls listed sideways and hissed as it slowly slid beneath the surface.

The carpenter walked up to Cortes and saluted. "As you suspected, sir. Wood-worm throughout. Definitely not seaworthy."

211

"Thank you, Mr. Madera. Head back to camp."

The men turned, gray-faced, from the horrific sight offshore, to face Cortes once again. Some looked at the *San Lazaro*, free of flames, anchored far off upwind of the fire.

Cortes knew what they were thinking. How many of them could crowd aboard her? She wasn't very big. "Mr. Alaminos."

"Sir."

"It seems we are going to need new transport – enough for several hundred men and all the treasure we are going to find. I'm ordering you to sail straight to Spain and send help. Don't stop anywhere along the way. Give the king the kindest regards of the Governor of his new colony, and give him my dispatches. Ask him to send us new ships at his earliest convenience."

"I need a crew, sir."

"Indeed you do. Select a small crew from this lot – I believe you will find *San Lazaro* is fully provisioned for a crew of fifteen. That should be plenty, wouldn't you think? We'll need the rest here to defend ourselves until help arrives." He handed Alaminos a list of names. "I believe you will find that these men, and only these men, will make trustworthy companions."

He turned back to the men standing and sitting numbly on the beach. "As for the rest of you gentlemen, it appears you have two choices. You can rejoin your comrades in camp and make yourselves rich. Or you can walk back to Cuba." He pointed out to sea. "It's that way, I believe."

CHAPTER FORTY

Alaminos began calling out names. Cortes mounted El Arriero and turned to head back to Centla. He stopped next to Felipe. "Don't let any of these men convince you to give your horse to them," he said. "Walking back will allow them to reflect on their sins. I'll see you back in camp."

"Yes, sir," Felipe said. For the first and last time he deliberately lied to his master.

As soon as Cortes was out of sight several of the men clustered around Alaminos. "See here," one said. "I will lose thousands if I don't return to Cuba immediately! Take me with you, I beg you. I'll pay you five gold *reales* the moment we reach Santiago!"

"I'll pay ten!" another said. "Twenty!" said a third.

"QUIET!" Alaminos shouted. He looked up to make sure Cortes was out of sight. "I will take four of you on board. Four! And since that is nearly a third more than we are authorized, we will be on short rations for the entire trip. The fact that you have money does not mean you get extra water, understood? And I will not be taking any of you for a promise of pay. Now show me: Who has the most on him right now?"

Hands disappeared into hidden pockets, stitches popped on seams and gold and jewels were soon gleaming in the sun in the palms of a dozen hands. Alaminos made a mental note of who had how much wealth. But he was examining the palms as much as the riches. In an emergency he would need men who were not afraid of calluses.

One fellow waited until the selection was finished. Then he took off his cap and reached into it. He pulled out a green stone as clear as glass, carved into the shape of a fish. It nearly filled his soft, white palm. "I think this might convince you to take along one more passenger," he said.

"Emerald!" Felipe said.

Alaminos looked at him. "You know what this is? You recognize it?"

"No. I just know the word. I never imagined I would see one."

"Señor," Alaminos said to the emerald man, "you've earned a boat ride." And he snatched the emerald from the man's hand. He directed two of the sailors to load the strongboxes from Lightning into the boat the carpenter had left on the beach, and to take the boxes and the emerald man out to *San Lazaro*. "Bring back an extra boat so we can get this lot loaded. The rest of you, except for my crew: You don't want to keep Señor Cortes waiting."

One of the men had a bandage around his thigh and was limping badly. Felipe handed him Lightning's rein. "Señor Cortes gave strict instructions not to let anyone ride back to camp," Felipe said. "But I don't think he would thank either of us if you make your injury worse." The man thanked him and led the mare over to a log so he could mount.

Felipe fell in beside Alaminos as he walked along the beach waiting for the sailors to return with the boats. "Where do you think you're going?" Alaminos asked.

"Back to Cuba, please."

Alaminos didn't stop walking. He just shook his head as his eyes continued to scan the ground. "You heard the captain," he said quietly. "I have strict instructions to go directly to Spain."

"You'll be sailing right past Cuba. Besides, you don't seem to be under Captain Cortes' orders anymore."

Alaminos didn't say anything. He just kept walking. They came to a stream emptying into the bay, and Alaminos turned and followed it inland. After a few paces he spotted some white clay similar to what he'd seen Majesty coated in the other day. He bent down and scooped up a handful of it. Felipe wanted to know why, but he didn't want to interrupt Alaminos' thinking.

The boats returned as Alaminos and Felipe got back to the shoreline. Alaminos climbed into one, and Felipe climbed in beside him. "Did you not hear me, I said no one else…"

"I heard you," Felipe said. "I also heard the Captain say he would see me back in camp. It seems to be a day for disappointments."

"I can take you with me, but I can't stop in Cuba…"

"I also heard you before, when you said you owed me. Twice, I believe you said. Once for Ana…"

"Alright, alright. We'll see."

It took two more boat trips to get everyone on board the *San Lazaro*. Alaminos was relieved that the fifteen men on the list Cortes had given him were all capable sailors and they made short work of rowing the boats back and forth to the ship. When the last men were on board, they tied the carpenter's boat to the foot of the boarding ladder.

Alaminos gave the order to weigh anchor. Then he approached the man who had given him the emerald. "Did you enjoy your boat trip?"

"I'll let you know when we arrive."

"My apologies, Señor. You misunderstand me. That," he pointed down to the rowboat at the foot of the ladder, "is a boat. This," he gestured upward expansively to take in the deck, masts and rigging. "This is a ship. You paid for a boat ride, not a ship ride. And now you'll be going ashore. Take the boat upriver to the camp. I'm sure they will need it."

"You – this is thievery! You can't do this!"

"You make a fair point, no doubt. But I'm a navigator, not a legal expert. Be sure to file a complaint with Señor Cortes when you see him."

And he pushed the man overboard.

***

Pushing the emerald man overboard had a galvanizing effect on the other supernumeraries. It brought brutally home to them that this was not a pleasure cruise. When Alaminos ordered all sails aloft to catch the light offshore breeze every hand jumped to work eagerly. Sails had to be hauled up from below and laid out on deck. The four gentlemen who didn't know much about sailing allowed themselves to be ordered around by sailors they had always viewed as beneath them. They allowed themselves to be guided to the right lines to be handled. They pulled mightily on them until someone yelled at them to stop. And soon enough the *San Lazaro* was bearing away north, out to sea.

Once they were settled into a routine, Felipe walked into Alaminos' cabin. "Don't you knock?"

Felipe shrugged, apologized and flopped down in a chair. He surveyed the cabin. The two strongboxes were on the deck under the stern-lights – the aft-facing windows that allowed light into the captain's cabin. A ring on the side of each strongbox was chained to a ring on the floor. There was a small iron stove in one corner near the swinging platform bed. Oddly, considering the mild climate, Alaminos had lit a fire. The lump of clay he'd collected from the creek was in a pan on the stove drying out. Alaminos picked it up and examined it, then put it back in the pan. "What are you doing?"

"Old sailor's trick." But he didn't explain more.

Felipe came to the reason for his visit. "I'm sorry to make more trouble for you, but I need to call in the other favor you owe me." Alaminos looked at him suspiciously but said nothing. "I thought I could get my father out of prison. I thought the strongboxes were bound for Cuba."

"I don't understand. What difference does it make where they are headed?"

"I stole the papers Cortes signed that ordered my father's execution. I replaced them with documents ordering his release. I assumed Cortes was sending the strongboxes straight to Velasquez. But if you take my letters to Spain it will take a year or more before word gets back to Cuba."

"Where did you get it?"

"Get what?"

"A paper ordering your father's release?"

"I wrote it."

"How could you do that?"

"Do what?"

Alaminos exhaled loudly, exasperated. "How did you forge a letter from Cortes? Wait – don't tell me: you can read and write Latin?"

"Yes, I can."

Alaminos gaped at him. "How – You can read and write Latin? You can read and write Latin!" He shook his head. "I'm rich!"

"I thought you were already rich?"

"I'm richer." He shook his head. "The boy can read and write Latin," he mumbled to himself.

"What does that change?"

"I'll show you." Alaminos went back to the stove. He picked up the lump of clay and squeezed it slightly, molding it to his fingers. "Perfect." He took the lump of clay over to the strongboxes. He knelt down and examined each of the seals. "This one's the best," he said to no one. He pressed the lump of clay against the seal. Then he gently peeled it off and peered closely at the impression the wax seal had left in the clay. Satisfied, he took it back over to the stove. "Now we wait," he said.

"Wait for what?" Felipe asked. But Alaminos just smiled and shook his head. "The child reads and writes Latin. Of course he does."

***

When the small lump of clay was dry, Alaminos picked it up and inspected it closely. He used a knife to gently scrape smooth a few rough edges and then he nodded. "Looks perfect." He stepped over to one of the boxes and placed a handkerchief on the deck under the wax seal. Then he smacked the wax with the butt of the knife.

"What are you doing! The king…"

Alaminos ignored Felipe's objection. "You want your letter back, don't you?" He scraped off as much of the broken wax as he could, allowing the shards to fall onto the handkerchief. He did the same with the rest of the seals. Then he wrapped up the handkerchief and set it aside. "Now, we'll see what we see." He pulled a small iron tool from inside his vest and tinkered with the massive padlock for a moment and the hasp sprang open. He lifted the lid and looked inside. "Oh, you beauty."

Felipe had gotten up and looked down in the box also. The blacksmiths had been busy. They had melted all the gold that had been turned in and formed it into small bars. The bars were stacked up nearly to the middle of the box.

Each bar of gold was stamped with the letters "HC", a cross, then "BDC", followed by numbers. The numbers varied on each bar. "What does that mean?"

Alaminos explained. "It's to keep nefarious sea captains from shaving any gold off a bar. Diaz weighed each one and stamped it with the weight, his initials and Cortes' initials."

"Someone could just steal a whole bar, couldn't they?"

"They could. But somewhere in here is an inventory – a list of how many bars and such are in here. If I showed up in Spain with ninety-nine bars and the inventory says there are a hundred, I'd lose my head before the day was out."

That made Felipe feel better. Much as he liked Alaminos, he didn't want to help the man steal. But then his hopes were dashed.

"All we need to do is write a new inventory."

"Won't Cortes and Diaz have kept a copy of the inventory? What happens to you when they report back to the king?"

"Hmm, good point. Oh, well. I'll think of something. Here, make yourself useful." He handed the sealed documents to Felipe. "Don't open them, just look in…"

"I know. I did it before." Felipe peeked inside the folded, sealed documents. He hadn't seen these before. This was the strongbox that had already been locked when he invaded Cortes' tent. He finally found the one that sentenced his father to die. "This is it. The ones I made are both in the other box. So is the inventory."

"Show me."

Felipe set aside the death sentence and went through the papers in the other box. He quickly found the two forgeries he'd made, and the inventory list. "Here." He handed them, still sealed, to Alaminos.

Alaminos looked at the three sealed papers. "How on earth did you get Diaz to seal your forgeries?"

"I didn't. You did."

Alaminos thought about the papers Cortes had signed and sealed at the last moment. "Okay, which is the inventory?"

"I'm not going to help you steal."

"Do you want your father to rot in prison?" Felipe said nothing. He just pointed to the inventory. Alaminos set it aside. "Why are there two papers about your father?"

"Because Diaz had two – one addressed to the king and one to Velasquez. I don't know what that means. But I decided I needed to replace both of them. Except one of the boxes was already sealed. So I put them both with the other papers."

"Okay." Alaminos stepped over to the stove and warmed the tip of his knife. Then he carefully slid the point under the seal of the death sentence. He eased the wax blob free from the parchment without melting or cracking it and set it aside. "Might be useful later." Then he unfolded the document and handed it to Felipe. "Is this the death sentence?"

Felipe read it and handed it back. "Yes."

Alaminos stuck it between a couple books on a nearby shelf. "Nice piece of parchment. Never know when I might need one." He turned back to Felipe. "Can you tell without unsealing them which of your forgeries is addressed to Velasquez?"

Felipe picked them up and peeked in the sides. "This one." He handed it to Alaminos.

"You hang on to it. You're going to personally hand it to Velasquez."

"He'll never believe me. I'm a child. Besides, Cortes defied him. He will tear it up."

Alaminos continued as if Felipe hadn't spoken. "While you're at it, go through the rest of the papers and find all of them that are addressed to Velasquez or anybody else in Cuba."

They spent the rest of the day working on a plan to get Felipe home and get his father out of jail. Alaminos never said so, but Felipe was sure that somehow Alaminos was going to profit from the arrangements. But he couldn't figure out how.

***

The trip back to Cuba was mostly uneventful except for a short but violent squall that hit them when they rounded Cape Catoche at the northern tip of Yucatán. The storm blew them far north of their intended track. When it died away they were too far north and east to sail along the south coast of Cuba to Santiago. So Alaminos set a course along the northern coast. If the wind turned favorable, he explained to Felipe, he could round the eastern end and sail back to Santiago. What could have been a two week trip stretched into three weeks.

Alaminos' plan was complex. He convinced Felipe he would have to forge a new inventory. "We're not stealing anything. All we are doing is delivering it directly to Velasquez. We just need the inventory to explain that: so much in the box going to the king, so much in the box for Velasquez."

"But why?"

"You said you want Velasquez to take you seriously, right? If he focuses on his anger at Cortes he might do something wrong – such as leaving your father in jail. But if he's looking at a pile of gold, he's going to be feeling generous. Now, we need to make you look less like a beggar and more like an important emissary fit for an audience with the Governor of Cuba. Maybe I can get one of the sail-makers to sew you up some new clothes. Although I doubt if they have anything other than sailcloth."

Felipe reached into his bat-wing bag and pulled out the gift from Taxmar – the bright scarlet tunic. "Perhaps he can make this fit me?"

218

"Perfect! Is that what you've been lugging around this whole time? Why is it so heavy?"

Felipe had never dared open up the garment to see why it was so heavy. He'd assumed Taxmar had wanted to give Felipe some gold and had hidden it inside the garment so Felipe wouldn't be robbed. Until now it had seemed safest to leave it there. Now he took his knife and cut open the bulky hem. Inside was a heavy gold chain of intricately woven links, each as big around as his thumb. He draped the chain over his neck and it hung below his waist. Dangling from the end of it was a pendant of carved obsidian. He assumed it was an image of some Mayan god. But when he looked closely at it, he realized it looked like what a talented Mayan artist might have carved based on Aguilar's description of a horse. It actually looked a bit like Majesty.

They stashed the chain and obsidian carving in one of the strongboxes and Alaminos sent for the sail-maker. "Take this and make him a garment fit for a king," he said, handing the rich fabric to the sailor. He also handed the man a pair of tall black boots. "Cut these down to fit him." Turning to Felipe he said, "You can't show up barefoot for an audience with the Governor." The sail-maker returned with a scrap of wood and had Felipe stand on it while he traced around his feet. A couple days later, Felipe struggled into his new wardrobe.

The sail-maker was a miracle worker. He had fashioned the bright red tunic into a doublet. It was tight across Felipe's chest, but puffed out around his waist like a bowl. It had long, close-fitting sleeves, stuffed and squared off shoulders and a high collar. It closed with a dozen bright white buttons down the front that looked like ivory. "Turkey bones," the sailor shrugged. "It was all we could do on short notice."

The sailor had used some lightweight sailcloth to add contrasting lines at all the seams and stuffed a square of it in a pocket like a handkerchief. He'd also sewn up some white leggings to fill the gap between the bottom of the doublet and the tops of the boots. The toes of the boots had been shortened. The tops of the boots had been taken in along their entire length. They had been shortened somewhat but they still reached halfway past Felipe's knees. The sail maker had used some of the left over red material to fashion a small cap that flopped down to one side of Felipe's head. It, too, sported a turkey bone button.

Alaminos looked at Felipe's knife. It was clearly a quality knife but plain. From a small box of his personal belongings he pulled out some gold wire and wound it around and around the grip. The knife's sheath was the one Felipe had carved his name into and wore, quiver-style, in the middle of his back. Alaminos directed him to carve it to look more like a real scabbard. After it was slimmer and smoother and more pointed Alaminos blackened it with ashes from the stove and oiled it. Then he dressed it up with more of the wire wrapped around it in a crosshatch pattern. If no one examined it too closely, it might pass for a dagger worn by a wealthy person. Then he directed Felipe to cut the bat-wing bag away from its belt. He showed Felipe how to hang the knife from the belt so that it draped properly over his right hip. When he was finished, Alaminos looked him up and down and bowed mockingly. "Your Highness," he said. "Even I would believe you were important."

"I look ridiculous. And how does a person walk in these things?"

CHAPTER FORTY ONE

As they approached the eastern end of Cuba the wind came more against them, until finally Alaminos came about and headed for a small, protected bay on the north shore.

"Even if I could round *punta Maisí* in this wind, I would lose weeks beating back out of the harbor at Santiago to pick up a fair wind back to Spain. I'm afraid this is as far as you go."

One advantage of his decision to disobey Cortes by stopping in Cuba would be to refill the water casks. Alaminos anchored nearly a league off shore and had his gig lowered into the water. He made sure the ship's only other boat was chained and padlocked in its chocks and he kept the padlock key on a chain around his neck. He would be shorthanded for the crossing to Spain. He couldn't afford for any of his crew – including the four who thought they would be getting off in Cuba – to jump ship. Then he, Felipe and four trusted sailors headed for shore, towing an empty water butt behind them. One of the strongboxes, sporting a new red wax seal and much lighter than it had been, rested between Felipe's uncomfortably booted feet.

The bay was not uninhabited as it had first appeared. Some Spanish settlers had taken advantage of the stream flowing in and the fertile soil it had deposited there. A well-used trail headed inland beside the stream. Several of the Spaniards were waiting on the beach to greet the visitors.

Alaminos introduced himself. "With this wind I can't make enough southing to weather the point. I just need to refill my water from your stream, with your permission."

"Certainly. Help yourself." Alaminos and Felipe climbed onto the sand, and the sailors towed the water butt over to the stream. One of the Spanish men looked at Felipe's brilliant red doublet and extraordinarily tall boots. "Who's this, then?"

"He is an important visitor…" Felipe raised his chin and his hand as he'd seen Cortes do many times and cut him off. "I am Felipe Ferrer y Mendoza de Arjona. I have business with Governor Velasquez. I need to be in Santiago urgently. Would you or one of your neighbors by chance have a horse I could purchase to ride south?"

"You're not from Cortes, are you?"

"I heard that Cortes sailed for Yucatán months ago," Felipe said. "Without the Governor's consent, from what I understand."

The Spanish man visibly relaxed. "We heard that, too. But we heard stories of his taking people's horses, so we need to be careful. I have a horse, but he is not for sale."

"Would it be possible to rent him for a few weeks? I can pay well."

"How well?"

Felipe reached into his waistband and withdrew a handful of gold chain links left over from modifying Taxmar's necklace. The chain had been shortened and was now chafing under the collar of the doublet. He offered the man two of the links.

"Why don't we make it four, and I'll give you back two when I get my horse back."

"Done. And if it takes me longer than I anticipate, I'll pay more."

***

While they were sailing along Cuba's north coast, after they had solved the wardrobe problem, they had turned their attention to reorganizing the two strongboxes and completing their plan. There were one hundred and sixty bars of gold in total. Cortes' instructions to the Spanish court were to turn around and send ten percent, sixteen bars, back to Velasquez – some of which money would probably have ended up enriching some court official rather than being passed on entirely to Velasquez. It fit with the narrative Cortes had constructed: putting himself under the direct command of the king rather than being under orders from Velasquez.

Felipe still had the blank parchment he'd taken from Diaz. Copying phrases from the other documents he wrote out a flowery letter from Cortes to Velasquez, congratulating him on his wise investment and the success of the mission he had authorized, and please find included your payment in full and my resignation. Neither one of them wanted to try to forge Cortes' signature. Alaminos solved the problem by simply slashing a quill-ful of ink arrogantly across the signature space, as if Cortes had been in too much of a hurry to sign properly. Alaminos used the fake clay seal to emboss a blob of red wax on it that obscured part of the signature.

The real inventory took more finesse. Felipe had seen his father work with parchment enough that he knew how to re-use a piece. He could use the same technique. He borrowed a holystone from one of the deckhands, normally used for scrubbing the deck. He laid the parchment flat on the deck and gently, gradually sanded away the ink marks from the part he wanted to change. With his fingertip he massaged some oatmeal into the blank spaces in the soft leather. When it dried it was as white as the surrounding surface. Then he wrote over it.

When he was finished, the king's inventory read:

144 bars of gold
26 red gems of unknown type
35 blue gems, possibly sapphires
74 greenish gems, some carved by Indian artisans, possibly emerald
1 gold face mask with jeweled eyes

Felipe had changed "160" bars to "144", and sixteen bars had been loaded into the other strongbox for Felipe to present to Velasquez. At Alaminos' suggestion he had changed "rubies" to "red gems of unknown type." Alaminos also had him remove a line that read "20 emeralds" and merge them with the next line, fifty four carved green stones. "Cortes and Diaz don't really know what kind of gems they are. They only know their color," Alaminos said. "We don't want them to get in trouble."

Lastly, he removed all mention of forwarding anything to Velasquez. He filled the space left by that removal with a couple sentences, uncharacteristic of Cortes, praising the heroic efforts of his men, including especially navigator Antonio de Alaminos, gun captain Diego de Ordas, and horsemen Pedro and Pablo Sanchez and Felipe and Miguel Ferrer. Felipe grinned at the knowledge that he, his father, Pedro and Abí were all going to be recorded in the official history of Spain under assumed names. Oh, and a horse; a tall black heroic stallion named Majesty, killed at the battle of Centla saving Cortes' life.

The revised inventory was re-sealed and returned to the king's strongbox. But Alaminos didn't re-seal the box. "I'll do it later," he told Felipe. "It's the best place for you to keep your chain until we get to Cuba."

"I appreciate all you are doing for me. I am truly grateful. But even with the gold, even with my new clothes, Velasquez will still see me as a child. A child handing him an order from his enemy Cortes. Why wouldn't he simply rip it up? He might even kill my father if he thinks Cortes wants to honor him."

"I'm sure you're right. Normally, he would gladly defy a request from Cortes. But he won't dare defy this." He pointed to the seal on one of the documents.

"Cortes' seal. So what?"

"Ah! Now I see why you are confused. Take a good look at this." He held one of the wax seals close to Felipe's face. Felipe looked: He saw a rough cross with a sword on one side and some sort of bush on the other. The Latin words surrounding the border were too blurred to make out.

"So?"

"You still don't understand what this means, do you? This is not Cortes' seal. It is Diaz's seal. Velasquez will not dare to defy the Church. But, if you're worried, we can offer Velasquez one more thing." He took down from his shelf the parchment with the death sentence inscribed on it. "Perhaps we can use the back of this, if you'll scrub the writing off the front."

Felipe sanded and whitened the parchment and the next day Alaminos began drawing. He drew a map of Yucatán, showing quite clearly that it was a peninsula, not an island. He included the Grijalva River and the region called Tabasco, and the city of Potonchan and the town of Centla. He drew in the mountains west of Centla and a guess of where the city of Mexico was. The water off its coast, west of Yucatán, into which the Grijalva River emptied, he labeled the Gulf of Mexico. And to one side he wrote a note suggesting that these lands were not India, but rather a previously unknown continent, perhaps a northern extension of the continent mapped by the explorer Americus Vespucius a decade earlier. On his map he took the liberty of naming it America.

"Here," he said. "Give that to Velasquez, too. It will mean almost as much to him as the gold."

"It's beautiful. But why will Velasquez care?"

"Because he'll use it to find Cortes."

***

Felipe spoke soothingly to the horse, a short pinto stallion called Diego, and fed it a handful of grain. "I wonder if you might be Hurricane's father?" he murmured, and the horse licked his buttons.

The Spanish horse owner was delighted to see that this dandy knew how to treat a horse, and he quickly saddled it. While he was doing that, Felipe turned to Alaminos.

"Thank you for all your help. When will I see you again?"

"Don't get sentimental on me. You've been very strong up until now. I'm sailing to Spain with a strong recommendation, thanks to you, even if it is forged. I expect I'll be seconded to the king's office of Navigation. Who knows where they'll send me. But since Cuba is already well-mapped, I'm sure it won't be here."

"What about Ana? I know where to find her. I could have her here in a week. You could take her with you."

"My wife in Spain might not be too happy with that arrangement. Tell Ana goodbye for me."

Felipe gave him a fierce hug and vaulted into the saddle, then waited while the sailors secured the strongbox behind him. While they were doing that, the horse owner's wife brought Felipe a canteen and a small sack of food.

"Turn left at the top of the hill," the Spaniard said. "Then take that trail all the way over the mountain, about fifteen leagues. As you go down the other side, you will find another fork about ten leagues down. The broader trail, the left fork, leads right to Santiago. About another ten leagues on. Shouldn't take you more than three days. If I need Diego to cover a mare sooner than I expect, where will you be?"

"Are you familiar with Miguel Ferrer's stud farm outside of Santiago? Diego will be there."

CHAPTER FORTY TWO

Outwardly, Felipe looked every inch a busy royal messenger having to take care of a task he considered beneath him. It took all his focus to maintain that air. Inwardly, his mind was screaming: What if Bernardo recognized him? What if Bernardo refused? What if his father gave the game away? What if his father was too sick to move? What if he had died?

As soon as he'd gotten out of sight of the farm where he'd acquired Diego Felipe had taken off the finery. He rode for most of the next three days wearing nothing but his belt. He arrived on the outskirts of Santiago in late afternoon. The town seemed to have doubled in size since he left. He dismounted beside a stream and washed carefully before getting dressed in the fancy red doublet, white leggings and black boots.

He'd arrived at the governor's office late in the day. He dropped the strongbox as soon as he got through the door and gave a curt bow to the governor's assistant. "Don Cortes sent me with a message for the governor."

The man was flustered. There had been no word of a ship from Cortes. If this messenger truly was from Cortes, how did he get here? Why had Cortes sent a child? Was it an insult? On the other hand, his eyes strayed to the strongbox. If Cortes was sending money, did he dare keep the messenger waiting? In the end, greed won out.

"Come this way, young man. Bring the box."

"I am not a servant. Send someone to carry it," Felipe said, and he walked into the room the man had pointed to.

Apparently the man had no servant available as he appeared right behind Felipe, puffing and lugging the strongbox. "Excellency, this young man claims to be from…"

Felipe cut him off. "Your Excellency, I am Felipe Diaz, recently of the Cortes expedition to Mexico." Since he was about to inquire about a man named Ferrer he didn't want to rouse suspicions by using his real name. "Don Cortes has assigned me to deliver his dispatches to you." He pointed to the strongbox. He suddenly quailed: What if Velasquez didn't have a key for the strongbox?

No problem. "Mexico, hmm?" Velasquez tried out the new word. "Mexico." He took a key out of his waist pocket and unlocked a small cabinet behind him. From that he extracted a huge key-ring, which he handed to his assistant. "Has Cortes returned?"

"No, Don Velasquez. I am merely a messenger."

Velasquez nodded. "Sit, sir, sit. So, where is he, then?"

Felipe gratefully sat down in the huge chair facing the governor's desk. His feet were complaining about the boots.

"The navigator, Señor Anton de Alaminos, directed me to give you this." Felipe opened the top button of the doublet, which was beginning to choke him, and withdrew the map Alaminos had drawn. He handed it across the desk. Velasquez snatched it eagerly and spread it out. "*Mexico,*" he read. "Tabasco, Centla," his finger traced the various names as his tongue experimented with the unfamiliar words. The keys continued to jingle in the hands of the assistant until Felipe heard the distinctive click, then the creak of the hinges as the box swung open.

The assistant pulled the pile of folded documents from the chest and laid them on the desk. He handed the key-ring back to Velasquez. Then he left the office.

"So what am I supposed to do with you? Did Cortes give you orders? Are you supposed to return to him somehow?"

"He directed that I am to place myself in the service of a certain man named in one of the papers, a Don Miguel Ferrer."

***

And now he stood beside the soldier, waiting impatiently as Bernardo tried to appear as if he were reading the governor's order. Felipe knew Bernardo couldn't read. The soldier knew it, too. "At once, man! Do not keep this gentleman waiting. The governor himself wishes the release of this Ferrer, so you have no say in the matter. Move!"

Felipe had held his breath when the governor cracked open the seal on the reprieve of his father. Did it look real? Had he written it correctly?

Velasquez had closed it again and peered at the wax seal, now broken. Then he nodded and held the letter up. "More of Cortes' perfidy, no doubt. It appears he somehow cheated this man, and now, for reasons he does not explain, his conscience has gotten the better of him. Juan!" he bellowed. The assistant came running in. "Write an order for my signature transferring title of one hundred caballerias of Cortes' land to one Miguel Ferrer y Mendoza de Arjona. No, make it two hundred. Also, write an order to the jailer to release the man."

While they waited on Juan, the governor had tried to ask Felipe more questions about Cortes' campaign, but Felipe stuck to his 'I am only the messenger' line. He was so close to seeing his father. Finally the assistant returned with the two documents. The governor signed them and started to hand them to Felipe, then stopped himself. He looked Felipe up and down. "The jailer might not believe you. Let me send a soldier to fetch the man."

Felipe had jumped up. "I'll go with him. I'm sure your time is valuable. Thank you, Excellency." And he practically ran from the room.

Bernardo slowly rose from his stool and scratched his backside. As he handed the letter back to the soldier Felipe found something interesting out in the courtyard to look at so that Bernardo was looking at the bright red cap on the back of his head. Felipe heard the evening bells ring from the churches in town. He knew his father would be expecting his supper now. Thankfully, tonight he would be eating real food. If he was still alive. Bernardo took the key-ring off its hook and lumbered down the hall.

"It smells in here," Felipe said. "I'm going to wait in the plaza. When the jailer returns, tell him to send the man and all his belongings outside to me." He couldn't stand the idea that he might ruin the whole plan this close to the end.

***

"Sir?" He heard the soldier address him from behind. Before he turned around he heard another voice, one he clearly recognized.

"Sir? My lord? Thank you so much…"

Felipe's throat threatened to close. He raised a hand and waved dismissively to the soldier. Nothing came out when he tried to speak. He cleared his throat and tried again. "That will be all, soldier. Thank you for your assistance."

He heard the soldier walk away. Only then did he pull the ridiculous hat off his head and turn and run to his father.

"Felipe! I knew that was your voice! Dear God, how I prayed…" His father crushed him to his chest. "You've grown a foot!"

"It's the boots." He looked up at his father. "You look – actually, you look very well… healthy." He did, aside from the pale skin. His father was back to a healthy weight. His muscles were perhaps a bit softer but they were still there. His hair was a bit grayer, but it was still there as well. "I wasn't sure you would live. Did Bernardo decide to feed you properly?"

"It wasn't Bernardo."

"Well who…"

"Hello Felipe."

He whirled around. "Ana!"

"I know you said I should hide in the mountains. But the more I thought about your father being fed nothing but cassava, I knew I had to help him as you helped me." She held up a small parcel. "I've been bringing him dinner every day."

Felipe hugged her, as his father looked on. Then he held out his hand to Ana. "Nice to finally see you, Ana," Ferrer said. "This woman saved my life, son. She brought food and tied it to that fishing line outside my window.

228

And not just food. Look! Paper!" His father brandished several sheets of paper, written on both sides. "I told her where to find my Latin Bible, and she went to the farm and brought me pages from it. I've been translating them to Spanish. I've nearly finished the gospels."

"Ana, I have to tell you," Felipe began.

"Antonio? Does he live? Is he well?"

"Yes, he is doing well but..."

"He is not coming back, is he?"

"No, I'm sorry. He is sailing to Spain. He said to say goodbye."

"Thank you. Don't feel badly. I knew he would never come back. Anyway," she sighed. "Now that you are here, Felipe, and your father is free, I should go."

"Stay," Felipe said.

"Yes," Ferrer said. "Please stay with us."

***

They reached the farm the next day. The senior Ferrer was frustrated to find he did not have the strength to walk. He rode Diego as Felipe and Ana walked beside him. As expected, the fields had nearly been reclaimed by the jungle. To the surprise of both Ferrers, however, the buildings and barnyard were in substantially the same shape in which they'd left them.

The caretaker that Cortes had promised was there. He had done his job well. The barn roof was still intact, as were the windows and the door of the small house. The small garden near the house was producing vegetables. The tree branch fence that surrounded the corral was in good shape. The caretaker had just filled Majesty's old watering trough that morning. Felipe wondered if the gold he'd hidden under it was still there. The two growing horses, Aquila and Priscilla, came over to the trough. Ferrer senior smiled. They were nearly full grown. He had never expected to them see again.

Ferrer slid to the ground and went over to pat Aquila's nose but the young stallion shied away. "Still unbroken, I see. That's all right," he said soothingly. "That's all right. That makes you just like the rest of us."

229

EPILOGUE

When the truce had been reached on the afternoon of the battle of Centla, Abí and her relatives had gone to assist with collecting the dead and wounded. As the daylight was fading she stepped into the small depression where the cannons had been, and movement caught her eye.

Majesty tried to stand. Startled, she jumped back and screamed. He flopped back down with a wheeze. She approached him cautiously. "Are you going to attack me?" she asked. He didn't seem so dangerous now. One of her uncles came running up with a spear, preparing to put the hated monster to death. "No!" she cried.

Her uncle lowered his spear. "Why not?"

She didn't really know why not. She had always been deathly afraid of Majesty. But she thought of Hurricane. "I don't know. He's pretty. We can't just kill him."

Majesty coughed. "What can I do for you, boy?" she drew close enough to gingerly pat his neck. She could see the wound on his chest and a large pool of blood on the ground. How was he still alive with all his blood gone?

The uncle lost interest and moved on. Abí pulled an obsidian knife and sliced off a piece of the cotton armor that Felipe had wrapped around Majesty. She ran to the creek and soaked the wad of cotton and ran back and held it in front of Majesty's nose. He stuck his tongue out and began sucking thirstily on the wad. She sliced off another piece of the cotton batting and made another trip. She lost count of how many trips she made before the horse seemed to finally have gotten his fill of water. His breathing improved. He seemed to be in less distress.

But what was she supposed to do with him? Her uncle was probably right. The horse would likely die slowly from his wounds. It was probably better to kill him quickly. But she didn't have the heart.

While she deliberated, Majesty stood up. She quickly stepped over to him and he nuzzled her hair. "Do you think you can walk?" She sliced away the remains of the cotton armor. "Come on."

It was midnight by the time they arrived back at the village where her people were. Majesty had stumbled several times. Once he had lain back down and Abí was sure that he would die there. But she brought him more water and eventually he stood again and they slowly pressed on.

His presence in the village was a problem. No one wanted him there. Some thought he was a demon. Others believed him to be a god. None of them believed Majesty was simply an animal. And they all, uniformly, believed his presence in their village was a bad idea.

Abí led him far enough away from the village to be out of sight and earshot. Majesty made it as far as a patch of lush grass with a small stream running through it. He drank deeply from the stream, then he sank down into the grass and closed his eyes.

Abí fell asleep with her head resting on his side.

When she woke the next day, he was still alive. She tried to feed him some of the grass but he wouldn't take it. She brought him some water and he drank. Then he lay back down again.

Abí went to the Mayan village and found the shaman. He wanted nothing to do with the horse but she insisted, literally dragging him to the small meadow where Majesty lay. The man looked at him and shook his head.

Abí whined, "Please, do something; anything!" The shaman snipped one of the long hairs from Majesty's tail. He threaded it through a tiny bone needle and stitched up the wound in Majesty's chest. He opened a pot of a vile-smelling potion and rubbed in on the wound. Majesty made angry noises but didn't have the strength to resist.

The shaman rattled off an incantation over the horse then told Abí, "That's all I can do."

"But he won't eat!"

"Cook some stew for him."

"Horses don't eat stew. They eat grass. Except when they are babies. But he won't eat any grass."

"Give him milk, then. That is all I can tell you. Do not bother me with this thing again."

Majesty lay in the shade most of the day. She carried water to him. He stood once and walked a few steps and urinated. He drank from the stream and lay down again. He ate nothing.

The next day she was back in the Mayan camp. She visited several of the dogs to collect a gourd-full of milk and carried that back to Majesty. He sniffed but refused to even taste it.

She went back to the camp and begged milk off of two nursing mothers. Back to Majesty. No response.

"This is why I don't like you!" she said. "You are just mean! Why won't you cooperate? I'm trying to help."

She could see he was getting weaker. She had to get him to eat.

Before dawn the next morning she snuck into the Castilanos camp. She was sure Felipe would know what to do. She quickly found the horses tied to the rope ring but Felipe wasn't there. In the dark she spotted Hurricane, nursing from a horse she assumed was Isabella. That gave her an idea. She untied Isabella, raised the rope and guided her under it. But even if Majesty would drink from Isabella, there might not be enough for both him and

Hurricane. She untied another horse. Was it a mare? She couldn't tell in the dark. Just to be sure, she untied another. She led the three horses away from the dark camp, Hurricane following behind.

HISTORICAL NOTE

The fossil record seems to indicate that horses went extinct in the Americas thousands of years ago. History is divided on where the herds of wild horses seen roaming the west in the era of the John Wayne movie actually came from. Some claim they came from Desoto's expedition from Florida to the Mississippi, which included 42 horses. That expedition left abruptly, abandoning their horses, when Desoto died in 1542. Other historians credit the Catholic monks that were spreading their version of Christianity in the American Southwest with also peddling horses to the natives from the early seventeenth century on.

But the first horses to set foot on the North American continent were the 17 brought ashore by Cortes' conquistadors in 1519 – the 16 they left Cuba with, and the colt that was born on board along the way, in a hurricane. The surviving records of the expedition don't specifically mention horses getting loose. But a few months later, when Velasquez sent Panfilo Narvaez to arrest him, Cortes was down to just five horses. I suppose twelve could have died, but I prefer to think some of them got away.

While this is a work of fiction, many of the details were drawn from real events. The list of who I made up is shorter than the list of real people: Felipe and his father, Ana, Pedro, and Bernardo the jailer; And of course Abí, Ox-Ha-té, Kabil and Chimalatl.

Cortes really did have a personal priest named Diaz. Alaminos really was his navigator, and he really was sent to Spain with orders not to stop in Cuba after Cortes had had all but one of the ships burned. Cortes really did lose a shoe in the muddy bottom of the Rio Grijalva while wading ashore under a hail of Mayan arrows. Avila really did lead the assault by the other half of the army on the back side of Potonchan. Cortes really did slash the Ceiba tree in the town square. Melchior was really the interpreter, and he really did run away during that first battle.

Aguilar and Guerrero were real, and their story was pretty much as retold here. According to one account Guerrero stayed behind because of his wife and children and the tattoos on his face. According to another, he stayed behind because he'd fought beside the Mayans against the Spanish and was afraid of being hanged for treason. You choose. The fleet really did leave Cozumel without Aguilar and then return because of a leak. Aguilar came ashore naked except for his breviary in Cozumel, really had forgotten how to speak Spanish and Cortes really did wrap his own cloak around the man. And Cortes did skip Yucatán.

Why were the steps of the pyramid up which Felipe and Kabil raced uneven? The Mayans had such a precise knowledge of math and astronomy they built at least one of their pyramids so that, twice a year, on the equinox, the steps throw a shadow that looks like a snake, their god Kukulkan, slithering down from heaven. Of course, this happens at Chichen Itza, not Yaxuneh, but who knows what they'll discover at Yaxuneh?

History records the names of many of the horses, including El Arriero. According to one account Cortes really did pull the trick of having a mare in heat positioned behind his tent when El Arriero was brought out front. According to a different account Cortes had used Isabella in a similar way on Cozumel, taking Hurricane away from her and causing her to neigh long and loudly to frighten the natives. He likely did one or the other. Perhaps he did both. You choose.

El Arriero really was owned by men recorded as "Ortiz the musician and Bartolome the gold miner," and they really were forbidden to ride their own horse. And Cortes really did continue on El Arriero when his own black stallion was wounded in the Battle of Centla. And some of the Spanish soldiers did claim afterward that they'd seen St. James on a white horse during the battle.

One result of the truce with the natives of Centla was the gift of the twenty slave girls; one of whom, Malinalli or Malinche, was fluent in Aztec. She was baptized and given the name Marina. She was able to advise Cortes how to win the Mayans over to his side and use them to defeat the Aztecs. She is credited more than any other single asset for Cortes' conquest of Mexico. She bore Cortes a son despite his having left a wife behind in Cuba. Over the centuries, history has at times called her the 'mother' of Mexico just as Washington is called the 'father' of America. At other times she has been treated as a traitor. A bit like statues of Robert E. Lee being built in one generation and then torn down in the next.

The Inquisition really was very active in the sixteenth century and the Bible in Spanish really was forbidden to the general population. Bonifacio Ferrer's Bible was translated from the Latin Vulgate to Catalan in 1478, from which Felipe and his father borrowed their last name.

There was also a Spanish translation of the Hebrew Scriptures made in 1422 by Rabbi Moises Arragel, but it disappeared around the time Miguel Ferrer made his hasty escape to the New World.

***

Your feedback is important. If you enjoyed this book please take a moment to go back to Amazon.com and leave a review. Thank you!

Made in the USA
San Bernardino, CA
14 March 2020